LONG FOR THIS
WORLD

Books by Michael Byers

THE COAST OF GOOD INTENTIONS

LONG FOR THIS WORLD

LONG FOR THIS WORLD

MICHAEL BYERS

HOUGHTON MIFFLIN COMPANY

BOSTON · NEW YORK

2003

For information about permission to reproduce selections from
this book, write to Permissions, Houghton Mifflin Company,
215 Park Avenue South, New York, New York 10003.

Visit our Web site: www.houghtonmifflinbooks.com.

Library of Congress Cataloging-in-Publication Data
Byers, Michael.
Long for this world / Michael Byers.
p. cm.
ISBN 0-395-89171-X
1. Geneticists—Fiction. 2. Genetic disorders in children—
Fiction. 3. Aging—Prevention—Fiction. 4. Austrian
Americans—Fiction. 5. Women immigrants—Fiction.
6. Suicide victims—Fiction. 7. Seattle (Wash.)—
Fiction. 8. Sick children—Fiction. I. Title.
PS3552.Y42L6 2003
813'.54—dc21   2002191292

Printed in the United States of America

Book design by Robert Overholtzer

QUM 10 9 8 7 6 5 4 3 2 1

THIS BOOK IS FOR

SUSAN

WITHOUT WHOM NO LIFE,

HOWEVER LONG,

WOULD BE WORTH LIVING

AND

FOR MY FATHER

WITH LOVE

ACKNOWLEDGMENTS

It is a pleasure to give thanks to the people who helped make this book possible: to Janet Silver at Houghton Mifflin for her freeing patience and exquisite guidance; to Timothy Seldes for his faultless encouragement and advocacy; to the Mrs. Giles Whiting Foundation, the American Academy of Arts and Letters, and PEN/New England for their support; to the enormous list of friends, family, and fellow writers without whom this would have been a most lonely project—and in particular to my father, Peter Byers, for his direction and to Virginia Sybert for her unfailing generosity and her cheerful attention to the medical details.

Most of all I am lovingly indebted to my wife, Susan Hutton, whose influence on this book is immeasurable, and whose beautiful presence in my life is a continuing inspiration.

ONE

I

I T WAS A BIG OLD pleasant high school gym, built in the twenties and not much disturbed by renovation. The iron rafters met
at a shallow angle at the roofline, and the tall windows were
made up of a dozen big panes, each reinforced with chicken
wire, and the two ancient clocks sat on opposing brick walls,
ratcheting their works forward with an audible *whir, hiss, clunk.*
The gym smelled nostalgically of varnish, sweat, and paint, but it
was not an obsolete or shabby place. An electronic scoreboard
reading GARFIELD — VISITORS — QUARTER — FOULS — TIME
OUT had been added on the east wall, and a recent grant from
FareWatchers.com had supplied the courtside officials with a new
Huston-Marke computerized scoring system, a sleek blue box that
sat beneath the long scorers' table and extended its heavy gray ca-
bles to an outlet hidden under the bleachers. The purple Garfield
bulldog, wearing its studded collar, snarled up from the court's
center circle, and the backboards were regulation glass, and the
nets were in good repair, and when the boys played here a riotous,
explosive sort of crowd would gather, and the breakaway rims actually got some use, and once in a while — once a decade or so —
someone would appear who was so obviously superior to the rest
of the boys that his future would be discussed with the frank and
half-informed calculation any phenomenon inspires. The boys'
team often played in the state tournament and had won it six years

ago, and its purple banners hung from the rafters, drifting sideways when the big purple entry doors were left open to the hall.

But tonight the girls were playing, and very few people were there. From his seat midway up the home bleachers Henry Moss could see almost everyone who had come out of the rain to watch — a hundred or so people, including his wife, Ilse, and son, Darren, who sat directly in front of him, a row below, so he was looking down into their hair; and Sandra, his daughter, who was on the court, holding the ball with her back to the hoop, wearing the stern and thoughtful expression of someone taking apart a complicated bomb. The girls' team was not nearly as good as the boys' — in fact, they lost almost every game they played — but Sandra herself was very good, the starting center, and despite the team's terrible record she carried herself up and down between the baskets with a kind of preoccupied confidence that plucked at Henry's heart and made him lean down now and then to grasp his wife's shoulders. She would pat his hands and hold them for a second before letting go. It was not an uncommon gesture there; the team was so bad — so unwatchably bad at times, really — that nearly everyone in the gym was related in some way to one of the players. So it was a tender and familiar gathering, on the home side, anyway, under the old painted roof, and Henry was faintly conscious of the fellow feeling that surrounded him. A girl made an unlikely shot, or rolled her eyes in some characteristic way, or wiped her mouth in a gesture of embarrassed happiness, and somewhere in the bleachers Henry sensed someone's heart rising; there would come a bark of surprised laughter or a few beats of applause while the team fell back ten points, twenty before halftime. Even Darren would applaud his sister when he felt like it, though Henry suspected it was largely to draw attention to himself. He cupped his hands and shouted, "Go, Moss!" when she had the ball in the post, and when she stood at the foul line, her knees bent and the ball resting easily in her big, practiced hands — resting, resting — Darren would wait in silence until she cocked her elbows and sent the ball feathering through the net, when he would shout down at her, "And one!" with his newly deep voice, the voice of a stranger.

Behind them at the top of the bleachers tonight were a dozen or so children too young to be left at home alone but old enough to throw crumpled-up paper at each other, and occasionally at Henry.

After being hit twice in the head, not accidentally, he had had enough, and he made his slow way up to the top of the bleachers, where the benches were deeply gouged with graffiti, blue and black, name after name: *Michelle Grigo Peeper LaShelle VeeVee Ashlee Adam Brad LaVonn.* The children, seeing that he was there to stay, moved off to the other end of the stands and eventually through the open purple doors into the long empty hall outside, where they could be heard chanting, "Got no money, got no friends, got nobody that he can —" and then something he could not understand.

The crowd below him was clustered into groups of five or six, with a small population that circulated from group to group, making the rounds. As he watched, Darren, just turned fourteen, stood and maneuvered down beside a clutch of three girls, who after a moment burst into laughter at something he had said. His boy! Darren was not a handsome kid — his jaw was too long and seemed packed with teeth, and his eyes sat very deep in his skull, as though someone had pressed them in with a thumb. Henry had looked exactly the same at fourteen and had spent most of his adolescence staring at girls longingly from across the room, but Darren was different. Fearless.

Henry's wife tipped her head back, looked at him strangely, upside-down. *What are you doing up there?* her eyebrows asked.

He shrugged. *Nothing. Enjoying the view.* Up close, the iron rafters could be seen to have been painted dozens of times, white over white over white, and a faint tapping on the roof was rain. When he peered down through the slats of the bleachers, he could see in the looming darkness below a discouraging litter of potato chip bags, soda cans, miscellaneous papers, odd articles of clothing, but it seemed to Henry a secret, alluring kind of place, way down there and out of sight, the sort of hideout he would have liked to investigate if he were not fifty-one, a father, and an eternal source of potential humiliation to Sandra and Darren. So he stayed where he was.

After a few minutes the chanting children came leaking back in from the hall, and one by one they ducked under the bleachers. Everyone knew they were not supposed to be there, but no one stopped them from running back and forth forty feet below him, ducking through the steel supports and laughing at the sight of a hundred asses on display in rows — laughing and laughing, until someone's mother finally corralled them and distributed them to their various parents in the stands.

At length Henry's wife rose and climbed to join him. She was tall — she had given Sandra her height — and wore a white turtleneck and white jeans. "I do not foresee a comeback," she announced. She was Austrian, her accent smoothed by eighteen years of American English. "You look very sinister up here, like that man in *The Parallax View* up in the catwalk. Did you see that?"

"I think we saw it together."

"I mean Darren. Did you see him go down to those girls?" She leaned closer. "The one on the left, farthest from him, has been looking at him all night. Isn't she pretty?"

"That's Tanya. She was at his birthday."

She put a hand on his knee. "He's not handsome, but he is smart," she said. "If it's done the right way, it can be very attractive."

"Does that count as a date?"

"I don't think anybody actually dates anymore, I think they just all clump together like that and go around in a big . . ." — she searched — "a big herd. He said he was going down to check on something and then he just went right down and sat next to them!" She shook Henry's leg in excitement. "He's so much braver than I was, Henry — he must get it from you."

"I think he gets it from your mother."

"What a terrible idea! Don't tell her, she'll just hate him all the more. How awful it must be to have us here in the first place. I'm sure the only reason he came was because he knew Tanya was going to be here too. Good for him."

"What's *she* doing here?"

"Maybe she knew *he* was going to be here. Or maybe he's developed some kind of mind control device. Henry, you should ask. I'm going to cry if they kiss."

"She is pretty."

"He'll grow out of that poor face of his," she assured him. "He'll end up looking normal."

They sat together in silence for a minute, listening to the rain overhead. It was a driving, solid rain; it had been raining for weeks and weeks. Sandra scored, then watched the other team race ahead of her for an easy basket while Marcia Beck, the Garfield coach, looked on with her arms folded.

"You realize if we stay too long up here together talking, people will think we're having some kind of marital troubles."

"I like it up here. Nobody chucks stuff at my head."

"I promise I won't chuck stuff at your head. Oh, isn't it exhausting, even thinking about being a teenager again? Please, darling." She stood, took his hand. "Come be old with me. We'll sit far away and not disturb him."

It was January, wet but strangely warm, unnervingly so, and with the four of them in the car the windows quickly fogged. "What were you doing way up there on the top step?" Sandra asked him as soon as they pulled out of the lot. "I looked up there and I was like, What is my dad *doing*?"

"I was trying to get onto the roof."

"So you could jump, I guess, thanks a lot." She leaned forward and spoke almost directly into his ear, too loudly. "By the way, that ref is totally incompetent. He used to do JV games and he was okay but now he's doing varsity and he thinks he's all that and he doesn't even know the rules half the time. He kept saying things were sideouts that weren't and we were like, That's not a sideout!" She had Henry's round bland face but Ilse's long, articulated body, and after games she was almost always hyper like this; other times she hardly spoke at all. "Who was that up there with you?"

"That was me," said Ilse.

"No, before you."

"Just a bunch of kids."

"No, I mean there was somebody else up there with you, some grownup."

"It was just your mom."

"*Before* her."

"No, honey," he said, "there wasn't anybody else up there."

"Yes there was," she insisted. "There was some guy sitting next to you with a white shirt."

Ilse turned to him, looked back at Sandra. "That was *me*, darling."

"I know what you look like, Mom, duh."

"She thinks you look like a man," Darren said from his dark corner.

"No I don't, Mom. I *saw* you going up there, but this was before."

Ilse turned to him again. "Henry?"

"You're seeing things, baby."

"I am?" Sandra's voice was quieter, confused. "That's weird."

They drove on in silence. Christmas lights were still up in a number of houses, and they bleared through the foggy windshield. It was a Friday night, not quite ten o'clock, and in the neighborhood around Garfield the low-riding cars were out in number, parked in the fluorescent glow of the gas stations or thumping past on their way downtown, the windows tinted black, the chrome wheels shining. Henry did not find them particularly menacing but someone must, he imagined.

"Seriously, there wasn't anybody up there?" his daughter asked.

"No."

"Really? It was some blond guy."

"Honey, that was *me!* Never mind. I can see I'll have to get a new haircut."

"I'm not trying to insult you, Mom." Sandra leaned forward again, her hands draped over the seatbacks. "I like your hair, it's totally feminine."

"It isn't too puffy?"

"No, it's nice! It's soft." She touched it. "I wish mine was like that."

The neighborhood got more expensive as they went toward the lake. The houses grew larger and were placed farther back from the street, and the trees were taller and included some truly immense firs and cedars, majestic old trees that had been spared the saw a hundred years ago and now could be seen from blocks away, towering over everything. The two hemlocks on Hynes Street were both enormous specimens, six feet across at the trunk and at least eighty feet high, with broad spreading branches that dropped millions of tiny needles all year long. Now and then during big storms, upper branches would come loose and fall to the street, broken, like huge green wings. The neighborhood had debated cutting the trees down, but so far they had both survived, and Henry was happy about this; he liked them, the oceanic sound they made in a good wind, the sheltering sense of them above the houses, the shade, the size of them, the way you could stand at the base and look up into them and let your eyes climb from branch to branch. *A big tree is like a house,* he would think, looking up into them, and like anyone else he had a fondness for big houses.

"You're lovely," he told his wife when they parked.

She smiled faintly. "Don't you start," she said.

Their own house, standing within needle range of the bigger of the two hemlocks, was a smallish, haphazardly kept, shingled gray structure that needed paint and possibly a new roof, though neither was likely to happen anytime soon. They were saving for college, and while they earned good salaries, they weren't rich, and the amount of maintenance required to keep any house in fighting shape was, for Henry and Ilse, not worth the money or the effort. Squirrels lived in the eaves, and the baseboards were all coated with dust and the plaster was crumbling, so a good hard rap with the knuckles could set off a long, disintegrative trickling within the walls, and the basement was a warren of unlabeled storage crates and defunct equipment that for some reason was too valuable, too interesting, or too loaded with sentimental value to discard.

Most of the sentimental stuff belonged to Henry, it was true, and though once in a while he felt an impulse to rid himself of unnecessary things, he could not contrive, when it came down to it, to really find anything completely unnecessary — not his high school graduation gown, though the purple polyester had gone brittle with age and smelled chemically strange, as though its component materials were gradually separating from one another, not the old corduroy driving cap he had worn to medical school but that was now too big for him (he had had a sort of Afro in the seventies), and not the keys to his first and now long-vanished car, a green Dodge Valiant station wagon on whose radio he had first heard "Here Comes the Sun" while driving across North Dakota. None of the things in the fifteen or twenty unopened boxes could Henry bring himself to discard. Did he love himself so dearly as this? He did, he supposed, but he felt it was a more or less harmless vice. And the children added their own things, their heaps of books and rollerblades, and Darren in particular seemed to undress himself at random around the house, so his long skinny T-shirts and battered sandals showed up everywhere, and Sandra had five or six gym bags and grabbed whichever one was at hand and left the others to sit and ferment delicately — she did not sweat much — here and there.

For all this the house was not disorderly, exactly; Ilse was precise with the family accounts, and Henry was a meticulous scientist with a famously tidy office. But their energies were spent elsewhere than at home, and though he and Ilse both noticed that the carpet was dark and grubby and the foyer was a heap of discarded shoes and the attic was a disorganized clutter of still more boxes and put-aside toys, Henry didn't care. Tonight he emptied the trash, and that was enough. He took a hat from the rack, carried the bag with him into the back yard.

It was a warm, wet January night, getting warmer. Above him, the mountain ash was bare of leaves, but how long would it wait before it was convinced that spring was on the way? Three pear trees and a ragged ditch full of ivy separated them from the Nilssons, whose back yard abutted their own; in the ivy lived a population of *Hyla regilla,* the Pacific tree frog, little inch-long creatures encased in a taut green skin that had the bright reflective glossiness of oil paint. The frogs shuffled through the ivy and lurked under the pear trees like a kind of fallen, inedible fruit, and often, especially after a big rain, they would arrange themselves in sixes and sevens on Henry's driveway, panting as if desperately sick, peeping with a frightened insistence, *Hell-o? Hell-o? Hell-o?* It was unsettling to see. Henry — he was a geneticist — knew that chemicals in the groundwater were breaking down the zona pellucida of the amphibian egg, and that increased levels of ultraviolet radiation were introducing into the amphibian helicase a deadly rate of mutation, and that there was nothing he or his wife or anyone could do about any of it, really, except sit around and worry about what seemed the precipitate decline of the world, which Henry already did plenty of anyway. It was too warm, the warmest winter on record, warm enough for the frogs to be singing like this in January. If he stamped his feet he could scare them all back into the safety of the lawn, but a minute later they would creep back out into danger, seeking on the hard flat concrete something Henry could not imagine. Their own demise. Their own relief. He hated to see anybody suffering, even these dumb old frogs who didn't have the sense to look after themselves anymore.

He lifted the lid of the plastic can and dropped the garbage in. Shuffled his feet to silence the frogs. But when he put himself to bed, their song had begun again.

"You're sighing," his wife told him.

"I am?"

"See? *That.* That was a sigh."

"Those dumb guys are out there again."

She rolled to him, lifted herself on her elbows, peered down into his eyes. From six inches away her big face was a dark moon, her yellow hair standing on end around it. "Henry, I don't really look like a man, correct?"

"Correct," he said.

"Do you really like my new hair? Sometimes I think it makes me look just a little bit like Michael Landon."

"He had nice womanly hair."

"But it's something about my face — it looks strange lately. I think my nose is getting bigger or something." *Zumsing.*

"I don't think so."

"But," she countered, "have you actually measured it?"

"Have you?"

"I'm afraid to. I think it will tell me two millimeters per week — welcome to Big Wide Nose Land," she said. "Now you have to stop sighing. You can't do anything about the frogs, sweetheart, they're lonely for love."

"They're out there right now, it's crazy."

She thumped his chest. "Don't I try to dress nicely?"

"You do."

"Don't I paint my toenails sometimes?"

"Baby, you're beautiful."

"Maybe I'm not beautiful, but I am *big* and *powerful*," she said, and levered herself on top of him. "I can squish you like a bug."

"Say that again."

"Like a bug," she said. *Lie-ek ay-a bugg-a,* exaggerating. "Did you know you were moaning in your sleep last night? Again?"

"I was not."

"You certainly were! You were lying there moaning like a mummy."

"I was?"

"You were."

"Like *the* Mummy or just *a* mummy?"

She considered. "I think like *the* Mummy. I think you were having a dream." She lowered her head to his chest. "Actually, you sounded very sad."

"I'm not that sad."

"Was it a dream?"

Her head was warm on his chest. "I don't remember. " Last night was a blank to him, but he worked with sick children, dying children, and it was possible the work had been spilling over into his dreams. A favorite patient of his, William Durbin, was going to die soon, and he was only fourteen — only as old as Darren. Fourteen! It was a horrible thing, but it was going to happen; there was nothing anyone could do about it, nothing in the world. "It's probably just William," he said.

His wife said, into his chest, "Poor William. I'm sorry, darling."

"I know."

"I don't want you to be sad," she said.

He reached behind his head, closed the window, embraced her again. She was heavy, but it was a nice weight. She was as tall as he, no taller. They matched. The room was quieter now, dark. Patterns from the streetlight danced on the ceiling. His wife, heavy on his chest, an anchor, a shield. "I know you don't," he said.

2

TECHNICALLY IT WAS Ilse's second marriage, though by
now she hardly counted the first, which had been so long
ago and so brief and so much less *wonderful* than her
marriage to Henry that she usually preferred to pretend it
had not really happened. In what she thought of as her prehistoric
era she had been married, at twenty-five, in Vienna, to an unfriendly fellow resident named Gregor Hals, who had eaten his
sandwiches with a knife and fork while mumbling to himself and
who had cheated on her with such regularity and resolution that it
seemed he had honestly misunderstood the marriage vows and was
doing his best to be a very, very bad husband, the worst there had
ever been. She had been young. So had he. Gregor was short, bald,
Prussian heavy through the chest, with a wide flat pie of a face and
an astonished, innocent look he presented whenever Ilse discovered his bad behavior, and she had married him . . . oh, for many
reasons, really, but largely because it had seemed inevitable at the
time. Their families were old friends, and two cousins had already
married, so the match seemed to be making itself, and Ilse was spe-
cializing in bone diseases while Gregor, a few years older, was going to be a dermatologist — skin and bones; it was a sort of joke
they could tell on themselves — and Gregor did have a kind of
mean-spirited wit that, when it was directed at someone else, made

you feel snappy and smart, if a little bit guilty at the same time, and they had a number of friends in common, so all in all it had seemed the easiest and most obvious thing to do, and she had gone ahead and done it.

But it was a terrible mistake. To her relief, the marriage lasted only fifteen months, and a week after the divorce was final Ilse Hals, as she still called herself, was offered a job in Paris working for Gruber, a drug company. It was a chance to do something different, to leave Vienna and her family and her confused and divided friends and especially Gregor, with his swinish capacity for drink and his thoughtless cruelty, so how could she turn it down? She accepted, though only after being assured that Gruber would let her see patients now and then. Yes, that was why they had recruited her in the first place, to attend to the medical sides of various trial studies, osteoporosis and so on. Lots of patients. Good research. No administrative work, no committees? No, no, no, nothing like that. So — okay, she accepted.

Aside from vacations and two nights on her honeymoon with the execrable, grunting, awful, really just inexcusable Gregor, she had never spent much time out of the country; she had always thought of herself as Austrian, and more particularly Viennese, and in fact she knew she had her share of the perfectionist striving and isolationist aloofness that had marked her countrymen and spoiled their national politics since before the war. The Austrians, it was plain to Ilse, still felt unsophisticated in the shadow of cosmopolitan Germany and had, as her mother would say, overcompensated. Ilse herself was not immune; nor was her family. Her mother Freda was an analyst; her reclusive father Leopold was a professor of pharmaceutics; her unmarried older sister Tannie worked for the government, managing a bureau that disbursed money to the poor. They were successes all, but a somber air of make-do prevailed among them, particularly Ilse's mother, whose low, biting voice was the last Ilse heard as she boarded the train: "So! You're running away. Well, it's to be expected — I knew you'd do it someday." She handed over a paper bag full of tangerines. "You might as well have something to eat."

"I'm going to eat on the train, Mama. I'm not running away."

"Take it." Freda shook the sack peremptorily. "It's not just food, it's money."

"I don't need money, Mama."

"Everyone needs money." She was a short woman, with stiff white curls and a long black coat. She had always been a small, well-kept creature. Ilse, in her height and breadth, was not. "You can spend it on whatever you want, I don't care."

"It's not that far away."

"I don't expect to see much of you from now on," her mother said. "Just so you know, I want to be cremated, not buried."

"Mama."

"Someone needs to be told. Your father doesn't want to talk about it."

Ilse accepted the sack, which was heavy with the pendulous weight of the fruit. She looked inside. Six tangerines and a stack of currency, hundreds of marks, bound in a rubber band.

"I don't care what you spend it on."

"I don't need it."

"You will." Freda leaned forward to be kissed. Her cheek was loose and covered with a faint, gentle fuzz, the same fuzz that covered Ilse's own cheeks and arms.

Ilse, at twenty-seven, was tall, broadly built, and in the clumsy tower of her body often felt awkward and uncomfortable, as though she were too far from her extremities to control them precisely. Her clothes tended not to fit, and her hair was never really where it ought to have been, and now and then after a meal she would find a napkin stuck to her cuff, and in general she felt she broadcast an air of distraction. She was not very pretty, she felt, and she saw her future life as a solitary one, the sort of life her sister had now, and though such a life was not the worst fate in the world and her sister had acquired a certain caustic charm that made isolation seem the only sensible thing, Ilse did not really want that kind of life for herself. So she was unhappy, generally. It was nice, in fact, to be leaving her family behind, especially her mother. The imperfect world gravely disappointed her mother; disappointment was her mother's way of demonstrating herself a person of good quality, and Ilse, as any reasonable and imperfect person would, had long since found it suffocating.

She turned, boarded the train, and counted her money. It was too much, vastly more than her mother could have possibly afforded, and for hours she burned with guilty resentment. She would never have to go back, she told herself, never.

*   *   *

Still, once in Paris she missed them all, missed her family's immense dark apartment on the Brucknerstrasse and the monthly lunches with her father, a mild man with a canny, assessing, pill-counting gaze and a tall bald forehead that wrinkled deeply when he smiled. In her new city, Ilse felt obliged to dress well, and in the days after she rented a little white apartment above a row of upholstery shops, she used her mother's gift to buy herself most of a wardrobe. As she did — it took a week or so to spend it all — she began to develop a new, halfhearted, divorcée's acceptance of her tall, big-boned body, its square hips and broad shoulders. It was not too bad. Her long frame filled the shop mirrors, and she fought the urge to wave. Ruffles and frills were in style, and small strappy shoes that showed her knuckled toes.

To spend so much in this silly and defiant way did something to cut the guilt over taking the money to begin with. And in the end she did look very nice. She had straw-yellow hair and a dark complexion, and it turned out she looked best in yellow and white. How had she not known this before? Every shopkeeper in Paris knew it at a glance, and the floorwalkers in Galeries Lafayette brought creamy butters and bright gray linens without prompting. While with Gregor, she had worn green. Glimpsing herself in a window, she would not for an instant recognize the woman who stood there. She seemed taller than she had been. Slimmer. Her reflection was brighter than it had been, maybe that was it.

In this way, slowly, as the months passed, she came to like her new life. Away from her family, alone, prettified. Away from Gregor. And the city, majestic in its benign neglect of itself, enveloped her without protest. Her apartment faced east, and when sunlight struck the floorboards the kitchen filled with a deep, organic tonic, the old wood releasing its ancient molecules to the air. The white tiles in the bath glowed, and outside her bedroom window a spiral staircase clung to the plaster wall, unsafe for anyone but the pigeons who clattered there in the mornings, fussing in their elderly, consoling way. The apartment corridor was lit by a semicircular pane high above the dim stairwell, and the handrail was thick with blue paint that had acquired, in its countless layers, the soft polish of ceramic. Outside, the gutters and drains were clotted with tiny feathers — white goose down that drifted from the upholstery shops — and when the shops were open, the rapid rapping of tack hammers seemed the noise of an enormous, irregular machine with its workings stowed everywhere up and down the street. Her street. Her heart grew, ballooned, with what was apparently happiness, and though her salary was not high she began to feel rich enough, the bolts of upholstery fabric arriving every morning — scarlet, green, gold — seeming vast, kingly rolls of a currency so large it had to be carried down the street on a shoulder. Was this how her sister Tannie felt, secretly, alone in her apartment — that the world was full of riches, full of wonder? Maybe so.

And she loved her new position, consulting on Testarossa's new osteoporosis trials. Old women filled her office, displayed their hunchbacks, offered their grandsons in marriage. Her office was halfway across the city, on the third floor of a glassy new research campus, parts of which were still under construction. Union-idle truck drivers used the unfinished plaza below her window to park their vehicles out of sight of the thoroughfares, so her metal desk hummed always with the constant rumble of heavy engines. She could smell exhaust fumes and hear laughter, and from her window she would watch the furtive trading among the drivers: electronics for clothes, wine for music. Then there were complaints that the engines disrupted the microscaling being done in the basement, and the plaza was bricked over and the trucks were banished. She missed them in a way, but her research subjects were relieved. The trucks and drivers had been a gauntlet in the muddy lot, and the old women who had made their way across the city were happy to have them gone — they had shouted things, they had made simply *terrible* proposals. But the women had continued to come to Testarossa anyway — more than one of them said so — because of Ilse. "You're a nice doctor," they told her, grasping her arm. "You like to take your time." She blushed, demurred. But it was true. She was good at her job. She was gentle and thorough, and the women seemed not to mind her big broad hands traveling over their crippled backs and tortured shoulders. Old soft skin draped loosely over failing bone. She could do no healing, but she could record their condition. It was something. And she was never a disappointment to them, a fact that dawned on her slowly. Was that why she loved it all so much? At the end of each visit she handed over a little green disbursement slip and directed that hour's woman two floors down, to be paid for her trouble. Testarossa, it turned out, was also rich.

*   *   *

By the time she met Henry Moss two years later she had enjoyed a few little romances but nothing serious. Already nearing thirty, settled in a life that she had come to love, she began to miss the family she did not yet have. It was a funny kind of longing, not disabling but enough to nag at her. It would not be accurate to say she went to see Henry Moss speak at the Conférences Internationales des Sciences et Médicines in the hope of finding a husband. No, she was there on behalf of Testarossa and had all the tedious forms tacked to her clipboard to prove it. But she thought of it once in a while, and her patients, with the freedom of age, were always asking what she was waiting for. "Love," she told them. "If you wait too long," they warned her darkly, "all your children will have clubfeet." No one in Paris knew she had been married, and she told no one. She was content to be the aging girl, the neglected innocent.

She did not fall in love with Henry at once. He was a six-foot, mild-looking man with thick red-brown hair and a lumpy potato nose. Slender. A little hollow-eyed. He stood at the lectern pushing the "next slide" button with the eraser end of a long green pencil; twenty-five of them in a conference room, Dr. Moss down in front facing them all, a young man going on about the aging process. Not just young but very badly dressed, in a cheap blue blazer and a purple tie that curled up at the edges, like the Chinese fortune-telling fish Ilse had been given as a child; but he was an American, so his wardrobe was not necessarily to be held against him.

She was here to listen to him talk about cellular senescence — the aging of the human cell. Was it in her field? Oh, just barely. But it was interesting, and there was nothing else on the schedule she wanted to attend, so she sat and listened. Aging, he told them, was a fall from a kind of Eden. Cells in a newborn infant were nearly perfect and replicated themselves almost flawlessly, and eighty-five years later when you died the cells were slow and inefficient and the DNA was cluttered with junk. Why did this happen? A number of reasons, most of which appeared to be unavoidable. For one, cytochrome oxidase, the free radical that was the natural by-product of digestion, was also — with its oxygen — a corrosive. A poison. In the delicate environment of the cell, this poison created disruptions in the DNA — disruptions that, when they went uncaught, as some of them inevitably did, were passed down the cell line, replicated in turn, and further corrupted with additional errors.

"So we're doomed to deteriorate," Dr. Moss said resignedly. "We eat to survive, but by eating, we end up poisoning ourselves with these loose oxygens floating around the cell. The more you eat, the more poison you produce. Mice who consume fewer calories live longer, as long as they're well nourished, but they die too, eventually. Just later." He had a way of weighing a proposition in one upturned palm, pretending to look at it, then doing the same with his other palm — it looked like a contrived gesture, something he had thought of himself; it had that sort of overscripted awkwardness to it.

But of course there were repair mechanisms too, he said, so it wasn't all downhill. Thirty percent of a cell's energy was devoted to maintaining the integrity of the DNA, weeding out errors as they occurred. The proofreading was done by complex DNA inscription helicases, many of which had just been fully described in the past five years. Most of their mechanisms were not yet fully understood — he weighed this with his hand — but if we knew more exactly how these repairs were made, we might understand how to hypercatalyze them in some way. He lifted the other hand. But how could you get into a cell and make it proofread itself better, more thoroughly?

His own work in helicase research had been promising. The gene that caused Hickman syndrome was being actively sought in his laboratory in Seattle and at a laboratory in Berkeley, where Gary Hauptmann had been searching for years. Hickman patients died of old age at fourteen, having become elderly children at five or six. Maybe this was a clue to how aging really worked. Maybe the Hickman gene, wherever it was, operated as a sort of switch. Maybe it disabled the cell's internal repair mechanisms, reduced the efficiency with which the DNA was surveyed and corrected during replication, allowing an unusual number of replication errors to end up in the strand. An old cell was like a Dark Ages manuscript that had become encumbered with misspellings at the hands of illiterate monks; after a while, it became totally illegible. It could no longer do its job, or it could no longer reproduce itself — or sometimes it began to reproduce itself without limit, becoming malignant. In fact cancer was very interesting in its reckless self-propagation, perhaps ironically holding in its clotted stinking heart some cellular ambergris. But probably if a cell was capable of getting older faster, as a Hickman cell was, then it was capable of getting older more slowly. It was just a matter of bringing to light the mechanisms in question and discovering how to manipulate those mechanisms. Dr. Moss poked the lectern with the eraser, his bad purple tie swinging back and forth across his abdomen. "But that," he said, "is the really hard part."

Afterward, to Ilse's surprise, he approached her. He had a cold. "I always get a cold," he said, "after flying all night. Listen, I spotted you," he said, dabbing at his nose, "out in the lobby. You used to be married to Gregor Hals, didn't you? You're Ilse Hals." He nodded at her nametag.

"Yes!" she cried, surprising herself with happiness. "You know him?"

"Yeah. Well, no, not really. Gregor studied with Arnie Leesmann, and Arnie and I worked on a paper together a couple years ago. Mostly it was Arnie's project."

"Yes, I know Arnie," she said. "I met him once."

"With the big ears."

"Arnie is huge, like the elephant," she said.

"Arnie is huge, like a chain-smoking elephant who should take more showers," he said. "But you're not married anymore."

"No." It pleased her, in a surprising way, to be recognized like this. Like almost no one in her present life, he knew about her past. Thrown into what felt like a sudden intimacy, she allowed herself to examine him. In fact the potato nose was not really shapeless, just blunt-tipped, like a cork, and his eyes, though deep in their sockets, were nice, pale blue with a black ring around the iris. Pretty things, even now, when he had a cold — he kept pecking at his nose with the corner of a heavily seamed white handkerchief. It was an American face, long mongrelized and undistinguished, entirely harmless. He looked very young. Only a faint web of wrinkles around the eyes and a graininess to the skin gave him away as being older than she. He had taken good care of himself. He was busy for dinner, he said, but what about breakfast tomorrow?

She met him the next morning in the hotel dining room, which adjoined, through glass sliding doors, a small courtyard. Waiters tended the hundred tables, their white shirts flashing in the sun, fading in shadow. Little grapefruit trees grew in plastic pots.

Henry, across from her, was dressed this morning in a gray shirt, the same curly tie, the same blue jacket with its black plastic buttons. His cold had cleared up overnight; he ate a bowl of oatmeal and drank a cup of coffee. (He didn't care much about food, as she would learn; he ate, as had been his habit as an resident, like a calorie-restricted mouse, and as a medical student he had lived for a year mostly on cafeteria hamburgers and Top Ramen and the kohlrabi he could grow below his window in Ann Arbor.) No, he wasn't married (she had to find out, for form's sake). No, he had never been. No children. She herself felt attractive in the glassy light, with the morning sun striking the tables and picking out the leaves on the grapefruit trees. Her hair was pulled back, her skin was clear, her butter-yellow, old-fashioned, bias-cut suit showed her figure well. But it would not do, she felt, to appear overeager. *The eager beaver,* she thought. She had just learned the slang, and its second meaning.

So she was a bone specialist; had she worked on osteoporosis much? She nodded. "I do the estrogen trials for Gruber now."

"That's who you work for?"

"Not too bad a place," she said. "Also they are good for their doctors."

"You see people?"

"Yes — you mean patients. It is a foundation section that I work in, called Testarossa, the Red Head, named for his daughter who died."

"Sort of guilt money."

"Yes, some. But we do good, you know?" A little offended, she said, "Not everybody can do only very pure research in some university."

"It's good you keep their feet to the fire."

"Yes. We make them pay their dues. It's the right phrase?"

"Sure. Pay your dues? Sure."

"I got it from *The Rockford Files.*" She shrugged. "A dumb show, but it has some pretty good English."

"I'll take your word for it."

"It's a dumb show, right?"

"I've never seen it."

"Jim Garner," she persisted. "Very strong. He's a detective in Los Angeles, so he has to go back and forth, back and forth, to the beach, in the car, around and around, into little places where the

Chinese live — it's good." But he looked completely blank. What was she talking about? Embarrassed, she pressed on, distracting him: "So, listen, would you like to have dinner tonight? There is a fine place I go to that is very nearby my apartment." She reached across the table for his hand. Searching for the words, she came out with "It has been a long time since I had a nice social dinner with some new friend from the past."

He accepted, and in this way she discovered — sooner than maybe was decent, really — that the body under his clothes was a nice surprise, not slumped but shapely and strong, even slimmer than she thought it would be. It struck her as very sexy that he could have a body like this and yet not flaunt himself; it seemed a masculine thing, a carelessness that both excited her and gave her tender feelings toward him. He could be taught a few things. He could be shown how to dress — oh, those terrible clothes!

"You stay in condition," she said afterward.

"Yeah? I used to run a little bit."

"Oh, runners! I knew a runner who ran marathons. An Ethiopian, a very little tiny thin machine. Up at four in the morning every day to do the running, fifteen miles per day or more. They are a beautiful people and good runners, you notice — it is a trait they have, like the Americans for driving and playing golf and the French for hanging around and talking. He told me," she remembered, "that I was too skinny for him! If you can imagine. The Africans have a different idea of fat and skinny. They do!" she insisted, seeing him shrug. "They have the different culture, where food is a symbol."

But he had become uncomfortable; his eyes shifted, the typical American reaction to race. They were all so sensitive, though the country had produced King and Malcolm X and all the interesting blacks, James Baldwin and everybody. "Where is he now?" he asked.

"Yes, you're jealous. Well, he has gone to Kenya. He married a Coca-Cola factory. He has maybe forgotten about me now, probably."

"Too bad for him."

"Oh, it was a short affair, nothing serious."

"You ever see Gregor?"

"Hn. No." She didn't smoke much anymore, had no cigarettes in the apartment, but would have liked something to do with her hands. Henry's palm kept caressing her stomach in a way that was not entirely pleasant but not worth stopping; then she reached down and put a hand on his. "He is in Zurich now with a new wife, so they say, but I try not to hear anything about him. He is not my husband any longer. I have no interest in him. I can be happy and not think of him for months, months, months."

"Would you ever move?"

"Move?"

"Come back with me?"

"To where?"

"To the States."

"Don't tease," she scolded.

"You want kids?"

"Yes." Of course she did. "It is right for a woman to have children — it is something we come to want, in a natural way. Don't you think? That has been my experience so far, with me, with my friends."

"You say something like that in the States you'd get your license as a woman revoked."

"So then, I do not want to move. Probably they would all think I was fat anyway. The ladies that you date and sleep with. That you *nail*," she said, proud to have the word come to her unbidden like that.

"Nail? I don't nail anybody."

"It means having sex with, so —?"

"Well, yeah, but it's got sort of nasty connotations. Like you're putting a notch in your belt."

"Yes, exactly."

"Look." He leaned over, picked up his pants, the belt still threaded through the loops. "See? No notches."

"So you are either a virgin or that is a brand-new belt, because the other was filled up."

"I haven't bought new clothes in two years."

She pretended innocence. "Yes? Well, Paris is the place, you know."

"Too fancy. Plus too expensive, with the exchange. Imagine me going back all dolled up."

"Who cares what people think? Let them think you are a mysterious man with a Paris girlfriend who knows what you like to wear. Let me get you something."

"Girlfriend," he said experimentally.

"Or mistress, if that is more romantic." She was fishing, she knew it. It was nothing, nothing, just sex between strangers, but she *liked* him. He had seemed — and on second thought maybe this was distressing — immediately at home here, as though he had seen a thousand women's apartments and hotel rooms and had grown entirely used to the whole procedure, to the nakedness and the fun of finding a new bedroom and a new bed with fresh sheets that she had changed that afternoon, rushing home from the conference to clean up and all the while thinking how silly it was, and how scheming too. Certainly she could not claim to be the innocent one here, the one seduced — how the old ladies would be scandalized! And she had felt slightly dirty, smoothing down the clean white percale, turning over the yellow fringed coverlet that had looked so good in the catalogue but that among her other things looked like something in a bad hotel.

Well, he hadn't noticed. Neither had she, when it came to it. She had been intent on watching him disrobe, the terrible, terrible jacket first and then the bad tie, and the all-right shirt, and then underneath this, a surprise, a nice old-fashioned scoop-necked T-shirt, the sort old Italian men wore, showing little reddish tufts of hair above the neckline. So — secretly he was an old man. The narrow black belt, the black pants, the nameless shoes, the bunched and humble underpants, and at last behind them the thick purplish veined penis on its nest of tan hair, stirring as he climbed onto the bed toward her. And as he did, a sweet, hopeful look, happy but not wanting to offend. The eager beaver.

The next morning she went out to get him the clothes he so desperately needed. But she could not get him everything, it would be too much. So what did you start with? Ties. She went immediately to Galeries Lafayette and bought one very nice green paisley on a gold field and one striped red, white, and blue. "For an American," she explained, and the clerk rolled her eyes and said, "He'll never wear it." She had them wrapped in a narrow white box, which she then delivered to the desk of the hotel. She was maybe in a giddy mood, but why not? She liked him. He was a doctor, not famous or anything but a young success, and he had liked her, after all, and he was not arrogant or too stupid, like most doctors. A good man. He was. She could tell.

But as the conference went on that day, a series of doubts rose in her. Had she been too forward? Had she come across badly? By the afternoon a burning shame had gripped her, made her inhale suddenly in her chair while taking her notes for awful old Gruber; it was true, they were mercenaries really. She put down her clipboard. The gray carpet extended everywhere. Oh, she had ruined her chance with him, she thought — she had leapt too readily at him, she had not valued herself enough, she had been too eager to have sex on just a tiny excuse, not even an excuse at all. Stupid old stinky Arnie. Her heart dropped, a black emptiness opened in her gut, and from it came a great tugging sensation, a sensation of falling, falling, falling into her spinsterhood, and when she called Henry's room he did not answer. Oh, he was with someone else already! Gregor had been right — she had not been worth keeping, not even for a day.

She went on like this until at last she found him, by accident, as he was emerging from the bathroom in a back hallway. He was buckling his belt. Hanging strangely from his collar was the paisley tie. Surprised by him, her heart swung helplessly open — oh, his nice plain face, his red-brown hair curling out over his ears, that mild, preoccupied shape to his eyes, as though he were planning a conversation he was about to have. She had startled him too. A look of real happiness flashed across his features. He held up the tie, dropped it again. "It's the nicest tie I've ever owned in my life."

"It looks good." She shrugged. "It's sort of . . . crooked, maybe."

He approached, took her hand. "Listen, I didn't want to miss you."

"You have two days still."

"Yeah. Come back with me."

"Not this second, I have one more dumb seminar to go to."

"I mean to the States."

"Esh." She was startled; he had been joking, she thought. Did he really mean it? "You say it to all the girls."

"Not really."

"So maybe half the girls, the ones who buy you things, plus the pretty ones who you buy things for?"

"No," he said.

Her heart was racing. She swallowed. Her hands, of their own accord, lifted to his collar. She adjusted him. "It is a lot to hope, only from a tie."

"But two ties," he said.

She didn't go. Not right away. But she kept in touch with Dr. Moss, with Henry, after he went back to Seattle — an outpost, or so it seemed in her mind, so far west and north. Up near Alaska, wasn't it? One of those American cities that had burned down a hundred years ago (she looked it up), when every single building had been made of wood. No brick, no stone. Why had all the buildings not just blown away in the wind before — were they all fastened into the dirt somehow? Yes, obviously, silly. And that volcano, Mount St. Helens, just last year it had made the sunsets red all around the planet, and although she had never noticed any difference in Paris, that sort of event did leave the impression that his part of the world was not really fit for human habitation, as though he had pitched up in a jungle full of pterodactyls. The roads, she assured herself, were paved. It was America, after all. But on the telephone he sounded awfully far away, as though he were calling from the moon, and there seemed to be a sort of wind on the line, an interstellar foamy hissing that made his voice small and feeble. In this day and age!

Really the whole romance, if that was what it was, felt old-fashioned. Sudden and entirely groundless, the sort of quick coupling her mother might have seen in the movies and laughed about. Was she being ridiculous? Her mother said she was. "Of course you are. Specifically, I wonder why you choose a man who lives so far away," she said.

"He's very nice."

"I think you are overcorrecting your past mistakes. Gregor was too close. He was practically family, so you find a man who is his opposite."

"Opposite in a good way, Mama."

"Oh," her mother fluted, "but there *are* no opposites!"

"That was your word!"

"Also, I do not like the way you talk about him as if he is perfect," said her mother. "It's a very strange idea, a perfect person."

"I don't think he's perfect, Mama, nobody is."

"Ha, but you talk, talk, talk about him, how funny and nice he is, how smart, how kind, et cetera, et cetera. But he lives so far away! I also think you do this because you have lived in peace all your life. If you got married in wartime you wouldn't think it was so important who you married, you wouldn't care so much. Now you have to find somebody you think is perfect, and you spend two years looking for him, and you find him in a hotel where he is visiting from a million miles away!"

"Mama, don't be rude. He's better than Gregor was. A hundred times better."

Her mother sighed. "But you can't move to America."

"Why not?"

"Because you're not American. You'll be miserable. Even the Americans are miserable!"

Possibly this was true. She could have hoped for more encouragement from her father, perhaps, but she did not go to him. As the younger daughter, the one to follow him into medicine, she had always felt too similar in temperament to really talk to him. What could be said? He would shrug, give his passive blessing, then retreat into his study. He had been a doctor during the war, and though Ilse's understanding of the details was fuzzy she had the impression he had been damaged by the experience and that he carried around with him a burden of guilt he could never really discharge. In his early photographs he was jaunty and dashing, he had owned a motorcycle, he had been a mountaineer. But no longer. She suspected he was innocent of anything too terrible, and read his sadness in the contents of his self-consciously broad library, in which were featured books about the Kalahari Bushmen and the Ebo and nudism. These had been her secret texts growing up, though after a while she began to think they were not so secret after all, that they had been intended for her all along.

What a strange modern childhood she had had, after all, born in 1952! She did not remember the years of four-power occupation — the Soviets left when she was three — but her mother informed her that she had cried to see the big Russian tanks rolling away. "You love everything too much," her mother explained, "except the things you should." Was this true too? Her parents had raised her well, as well as could be expected, anyway, and now this was how she was repaying them — by falling in love with an American who wanted to take her away from her own country, and by becoming her own grandmother, that itchy impulsive kindhearted romantic lady who had been married at nineteen to a penniless medical student from Klagenfurt! Ilse's grandfather. Both dead now.

Henry's letters were typed — she had never received a typed letter before except from businesses; it was simply not done, in her experience — and enfolded in long opaque white envelopes, very rich, the sort that Testarossa might use, bearing their airmail stamps in the corner like tiny pieces of foreign currency. Her own letters she preferred to write longhand, in blue ink on small white paper. Fussy paper, when she looked at it again out of the drawer. (Oh, she could hear her mother snicker.) Henry's signature was large, blue, and not very elegant, but his letters were charming, and he still wanted her to come visit. He hadn't changed his mind. He wanted to buy a house; would she come help pick it out? It was all quite fun; certainly it wasn't very real at all. She wrote back all sorts of wild things, not really believing she would ever go, but six months after the conference she was due for a vacation and decided to go to the United States, because after all she had never been, and to fly to Seattle, just out of the corner of her eye, as it were, though it was a long way from New York and Washington, D.C., where she had intended to go years before.

"You're going," her mother said over the telephone, "to prove me wrong."

"I'm not, Mama."

"That's good," said her mother, "because as you know I'm never wrong about anything, especially about people."

"What about Papa?"

"He's not a person, he's my husband."

"No, I mean what does he think?"

"Oh, well," Freda said, "he loves you."

"For reasons you cannot understand."

"No," Freda said, subdued, "I understand him very well."

As Ilse had expected, she liked New York for its grubby friendliness and the very American sense of danger that loomed down the side streets that never got any sun. You did have to know where not to venture; it was like the Third World in that way, or like Jerusalem or Rome, or Paris, she supposed — there were cities within cities, and no one lived in all of them at once, except possibly for aid workers. She liked Washington too; it was stirring to stand in the Lincoln Memorial and read Lincoln's speeches carved into the marble. He had been so fine-hearted and decent, and her English was almost good enough now to appreciate it all, his big hand-made Roman sentences. She liked the littleness of herself in there, the way she had to crane her head back to see his face; he was like Jupiter looking down the long green mall with that expression of fierce worry, as though he were still concerned for all of them, all the slaves and the poor farmer boys, the blacks and the whites, and not thinking for a moment about himself, and so he had allowed himself to be ambushed while watching a play. Oh it was sad, the dead king! You felt you would have to invent him if he did not exist already. And so recent too. By Lincoln's day in Vienna cavalrymen were parading with their draft horses on the cobblestones and Metternich was studying his maps, and you felt there was no way out, that history would lead you right to Sarajevo and the bullets in the archduke's motorcar, then to Versailles and Hindenburg and Hitler and Stalin and the Wall, it was all set and ready like cards waiting in a dealer's shoe to be dealt. But there was something different about America, as though it existed outside of time, so it could be imperial already, with a grand past and marble monuments and gigantic armies and nuclear missiles and a man on the moon, and now a new space shuttle, yet still have volcanoes going off and forests with bears and lions still living in them, not just in old heraldic signs but actually alive in the wild, as though it were India, and also oil wells and football teams. It could be everything at once — it could have cowboys who still rode horses every day and also all this traffic, and incidentally no sense of how to organize a city, with everybody driving everyplace and never walking. And the suburbs! When she took the train from New York to Washington they seemed to follow her all the way down the track, patchy and persistent, like hyenas, half-built horrible noplaces with shabby falling-down architecture. Yet also she saw the fine colonial houses that looked as though they had been built from picture books, and oak trees standing in the middle of city parks, parks that all appeared to be empty. Why oh why were these beautiful parks empty when there were these grand trees to enjoy, planted out of fine municipal civic-mindedness? Where was everyone? At home watching television. But people did that everywhere; she ought not to hold it against Americans — though they *had* invented it. Oh, it was the same exhilaration and disappointment that everyone felt when coming to America, she supposed, it was all you had hoped for but it was other things too, dirty and hurriedly made and sort of tacky, and grander than you had thought, and less friendly. And bigger.

Much bigger: six hours to fly to Seattle, and it was all, she had to keep reminding herself, the same country — Ronald Reagan was the president of that lake and that little circular set of fields and that butterfly highway exchange and all these clouds and all the mountains too. All of it, on and on, like a god. She flew over it for days, it seemed, and at last began descending, descending, into a mountainous green country where the hillsides were barbarously shaved of their trees, as though marauding armies had passed through recently, and then she began to see green islands in a sinuous piece of water — Puget Sound, she surmised — and at last she saw a trim, shiny, glass-walled city sitting on the water, and her heart leapt into her throat. Oh, she was suddenly terrified! She was landing to meet a man she had slept with only a few times, who had more or less asked her to marry him already, but all right, she was quite capable of handling this, she was an Austrian woman who spoke three languages well and also some Italian that was good for traveling. She had on a new suit and had just finished her period and if things didn't go well what on earth would prevent her from having a good time anyway? She walked up the ramp with a brave step. She had never been this far west, and if she wanted she might just keep going on to Japan or somewhere and then into one of those little South Asian countries, the ones with the wiry alphabets, and go home to Paris the back way, and then she could say she had been around the world for love and not found it and that would be that, she could live with Tannie and raise a million cats.

But no: he was waiting at the gate, wearing his red, white, and blue tie. In relief she began to cry very quietly onto his shoulder, and when she had finished she was happier than she could ever remember. Oh, so old-fashioned, it was embarrassing! But here she was, in America, in love. "I'm sorry" were her first American words to Henry, and his in return were, breathlessly, "You're here."

3

HENRY'S LAB — he got his own when he became an assistant professor, in 1986 — measured thirty feet long and twenty feet wide and smelled, usually, of heated electronics and overboiled coffee, and the spice of Victoria's cinnamon gum, and the leavings of the tuna fish and bananas the postdoctoral fellows brought for lunch, and his longtime assistant Gretl's floral, grandmotherly soap. The high ceilings were hung with acoustic tile and fluorescent lights and an intricate, red-piped sprinkler system, and three black PermaCote workbenches stood along the length of the room. Workers faced one another through shelves stacked with beakers and agar dishes and racks of slender plastic pipettes, and down the western wall of the laboratory ran a row of thick, narrow windows which could be swung open a few inches. From these windows you could see a slice of Lake Union and the rusted old boilers at Gasworks Park and, over the water, the green iron span of the Ship Canal Bridge. The western exposure gave the laboratory a pleasant, airy feel, and Henry enjoyed the early mornings here in his clean adjoining office, with his desk free of clutter, the expensively archived volumes of *Age* and *New England Journal of Medicine* and *American Journal of Human Genetics* standing in neat rows of white and green above him. This is where his work had brought him, and he felt, in an unembarrassed way, that he had earned it.

Earned it. He had finally found the gene that caused Hickman syndrome, beating Gary Hauptmann to the punch, finding the six-teen-nucleotide deletion at last on the short arm of the eighth chromosome. It had been a breakthrough, the biggest in the history of the disease. It was hard to study such a rare disorder; only seventy-five children with the condition were alive at any one time — on the average, anyway; at the moment there were only sixty-eight — and when you ballparked the numbers out, with an average life-span of about fifteen years, you had a worldwide birthrate of about five new cases a year. Hickman was a classic autosomal recessive condition, so two people who both carried one copy of the Hickman mutation not only had to come together by chance, but each also had to pass on his or her one defective copy of the gene to produce a child with two defective copies, and therefore the condition. Long odds, but they did come home, and genetics was still an obscure enough science that most people discovered there was such a thing as Hickman only when their child began to look funny at the age of two or three. Hair turning gray and falling out. Weird folds around the eyes. Then it was arthritis at ten, osteoporosis for the girls at eleven, straight into senility before hitting puberty, and death from heart failure or simple old age by nineteen at the very latest. The kids were stoic, by and large, and happy enough at their annual picnics, but they were doomed, trapped in their elderly bodies. It was a peculiar disease in that the carrier state was almost totally neutral, meaning that the condition was distributed very evenly around the world, with a slightly elevated rate of incidence in Western countries — and this just because of better reporting, or so Henry suspected. French, Japanese, Nigerian, Mongolian, it didn't matter. This kind of homogeneity was rare in an inherited condition, and suggested that the mutation was a very old one.

What might the survival advantage have been, Henry had long wondered, to owning only one of these broken genes? Immunity to some long-extinct virus — something the Neandertals had come down with, or *Homo erectus,* or the Australopithecines? If half of sickle cell anemia gave you immunity to malaria, what did half of Hickman give you? He had never found even a suggestion of a pos-itive effect among carriers, but it didn't keep him from wondering. The ability to digest a now vanished plant? To hibernate?

So Henry saw his two or three new patients a year — children referred to him by some spooked pediatrician who had gone to the reference shelf and pulled down the third edition of *Genetic Disorders in Development,* eds. Palmer and Lyman, and discovered Henry's name at the top of the Hickman bibliography. In fact the diagnosis was very easy. As was true of many genetic disorders, Hickman patients all looked alike; they lived and died as a recognizable group, as though they had signed away the bulk of their genetic birthright in exchange for ownership of their one small mistake, a mistake their bodies cherished and preserved. By the time they died, all showed the same sluggish bowels and varicose veins and pure hairlessness, like pigs that had been scalded. All became very frail and thin, with extremely low muscle mass, bulbous heads, wasted limbs, sunken jaws. Jews in the concentration camps, you couldn't help think. Or aliens, enfeebled by a gravity too heavy for them. And they all died young. The longest anyone had ever lived with Hickman was nineteen years and two months: a Libyan girl named Hara Haraj. She had died in 1967, senile, toothless, and incontinent, the last long year of her life an endless terminal century of aging. No one since then had made it even to eighteen. Not necessarily a bad thing, in Henry's book.

Despite all this gloomy stuff, Henry didn't feel much about his own dying one way or the other. He had been orphaned at twenty-two, and he suspected this had something to do with it. His parents' car, with his mother and father inside it, had been destroyed by a logging truck many miles from anywhere his parents should have been — for some reason they had been way out in the wilderness, deep into the nearly roadless hills west of Chehalis. Why? It was as though they had been sent out with a map to discover their own destruction. Where had they been going? What had they been after? He would never know. They did not take such trips. Crushed, killed instantly, the car a hideous mangle of steel. He never saw the bodies; he had been advised not to.

Their deaths were, as it turned out, a spur to Henry. Life, he could see, was serious. His training in medicine was a steady rise from Ann Arbor — medical school — to Oakland for his internship, then to hot, blighted Dallas for his residency. As an only child he had always had a sort of speculative, off-the-rails kind of mind — Henry had read his share of science fiction as a teenager — and the notion of extending human longevity had attracted him as a scientist. It was an interesting problem. Why should organisms die? What good does it do? Hickman had seemed an excellent way into the subject. People were still asking those big questions, and as with any complex problem the answers were various and bewilderingly interconnected, but these days Henry's research was entirely focused on the Hickman gene and how it worked, how its disordered enzyme functioned within the body, and how the condition manifested itself at various stages. On his wall he had a framed copy of Lincoln Hickman's very own two-page description of a girl suffering from *precocious senility of striking degree,* filed with the Hospital of St. Michael in London in 1882. It was all there from the beginning: *exophthalmic eyes, significant osseous erosion of mandible, general fragility, high and unusual voice.*

So Henry was a specialist. He got suspicious blood in the mail from all over the world, chilly dark vials emerging from their Cold Crates with a ghostly whiff of dry ice, packages addressed to Doctor Henri Mosh, Dr. Henrie Mosse, Dr. Henry Moth, Dr. Harry Roth, Dr. Howard Mouth, Dr. H. M. Monk, Dr. Henry Hickman. Him.

And, all in all, he was happy where he was. But occasionally when shuffling grant proposals in his office on a Thursday night he would think nostalgically of his days in Oakland, those early days when he had swabbed sore throats, attended pulmonary rounds, observed the bloody gymnastics of cardiac surgery, and in the emergency room stitched black thread into the jagged knife wounds of muggers and drug dealers. Real work, as his father would have said. Henry missed it sometimes. His sewing hand was very good, having been trained on socks and pillowcases by his mother; his tight black stitches received compliments. His father, a planner for Seattle City Light, had strung miles and miles of telephone line in his own distant youth, and in the middle of a suturing Henry had liked to think that the old man would have appreciated the tension and friction of the sewing — the long give, the pull, the hard, terminal knot.

But this too was something Henry would never know. His father had been painfully cautious and reticent, and after his two summers on the poles the man had worked at a planner's desk for decades, and his mother had kept house and pursued, in the sincere manner of the times, the higher-toned crafts: woodcuts, quilting, and watercolors. Henry had been born late, and his parents' habits of married solitude had long since been cemented. As a boy he had often felt like an object of polite surprise between them, and of pity, the pity of the insider for the newcomer. What had the two of them thought in that last crushing instant? Had they thought of him, their son? Or of each other, born within eight days of one another in two prairie towns separated by a thousand miles? Their mild, measured blood moved in his heart, as always, but like them it had little to say. Their premature disappearance had taught him — early — that he too would someday disappear. It was not his favorite idea, but he felt the universe had offered him a fair deal. More than fair. Work hard. Love his wife. Have children. Then perish, having used up his telomeres and polluted his DNA with the free radicals contained in two thousand cafeteria hamburgers. He needed no solace from religion, and anyway he knew too well the means by which a primitive strand of chance molecules might have been electrified into life while no one was watching. It had taken eons to occur, probably, but geological time was vast. If the universe had any blessing at all to bestow, it was the blessing of time. In all that vastness he would be forgotten, as so many others had been before him, and the idea did not bother him that much.

On the other hand, his kids worried him a little. What did they think of it all? "I am a molecular geneticist," he told them, and they accepted it with solemn nods. He gave harmless little demonstrations of Mendelian genetics at the elementary school, conscientiously treating his own children as politely, as distantly, as he treated the other students. He was careful, especially when they were young, to limit the table talk. But they both knew what he did, and seemed to have a good idea of what it meant. "What the hell is *that?*" Sandra had cried once, after opening a folder he had left on the kitchen counter. She was backing away, cringing. Inside were photographs of a thirteen-year-old girl, toothless, globe-headed, bald, her eyes popping from their sockets, her chin sunken and her neck wattled. "That's Carrie McDonald," Henry said softly, and his daughter — eight or nine years old at the time — shuddered, turned away in terror. *It had a name!* He was more careful after that. But he couldn't protect them completely. The reference books around the house were long catalogs of horror. Collodion babies, ichthyoses, disturbing malformations of the scalp and face, freakish flexible elbows that could bend nightmarishly backward, chaotically speckled skin, fused and eroded fingers and toes, people missing shoulders, eyes, ears, brains. He and Ilse kept the books sequestered in their bedroom, but Henry knew Sandra and Darren could get to them if they really wanted to.

As it turned out, they did not want to. The people in the pictures were too grotesque, too real and frightening, to be examined with anything like delight. And most of the people pictured — the kids must have known this — had since died. You didn't live long with this stuff. "I think it's okay," his wife said. "They don't want to see it."

"She's going to remember that girl."

"She saw worse when we rented *The Fly*, and that only bothered her for a week."

"If I was a shepherd or something," he said, "we wouldn't have this problem."

"But then" — she gestured hopelessly — "disgusting sheep everywhere. Plus, mutton. You can't win, darling."

The only local Hickman patient, William Durbin, was almost exactly Darren's age. Their birthdays were five weeks apart, but while Darren grew from a solid lump to a skinny toddler to a regulation-size boy, William Durbin did not. At two, when Henry first saw him in clinic, he was a smallish, polite, fragile kid, just beginning to show signs. It was unusual to see a Hickman patient this young, and a Hickman baby had never been born in Seattle. So it was natural, Henry would think later, to become attached to William; he couldn't really be blamed for it. And William was a winner from the start: a nice kid. When Henry first propped him gently on the black vinyl stool in front of him, the boy was the first to speak. "Thank you very much," he said.

"Well, you're very welcome." Henry felt the neck, the musculature across the shoulders. Weak, but not terrible. Examined his eyes, his ears. "This is my magic eye light," he said.

"No it's not."

"I think it is," Henry said. "See? It goes blink! Blink!"

"That's just normal!"

"Smart kid," Henry said to the parents. "Can't fool him."

"No, you can't." Bernie Durbin was a dark, stout man of thirty-five. He was nearly bald and kept his remaining fringe of black hair very short around his ears; his face was tight with grief and confusion. His wife, Lillian, was watching Henry closely, restraining herself. She plainly wanted to reach out and retrieve William, gather him up, but instead she folded her arms against her chest. Blond, her husband's age, with gold bracelets. Waiting. Henry helped William off the stool and Lillian snatched the boy up, inhaled the scent of his hair. Closed her eyes. *Please, please, get it over with,* she was asking. They had been given the diagnosis a week ago by Charlie Calens, their pediatrician, who had an office four floors up; Henry's lab had done the blood work. And now the Durbins had come to him so he could explain it all. So he did.

"Charlie told you a little something about the condition," he began, "so you know the general prognosis."

"A little," said Bernie. "It's still about fourteen years old, the average — you know, expectancy?"

"That's about the average."

The parents blinked. "We thought it might have gone up a little since the stuff we read," Bernie said finally. "But not yet?"

"Not yet."

Bernie exhaled heavily through his nose. "Okay," he said, and grappled for his wife's hand, found it. "So? You probably have a list of stuff to tell us."

"We can go as slow as you want," Henry said. "We can talk now, or next week, or next month. It's up to you. If you want to talk now, we can have Victoria take William upstairs to the playroom for a few minutes so we can do this in private. They're very germ-conscious up there, so he'd be okay. He wouldn't catch anything."

"I'd rather have him stay," Lillian said, shaking down her bracelets.

"That's fine. It's up to you."

"Up to you," William mimicked.

"Go ahead," said Bernie.

Henry took a deep breath. How did you do this? You made it as plain as possible, as unadorned, and let them handle it as well as they could. It was never easy. In fact as the years had passed Henry had found this particular speech more difficult to give, feeling as the moment came that he was presenting parents with a terrible, elaborate gift, one sheathed in dozens and dozens of layers of wrapping paper, boxes within boxes, and containing at its heart a magnetic black nothingness. It had to do with having your own kids: you understood exactly what you were telling people.

"So you know it's a very rare condition. Which means, among other things, that research can be slow, because we don't have a lot of patients to study. We're better off than we were a couple years ago, because now we know what causes it. But it's a condition that still results in a shortened lifespan, and right now we can't do anything about that."

"Yeah," said Bernie.

"It's basically a global, cellular condition. So it's not as if there's just liver failure or kidney problems, although there are. Every cell in every organ system in the body is affected. Every time any cell divides, its DNA has to be copied, and there are special enzymes that do the copying, and in William the rate of cellular replication is turned up very high, and at the same time the normal copying and repair mechanisms don't work very well, so the aging process happens much more quickly in him than in you or me. We don't really know how it happens, and we don't know how to stop it."

"Does it hurt?" asked Bernie.

"No. Not in itself. The symptoms can, sometimes."

"He seems tired all the time," said Lillian.

"That's common. There's usually a nice little upswing around three or four, and the condition's usually pretty stable until eight or nine. Then there'll start to be a slow decline. There's a large variation in how quickly that happens. Given the state of the condition as it looks today, I'd predict it'd be slow, and that you're on the higher end of the average age. But we don't know. That's just a guess."

"What happens at the end?"

"It depends."

"Will it hurt then?" Bernie was spinning a heavy silver ring on his finger. "Is that something we need to get ready for? Is there something we're supposed to do now, to get ready?"

No, there wasn't. "We'd like to be able to see him fairly often, if you're comfortable with that. Just to monitor him. Since you're local, that might be as much as once a month, but it's up to you. We can recommend a diet that seems to be the best thing. He can go to school if you want, when he's old enough. And he can play, but he'll want to be careful, because he's going to experience some bone fragility starting around seven or eight. He's okay now, but he'll start to look very different from his friends in another year or two, and everybody'll know there's something different about him, and he'll know it too, and you'll get a lot of questions from people, and probably some comments that you'll wish you hadn't heard. But he's not *sick,* exactly. He's just going to get old very fast, and there'll be the usual frailties that accompany getting old."

"How do we break the news?" Lillian asked. "What do we say?"

"To him? Whatever you want to." William, in his mother's lap, was reaching idly for the cartoons on Henry's door. "That's up to you."

"What would you do?" she asked.

His heart sank, as it always did. How would he react if he were told that Darren was going to die, or Sandra? Like any father, he had imagined getting the news over and over — practicing, maybe, for the worst — and most of the time he could imagine a desolate, mute, catastrophic sort of grief; but it wasn't the real thing, and he knew it; he knew he didn't really know what it felt like. So he told the Durbins what he always told the families who sat on that sofa, facing him: "It's going to be very hard. But I'd make sure it's not a secret from anybody, certainly not from him. Not from your parents, not from your families. But there'll be a moment when he gets it," Henry said, and he saw Bernie gulp, "and that'll be very hard. There's the Hickman Foundation in San Francisco, which can help with a lot of this — Victoria can get you all that information. Other families, counseling, that kind of thing. They're very good."

"It's fast at the end?"

"It depends on what happens."

"Which is usually what?"

"Usually it's congestive heart failure."

"Oh my god," Bernie said, putting a hand over his eyes.

Lillian, rearranging William on her shoulder, said, "We waited a long time to have kids. I keep thinking if I'd just had kids when I was younger." She licked her lips. She was pretty, well kept, looked rich. "But that doesn't have anything to do with it?"

"You two could have had him when you were seventeen. He *is* one of the younger patients I've seen. We don't usually see them until they're around three."

William turned and examined Henry now. He was barely beginning to show the phenotype: forehead subtly enlarged, eyes a trifle bulging, his chin just marginally weak. His teeth were small but intact. Charlie Calens was good. Observant as hell, to catch it so early.

"I'm two," William told Henry.

"I know," Henry said. "That's a very good age."

"Two is more than one."

"It's one more than one."

"One is the same as one," William answered.

"But when you put one and one together you get two."

"Exactly," said William. He was an intent kid who now regarded Henry with a new air of respect: *This guy can do math.* "Very good," William said.

"Thank you."

"He's very talkative," Lillian said apologetically, and, embracing her child, she began to cry, then gritted her teeth and stopped herself. "God, he's so smart," she said angrily. "It's not fair."

It wasn't, it was just a terrible thing, and Henry had never come up with anything that would make this moment easier. He talked to the Durbins that day for hours. As most parents did, they asked why, and he had no answer. He could show them the printout of the Hickman gene and point to the deletion, but that wasn't why, that was how. For religious parents, their beliefs were usually a comfort, and Henry had met his share of devout eleven-year-old Hickman patients who in their baldness and accomplished serenity reminded him of Buddhist monks waiting for their existence to pass, as if in their holiness they had received permission to die more swiftly and return again to perfect nothingness. But for nonbelievers like the Durbins, it was a bizarre, frightening, highly unnatural condition, the child dying visibly for years, dying before his parents; and though Hickman parents eventually grew accustomed to the idea, it never grew less bizarre. The human mind had not evolved to be able to compute such a thing, Henry thought, and although parents were resilient and made the best of it, and were capable of feats of wonderful grace and delicacy in the middle of terrible sadness, Hickman never seemed normal. *It's like something out of a dream,* the parents often said, *but we can't wake up.*

But Bernie and Lillian, after the first months of shock, did well. They agreed to let Henry see William as often as Henry wished, and as Henry grew to know the Durbins he came to admire them. They were rich. They gave big checks to the Hickman Foundation and to the March of Dimes. They hosted fundraisers. They were both lawyers, and Lillian's family had money from somewhere — Henry never found out where, exactly, but there was a lot of it. Their big old house on Capitol Hill sat on a corner lot, with a deep green lawn where two tall dogwoods opened tender white blossoms every spring. A porch wrapped around the side of the house, and a row of wicker chairs stood in the shade, offering a view of the city below: Lake Washington, the floating bridge to Bellevue, the university hospital, and, if you knew where to look, Henry's office window, one gray square among a thousand others.

Inside, the Durbins' house was quiet, dim, and smelled richly of historical pampering — mineral oil on the woodwork, smoke in the fireplace, the carpets giving up the scent of old Turkish dust — and there was a cool, preservationist quality to the air. It was a big stone house, with plaster walls chill to the touch, lace curtains that filtered the light, and a marvelous endlessness to the rooms — closets and back staircases and tiny octagonally tiled bathrooms, eight bedrooms piled in three stories, and sun porches where the light fell on the cushioned sewing chairs. Henry's heart, in these rooms, would fill with a happy serenity: it was a perfect place, it seemed, a place that would make anyone happy, and as William grew up he did seem happy, as happy as could be expected. When fundraisers were held here the house was full of fancy, well-dressed people, and William could be seen walking among them with a tray, serving drinks. "Booze?" he would ask. "Booze for the lady? And booze for the doctor?"

William's bedroom was down the hall from his parents' room and overlooked the front yard. "My domain," he would say, sitting by the window and waving his arm stiffly at the view. A certain air of invalidism was unavoidable, Henry supposed, but it was kept to a minimum. Medical supplies were stored out of sight in a closet. There was a nurse, Elaine O'Donnell, who took care of William during the days. "He's been looking forward to seeing you," she might say, showing Henry upstairs.

"How is he?"

She was a tall, stooped woman who moved with an athlete's unthinking vigor. She took the stairs two at a time; stopping, she might turn to him and say, "He's doing all right," if William had been corresponding with a Hickman friend over e-mail. Or "He's been in the dumps," if he'd taken a fall.

"Buddy," Henry might say, entering the room.

"Pal."

"This is going to shock you, but I need some blood."

"Do I get it back this time?"

"We put it on our ice cream," Henry might say, or "We sell it to hot dog manufacturers," or "We just put it out in the hall in a box that says *Free*." He had taken a lot of blood from William, it was true, probably gallons of it by now, and as the years had passed the skin on William's forearm had sagged and puckered, lost its elasticity, and the veins had sunk into the tissue, so discovering them with a needle was impossible; later Henry moved on to the boy's feet, the backs of his hands, the tender skin of his ankles.

Bernie and Lillian never had any more children, though Henry explained how early in a pregnancy genetic testing could be done. "Okay, but what would William think?" Lillian had asked. "Imagine he gets a healthy younger brother suddenly."

"There is that."

"Yeah," Bernie said, twisting his ring, "and what if we end up ignoring the kid then, and just focusing on the healthy new one? I personally can't imagine that, but — it might happen."

"I doubt it."

"On the other hand," Lillian said, "maybe he'd really like a brother. Or a sister."

"But by the time they got old enough for him to play with . . ." Bernie began. Bernie was completely bald now, and resembled a younger, more vital version of his son. "I don't know. He's a fun kid. I don't want to give him anything else to think about."

Charlie Calens was around a lot too, taking his own blood samples, administering his own tests; Calens was also bald, with high pointed gargoyle's ears and a Gothic height to the dome of his skull, as though the brain's effort in carrying the secrets of pediatric pathology had caused its tissues to swell. A good doctor, he was liked by children, who were attracted, Henry thought, to his cartoonish looks. When he was examining William, the man's eyes would unwittingly bulge — more pressure building within his head, pressure that would dissipate in a long, breathy, tuneful whirring through chipped teeth. "Beeeeeej," Calens would say, feeling William's wrists and elbows. "Whoooooorrrrr," while palpating his scalp. Henry liked Charlie, admired him, but really they had little to say to each other. There was nothing either of them could do, after all. There was no magic undiscovered gland to be massaged with radiation. No gold-flecked tonic to administer. Every month William looked more and more like a Hickman patient, as the boy he had been vanished into the phenotypic signs: bulbous head, sunken jaw, ragged teeth, wasted body.

Meanwhile Henry's own children went ahead and got older in the normal way: first they couldn't climb down the stairs except backward and one step at a time, and suddenly they were keeping secrets from him, Sandra especially, with her big Aztec face and its wary, pagan expressions when she came in at the end of the day, this big piece of Henry wandering around in the world. His daughter's name, written in ballpoint on her Pee-Chee notebooks, seemed a message from the gods inscribed directly on the surface of Henry's big soft fatherly heart, and Darren's hard little bristly head in Henry's palm was hot, steaming with the energy of boyhood, and felt as therapeutic as a water bottle. It was a good life, and Henry knew it. How perfect his children's skin was, how clear their milky scleras! How dainty the golden hairs crowded along their earlobes! How perfectly supple their flawless lungs! It stirred him to tears. When Darren played soccer as a nine-year-old, Henry and Ilse stood outside in the November cold, their chins in their jackets, and watched their boy run up and down the grass. Late afternoons over the field, the sky would turn a bright, northern pink, and the jets coming into Sea-Tac would circle over the sound and fly southbound over the city, pinpoints of light that seemed held up — suspended — by the sky itself. Alien craft, Henry would think, standing there. And then suddenly he would be thinking of William again, even as he stood there with his wife, appearing in every way to be a normal, attentive father; it happened all the time. *I wish I was an alien,* William had said once, recently.

"Oh yeah?"

"Well, there would be some obvious advantages."

"Like what?"

"Well . . ." The boy had paused. "Like number one, I would have advanced technology that might get me out of this mess. Number two, I would have seen a lot more of the universe than I have. Number three" — he shrugged — "I would be supposed to look like this."

"Good point."

"But I'm not, right?"

"Not an alien?"

"Right," William said.

"Yeah, no, you're not."

"I thought it might just be conceivably possible," William said. "And how would I know? Unless somebody told me."

"Another good point."

Henry hadn't meant to, but as the years had passed he had come to love William as much as he loved anyone in the world. And now, as the last spring of the century was beginning, William was fourteen and dying, and Henry's heart was breaking. In bed at night the frogs sang him to sleep, and his wife embraced him, holding him safe against the darkness, while the warm rain dashed from his gutters and the frogs sang their endless, desperate song. No, there was nothing he could do about it, nothing at all. He knew this, and sometimes he felt this knowledge should have been a kind of solace. But it wasn't.

4

ILSE WAS THE DIRECTOR of medical staffing at Kreutznaer General Hospital, across town from Henry's university, which meant basically she did a lot of hiring and firing, which was sometimes fun and sometimes not. Additionally, she was in charge of running the residents in and out, making sure no one too crazy was taken on, making sure they got paid and fed, that sort of thing. Minding the troops, she called it.

She had not been able to find work as a doctor when she had arrived in America, and once at Kreutznaer she had never gone back to practice — which meant she was not a doctor anymore really, except in title, and lately she had begun to wonder if this had been a mistake. She was good at her work, as her native bureaucratic talents had risen in her — she was a perfect *beamte,* meticulous and stern and selfless; she used a plain old glass-topped desk and brought her lunch in a bag, and therefore she was able to say, No, don't buy shrimp for the party, parties are for home, not for work, if people want to celebrate something let them do it down the street at the Garage Bar, not up here where the janitors have to come in afterward and clean up the cheese triangles. Instead, residents should have a nicely painted dormitory, and once in a while the sofa cushions should actually go to the cleaners so they don't smell like someone's head.

And without ever making an explicit point of it, she directed favor to blacks and Indians, the blacks especially, the men in their jackets looking very handsome and serious, some with symbols carved on their arms, the keloid scars raised like welding seams. Five hundred years from now, who would remember that people did this? Slavery had not been that long ago, and when she saw those scars she could not help but think of branding, and how defiant and brave the act seemed in that light, how praiseworthy! Recently she had touched one resident's arm and felt the hard ridge of his scar: a Greek letter, an omega. "Did that hurt?" she asked.

"Actually, I was pretty drunk," he answered sheepishly. "Didn't feel much until the next day, I guess."

"What does it mean?" Her accent, even faded as it was, identified her as a foreigner, so she was allowed to ask questions like this. Americans, polite people. "Is it religious?"

"It's my fraternity."

"Who did it?"

"My brothers. My fraternity brothers, I mean."

"In Austria we had societies. The International Relations Society, the Historical Society. No scars, but very serious, you know, because if you were too heavy a drinker you were left behind in the courses. Then you had to enter a trade school, which was worse than death."

"Probably got a better education than we did."

"Yes, but out of fear," she said. "In medical school we were expected to travel on outings together, to the library, to the park, for our enjoyment. But that was many years ago. Now it may be different. I was an orthopedist." *Was;* the word still stung.

"That's what I hear."

"Oh, I was, and then I was dragooned into this job, you know. They thought I was so bossy I might as well be put to use, in bossing the maximum number of people."

"Yeah, I like the way this place works. It's humane."

"Is it?" she asked gratefully.

"Yeah." He shrugged, began shifting away. "You actually let us get some sleep."

"It's only the stupid old men who want to make medicine an endurance contest for some reason. Like the twenty-four hours of Le Mans. Isn't it ridiculous?"

"I guess so."

"You're Dr. Edmonds?"

"Edwards," said the resident. "But pretty close. I'm impressed."

"Close but no cigar," she said. "No prize for that. I'm sorry. Dr. Edwards."

"No, it's cool. Really."

"Dr. *Edwards*. Shame on me!"

"It's cool. You can't know everybody, there's like sixty new people every year."

"No, I'm very sorry," she insisted. "Edwards."

She did her best to wave the guilt away, from this and a hundred other little mistakes, because she *was* good at her work. Oh, she recited the facts to herself all the time. She gave time off for Kwanzaa, though she had her private doubts about it as a holiday. She sent black doctors into the local high schools. She made herself visible as a woman in charge, which she believed had some effect. And she was kind to people.

But it wasn't medicine. She had been doing research in Paris, and administrative work had seemed an acceptable temporary measure in America — she had not wanted to be too picky, not wanted Henry to support her — but she had not gone back to real doctoring, and now it was too late, and lately she had been growing unhappy with herself in a fairly serious way. She had not become the brilliant and capable doctor she should have been — not become herself, finally. At the end of the day her glass desk showed her fingerprints everywhere, but in the morning the surface was always clean again. She had been there eighteen years and she could be replaced in an afternoon, she felt. Too much longer at Kreutznaer, she feared, and she would lose herself altogether.

It was something she would have liked to have asked her father about, but he had died twelve years ago, leaving behind his African masks and photography books and, unsuspected in his papers, a thick stack of pencil drawings — nudes — at which he had been secretly at work for years. "I guess we saw it coming," her mother had said, her voice tight over the telephone, "except for the naked ladies."

Ilse, pained to the heart, had bought a ticket and packed a suitcase. "I won't be long," she promised Henry. Her poor papa. She flew all night and landed with a bump the next day in a state of dread. He had died without warning in his sleep. A heart attack.

She cried all the way into the city, standing at the window of the tram and trying not to attract too much attention, watching her old city roll past. Vienna, and her parents' enormous apartment, were exactly as Ilse remembered them: beautiful, pompous, and perilous, with the hostile undercurrents of Waldheim's recent election still stirring. Her father's belongings, abandoned in the dim yellow light of the Brucknerstrasse, were just as sad and terrifying as she had expected. His tortoiseshell glasses lay on his desk with no eyes to look through them, and his silly pipe for which he occasionally reproved himself now sat cool and stained on the shelf. His miniature ivory Buddha still contained its unexpected heft, as though made of lead, and his precious never-used leather doctor's bag, initialed with its touching leonine L, still sat ceremoniously on a high shelf, and the row of white shirts waited in the narrow closet, as faithful and patient as valets. The place still smelled of him, smoky and assured and very old. It broke her heart.

"You're welcome to stay as long as you wish," her mother said, stalking through the apartment, room after room, as if to demonstrate that she was alone, that the rooms were in fact empty. "Although I don't expect that to be very long."

"I'll stay as long as you like, Mama."

"Pah," her mother said, her chin quivering. "I never wanted you to leave in the first place."

"Where is he?"

"At Rieger. We can go look at him if you want."

"Did you find him?"

"Who else do you think lives here? Of course I found him. He was in bed next to me!" Her mother lifted her arms and then dropped them helplessly to her sides. "It was just as he would have wanted."

"To go quietly."

"No, to give me one last awful surprise," her mother said, scowling.

Tannie arrived from Berlin, her hair coiled in tight brown curls against her scalp and her mourning suit prim, well cut, and expensive. In the kitchen she greeted Ilse with "You're really here," and then leaned down to kiss their mother. She embraced the old woman with a rattle of jewelry. "And Henry?" she asked.

"They're all at home."

"Home." Tannie nodded. "You should bring them over to visit."

"They're too young."

"And soon they will be too old."

"You can always come see us," Ilse suggested.

"Because I haven't any encumbrances?"

"Well," Ilse pointed out, "you don't."

"Not as you would see them."

"Oh, leave her alone. The baby," her mother said, and pressed her soft palm to Ilse's cheek. "She misses her father."

"We all do," said Tannie.

"Ilse more than you or I," said Freda, looking up at Ilse fondly. "They were two of a kind."

"How true," said Tannie.

Tannie did not mean this as a kindness. But was it true? Ilse hadn't seen him much since departing for America; she had been back only twice since leaving Paris for good. The quiet, careful Henry had been a substitute, in some ways, for her father, and nothing had ever seemed to change here in this big apartment, with her mother chattering on the telephone at one end, looking out between the red curtains onto the street, and her father with his feet up in his study at the other end. Her two visits had left Ilse unsatisfied. Maybe she had expected her absence to have wrought more change. But her parents had long since been beyond changing.

Leopold Entwitten had been eighty-two. His body at Rieger was small, seeming to end halfway down and vanish into nothing, his legs indistinguishable from the white folds of the sheet. The skin of his arms hung loose and dark, flecked with moles and impressed here and there with huge liver spots, as though someone had repeatedly pressed an inky thumb to him. His neck was arched just slightly and his mouth was ajar, as though he were craning up to be fed. The face was grayed by death but stronger and more defined than it had been in his later life, the loose skin of his cheeks and jowls sliding away and down to reveal a big Roman nose and the sharp point of a chin. This was the young face her mother had known, the face that had worn the cycling goggles. In the little viewing room Tannie began to cry, her square shoulders jumping, and this caused Ilse to begin as well, turning to her mother, who accepted her, without remark, into her old arms. A hand on his forehead: not cold but cool, the skin waxy and stiffened. Her papa, who had slowed and slowed over the decades, had finally stopped moving entirely.

"He had been closing down for a year or two," said Freda afterward, back home. "He was finding his cave to die in, as they say. He spent all day near the end in that room of his. Those awful drawings."

"Can we see them?"

Her mother glowered at her cup and saucer. "He must have been feeling it all very keenly, the diminishment of his powers. I think for men it's much worse at the end than it is for women, as we're used to diminishment on a monthly installment, and they have it come at them all at once, a whole life's worth."

"I don't know about that, Mama."

"Of course you don't, Tannie."

"You don't want to show them," said Ilse.

"No, I don't."

"Why not?"

"Because he's dead, and that's humiliation enough." Her mother blinked, tearing up. "He might deserve it, but I won't be the one to deliver it. You've always been one of the romantics, Ilse. We could have used more of you here a little while ago — we might have elected Steyrer instead. Or maybe that was the trouble, our nasty romanticism. Which never believes anything is *real*. Or serious," she added. "Even ridiculous people are real. I am real, even though you think I'm ridiculous."

"Mama," Tannie began.

"I am," her mother insisted. "What do you think, that I was married for so long and didn't care?"

"No," said Tannie.

"You, I know about you, Tannie, you're a reasonable person. It's your sister who thinks all this. What is it about me, Ilse, that strikes you as ridiculous?"

"Nothing, Mama."

"Nothing." Freda scowled again. "I can never get a straight answer from anyone anymore. Those people at Rieger wanted me to sign a form and wouldn't tell me why — they thought I wouldn't understand. It turned out they wanted to cremate him right away, before either of you got to see him! Well, I'm not *senile*. People like us, we don't wear out like that, we just" — her voice caught — "stop working."

His study door was kept closed now, as it had never been in life. But Ilse could not keep herself from creeping inside. The view, as it always had, filled her heart with a beautiful, untouchable longing. What happiness he must have felt here! The upper corners of the dark room shivered with cobwebs, and the shelves were shadowy with *Zeitvertreiben den Amazonen,* the works of Basquiat, and *Tinker, Tailor, Soldier, Spy.* The dark carpet was filled with maroon arabesques, and the desk contained tiny leather and rubber and bronze objects with which a perfect Ilse could, in an ideal world, cut her fingernails, erase her mistakes, open her letters, contain her keys. She sat down. Her instincts for order and care originated in this room, she knew, and it felt like home. One enormous window looked out over the slate rooftops. A sea of chimneys extended in all directions. Trees showed their shifting heads, newly green, along the Ringstrasse. Her father's things around her. The shiny mantel clock. The brass bowls on the stone windowsill. The empty blue jar. The square dish of tight pinecones. The cardboard boxes full of old clippings arranged in chronological order on the shelves. Nothing had changed. Nothing did, while she stayed. Her mother kept away except to peer around the door. "You're getting dusty," she warned.

Ilse's old bedroom, where she slept, had been kept in order. The ceiling was high, though the room itself was quite small and windowless. It smelled of rosehips, which were to be found in a bowl on her bureau. Her journals stood in their blue row on the shelf, waiting to be read again, and her fountain pen, whose transparent barrel she had admired so much as a girl, was waiting to be taken in hand. But she didn't dare. The journals stayed where they were, their fabric bindings loose and thready, their lined pages containing the daily record of her old life. What perilous things they seemed to her now! What heartbreak they promised to deliver! Her journals had ended with her marriage to Gregor, and so had, she feared, some contact with her truest self. Like so many other people, she felt she had a core of radiant selfhood whose loveliness had been, inevitably, dampened by the life she had led. But it was in this room that she had begun to learn the odd idioms of English — *tongue in cheek, throw the book at him, bury the hatchet, skeleton in the closet, bite the dust* — that had in some way prepared her for Henry's letters, his boyish signature, and the life she had chosen. Despite her tumult of feeling, she slept soundly. In the mornings she woke with a guilty start: how could she be so cool, with her father dead? What sort of daughter was she?

Ten days passed with the drinking of a thousand cups of coffee and the eating of a hundred slices of cake; her father had had countless friends even into his eighties, and they all seemed to visit in their beautiful clothes, filling the long rooms with the sound of rustling silk. At last her father was cremated and installed behind a block of marble. Ilse and Tannie cried while Freda stood in curatorial silence, her black dress shifting around her ankles. "He would have liked that," Freda told them later, "being put on a shelf like that, where we would always know where to find him. Filed under L, for Leopold. Next it's my turn."

"You've got a long time," Tannie said.

"I'm afraid you're right. Now, Ilse, I am coming to visit you. I don't want to stay here alone at the moment. I want to leave the country for a while." She gave Ilse a hooded look. "I find it helps to clear the mind. Would you object?"

"Well," she said, "no, Mama."

"I won't be in your way, and I suppose you've got the children to keep you busy. I remember what a burden you both were to me when I was trying to work. I still think I would have had a much larger practice had it not been for you. And now, of course, no one wants to see me professionally, because I'm much too old. I was obviously too old for Leopold," she said sadly. "He wanted those girls he drew."

"Of course you can visit, Mama. No one ever said you couldn't."

"Well, then, I'll just come home with you when you go on Friday," Freda said, skipping off to the telephone, "if that's all right. I'll call the airlines right now and see if I can get a seat next to yours."

She did, and they flew back together and were picked up at the airport by a polite but querulous Henry, and for two weeks she stayed upstairs in their guest bedroom and walked up and down the hills in the mornings. She complained about the shower, which she thought was too hot, while poor Henry and Ilse ate, obligingly, her antique and lard-laden cooking, and then one afternoon she announced that she would be staying in Seattle for good and would find herself an apartment. "All at once, dear, I just don't want to go back to that place. Such a dead, dead place, Ilse — I'll die too if I have to go back." Dramatically, wearing a stern and menacing expression, she held out her arms as though crucified, so her black dress lifted around her bosom. "I'm seventy-eight years old, and I don't want to go back to that place. You maybe mind if I come to live in your city, Henry?" she asked.

"Of course not."

"Your children are beautiful." This she plainly forced out. "They are very polite."

"Yeah," Henry said. "Well, they can be."

"Mama, what about the apartment?"

"Pah. Let Tannie stay in it. She is an old lady too, she always wanted it. She likes all the corridors," she said, turning to Henry. "It is a silly old mind that likes a corridor for looking at. To me it is more like a hospital, something always waiting at the end of the hallway to frighten me. And I have the money," she said serenely, "for a nice condominium."

"Okay," Henry said.

"You don't mind? I know it is not what you imagine, as a married couple, that this old lady comes to stay in your city forever."

"We're happy to have you."

"Don't be polite. Say what you think."

"No, I think it's fine," he said, still studiously avoiding Ilse's eyes. To exchange a look, they both knew, would be insulting. "We love you."

"Possibly you like me. Okay, it's enough. I like you, you like me."

"Deal," said Henry.

"That's better. At least you don't hate me."

"Of course we don't," Ilse said, and was caught by a gust of daughterly affection, which blew her forward to embrace her mother. Hard and bony, her bones cabled together with steel, Freda was an uncomfortable package. *A sack of hammers.* "We love you, Mama," said Ilse.

"You do? Well, it's nice to hear, anyway," she said. "But I don't believe a word."

Six days later she bought a condominium downtown, above the Pike Place Market. The children did their best but could not call her anything nicer than That Lady. "She is my mother," Ilse explained patiently, but for years they didn't quite buy it. "She looks at me like I'm a rat," Darren said. "You know why?" his sister asked. "Because you *are* a rat."

*   *   *

So it was to her mother that she was forced to go now — a poor replacement, in Ilse's mind. Her mother's condominium had a little pink tacked-on balcony, where in the late afternoons the old lady could sit in one of her white plastic chairs and look out over the water, drinking her day's single cup of resinous coffee and counting the clouds. The balcony, sixty feet above the sidewalk, did not seem entirely stable to Ilse; the railings were narrow and could be made to shiver under her hand. But her mother, at ninety-five pounds, could never generate enough momentum to crash through the railing, and at any rate the five-story drop to the pavement would have been softened by the green awnings of Il Cioppino. And Freda, Ilse had no doubt, would not be killed by such a fall, only annoyed at the indignity.

"Of course it's really the *children* who suffer," her mother told her. "I know it's a cliché, but that's who suffers when a marriage begins to disintegrate."

"Mama, it's not disintegrating in the slightest. That's not what I'm talking about, I'm talking about my job."

"So you say! Henry has always struck me as a man who lives almost entirely inside his head, even more than most men. He feels he can because you allow him to." Now ninety, Freda had not slowed much, just become smaller, more sinewy, like a carrot left in the back of the refrigerator. "Your children don't deserve a romantic for a mother, they deserve someone with a harder head."

"Like you?"

"I would be very suited to being their mother, but that boy would try to tie me up and put me in a closet."

"Darren's very sweet and serious. He would never."

"Ha! He's a menace."

"Mama, he's fourteen! He goes to school all day and does homework all night."

"If he had a job," her mother stated, "he wouldn't be such a *menace.*"

Ten years ago downtown property had been cheap and plentiful, and if her mother had wanted to she could have bought heroin within a block of Nordstrom's, and First Avenue had been a series of blind, boarded-up shop fronts and sinister pawnshops that had sold musical instruments, power tools, and pistols from behind bulletproof glass. The last remains of the old frontier town had been still visible then, in 1989, and her mother's instinct for the genuine and her attraction to the marginally unpleasant had drawn her here. But money had done its relentless polishing, as it had done almost everywhere, and Freda was unhappy about it, or pretended to be; her neighborhood had gentrified around her, to her displeasure. "I'm sure you think this is all wonderful, but it won't last, it's all based on imaginary things. I hope you're not involved in all this" — she gestured — "froth."

"We don't really have any money, Mama."

"You have to have *some* money. You don't work for free. Henry doesn't. You have a house."

"But we live there. It's not an investment."

"Maybe, maybe not." Freda shrugged in her plastic chair on the suspended balcony; her white sweatshirt rose stiffly around her, like a pastry shell. "Nothing is ever firm," she said, settling her coffee cup into its white saucer.

"Some things are."

"The other problem is that you married him so quickly!"

"Oh, Mama, I'm sorry I said anything. We're very well suited."

"Well suited!" She laughed. "You would have married anyone with a plane ticket."

"I would not have."

"When you come to me with trouble, I try to give you the best advice I can, and if it's not to your liking, I don't know why you come at all."

"You haven't given me a single word of advice! You've just insulted me about fifteen times."

"Your mother can say things to you," said Freda, "that no one else will dare."

"Oh, please. You're trying to be funny or something."

"*Funny,*" her mother repeated. She fixed Ilse with a fierce, mocking look; then, with a single swift gesture, she tossed the empty white coffee cup over the rail. Its arc was not high, and it dropped harmlessly into the middle of the street below, where it shattered like a star on the asphalt. A few people looked around to see what might have caused the noise, but the two women were high enough off the ground to be inconspicuous. "That was just a cup," she said, wagging the empty saucer on her lap like a discus. "In a minute I'm going to throw this at that man with the accordion.

Speaking of husbands, he proposed to me yesterday. Maybe you would like me to get his attention for you."

Ilse had to laugh. "Mama, you're crazy."

"He did ask me. I gave him the evil eye."

"You can't throw anything that far."

"I can. I've hit that man who plays the paper trumpet with the monkey on his head. They don't hurt anyone, they're very cheap dishes."

"You're trying to make a point of some kind."

"I am not trying to make a point of any kind," Freda said lightly. "I'm just doing what I want to do. I'm old enough and rich enough to do that."

But no, that wasn't it. Ilse's father had certainly never been rich, and her mother's professional life had been halting at best since the forties. Freda had a pension from the Austrian government, but it did not amount to more than a few hundred dollars a month. She never asked Ilse for money, but she lived on very little; it was an old woman's spare and punctuated life: coffee, zeppelin bread, pears, chocolate. And wine, now and then. No; to destroy a cup like that, Ilse thought, was more than just bravado. It was, in effect, her mother's advice to her. *Do whatever you want to do,* she was saying.

Beyond the rail the balcony's view was wide and encompassing, and while you sat there you smelled the salty blue air and the marine creosote and the smoke from the alderwood fires from Etta's below. The ferries hooted across the water. Full of light and air, the apartment was as unlike the dark warren of the Brucknerstrasse as could be. Her mother's furniture, from Ikea, was lightweight and featureless. Only a few old mirrors had come along to Seattle and had ended up in Freda's bedroom, heavy and unusually dark, as though some internal light had long ago leaked away from them. Eight framed photographs hung in a bright hallway: old photographs of Freda herself, young, posed here and there in the sooty old city before the war. "It is my wall of personal vanity," she would say in her fine early-century phrasing. Ilse and Tannie and their dead, beloved father were nowhere in evidence. Leopold had taken all the photographs, and in some of them the dead man's shadow could be seen sloping against the sunlit stones: more soot. Poor Papa!

Would Ilse be capable of the same thing at eighty? Would she have the nerve to leave everything and move a world away, to be with Sandra or Darren in her unloved dotage? She didn't know. She did not have her mother's toughness — her sinew, her venom. Even now her mother's sudden grip was firm, painful, on her forearm. "Remember, a husband is not everything," Freda hissed into her ear. Here it came, the advice. "And remember, there is a life to be *lived*."

This was about as much help as Ilse could expect from her mother. But she did need to do something soon; her work seemed a sort of glacial, grinding, crushing, irresistible process from which one could never hope to escape, and like weather, or time, it had a plodding sameness-with-a-difference every month, every year. Certainly compared to Henry's research it was nearly meaningless. How nice it would be — how *useful* — to start a little private practice in a tiny office, somewhere in the Central District, where she could treat the poor! But the world had moved on, and she had chosen a path, the wrong one. She spent hours watching the workmen finishing the last of Safeco Field — tethered men in hardhats and boots fastening metal panels together three hundred feet in the air. Could she do that herself? No, probably not. So high, and nothing to hold on to.

Now, at the end of March, she had long since looked over next year's new residents, she was nicely under budget for the year, and the new projections weren't due for another six weeks, one of the many annual exercises in sternness and conciliation that she had come to hate. How many cardiac surgeons could they train? How many debt-burdened residents could she manage to turn into GPs against all odds? How much medicine could they afford to distribute to the poor, the insane, the aged, before the accountants began to get nervous? Not enough, not enough, no matter how hard she tried. As she always did, she complained to Henry. "I'm *nothing*," she said over the phone. "What do I do all day? Nothing."

"You don't do nothing."

"Guess what's on my desk right now."

"Nothing?"

"Worse! A stack of reports about the kitchens for some reason. They want my opinion about the food!" It wasn't really a stack, just a single sheet of paper, but it meant a day's worth of phone calls, another dumb meeting where she would be only tangentially relevant. As good as a stack. "Everyone knows the food is bad, they make standup jokes about hospital food."

"You could go work at Amazon or something. I bet they're hiring doctors. They're hiring everybody else."

"I want to go to Chechnya and be a doctor for refugees."

"Or Chechnya," he agreed.

Why not? She sat pinned in front of the television, watching what spotty coverage there was. She could do good there, couldn't she, for three months? Couldn't Sandra and Darren get along without her for ninety days? So what was she doing here? The e-mail arrived, was answered; her secretary, Miriam, handed her the morning's little folders, which she efficiently dispatched; decisions were made, compromises borne. Like any life, she supposed, hers described itself by what lives it was not. She was not an itinerant doctor among the poor in Alabama. She was not an operagoer. She even had — what a strange thing to admit — no real friends; the women she had known in childhood were thousands of miles away, on another planet. Not hers. How long had it been since she had sensed that particular — how would you say it in English? *Liftingness?* That complicated, palpable sensation of life that had seemed to rise like a scent from the rooftops below her father's window? That nutritive, sunny air of possibility? "Sooner or later you forget about all that stuff," Freda had told her. "You stop worrying about being happy and just get on with things."

"But are you happy, Mama?"

"The question is not happiness but pleasure. I take pleasure from things. I am not happy as you speak of it. There is a difference."

"What do you take pleasure in?"

"Oh, things."

"Like what?"

"This and that. Things. Things. I have my secrets," her mother sniffed.

In the throes of this difficult mood she decided to buy herself a motor scooter. The ad was on one of the hospital bulletin boards, a sheet of paper with a photograph. She had owned one just like it, a

Vespa 50SR, and driven by nostalgia and a kind of mounting desperation she removed the pin from the paper and took the flyer down — the bulletin boards were for official announcements only, after all — and made arrangements to see it.

The man who had placed the ad was in his forties, with a beefy British face and a hefty brown mustache, and was one of the building's cafeteria supervisors; they had met briefly once, years ago. Terrence. His Vespa, stowed on the bottom level of the hospital's parking garage, was an old white machine with a modish convex knee guard. "I just got it used last year," he told her as they stood above it. "Thought I'd use it to go to the grocery store. But. Rain and whatnot. Also you get on the bigger arterials and it just doesn't feel safe."

"I had one as a girl," she said. She sat astride it, eased it forward off the stand. "It's what you had instead of a car."

"Suits you."

"You think?"

"More than me." Wordlessly Terrence reached over and turned the little minnow of a key, and the Vespa rasped to life. In the concrete cavern of the underground garage the sound of the scooter echoed and was amplified, but otherwise it was the same sound as it had been the last time she had been on a scooter, years ago, in medical school, when she had been wearing a green skirt and telling herself she was at least a little bit in love with Gregor. Up and down the Stadtpark she had gone, wind in her face, almost convinced. The recollection was so immediate that she fumbled with the controls and the Vespa stalled.

"Clutch is on the handlebar."

"Yes, I know." The soft-firm grip, the notched controls. She turned the key off. "I brought my checkbook."

"You actually want it? You getting it for your kid or something?"

"You said it suited me, yes? And I want it, so I'll take it."

"Seriously? Why?"

Because she was sad, because she regretted certain things about her life, because she had been young once? "For going to the grocery store. I don't know, exactly."

Together they loaded the thing sideways into her Honda's empty trunk. "You definitely want to watch it in the rain. Personally, I never drove it in the rain. Didn't like the feel of it. Tended to get squirrelly." He held up his two palms. "All I need is a little more brain damage and that'd about do it for me."

"I almost hit a bus once. As a girl."

"Yours," he said with finality, folding her check into his back pocket. "Keep it off the pavement."

Laid on its side in the back of the Honda, the Vespa had the skewed, upended look of a deer. Its two tall mirrors, like silvery antlers, poked out above the bumper. Where to store it? The driveway was a murderous slope, with a blind entrance to Hynes Street below, and their garage had become over the years a clutter of ladders and old boards and windows salvaged from a basement remodeling, plus rakes and shovels and bags of fertilizer and rusty cans of old paint, like a row of squat candles on a painted shelf, and long quivering lengths of baseboard trim, extra from when they'd had it specially milled in the first ambitious years of owning the house: junk upon junk. But the Vespa would fit in there, she thought, if she moved a few things aside, which, together with Henry, she did.

"What's the idea?" he asked.

"Oh, no idea," she said. "I just think it's stupid to drive the car to the video store if it's only to carry back a video that weighs a pound. We're too lazy to walk. You used to ride a bicycle."

"Hey," he said, "you okay?"

"Me? I'm fine, la, la, la, Henry, you know. La, la, la. Oh, I don't know."

"Just so you don't kill yourself."

Gallantly, she said, "Maybe that's it. Maybe that's what I secretly want and my job is too slow to do the trick."

"So quit."

"We need the money, don't we?"

"Well, we *use* the money. How much was it?"

"Free. Almost free. Try it." She thrust the handlebars at him. Dear, sweet Henry! He didn't make fun of her, didn't press. He did not know how to ride it, and proved this right away by rolling down the driveway into the street and steering into the back of their parked Honda at two miles an hour. "Did you get whiplash?" she called, giggling, from the sidewalk.

"I think one of my eyeballs fell out," he said.

Darren — pale, adrift in the Saturday house — appeared at the top of the driveway. "Hey," he said, "is that yours?"

"It's your mother's."

"No way."

"Way," said Henry.

"There's this guy at school who got one of those dirt bikes? And he broke his leg in like eleven places and his leg turned out like an inch shorter than the other one." With a look of beady curiosity, Darren turned to her. "How much was it?"

"It was free," Henry said.

"Yeah, right. Can I try it?"

"No," said Ilse. But the press of nostalgic longing was at her back, and in the end she agreed to drive her son around the block, Darren sitting behind her and grasping her waist. Neither of them was wearing a helmet — what a terrible mother she was; really, it wasn't funny at all. But these were very quiet streets, not dangerous, and after turning the corner twice she said, relenting, "Okay, just once." He was young *now*, after all. They were in the empty middle of a flat block, no cars in sight. He missed the clutch a few times, accelerated too quickly, and nearly fell when he ran into a curb, but he got the hang of it soon enough.

"Now I can go rob banks," he said when he pulled up, idling, beside her. "I saw this thing about perfect crimes? Like how to commit a perfect murder?"

"You have to watch these things."

"They said that for it to be perfect, you have to kill somebody you don't have any connection with, and they were like talking about gloves and everything, and like use a gun and then throw it in the ocean, but you know what the perfect murder is? I thought of this myself. Like if you want to murder your wife? You just push her off a cliff." He revved the engine. "If there's no witnesses it's totally perfect. You don't have to worry about evidence or anything, and if there's a scratch or something on you, you can just say you were trying to catch her."

That plunge off the stadium's roof, she could feel it in her bones, suddenly. A dark sadness dropping through her gut. "But you're such a nice boy, darling, you *would* try to catch her," she said. To her surprise, she found herself close to tears. Oh, no, no, this would never do.

5

A T THE END of March a three-year-old boy was flown in from Detroit with his family. Giles Benhamouda showed all the classic Hickman signs: enlarged head, thinning hair, the beginnings of mandibular reabsorption, senility in the skin and structure of the face, a basic bodily fragility. The Benhamouda family was Algerian but had lived in Detroit for twenty years. The boy's name was pronounced in the French way; the parents were Théodore and Hélène, and there was a handsome older son, Thomas, a normal seventeen-year-old. Théodore was a big-shouldered, gray-eyed man, and his wife had dark, loosely kinked hair that fell to her shoulders and a slim, shifty figure under a long printed dress. Nice people. Hesitant, as everyone was at first, but also happy to be with someone who knew what was wrong, who understood and could explain Hickman. After twenty years in America they had good English, which made everything easier. They knew — had known for a month — that Giles was going to die.

Giles's digestion was sluggish, his muscle tone was slack, and his heart, when Henry listened to it briefly through the stethoscope, was weak, making its weary footsteps one after the other in the echoing room of his chest. A sweet, trusting kid, pulling up his shirt to show a fragile ribcage and a soft, gently swollen belly, the skin dry and beginning to scale. Doomed, doomed. "No other cases in the family," Henry said.

"No," said Théodore.

"You two aren't related to each other in any way, even distantly?"

They shook their heads.

"Had you ever heard of the condition before Giles began to show these signs?"

Théodore shrugged his heavy shoulders. "No."

Thomas had not been tested yet to determine whether he was a carrier. "They never ran you as a family?"

"You see," said Théodore sheepishly, "we didn't want to. We didn't want to know."

The older boy was handsome. Striking, really. Finely made, constructed on the same small scale as his mother, with his mother's slender, slinky trunk. Dark-eyed, he sat between his parents on the yellow couch. He had been dragged along recently on a few of these trips, it was obvious; with an expression of bored and practiced consideration, his gaze traveled over the bookshelves, the computer, the pictures of Sandra and Darren and Ilse. His skin was a pretty, glowing, middle-range tan, darker than his mother's, lighter than his father's, his face already rising out of babyish roundness into its adult planes: high cheekbones, a square chin, a high forehead. Full lips. Pretty. It was the sort of face you saw in the perfume ads: dark, androgynous, watchful. It was meant to look like a universal face, Henry supposed, though it was still unusual enough to catch your eye.

It was the middle of the afternoon, and quiet. Seaplanes could be heard feathering the air on their way down to Lake Union. "And you, Thomas?" Henry asked. The accent on the second syllable, where the parents had put it.

"It's *Thom*as, man." A clear, unaccented voice.

Henry glanced at Hélène, who rolled her dark eyes. "Sorry," he said, "*Thomas.*"

"Sha." He shrugged. "Whatever."

The next day they were all gone, back to Detroit, leaving behind their blood: sixteen dark upright columns on the top shelf of the laboratory refrigerator.

By now, in the twenty-fourth year of his career, Henry was able to count on funding from the March of Dimes and the National Institute of Genetic Research and a few other, smaller organizations that were regular donors, and the university matched whatever he could bring in. With this money he paid his own salary and hired the postdoctoral fellows who were beginning their careers in cell senescence — a funny place to start a life, he had always thought, studying its end, but what had he himself done, after all? Exactly that. The fellows stayed for two or three years, and occasionally they were brilliant, but more often they were just useful additions to his staff, men and women to whom he enjoyed demonstrating the PCR machine (they had all seen them, but to Henry it was still a fairly recent invention, and he got a kick out of showing it off) and for whom he tried to model the delicate balance between research and compassion that was required to do good, useful work with sick children and their parents.

The fellows were crucial, as they did about half the grubby trial-and-error stuff, the centrifuging, the data compilation. Much of this sort of thing was also done by Gretl Johns, his laboratory assistant. Now in her sixties, she had a cap of straight white hair and a slow Scandinavian way of speaking and very steady red hands with long flat fingernails — agile, practiced, professional hands. She took the postdocs in, made them comfortable — steady as a rock, she was, and she'd been there for years. It was she who screened the blood they received and she who came back with the verdict: Hickman or not.

Giles's results were no surprise: the classic defect in the eighth chromosome, fatally missing its sixteen crucial nucleotides — the ghostly gray bars of DNA appearing in the plate of polymer like a vertical bar code, not sinking away from the electrolyzer as they should have but sitting there almost unmoved. Missing those nucleotides made the gene lighter, less subject to electrolysis, and fainter in the plate. The parents, as carriers, each showed the broken allele on one chromosome and not the other. But Thomas's test was strange. Alongside his brother in the dish, the boy appeared to have Hickman — to have two copies of the defective gene. It was a mistake.

"This is the brother's?" Henry asked Gretl.

Gretl was certain. "I put him on the right." She pointed with her red Bic. "Sibs go to the right of the parents. Kid, mom, dad, sibs. As usual."

"Try it again, maybe."

"This is the second plate. First one was just like this one."

"You have a lot to drink last night?"

She held out her hands. Steady. "Not so's you'd notice."

"Whose mistake is it?"

"Not mine." She looked up at him.

"Whose, then?"

"Well," she said, "I don't know."

"Okay."

"You're assuming there is one," she said carefully.

"I think we have to."

"But it wasn't my mistake," she told him. "I don't make mistakes."

It was true. He nodded. "I know that."

"And if it wasn't mine" — she searched his face — "and it wasn't yours, because you didn't touch it, and it wasn't Chin's, because neither did he, then whose was it?"

"Let's do it again."

"That'll be the third one."

"I know," he said.

"It's going to be the same, I bet you dollars to doughnuts."

They ran the test again, this time in isolation. The boy's blood had been mislabeled. Or contaminated. Something was wrong — Thomas came up positive again.

"Maybe we need another sample," Gretl said cautiously.

"Yeah. Send for samples from the whole family again. We don't want to spook anybody."

They did, and the pack arrived from Detroit two days later in the ten o'clock delivery, giving off a clean clinical smell when they lifted off the squeaking Styrofoam lid. The four neat vials, stoppered with plastic, were labeled with black marker in an angular hand.

"Just his?" Gretl asked.

"Do them all again."

"You think this is something?"

"No." He kept his face steady, neutral; it had to be some kind of mistake, and he didn't want to get his hopes up. "It can't be, right?"

She held the blood in her hand, a vial so dark it was almost black. Held it up to the light. "You notice what he looked like? Young. Younger than he should have."

"So did the parents."

"True," she acknowledged, and turned away into the laboratory.

He went into his office to sit down.

No: it could not be anything. Of the sixty-eight living children with the disease, all fit the classic profile. He knew this. He knew everything about Hickman, everything there was to know. There were no asymptomatic positives. Everyone with two copies of the altered gene was sick, and everyone with one copy was a healthy carrier. A classic autosomal recessive condition. So the test was a mistake. The blood had been mislabeled somehow. In fact this had happened once before — but in that case it had not been Gretl who had taken the questionable blood, it had been a postdoc who was afraid of needles. No, Gretl did not make mistakes like that, she never had, and though she was nearing retirement she was just as sharp as he himself was, if not sharper.

It was a mistake. It had to be. You could not be seventeen and healthy and have Hickman at the same time.

Well — you could, theoretically. You *could,* just conceivably. But in that case you had to be doing something to compensate for the Hickman. You had to have a back-mutation, a corrective, something that restored the proper functioning of the Hickman gene and made you, against all odds, asymptomatic. The idea — the possibility — was a sudden swinging heaviness within, a weighted bag. But it wasn't much of a possibility; the odds were gigantically against it. One in — what? You had the Hickman mutation and then you coincidentally had a second, spontaneous mutation, which just happened to correct for Hickman somehow. A mutation that just happened to make you normal again. No, the odds were unthinkable. Incalculable.

But Thomas *was* perfect. Young-looking for his age, as Gretl had noticed. Not much facial hair. Lithe. Radiantly handsome. Henry stood up, went to the window. The implications — the possible implications — were spectacular. If — if — if he was what he appeared to be, then he had to be producing something weird, some unseen enzyme that managed to compensate for the Hickman. And if this was true, then certain things became possible, suddenly. Postnatal therapy for Hickman patients: take an injection every day and fend off the disease. Take a boost of whatever exotic enzymes this kid was producing and have a normal childhood. No stranger than being a diabetic. Expensive as hell, and the HMOs would hate it. But maybe Giles wasn't doomed after all. And maybe William Durbin wasn't doomed either.

There was something else too, something that was dancing at the back of Henry's mind, which he now allowed himself to consider. It was this: if Thomas's enzymes completely blocked the process of aging in Hickman patients, what would they do for people without Hickman? Were they — could they be — the body's natural preservatives? An organic restorative that traveled along the spiral of the DNA, undoing the damage of time? Why not? Why on earth not? How long would Thomas Benhamouda live? A hundred years? Two hundred?

But if that was the case, why wasn't anyone else known to be that long-lived? Why, in the reliable human record, was no one known to have lived more than 122 years? Henry sat down at his desk, pulled a blank sheet of paper from the printer, then set it aside. Well, no, it made sense: the particular enzyme, if it existed, worked only on Hickman patients. It was a corrective, a back-mutation, and nothing more. That was most likely; it was by far the most elegant solution, anyway. However — and here Henry had to stand up again and go back to the window, watch the boats travel past — maybe not. Maybe the only reason no one had yet lived to be five hundred years old was that no one had yet been born with both Hickman and whatever secondary mutation this kid was carrying. The new mutation was a lucky shot, a random recovery from an apparently unsalvable position, and this kid was the first one to get lucky in that particular way, and his particular enzyme had never been seen before because the sample size of Hickman patients was too small to expect such a thing ever to happen. Five new cases a year, times maybe fifty thousand years of Hickman, equals a quarter million Hickman kids in the history of the species, and asking someone in that small a population to hit a jackpot like this was ridiculous. Like buying one lottery ticket a century and hoping for the best.

Gretl did appear, finally. At the doorway she wore a neutral, unreadable expression — his own, he saw. "So," she said, "some weather out there."

"Jesus Christ, Gretl."

"It's the same. Same as before."

A current of joy ran through him. He clapped his hands and whispered, "Holy shit."

[67]

"Funny, that's exactly what I said."

"Let's run him through the sequencer."

"He's in there already. He'll be out in half an hour."

"Oh boy," Henry said. "Oh boy, oh boy. Jesus Christ."

"You want me to tell Chin?"

"He starting to wonder?"

"He's busy with his AIDS thing."

"Then keep it under your hat. For today. This is ours. Yours and mine."

"Shame on you." Her wide face reddened with pleasure. "But all right."

The sequencer was across the hall, a nearly featureless black box attached to a Melf-Ponora synthesizer, which was in turn attached to a PC and a monitor, where the new sequence would eventually be displayed. It was another of his favorite machines; you fed DNA into the self-sterilizing chamber and the Melf-Ponora silently did its work. As he stood there next to it, watching the red status bar inch to the right, little flutters of disbelieving joy kept rising in him, and he went up on his tiptoes and back down again, over and over. "Jesus," he kept saying. Gretl flashed him a tiny, anticipatory smile. "But it's impossible," he said.

"Probably," she agreed.

Chemically the machine was snipping the eighth chromosome from the pack, isolating on it a sequence of ten thousand nucleotides or so on either side of the Hickman gene, then replicating and reading the nucleotides on a smaller section of that sequence, like a magnifier moving closer and closer to the strand itself. After it was read, Thomas's Hickman gene would appear as a series of letters — A, G, T, C, standing for adenine, guanine, thymine, and cytosine, the four building blocks of the double helix, with its sixteen nucleotides missing. Without those sixteen nucleotides the gene should have encoded, fatally, for Hickman. But somehow not for this kid. Somewhere near the Hickman sequence, Henry was guessing, there would be something new. A new flaw, something never seen before. A deletion, an addition. Something. That was his guess, though of course theoretically the new material could have been added or deleted elsewhere. It could be anywhere on any of the twenty-three chromosomes, really, anywhere in the vast and still uncharted reaches of the genome. But he didn't think so. He had a hunch it would be right there.

What the new sequence meant would be another story. You couldn't just look at a strand of DNA and see what it did. You had to watch it in action. What enzymes it produced, what they did, how they interacted with other enzymes in the body — all these things were impossible to know at a glance, and often impossible to know at all. It would take years of work to begin to understand why this kid was still alive, and they might never know, not precisely. Anyway, it was a hell of a project.

And he could make a killing off this sort of thing, it occurred to him, standing there in the sequencing room. If he played his cards right.

Finally the sequencer came back with its readout. He and Gretl leaned over the monitor. Yes, there it was. Forty-two nucleotides after the classic Hickman deletion, a single cytosine had been inserted — an errant cytosine between two guanines in the middle of the third exon. Another mistake. But this one was a good one. A lucky one. A little footnote added mistakenly during recombination — a correction that reestablished the right reading frame for the rest of the gene, saving Thomas's life and encoding between the two errors a brand-new protein, something no one had ever seen. Henry's heart leapt. It was true. The kid was a fluke, a freak, a wonder.

"Oh, Jesus. Okay. Let's fly him out again. Jesus, let's get them to move out here. We can get the foundation to kick in some money. This is it," he said, realizing the truth of it. "This is what we've been waiting for."

"Congratulations." Gretl's arctic-blue eyes were shining.

"Let's order out for martinis. Can we do that?"

"We can," Gretl said, and flushed again. "Kozmo can bring us anything."

"Liquor?" What did you do to celebrate such a thing? "Or — a cake, or something?"

"Anything we want," she said. Girlishly, with a pounce, she embraced his neck. "Congratulations, sweetheart," she whispered into his ear, as the machinery hummed around them.

"Oh, Henry, that's wonderful!" Ilse said, standing in the kitchen, holding an apple. She had frozen mid-chew and now continued, her jaws working. "That's an incredible thing. What will you do?"

"I don't know. It sort of depends."

"On whether you can get them to move out here. Of course you can. The foundation can pay." His wife, personnel manager, began calculating. "Or the Durbins might be interested. It wouldn't cost that much — I'm sure they'd be interested." Now she laughed, a healthy bark. "My god, what a shock! Gretl found it?"

"I let her. And then she kissed me."

"You're very kissable, Henry, even still." She leaned forward and kissed him too, a sharp, ceremonial, administrative peck. "You should see yourself, darling, you're in a daze. And is he normal, he looks normal?"

"Completely." Although that odd subdermal illumination — that glow, or whatever it was — had caught his eye. "He seems to be, anyway."

"We need to celebrate."

"All right."

"What would you like to do?"

"I think I'd like to sort of sit down and think about it for a minute. It's just . . ." How could he describe this? "It's unreal. I mean, it can't really be true."

"Is it?"

"Well," he said. But it was, wasn't it? That little red C. They'd even sequenced him a second time, a third time. It had not gone away. They'd gone back through the files, double-checking against other Hickman sequences they'd run, and no one else had shown that anomalous cytosine. "Yeah," he said. "Seems to be."

She was peering at him closely. "You *are* in a daze. Maybe you should jump up and down a little."

"I know I should."

"Well?"

He jumped up once, landed heavily. "Hooray!" he said.

"Okay, that's a start. You're really very even-tempered sometimes, Henry — it's a little alarming."

"Maybe I should go on a six-day bender."

"That would be fine with me." His wife blinked at him. "I would come for the first day."

What was holding him back? Disbelief, mostly. Superstition. And he had never been very good at celebrating anyway. "I feel like it's bad luck or something, I don't know. I don't want to count my chickens."

"But the chickens are hatched!" She grabbed his shoulders, shook him. "Listen, everybody else celebrates. Jackie White just bought herself a new Suburban, if you can believe it, she saw my scooter and said, 'What a cute idea, you know, I should do something fun,' and she did. And that's her idea of a scooter."

"It is?"

"I guess so. I'm sort of joking, Henry, although actually I'm also trying to get Darren to put one of those stickers on it. You know? 'I'm changing the climate, ask me how'? 'I have a small penis'?"

"You are?"

She leaned forward, kissed him heavily. "Congratulations, darling, that's wonderful. I'm terribly jealous. Now you're going to be famous and I'll just be your wife, when it really should be the other way around."

Jealous? "Don't be."

She shot him a stern, embarrassed look. "But of course I am, sweetheart. I can't help it." She kissed him again. "It won't last forever."

"It was completely an accident."

"Don't feel guilty! It's a wonderful, wonderful, wonderful thing," she insisted, and he knew she meant it. "Think how happy everyone will be, Henry! Think how happy you're going to make everyone when they find out."

"It will, won't it? Even if it doesn't come to anything right away."

"Of course it will. It's *progress,* which is what everyone's been waiting for. It's wonderful news." She pressed herself against him. "He's really asymptomatic?"

"He's perfect."

"Are you going to announce?"

"I need to think about a couple things first."

It took her only a moment. She nodded against his chest. "You're going to try something, aren't you?"

"I might," he admitted.

"Something with William?"

"I need to think about it."

"You think you can help him?"

"It's possible," he said, and the thought — the thought that he could really save William Durbin — passed electrically through him. He had never dared hope for such a thing, but now it was a possibility — faint, but a possibility. "I don't know. I want to, but I don't know if I can."

Ilse pushed herself against him, burrowing. "Don't do anything too silly," she said.

"I won't."

"It's wonderful news," she repeated, and he felt her sigh. "Oh, Henry, think about all those people you can tell!"

But no, not right away. If he were to help William, it would have to be in secret, and it would be against all the established ethics of his profession. So — he promised himself — he would think about it. Not decide anything right away, but allow himself to consider the idea. At least that: to weigh his options.

He sat almost wordless through dinner, trying to surprise himself with the fact of his discovery — trying to forget it for a minute and then remember it again. It was an artificial exercise, but it worked — he could induce that first fluttering upward sensation whenever he wanted. *They had found it. The cure.* Oh, it was spectacular! His children sat innocently, his wife cast him an occasional conversational softball, but mostly he was left alone in his reverie. *The cure!* Flutter. Outside, beyond the kitchen windows, the pear tree leaned in the wind, and the leafless ash filtered the air with a hollow rushing sound. Henry thought of William in his exposed aerie, looking out over the lawn on this dark night, listening to this same wind. When would he tell the Durbins? Soon. Not right away, but soon. As soon as he really knew what he had.

Ilse came to him after dinner and led him outside, into the night. "You need to walk with me somewhere," she told him, and snaked her arm through his. She knew how his mind worked — that he was reflective, slow to show emotion, too likely to miss his own feelings of happiness — so here she was, his wife, taking him out into the night air to let him breathe a little, to let the news sink in. The gusts had strengthened, and a titanic roaring sound had begun in the tops of the hemlocks, but it was warm, too warm for April; they shed their coats and left them at the mailbox. "I'll show you Jackie's new Suburban," she offered, and guided him down the sidewalk.

The houses on their side of the street were small; those across the street were much larger and more imposing, and had better views of the lake. The rooms of Saul Harstein's big green house, which he occupied alone, were illuminated here and there as though by candlelight. Jackie and Kevin White lived next to Saul in another enormous house, with white clapboards and three stories of sprawling porches. Their new black Suburban sat at the curb, gleaming, next to a green dumpster. "There it is," Ilse whispered. "The beast. Do you want to know what it cost? Thirty-nine thousand dollars, plus extras!"

"They can afford that, can't they?"

"To hear Jackie tell it, they don't even blink about spending that kind of money anymore. She came and told me all about it." Flaring, she said, "You should have seen her drop that number. She's really becoming awful. And why do *they* have all the money? He's such a moron! They both are!"

"He's not a moron exactly, he's —" How would you describe Kevin White? "He's a good technical person."

"But why did *he* get to be so rich? What did *he* ever do?"

"He spent twelve years crossing that bridge every day, I don't know."

"You know what he did, Henry — he wrote stupid, stupid *code* for that stupid, stupid company. And here you are, doing really important things, and so am I, for that matter, but *they* get the money. And that remodeling they're doing! It's a crime. They had such a nice pretty kitchen before, with all that nice old tile, and now they're getting that dumb green one that *everybody* has now, the one in the magazines. People like that shouldn't be allowed to have nice houses."

The Whites' porch light was on. Brick steps, leaded fanlight. The knocker, gold eagle, glowed beneath the peephole. A long laurel hedge ran along the parking strip, separating the house from the street. The dumpster was half full of old drywall and stained timbers, and a big ceramic sink sat upside down on the floor of the container, neatly cracked into two halves. The Suburban sat on its four gigantic tires. Black, with bright highlights of chrome, it gave off a powerful impression of mechanical strength. The street was silent, dark.

"If I had any dignity, I would go up there and tell her to take it back." She pulled him closer. "If *we* had that money, Henry, what would we do?"

"Get a Suburban."

"I'm serious."

"I don't know." Slowly, as they stood there, his heart was beginning to shift, a rich, textured, pleasant feeling — happiness — spreading with glacial patience from beneath his breastbone. "Maybe go to Paris," he said, as the thought occurred to him.

"*Yes*," Ilse cried softly, and pulled him aside into the laurel hedge. The long polished leaves brushed his face. "What a good idea! We could sit around and eat lunch all day. And Mama doesn't speak French, so she couldn't follow us." She brushed his hair off his forehead and kissed him again, a hard, quick, grateful kiss. Something sad was at work in her, Henry thought; he could see it, suddenly, in the still pond of his mind: Boredom. Disappointment. A burst of midlife vigor, as the long stretch toward retirement grew visibly shorter. There on the sidewalk she gripped the lapels of his parka and held him in place. "Still kissable. Well, it is *such* wonderful news," she told him now, her eyes happy and wide. "Is it really going to be something? Tell me."

Flutter. "If it's what we think it is, it's going to be great. Better than great. It's everything. It's exactly what we never thought we'd get. The key to the kingdom."

"And here it is?"

"And here it is. It doesn't make any sense that it's there, but it's there. It's impossible, but it's *there*. The odds against it are ridiculous."

"That's *wonderful*," she repeated, and shook him slightly. The wind continued in the trees. "I have to tell you, Henry, it does make me jealous. Just think what *I* would have discovered if I had kept going! Oh, you have stuff in your hair, all these twigs, I'm sorry."

He allowed himself to be groomed. "It's just luck," he told her. Which was true.

"It is *not* luck." She dropped a collection of sticks to the sidewalk. "Not *just* luck. You are a good man and you have worked hard all your life doing exactly the thing you are best at, which you *are* very lucky to have been able to do, but you must be *happy* about it, eventually you *must*, or I will get angry with you for not appreciating how very, very wonderful it *is*." She fixed him with a serious look, full of longing. "It *is*," she repeated, "and if you aren't happy about it I will take it as an insult to all of us who don't like our jobs at all." Then, before he could respond, she came forward and kissed him passionately there in the hedge, pressing herself against him until he was forced to exhale.

She was right, of course, but his caution was part of his character, and though the happiness was still there in the middle of his chest, it was not spreading any faster than it had been. It was a guilty feeling, this caution; back in the house, Darren, canny boy, eyed them closely over the banister: windblown, flush-faced, they were obviously hiding something. What did Darren think of them, his ancient and mysterious parents? Whatever it was, he wasn't saying. It was another little pluck at Henry's heart, and all at once, abruptly, he thought of his own dead mother and father, crushed without mercy. There in the bright cluttered foyer, their eternal absence seemed a rushing updraft, a wind that poured up and out of the room, through the plaster ceiling and away from him. How he missed them! How proud they would have been of him today! How badly he wanted to tell them everything! And how alone in the world he felt! "Just out on a prowl," he told his son, who nodded, shot him a secret grin, and crept soundlessly back upstairs into his room and shut the door. Henry, in tumult, almost cried out to him; but instead he went to the dining room table and sat down with a pad and began to work. Suddenly there was a lot he had to do.

The matter of moving the Benhamoudas west was settled quickly. Yes, the foundation would pay. Théodore had been intending to move the family in any case, move them out of Detroit. He was tired, he said, of the city, its summer heat and endless concrete, its violence.

"You know it rains out here now and then," Henry warned.

"Hey, you know? We like a change. It's good to change. Plus, you know, I like it out there. Live a good life. Take it easy a little."

"How's Giles?"

"The same. You know, the same."

Henry was shy to say the name: "And Thomas, he's still healthy?"

"Oh, yeah," said Théodore. "You know what he is? He's a behavior problem. At school. It happened slow, and he just got, you know, worse and worse. He don't go to class unless I call and make sure he's there. That school don't call us, they don't care. You ever heard of this school Garfield?"

"My daughter goes there."

"That's where we're going. It's a good school?"

"Sure," Henry said.

"Safe?"

"Pretty much."

"It's in the city?"

This was code, Henry knew. "Yeah," Henry told him, "it's right in the middle of everything." Blacks, whites, whoever.

The Benhamoudas had a neighbor in Detroit who had a cousin who lived in Seattle, and this cousin knew about a house for rent a block or two away — a house that was actually just a mile up and over the hill from Henry and Ilse, but away from the water, in an old black neighborhood that had been neglected for years because it was without views but that now, under the pressure of the city's new money, was quickly gentrifying. It was here, the day before tax day, that the four Benhamoudas settled, Théodore with his wide coat-hanger shoulders and Hélène now carrying an umbrella above her slender figure in the gray drizzle of this Seattle April. Giles was enrolled in the local preschool, a late introduction to Madison Valley KidPlace, and was understood at once to be a sick boy — did he maybe have cancer? How many days did Hélène expect him to miss per week, on average? It was not uncommon; there had been a boy last year who'd died of leukemia, and a boy the year before who'd died at home of an asthma attack, though that wasn't the same, exactly — he'd been healthy otherwise and had carried an inhaler. DeVon had been his name. Sometimes he'd had to sit at the side of the play area when the pollen or pollution was too thick.

And Thomas, to a murmur of appreciation from the girls at James A. Garfield High School, entered the eleventh grade, a boy of middle height and slender build curling himself into the one-armed desks as though he had been expecting this westward move all along, though it was a move that had rendered him friendless. The white boys distrusted his foreign looks, and the blacks distrusted his quiet and his feminine eyes, and the girls were shy of his beauty. In his friendlessness he stood out even more than he might have otherwise, with his dark Benetton gaze and limber, sexual mouth, and his father's shoulders still bony under his white T-shirt and black puffy jacket as he walked alone through the hallways to his battered locker in the third-floor annex. He was unusual — calm, slow of gesture, scornful of what attention came his way. He said very little. The adults noticed him too — even in the jumbled mass of students he distinguished himself; was he Indian? Indians were everywhere in town now, imported for their computer skills. Mr. Redmond called him Tom, and a little wave of laughter went through the class. Only the girls laughed. The boys knew a rival when they saw one.

Sandra noticed him too. She knew who he was, knew that he was from Detroit, that he was an unaffected carrier of Hickman, that he now visited her father once a week to have his blood sampled. But it was information she was not supposed to know, so she pretended she knew nothing. And Thomas in turn knew who she was; Sandra had seen his attention caught when Keisha McDonald greeted her in the hallway: *Moss!* It was a small thing, maybe, but she held it dear: a connection between herself and Thomas, this beautiful, flawless, lithe, foreign, American boy with the dying brother.

Treatments for Giles, as for any Hickman patient, amounted to addressing symptoms: the slow bowels, the coronary blockage, the problematic pancreas. But really there was little to be done except make the patients comfortable and watch them go. Giles was weak, weaker than most of them were at three, and submissive — he had been touched so often recently he was used to it, but Henry still approached him the way he would approach a cat: nothing up his sleeves. With the twin pads of his thumbs, he smoothed the skin beneath Giles's eyes, let his hands travel down the boy's face, over the beaky nose, the Mickey Rooney chin, the sagging skin of the throat, the slender bones of the neck. He spun Giles gingerly around on the stool and ran his hands up the back of the boy's skull, over the veined scalp, where the last elderly tendrils of hair remained. Applied the diaphragm of his stethoscope to Giles's thin, papery chest; the heart within shuffled, shuffled. Giles looked up at him, at the plastic tube snaking between them, and looked away. *The usual,* the boy seemed to be thinking. "He looks okay," Henry said. But not good.

"He had a little accident," said Théodore. "He can't sleep."

"What happened?"

"I can sleep," said Giles in his piping, reedy voice. "No problem."

"You were on the stairs," said Théodore patiently, and he turned to Henry. "He fell. He said his neck hurt him."

"Your neck hurts?"

"No," said Giles.

"Your neck doesn't hurt you?"

"No."

"Nothing hurts anywhere?"

Daintily, the boy sighed. "No."

Henry felt the boy's neck again, his shoulders, the knobby spine. "He's not protective of anything."

"I want some pills for him," said Théodore. "Sleeping pills. He wants to turn the light on all night. And in the morning he's too tired to get up."

"Does he complain of pain?"

"He doesn't complain."

"Are his bowel movements all right?"

"Fine," said Théodore. "Every two, three days, he goes."

"Please," said Hélène. She twitched her hair over a shoulder. "I want him to sleep."

"He's not bruised. He's not flinching at anything."

"He doesn't like to have the light out," she explained in a low voice. "He's afraid."

"Sure."

"He's afraid he won't wake up."

What could he say to that? "I'll write him up some sleeping pills," he said.

Giles lowered himself carefully to the floor and walked with his elderly limp to his mother's exposed knees. Though he tried never to do this, Henry found it was impossible not to feel pity for him, and a strange, sad disappointment, too: if Thomas could beat the odds so spectacularly, why couldn't Giles? Instead, he looked tired, tired — an old man on a park bench, a bag of bones. Patient 22-99, not long for this world.

Thomas — 23-99 — got a brand-new green folder, the color Henry used for control patients, which wasn't quite right. But what would be right? A rainbow folder. A gold folder. "You're quite a case," said Henry the first time the two met alone. "You know what the story is?"

"Yeah." He was wearing sunglasses, though the day was gray, rainy. "I'm a mutant. I always thought I was different. Like the things that people get all excited about? Like sports — you care about sports? I don't see the point. A game, you know? All that for a game."

"What do you care about?"

Thomas smiled. "Booty. But I'm picky. I like to pick and choose. You want to hear about it?"

Henry daubed the boy's arm with alcohol, readied the syringe. He was nervous, he discovered; a tiny tremble in his hands, as though in the presence of celebrity. He laid the point against Thomas's skin, guided the needle smoothly into the vein. In, wait a beat, out again, the vial full. "Not really."

"Sha, I know you old guys. You're older than my parents, man."

"Yeah. Hold that there for a minute."

"I had this one girl," said Thomas, "she was Puerto Rican, who used to come to school with no panties on, and she'd wear these like long skirts and everything because she was a Catholic, but she had this ass, this little perfect ass, and it used to just like stick out like that, and she'd wave it around when she was walking in front of me and then sometimes she'd pull her skirt up and show it to me in the hall, if nobody was looking, this little ass she had." His expression hadn't changed; thoughtfully, he examined the gauze on his puncture. "She was okay, but from the front she wasn't actually all that nice. But some things you can't turn down, you know?"

"I actually don't want to hear this."

"Yee, don't jump down my neck. Just making conversation. Nobody at that school talks to me."

At Henry's request, the hospital in Detroit had run Thomas through a series of tests. He had come back on the very high end of healthy: lung capacity high, heart slow and powerful, blood oxygen excellent, cholesterols ideal, eyesight perfect, digestion unremarkable, joint cartilage intact, bones fine. "We're going to be running a bunch of studies on you," Henry said. "On your blood, mostly, but also having to do with how your body's working. What it makes, what it does. So you'll be coming in here a lot."

Thomas folded his arm, pinning the gauze, and removed his sunglasses. "Tell me I'm not about to die, that's all I want to know."

"Not for a long time."

"Because like Giles knows." With a studied gesture Thomas

slipped his sunglasses back on. "It's weird. It's like he's not really my brother, you know? Like what are you supposed to say, exactly? He's just this little old man, basically. I mean that's what he is, you can look at him and see it."

"Is that upsetting?"

"Sha, what do you think? I mean I'm mostly used to it by now. But sometimes it just like *hits* me, like there's this total freak at the table sitting there eating or whatever." He scowled. "I guess that's rude too. You see these freaks all the time?"

"That's what we do."

"You ever feel like you just want to drown them? Put them out of their misery?"

"No. Come on. Of course not."

"I'm serious. Like they know they're about to die anyway."

"Yeah. Well, look, it's a really sad thing that happens to people like your brother. But it doesn't mean they don't have a good time on earth, like you do."

"They can't ever have sex, right?"

"There are other things to enjoy."

"Sha, like what?" He looked over Henry's head, scanning the shelves. "If I was like that, I'd say just put me in the bathtub and drown me." Unthinking, he lifted the gauze from his arm. A tiny prick of blood on the gauze, but on his skin no mark whatsoever. No redness, no puffiness. As though nothing had happened, nothing at all.

Once Henry had adjusted to the unfathomable fact of Thomas — and to his snarling, defensive way of interacting with everyone — he was able to settle down a little and really begin to investigate him. It was striking how beautiful he was. His skin had a seductive velvety fineness to it, a supple softness that Henry had to resist — his hands would linger on the boy's forearm just a moment too long, and Thomas would give him a glance of knowing disgust. Milky brown, perfect. It was intriguing, because the eighth chromosome seemed to be involved not just with aging abnormalities but with certain small dermatological oddities — none of the really deadly collodion disorders or ichthyoses but funny random things, unusual frizzy hair that broke easily, and fingernail dystrophies: the management and removal of dead cells from the surfaces and shallow subsurfaces of the body. Petronov was on eight, Hickman was on eight, Berteuil-Unsendt appeared to be split between eight and twenty. But what did it mean?

It was going to take him a long time to figure any of this out. The first order of business was to determine what the anomalous C made — what unprecedented enzyme the newly configured gene encoded. That part would not be hard — a matter of cloning the sequence into bacteria and allowing the gene to produce its enzyme or enzymes in a petri dish, where they could be gathered and examined. But then came the difficult part: determining what the new enzymes did alone, what they did in concert with other enzymes within the body, why, how, and how often. He would give them to progeroid mice first, and after a year or two there might be reason to do a primate study. But first he would have to put together the funding to buy the primates, and then he'd actually have to create progeroid primates to experiment on. He hadn't done that yet, and he didn't know if he could. He thought so, probably. But it was a hell of a long road. Human experimentation would come only after the protocols were established, which in the normal course of things took years and years.

Which meant that unless Henry acted quickly, and in fact illegally, William Durbin was out of luck. By the end of April, William was back in the hospital. He had collapsed while watching television, and when Charlie Calens looked him over, he found that William had had a small heart attack. So William was up in the pediatric ICU for an extended stay, and there was every chance that he would never leave the hospital again.

"Buddy," Henry said, looming over him in the hospital bed, "can you hear me?"

"Only when you talk." William's eyes opened slowly.

"I could sing instead, if you want." Henry put his hand on William's forehead. The round bones were rising through the skin, as though his skull were trying to be born. "Or maybe not."

"No thanks," said William, and closed his eyes.

"Henry has a very nice voice," said Lillian.

"Except," William began, and stopped. They all waited for him to resume; he swallowed, exhaled sharply, and said, "For the singing."

"From what we can tell," Charlie Calens said, "the damage

wasn't that bad. You've still got pretty good blood pressure. Your heart's still working on all four cylinders."

"Hear that?" Bernie said.

"Your heart's still working okay," Charlie repeated.

William lifted his head from the pillow, looked down the bed at the four of them. His parents, each holding one of his hands; Henry and Charlie at the end of the bed. Dropped his head again. "How come I can't breathe, then?"

"You've got some fluid in your lungs."

A few seconds passed. "Why?"

"Because there's some stenosis," Henry told him. "We've got you on some Nifedipine. That'll help clear your lungs. It probably feels like you've got some weights on your chest."

"I can't," he said, "talk."

"Don't try," Lillian told him.

"You lost a little bit of heart muscle," Charlie explained, "but just a little. It was minor. But your system's compromised already, right? So you're going to take a while to get back to where you were." Charlie glanced at Henry; Henry shrugged in agreement. If he ever would. "So you should get used to that ceiling."

"I've been in this room before," William said.

"When you broke your ankle," Henry remembered.

William nodded briefly, said nothing, but looked at Henry gratefully. The flesh of William's throat was seamed and folded; his bony shoulders were milk white. The adipose tissue had entirely wasted away. He was an ancient boy with the body of a hundred-year-old man. "I knew I'd been here before," he said, satisfied.

Outside in the corridor with Charlie, Henry exhaled raggedly: what good was his happiness, finally, when this was happening to William? Around them the linoleum glowed yellow under the fluorescent lights, and the measured quiet of the ICU extended in all directions. Poor William, failing in his final room. A terrible sorrow swelled within Henry, an underground cavern filling with water, growing heavier, colder. His own water on the lungs.

"You think this is it?" Charlie asked. "It's got to be getting close."

"This is the beginning," Henry said.

"Of the end." Charlie puffed out his cheeks, whistled: *zeeee.* "Seems like it's about time. He's exhausted."

Another blow. "Yeah," Henry said.

"This is going to be terrible, isn't it?" Charlie peered at him. "He's still so fucking aware of everything. I thought they were supposed to have a kind of sundowning."

"They do, usually. But he's always been cognitively ahead of the game."

"Or," Charlie said, "he might not be as bad off as we think."

Don't make me say it, Henry pleaded silently.

"But maybe," Charlie asked softly, "six months?"

"Maybe."

"Less?"

"Probably less," Henry said.

Passing the door again on their way out, Henry glanced in, saw that William had closed his eyes, and that his mouth now hung agape, and he looked for all the world like someone's tiny, wizened father, an old spent farmer, a veteran of wars forgotten. As Henry passed the door, his heart turned sorrowfully in his chest. He loved William, loved him as helplessly as he loved his own children, and by the time he reached the elevator he had decided. He would try to save William, no matter what the risks turned out to be.

He met Bernie Durbin for lunch the next day in the smaller of the hospital's two cafeterias, a bright new room on the western edge of the science complex, frequented by postdocs and researchers like himself and some of the marina workers who walked up from Boat Street two blocks away. There was a pleasant, wholesome odor of coffee and fried food.

"You hear this, they're trying to build a fucking hotel in front of Victor Steinbrueck Park?" Bernie asked, sitting down across from him. "People, Henry, in this city! Smell a little money and they lose their minds. Run around blocking the views. Always was a gold-rush town, you know? Boom and bust." He unwrapped a sandwich and began eating. "I tell Willie it's all temporary, he tells me there's a new economy. But I say, if somebody's making money, somebody else is losing it. Productivity only goes up so much. I think he's coming around to my point of view finally."

"How is he today?"

Bernie tipped his head, chewed. "Down. You know? A little more scared. He had a pretty bad night."

"How are you?"

"Shitty, Henry. This whole thing is just the pits. Sometimes?" He swallowed, lifted his eyes in appeal. "Sometimes I just think I'm done. I mean, Lil's up there all day, and I'm up there, and you get to the point where you just think, I'm going to be here for the rest of my life, and he's going to be lying there like that for the rest of his life, and I just want to go out and chop down a bunch of trees or something. You know?" He clenched his fists around his sandwich, shook it. "Just fucking go knock over a bunch of mailboxes with a baseball bat."

"Yeah, so listen," Henry began. "I think we've got something interesting happening. It's sort of good news, possibly."

"Yeah?"

"I think we found an asymptomatic positive."

Bernie stopped. "That is good, isn't it?"

"Could be."

"You found this yourself?"

"He came to us a few weeks ago," Henry said, and described the boy, the family.

"And he's really healthy?"

"He's perfect. I mean he's strangely perfect. Like a mannequin."

"He's got it?"

"He's got the gene, but he doesn't have the disease."

"No shit."

"Exactly. We didn't believe it at first, but it's true."

"Yeah." Slowly Bernie put his sandwich down, pulled his coffee cup to him. "I don't know exactly what you're telling me here, Hen."

"Well, I guess I'm sort of half talking," Henry said, "and half thinking."

"Okay." Bernie's eyes were wide, fixed on him. "You should probably keep going, then."

"I'm not trying to get your hopes up too much, because anything that would actually come of this is probably at least a few months off at this point."

"Okay."

"And there are certain actions I can't consider, legally. I don't even know if I can talk to you about considering them."

Bernie was still staring. "What exactly are we talking about?"

Here it was. Say it or not? Say it. "Theoretically, I might be able to give William a dose of what this kid's making for himself. Once I isolate it and stick it in a transport virus, I might be able to convince William's cells to do the same thing this kid's cells are doing. But I can't do it legally."

"Jesus Christ." Bernie's eyes filled with tears. "What do you need — you need money?"

"That's not the problem."

"You could just give it to him in secret, right?"

"Maybe."

"This other kid is seriously healthy?"

"Looks like it."

"He's *seventeen*?"

"Yeah."

"And he's got a sick brother how old?"

It was the question every Hickman parent was constantly asking: how much time was left? "Three. He's in bad shape already."

"How —?" Bernie wiped his eyes, lifted his cup, put it down again, leaned back, his arms rising in astonishment. "How is that possible?"

"Chance. One in a billion. He's got a second mutation in one of his altered copies. I don't know what it does, but it looks as if it's correcting the defect and making a better enzyme at the same time."

"So you could just give it to Willie?"

"In so many words, probably. But not legally."

"What would happen if they found out?"

"I'd lose my job. It's the worst thing I could do as a doctor. Human experimentation without an experimental protocol."

"You couldn't just get one set up?"

"Not in six months. Not in twelve months. The Institutional Review Board would want to see probably three years of study before we got to humans. Maybe two, given the nature of the condition. But I'd be surprised if they let us off that easy."

"Isn't there an emergency provision?"

"No."

"Do I know anybody on that board?"

"Maybe. Probably. Knowing you."

"So I could just go in there and raise some hell, couldn't I?" Bernie, red-eyed, was rising out of his chair. "Wouldn't they let me do that?"

"Yeah, no, they wouldn't. They turn people down all the time for things like this, and patients die because of it, but that's how you do the science."

"What if I just gave it to him myself?"

"That's just as bad for me legally. And then you're in trouble too."

"What if I said I stole it from you?"

"Still my fault. And nobody'd believe you."

"You can't give it to him because you don't know what it does?" Bernie said. "What the hell is that? We know what's going to happen if we *don't* give it to him."

"If there's no animal research, there's no profile of what it does in a mammalian system, so there can't be informed consent. And you can't treat a patient without informed consent. It's against national and international law — I mean it's a seriously bad thing to do. And we couldn't start to build a case for consent for a year at least. I mean it might do nothing. But there is a chance it might make him worse."

"You think he could be worse?" Bernie, seating himself again, with a look of naked sadness in his eyes, appealed to Henry across the table. "How the hell could he be worse?"

"Well," Henry said, "that's the other part of this. That's why I bring it up."

"You want to do it."

"I want to give you the option of saying yes or no."

"Okay, I think I'm getting the picture. Lillian's upstairs right now, you want to come tell her about this? Come on. Up. Up." His voice was suddenly tight, strained, peremptory. Henry hesitated. "Get up!" Bernie shouted, rising, his hands shaking, his coffee spilling across the table.

They rode four floors up in the elevator with the mirrored ceiling. Silence. Bernie wiping his nose. His eyes. "Yesterday" playing on the Muzak. Stepped out onto the pediatric floor, with its sad yellow suns and bears and posters of baseball players above the water fountains. In his room, William was propped up with an IV in his arm.

"Lil, there's an asymptomatic positive," Bernie said over Henry's shoulder. "Henry found some kid."

"Keep your voice down," Henry told him, and shut the door.

"Am I yelling?" Bernie faced him. "What the hell do you expect me to do? This kid's healthy, sweetheart. He's seventeen."

Lillian put a hand to her throat. "Who is he?"

"They've just moved here," Henry said.

"When? They're here right now? They're in town?"

Henry explained. William watched from his bed. Henry checked him now and then for a reaction. Not much. His color was worse than Henry had ever seen it, chalky gray with a rubbery under-tinge. Worse than yesterday. Horrible. But he was listening, and following, his gaze flitting back and forth among the three of them as Henry talked. Henry watched him take two or three calculated breaths; then the boy asked, in his reedy, drowning voice, "What's the problem?"

"There's no problem, honey."

"How old is he?" William asked.

"Seventeen," Henry repeated. No way William would ever get there, they all knew. Unless.

"Henry." Lillian eyed the door. "We don't even have to tell Charlie."

"Yeah, and listen, we'll find you a fucking patent lawyer. I know two right off the top of my head. You could make a lot of money off something like this. Two birds with one stone."

"You didn't tell anybody about the steroids you were giving him," Lillian said.

"That wasn't experimental in the same way. We're always giving people steroids for one reason or another. This is totally different. We have no idea what'll happen in this case."

"*We* certainly wouldn't tell anybody."

"Also, you have to know, it might be harmful," Henry said. "That's why we have all the protocols in the first place, so everybody at least has a sense of what to watch out for. We could do some rodent studies at the same time and keep an eye out, but it wouldn't necessarily tell us anything. We'll be totally blind."

"But you want to do it." Lillian touched his arm. "Isn't that why you told us? You want to do it, don't you? Don't you want to?"

He did. It wouldn't be hard. Cloning the sequence was mostly a matter of routine, and once that was done they'd have to retrofit it into a transport virus and allow the virus to carry the sequence through the cell membrane, where it could do its work from within. Still. It wouldn't take long. It was a terrible risk, for Henry, for William, for anyone who knew what he was doing. But he loved William, loved him ferociously. The three of them sat watching him, waiting for him to answer. Didn't he want to do it, after all? He did. "God, I really do," he said abruptly, and something broke all at once in him; his eyes were wet; he turned blindly to the window, saw only light; someone embraced him.

6

ALEXANDRA ENTWITTEN MOSS, Sandra to anyone she cared about, was a plush, very tall, broad-faced, fairly pretty girl with a head of blond hair that was limp and fine like her mother's but worn long over her shoulders, and a wry, suspicious manner that, combined with her size, led people to believe she was older than seventeen. Her height, everyone said, came from her mother, like her hair, and Sandra was happy to have it. When she stood up from the high school's cramped desks, she enjoyed the sensation of things dropping away and her legs elongating like industrial cranes, with that same mechanical sort of strength. Now, nearing the end of her junior year, she was at least five foot eleven, and she was not done growing. Secretly she hoped to be over six feet by graduation, and already she towered over the other girls and almost all the boys too, a fine fuck-you feeling even when her hair was shitty or her skin had broken out. She liked the height, would not have given it up for anything.

It was a freakish body, she knew that. No hips. No breasts either, really. She was a 40B, and on the great tower of her torso her breasts appeared, to her eyes, an afterthought, brown-tipped and actually pretty nice but totally out of proportion to the rest of her. But that was okay. She'd seen breasts get in other girls' way, and she liked the sleek powerful look of herself in the mirror. Like a seal, sort of, all smooth muscle, as if she'd been made for some different element, although she didn't like swimming much: the stink of the chlorine, and she was prone to sinking — too much muscle — while others just floated on the surface. Plus it was hard to get a suit that fit her.

But with her height and strength she was a natural at basketball, and her big soft hands, in which the basketball rested as comfortably as a rock in a hole, seemed made for the game. She liked the post and the flitting of the ball back and forth, down to her and then back out to Keisha McDonald, and the companionable bumping the other center gave her as she backed down into the key, and the act of turn and release, up and down: pivot, back-step, raise, shoot, use the glass at an angle if she was deep or let the ball find its own way if not, don't think about it too much as you're shooting, just look at the rim and feel the rough texture of the ball in your hand and don't think, don't think, just act.

It was totally the opposite of schoolwork. But she was good at that too. Which wasn't superhard at Garfield, though she took the AP classes, the marine science and the trigonometry and the AP English, in which they read Shakespeare and *1984*, including the part where Julia took off her blue overalls out in the country and she and Winston had sex, poor dumb sad Winston, with the disgusting ulcer on his leg and his cough and his pitiable doomed longings. After the sex it was plain that nothing could go right for him, they'd get him eventually, and it would be a relief, a relief to him and to Julia and also to Sandra herself that she wouldn't have to worry about the man anymore, that he would be gone, erased, forgotten. She knew her grandmother had grown up in Austria, which had become a Nazi country after the Anschluss, and wondered, was this what it had been like? That doomed feeling, as though nothing you did could ever matter? No one never talked about it. Everyone always said *Never forget, Never forget.* But who could ever forget? What on earth did they mean? What kind of person could ever forget something like that?

She didn't ask a lot of questions in class. It wasn't that she didn't have them; they just weren't the sort of questions people answered.

Thomas Benhamouda, she saw, continued mostly friendless. At lunch and after school he wandered the grounds of the school: along the chain-link fencing that surrounded the football practice field, down the covered walkway to the lower parking lot where the teachers parked their Subarus and Skylarks. Then he walked out onto the wide grass of the baseball diamond, where he sat in center field if the weather was decent, or if it was raining he kept going until he reached the overhang of the gymnasium, which is where Sandra found him as she entered practice one wet afternoon. He was standing dark-eyed and idle against the cinderblock wall. He glanced at her: her height, the gym bag, her high-tops. Air Pegasus, her second-best pair.

"Hi," she said.

"Dr. Moss is your dad," he said.

"Yeah."

"You know about me?" His voice was soft, not very deep. Wary.

"Sort of."

"You know about my brother?"

"Yeah."

"You tell anybody?"

"No," she said. "I'm not allowed."

"They think I'm gonna die too, right?"

"I don't know. I don't think so."

"Nah, they do," he said.

"Really?" She didn't believe it. "That's too bad."

"Sha, it's true. They don't want to bust out and tell me, but it's true. I did my own research."

"Oh," she said politely.

But he heard the condescension. "Sha, girl, I know things you don't even want to know. I've got all this information." He pushed himself from the wall sinuously, using his shoulders. Upright, he was obviously shorter than she. "You play basketball."

"Yeah."

"You're not even black."

"Hey, you're right," said Sandra, looking at her hand. "I didn't even notice."

Thomas shrugged, turned, began to leave.

Too abruptly she called after him, "You should like ask somebody out, you know? There's girls who would like you. They think you're interesting. You should just *talk* to somebody once in a while."

"You want to go out with me?"

"No."

"You a lez?"

"No!"

"Sha. Your dad tell you not to date me?"

"No."

"I was telling him about all my girlfriends, and he was getting all like nervous and whatever, like he didn't want to hear it. And I'm like throwing him all these stories and he's looking at me with this fucked-up look." Then Thomas imitated her father with such perfect fidelity — his patient, cautious look, his eyes widening in alarm — that she had to laugh.

"Don't talk about my dad," she said, smiling.

He came forward a step. "He talks about me, though, right? To you?"

"No, I just hear things. My parents talk, but it's not like gossip." She found herself imitating his accent, his speech, and restrained herself. "They don't do that."

"Sha, he shouldn't be talking about me to people, man. I've got confidentiality, you know? What's he say, I'm going to die?"

"He doesn't really say anything. All I know is your brother's got Hickman."

"You think you know something."

"That's all. And that you should have it, but you don't for some reason."

"He thinks I'm going to die. He told you not to say anything."

"No, he didn't."

"Sha, he *did*," he insisted, and walked away. Under his breath, he said something like "Dumbass fat bitch."

Whatever, Sandra thought, and went in to practice.

Marcia Beck, the basketball coach, *was* an obvious lesbian. She'd played for the University of Connecticut and been to the Final Four twice, and like other lifelong athletes Sandra had known, she had a body she used unconsciously, like a familiar tool, and she watched the fifteen girls she coached with a hard, suspicious eye, and could be seen constantly to be rejecting romantic advances that never occurred. Sensitive about being thought a pervert (so they all figured), she had cut herself off from any possibility of camaraderie, and with her funny bifurcated nose and broad forehead and short, lifeless hair, she spoke only in the plain, literal sentences that a missionary might use, her silver whistle hanging like a padlock around her neck and her figure hidden prudishly in a gray tracksuit. She never showered with the girls, and the notes she sent home were primitively composed and full of misspellings and illiteracies: *tornament, permition, atitude,* and even, though they played all season below a purple banner on which the word was correctly printed, *Go Buldogs.*

But in fact she was a good coach. A good coach, doing her best with bad players. She stuck to the basics. Sandra liked it, actually. Routines became automatic — layups, pick-and-rolls, defensive rotations — and so were removed from the brain and given to the body, where they could be performed without thinking. It was strange the way it happened — not all the time, but sometimes during a game, say halfway through the first quarter after the jitters had disappeared and Sandra was nicely warmed up. It was mystical, sort of — some higher intelligence seemed to be at work, letting her know where Keisha would be, whether she had made her way free on the cut or had worked herself off a pick, or whether Sandra herself should turn and lift and shoot. It was not something that lent itself to explanation. Step, rise, shoot, follow.

Sandra wasn't fat, and she knew it, and she definitely wasn't a dumbass fat bitch, but still the words hurt. Well, fine. Who cared. Whatever. But it bothered her. After practice, in the heat of the locker room shower, surrounded by the muscular imperfect shapes of Yolanda's thighs and Theresa's chunky back and Keisha's unpretty face and Simone Whitman's big purple-veined breasts swaying in the hot water she felt abruptly as though she were seeing with Thomas's eyes; that he had, perversely, entered her when she hadn't noticed. She was faintly disgusted by these girls suddenly, when she had hardly noticed them before — disgusted by their unsightliness, their straggly hair, their creased and dimpled stomachs — but she couldn't stop looking. The nipples, the dark clefts behind the hair. Upset, she turned off the shower and went self-consciously to her locker. She'd never had a boyfriend exactly, and she was still a virgin, but she wasn't lesbian, not at all. So this momentary vision seemed to have been imported from some other brain, some other consciousness. His. She slipped quickly into her clothes and left without a word to anyone. How had he done that — got inside her like that?

*   *   *

[93]

Her friend Colleen wasn't much help, as she never had boyfriends and her family belonged to some kind of strange Christian sect that required her to wear a square white cap and long denim skirts to school. Not Mennonite. Austerian. Or Mousterian — no, that was the anthropological era, but Sandra had heard the name just once, and having heard it she had sensed, there in Colleen's kitchen — while Colleen's mother stood before her, a very fat, friendly, pretty woman with a permanently steamed-open complexion — that she had inadvertently been admitted to a secret room of the house, that the name of a sacred aunt or missing brother had been mentioned, and thereafter she had asked nothing else about it. Colleen's house was small, cozy, and smelled of baking. Clean. In the daylight, during this rainy spring, Colleen's bedroom under the eaves was a snug, tidy little space where a badger might have lived in a storybook.

"I think maybe it's because he's so cute, I just automatically think about him more than I want to," Sandra told her quietly. By rule, the door was always open. "I just wish he wasn't such a jerk. I think I could ask him out probably, but then, you know — he was just really rude to me."

"Is he smart?"

"I don't know. He's so *beautiful,* my god."

"That's typical. The cute ones are always assholes."

"They totally are," Sandra said.

"Pretty people are self-centered. He probably thinks he's being funny by ignoring you. You should just ask him out."

"Why don't you?"

"I would, but then I'd blow my cover," Colleen said. A year ago, seated near each other in Geometry, they had each felt a sort of curiosity about the other — Sandra couldn't stop looking across the aisle at Colleen's strange penitent outfits and flat canvas shoes and uncut brown hair braided and coiled under that lacy white cap, and despite all this staring Colleen held herself with a cosmopolitan poise, her back straight in the uncomfortable chair, and seemed not to notice the attention she drew. And Colleen, it was obvious, was surprised to find Sandra so diligent at her schoolwork and quick to answer Mr. Garr's ranting *Whogotta numba, whogotta numba?* In her heavy purple letterman's jacket Sandra knew she did not exactly give off an intellectual air, but what was she supposed to do about her body? They each saw in the other a hidden person, and both were smart, and both, it turned out, traveled on the peripheries of several social circles at once, two outer gears that now found each other and meshed. Colleen could not date, though she talked to plenty of boys and laughed all the time, and Sandra grew to like her, to admire the lightness with which she bore her imposed costume, and Sandra tried to copy her composure during all the dumb stuff she had to do — like stand onstage before a crowd of seventh-graders to talk about Motivation and Sportsmanship. Awkward, awkward, not her style. But her duty, it had somehow turned out.

Today Sandra was bursting with precious information and found herself spilling over in Colleen's quiet room, though she knew she shouldn't. "He's actually a patient of my dad's," she said, hushed. "His brother's got this really rare condition where he gets old really fast? And Thomas supposedly has it, but doesn't have the symptoms. They're trying to figure out why."

"Really?"

"But I'm seriously not supposed to know. So seriously, seriously, don't tell anybody. It's really rare, it's like one in forty million births or something, that's why they moved here. My dad got them the money to move, and now they're doing research on him. On Thomas, to figure out why he's not sick when he should be. But I'm not supposed to tell anybody this, so."

"I've seen that on television. He has it? Thomas?"

"Supposedly. But like he's got some glitch? So like it's not showing up like it's supposed to." *Like, like, like,* she heard herself. Her mother would make fun of her for talking this way, but away from home it just blossomed. "My dad says he's got these like instant reflexes. Instantaneous," she said, correcting herself.

"He looks really young," Colleen murmured.

"I know. I guess his brother's like three and looks like he's about fifty."

"That's so sad."

"Yeah," Sandra said, knowing it was true, that it was sad, but still not quite feeling it. Her father had always dealt with dying people and at the dinner table had talked about some kid's dying, somebody's heart giving out, somebody's brain hemorrhaging, for as long as she could remember, and though her father had been somber and quiet in telling the news, he had never been noticeably sad, exactly, and so neither had she. But he probably was, wasn't he? It was just that her father was only rarely noticeably anything except just plain normal, *the usual,* his own steady self who went off every day on the bus with his briefcase full of medical magazines and his too-big glasses, and whom she sometimes caught standing somewhere in the house in a wordless spell, gazing down from a window into the street or staring at his fingertips as they circled in the air before him, as though he were building something in his brain, which maybe he was. Who knew? She had never worried about growing up, not really, but she had recently begun to see that being an adult of any respectable description meant working pretty hard most of the time.

Not that this bothered her either. She and Colleen were studying — at least they were supposed to be — trigonometry. *13. The Leaning Tower of Pisa was built to be 184.5 feet high. If the angle of elevation to the top of the tower is 60 degrees at a distance of 123.4 feet from the base of the tower, how far from the vertical is it leaning?* Find $\sin\theta$, so find θ; and side-side-angle means use the law of sines. It was not so much that she could do it in her sleep but that the joggings of trigonometry came naturally to her; you passed facts from one hand to another, like water falling down a long train of buckets, and at last came out with what you needed — it was just a matter of turning your hand in the right way. Trig had always been that way to her, and last year geometry had hardly struck her as something you needed to study at all, consisting as it did of a very forgiving stairway of proofs, one after the other, beginning on an immense flat prairie where nothing was true but six or seven facts, and then you just walked up gradually into $\frac{1}{2}h+b$ and into conical sections and parabolas while above you, like constellations, hung things like the trisected angle and the squared circle, unattainable mythologies but nonetheless there to be seen. Trigonometry was more involving, she thought: something to grab on to and manipulate. *14. Use a half-angle formula to find a) sin 22.5, b) cos 22.5, c) tan 22.5.*

"But Thomas is supposedly normal," she said, "or not normal, just not — you know. Affected."

Colleen leaned forward. "My mom would say it's a miracle."

"Yeah."

"She would say" — Colleen tipped her head back and looked into the air to find her mother's voice — "'He's been blessed by God.' And then I would ask, very calmly, 'Well, what about his brother, is he *cursed* by God?' And then she would say, 'We can't understand everything God does, He sees everything, He has a purpose for everything.' And then I would ask, 'How do you know?' And then she would say, 'Because He gave us His Word.'" Her voice fell into a mocking rhythm, the words coming out in a ferocious whisper. "And then I would say, 'How do you know that's not all just invented by men who were out to control society and keep the poor from rebelling and killing them?' And she would say, 'Because it's written in the Bible.' And I would say, 'How do you know the Bible's true?' And then she would say, 'Because I know.'" Colleen exhaled with a sudden gust. "And I would say, '*Whatever,* Mom — you're a moron.'"

Sandra whispered back, "You can't tell anyone I told you about him."

"I won't. I'm just" — she gestured with her pencil — "sort of like sick of it at the moment."

Sandra groped for some similar imposition she could offer, something she could complain about in return. But the only impositions she felt, occasionally, were those that arose from her own body: its size, its weirdness. Her parents were no problem, not really. Thomas's sullen, clumsy approach had been mostly unpleasant, but not entirely. What would his body be like, she wondered, once those skinny black jeans were taken down? "You could tell her what you think," she offered.

"No." Colleen shook her head. "She'd kick me out of the house. I'm lucky I even get to go to that school. If I start, quote, rebelling, unquote, they'll start home schooling me again."

"That'd be cool."

Colleen gave her a look of flat dread. "You have no idea," she said, "how awful it is. It took me so long to convince them to let me go to Garfield. You know what they think?" She drew a quick shuddering breath. "They actually think the earth is six thousand years old. I'm not even kidding. And I just have to *sit there,*" she whispered, "and listen to them talk about things like dinosaurs and shit like that, and it's just *infuriating* because they're just so *stupid,* and I have to pretend like I agree with what they say. And obviously they don't let me go on dates, they like totally keep track of who my *friends* are — you're the only one they even allow in the house, practically." Her pale forehead had gone hot with anger. "You know what they said? They said they think you're safe."

[97]

"Me?"

"Isn't that insulting? I mean to both of us?"

It was. It felt like a slap. "Totally," Sandra said. It was always insulting, it occurred to her, to be judged at all, even favorably — an invasion, a stamp of approval when she hadn't asked for one. "I must be a total loser."

"Believe me, they don't know the difference, they think I'm little Miss Perfect Innocent, you know, Vessel of Christ. As if they have any idea what I actually believe, which they don't, and the reason they don't is because they never even bother to *ask* me, they just assume they know because they've told me blah blah blah, and they're too stupid to see that I actually might have opinions of my own."

The question hung in the air, and after a second Sandra saw no reason not to ask. "What *do* you believe?"

Colleen rolled her eyes. "Right now? I don't know. I think there's maybe possibly a God of some kind, but I don't know what kind. Like," she enumerated, "obviously evolution is a fact, and so that takes care of people and animals and trees and, you know, *life,* et cetera. But I don't know exactly what . . . what's out there. Up there. Whatever."

What did Sandra think? 16. *From a remote point 50 feet above the foot of a tower, the angle of depression of the base is arctan ¾ and the angle of elevation of the top is 45 degrees. Find the height of the tower.* She hadn't thought about it much, and didn't really care to, and found, when she turned her mind to it now, that a gray blankness hung where her opinion should have been. She did not believe, did not disbelieve — the question did not interest her at all. Blankness. "You should just tell your parents," she said.

"Right. Then I'd have like no friends over, ever," Colleen said. "And they'd definitely take me out of school."

They were obviously both a little weird. But there was really no way of ever telling how normal you actually were. Did other people have those sorts of blanknesses hanging in their heads? Sandra felt that blankness about a few things, like history: she just didn't care, and in Government class she sat listlessly in the back accepting her A-minus with its sniping little deduction for lack of participation. Fuck you too. Pep rallies and her enforced attendance at the weekly Spirit Assemblies were stretches of utter nothingness, featureless deserts of time she had to cross. The campaign signs that showed up every spring, the white butcher paper puckering with its load of poster paint, triggered in her mind corresponding sheets of emptiness, antiposters of complete indifference, though her classmates seemed to actually care who was secretary and treasurer. Or were they just being suck-ups? She couldn't tell.

But some things did affect her. The idea of going away to college was a frightening slash of color rising on the horizon: a band of light beneath a ceiling of clouds. It was coming, like it or not. She could probably get a scholarship for basketball — nowhere like UConn or Tennessee, but if Tameka Galloway had got one to Pepperdine, she could get one at least that good. Her grades were excellent, and each semester's report card, arriving in the mail with its freight of A's, pleased her. She did take satisfaction from scorecards and registers and reports. It was her mother, she thought uneasily, showing in her.

She would miss her family, though. Her house. Her street, where she had lived all her life. When she was younger, the rise of the driveway into the garage had seemed a sloping domestic mountain, gravelly and oil-spotted, where anything might happen. Behind the garage, against the fence, funny pockets of old time still lingered. A green filtered light had lived under the rhododendrons when she was four, the light of a secret cave. She was too big to crawl in among the shrubs now, but the light shone in her mind. What was unseen was as valuable as the seen, if you really felt it to be there. Was this some version of religion? She didn't think so, but who could she ask about such things? In the same way her quick pulse of unwilling lust for Thomas could not be discussed. Who would she tell? And why did she have this itch to touch him everywhere, to overpower him? He was beautiful. But obviously stupid. And it didn't seem right somehow to be lusting after one of her dad's patients. Still, it stayed: the urge to peel down his jeans, his underpants, to grasp in her two big competent hands the small round perfect halves of his ass — smooth, hairless — and pull them toward her.

7

FOR HIS FOURTEENTH BIRTHDAY back in January he'd had a party, which had struck him as wrong the moment people started to ring the doorbell. He was too old suddenly, and it felt totally strange: ten of his friends over for cake and ice cream and the friendly impolite razzing he had recently started to hate. Pete, Zach, Josh Lee, Josh Price, Jeremy. And Kendra, Winnie, Ashlee, Olivia, and Tanya, the eleven of them crowding into the kitchen, where they stood around and drank Sprite and looked at the cake with its blue icing before sitting down in the living room to eat it with plastic forks. They all knew one another, but it had been a mistake to have everybody over like this — one birthday party too many. Darren cringed. They all felt out of place, and it made them half strangers. Ashlee was seen to be very tall among them, her black hair unusually long and shiny, and Josh Price's voice hooted from the green sofa under the window, where Darren had spent a whole year, sixth grade, reading Tolkien. The pile of presents — most of them jokes: an 'N Sync CD, a plastic hand with creepy lifelike fingernails, a container of rubber dog shit — was a heap of embarrassing stuff he hadn't asked for, didn't want. "Oh my god," Winnie shrieked when he threw the dog crap at her.

Josh Price got him *Dizzy Up the Girl,* which he liked but already had. Only Tanya Schiffer had got him anything serious: a palm-sized iron horse that sat heavily in his hand. "It's supposed to be like Etruscan," she told him.

Etruscan. It rang a bell, but he must have looked blank.

"Sort of like Greek?" she said. "My dad got it last summer, on a trip? It's just like a replica, it's not actually real."

Not real. For a brief uncomfortable moment he had imagined it was, and valuable. But duh, of course not. "Cool," he said. Not real. But it felt like a message as he weighed it in his palm. An offering. The iron horse was gaunt and almost two-dimensionally skinny but could be made to stand upright. On the glass tabletop its little hooves clicked. Its head was held high and stiff, one foreleg uplifted. Everyone fell silent. They picked it up, passed it around, examined it.

"It looks old," Olivia said respectfully.

Tanya shrugged. "It's not actually real? They just made it look that way somehow." She watched it travel around the circle of hands. "I just thought it was sort of cool."

"It is," Darren said.

"You actually like it?"

"Totally," he said.

"Cool," she said.

It was behavior that could make people hate you. Goody-goody, snooty-snooty. But Tanya knew that, obviously. Which was why she wasn't making a big deal about it. Plus she was pretty, so she could — Darren thought — get away with whatever she wanted to. In the living room a calm had settled. Her brown hair was piled up on her head, and around her slender throat she wore a plastic choker, and the way she looked at him — her head tipped, her dark, slanted eyes widening, the tip of her nose bobbing up and down — well, it was devastating. She had on a blue tank top beneath which her little breasts rose in soft desirable mounds that he couldn't keep from looking at.

"Thanks," he said. "It's neat."

"I thought you'd like it," she said.

It was an opening. He took it. By sticking close to her among the circling bunch of them, he managed to sit next to her in the back of Zach's mom's van on the way to the Crest Discount Theater, with just Olivia to fill out the bench seat. More maneuvering and he was able to sit next to her in the theater. The rest of their chattering friends noticed this but pretended not to, and at last, with a hysterical daring in the velvety red darkness, he reached out and touched her hand. She let him. He traced the ridged tendons and deep softness of the inside of her wrist, where the delicate pulse moved beneath the perfect skin. No one could see them. He kept this up for a while. Then he half turned to her and put his cupped hand up to feel, for a total of five seconds before she started to cry silently, the funny hard-softness of her left breast. It was a terrible, riveting moment: her pretty freckled face with its sculpted cheekbones and dark eyes crumpled into an expression of self-disgust visible even in the low light of *Antz*. He pulled his hand away and sat straight up in his seat as though nothing had happened, and she stopped crying, and ten minutes later she reached out and held his hand again. Permission. *That* was as far as he was supposed to go. Another message to him. And he would take it. Hell yes he would.

So anyway, he was getting a lot of messages lately. He was turning on or something. Noticing things. His mom in front of him on the scooter had been patient and shy and like *human*, not a permanent faraway entity as she had been just a year ago but now an actual person. It was a little unnerving.

"You would try to catch her," she had said, as though she weren't sure. But he had just been just saying, *theoretically.* "Theoretically or not," his mother had replied, "it's a terrible subject."

He had revved the engine again, feeling the exhaust catch and spit. "What if I wanted to like write a movie or something, then wouldn't I have to know about like perfect murders and everything?"

"Now that," she had pronounced, "would be fine with me." Her nose in the air. It was a joke, her kind of joke. He had smiled, to be nice. She was human, after all.

Another thing: he noticed now, when Freda came around, that his mother developed weird moods and tones — particular noises and tilts of the head — that were visible only in the old woman's presence. This alternate version of his mother was slower, more sympathetic than the everyday version. Younger. Foreign. When Freda was around, his mother's broad white face had a way of going as blank as a balloon, as though the nerves had been cut. As though she were barely containing herself.

And another thing: Freda was a serious pain in the ass. How had he not noticed this before? "You're not very nice to your mother," she accused him a week or so after the birthday party. "You make her life very difficult. You're too much of a boy."

"Me? What else am I supposed to be?"

"A man."

"I'm fourteen!" He looked around the kitchen for defense, but they were momentarily alone. "Just like barely. I'm not supposed to be a man yet."

"That's old enough," Freda spat. "You should be ashamed."

"Of what?"

"Of the way you act," she hissed.

"How do I act?"

"You know how you act."

"I seriously don't know what you're talking about."

"*You!*" She closed her eyes in disgust. She was theoretically forgivable, he supposed, just because she was old and bizarre in a spectacular way. Still, she was a nasty, scary old lady. On her chin grew six or seven long wispy hairs, lightened but not made invisible by her powdery makeup. Her accent was hard to understand. She was a tiny brownish woman with bright white curls and an impressive set of teeth, her own, below those stupid gigantic glasses with the swooping pink plastic frames. When do you get so old you stop paying attention to what you wear? Those glasses had gone out of style the year he was born. Her pupils through the lenses were magnified to the size of quarters, and stared angrily out at him. "Like a *monster*," she concluded, and shoved her rough way past him to the living room.

But he was no different than he ever was. Or so he thought. He was just seeing more. His mother was shy. His father was spacey, a mumbler, and had recently been giving him looks of such mournful love he could hardly meet his eye. His sister was a piece of thick muscle who without complaint or effort got straight A's and played varsity basketball. Not fair. And he himself? Not sure. He was seeing more, and maybe somehow the old woman had sensed it, sensed it in him, and not liked it. So maybe Freda too was sending him a message of some kind: *Keep it to yourself.*

Beyond all this, he had begun to notice a sort of pull in things. Or a fullness. Something. It was difficult to describe. He first began to notice it — to receive it out of the air, it felt like — a few days after his dumb party and the incident of the tank top, when it occurred to him that there *were* actually girls who *liked* guys, that most of them did, actually, that there were girls like Tanya, who were, like him, living in a body that really did want more than anything else contact with other people. These girls really did exist, and suddenly it felt as if he could sense them somehow — they took up space somewhere in the universe, and by taking up space they created gravity. Density. A roundness. And it seemed he could feel that density as these girls sat caught in the web of space, a web which, according to the latest superstring theory, consisted of a sort of humming field, like that produced by a rubber band stretched between two fingers and plucked, through which all the universe's details — buildings and trees and electrical wires — were woven and held.

Actually, this was the strangest thing of all to think about: the fact that the world he could see and touch was not just a presence in the mind, but that it held within itself some hard, true realness, and not just the realness of girls who would want him eventually but also a fundamental *presentness,* an actuality. Things existed. The heavy matter that had been created inside supernovas billions of years ago on the other side of the galaxy, and that through a series of irreproducible accidents had come, randomly, to make up his body, was *real.* He was *real.* Alone in bed at night, he felt he was almost able to detect the individual atoms jostling in the dark air around him, like marbles dancing on the membrane of his skin. *Real.*

Still, Tanya would only let him hold her hand once in a while, and he'd never felt her boob again after that one time, although they talked on the phone once in a while, late at night; the phone's green dial glowed against his face, illuminating, out of the corner of his eye, the fuzz that had recently sprouted high up on his cheek. The conversations were long, full of pauses. He asked her out whenever she called, and she would say driftingly, "I don't know," and let the line go quiet again. "You still there?" he would ask, to break the midnight hum of the line. "I'm here," she would say. Calm. The horse, with its judging eye stamped deep into the metal, stood watch on his desk.

He had also begun to talk with William Durbin. It started accidentally. He answered the ringing telephone one night, thinking it was Tanya, and a high, reedy voice asked for Henry Moss.

"This is Henry Moss," Darren said.

"I don't *think* so," said the voice.

"Seriously."

"I dialed the right number," said the voice, "because I always dial the right number."

"Seriously, this is him," Darren insisted. But the idea of becoming his father, even for a second, filled him with a dreadful hollowness: how did you do it? He laughed. "Nah," he said.

"*Obviously,*" said the voice. It was prissy, sort of. Smart. Strange-sounding, but familiar. Then a second later he got it: a Hickman patient. His dad received videotapes in the mail, and Darren had seen a few, not on purpose. Nasal, wheezy, with a weird musical hooting underneath, like a clarinet. "Who is this?" the voice asked.

From the beginning the conversations were kept secret. There was no reason for this, exactly, but since it started that way, Darren saw no way to make it otherwise. So now every couple weeks Darren would pick up the phone and dial — afternoons, before anyone else was home — and reach William on the other end of the line. It made him proud, sort of, to have begun a friendship with someone like William, and though at first it felt like a kind of charitable obligation, Darren quickly grew to like him. They thought alike in some ways, and were interested in the same science-club type of things, and obviously the science-club people you just had to stay away from permanently if you had any self-respect, but with William it was safe.

Darren felt he was testing himself, too, by talking to William. How much of this could he do? What was he capable of? Could he talk to William without freaking out too much? Usually he could. William talked fast but kept running out of air.

"You know about this thing," William had asked recently, "called NEAR?"

"I've heard of it."

"You have? The Near Earth Asteroid Rendezvous? You think it's going to work?"

"How would I know? Probably."

"You know about this new theory about the tenth planet?"

The afternoon view from his desk included the top of Mr. Harstein's big green porch and a tiny gray slice of the lake through the green trees. A booming thud issued from the direction of the

Whites' house; occasionally he would hear a crashing of debris into the bashed-up dumpster at the curb. "Planet X or something."

"Yeah, but that's old. This is a theory that there was this tenth planet between Mars and Jupiter, but that it was shattered when it got hit by an asteroid, or possibly a comet, which is why there's such a concentration of matter in that one ring, like Vesta and Ceres and Gaspra, all these big" — William gasped — "objects. And that possibly the reason for the Precambrian explosion of life on earth was the importation of new life forms from a planet like that, which was possibly big enough to have an atmosphere which was like ours was at the time."

"I think there's probably life on Mars," Darren said.

"Not anymore. Possibly there was once, but it's too cold now. Well, maybe under the surface possibly, they're discovering a lot of things about geothermal vents, but it's too cold on the surface."

"There used to be, I mean," Darren said. "There used to be water, so."

"That doesn't mean life automatically shows up."

"I know."

"You can have water without life."

"Yeah, I *know*," Darren said, "but they had all those like rivers and lakes and oceans, right? So, not like *The Martian Chronicles* Martians, obviously, but fish or something. Or amoebas."

"Fish are more advanced than amoebas," William said.

"Duh, I know that. I just mean like it wouldn't have to be people walking around and talking and whatever, but it'd still be life."

"Possibly. But if it was ever there on the surface, it's long gone now."

"We could find fossils."

"Maybe," William said quietly. He tired easily, just like that: suddenly lost all his steam. "It's possible."

"If they're up there, we'll find them eventually," Darren said, and the wonder of it struck him, the overwhelming tower of time that was to come after them both, as though they were standing on the deep floor of a mineshaft, looking up at the light. It was a frightening, helpless feeling — the way William must feel all the time, Darren guessed. Sinking, falling away from the future. Two years ago he would have shut his mind to this idea, but now, testing himself, he forced himself to think about it clearly. The end of you. The end. Nothing more of you forever. Moldy bones. Graveyards full of caskets populated by people just like him, people who had been young once but were now forever dead. If they could die, so could he.

But it was too big. Too big to really think about for long, even when he wanted to. His mind kept slipping away from it. A ball too huge to be grasped. He wondered how William did it, or if he did, or if he had already figured everything out and didn't have to think about it anymore.

Now that William was in the hospital he sounded much worse than he ever had, and their conversations had become halting, uncomfortable. William's attention wandered, failed, and there were long pauses when Darren wasn't sure if anyone was still on the line. "What were we talking about?" William would ask, finally, and Darren would remind him. The Big Bang. Type 0, Type I, Type II, Type III civilizations. Distant past, distant future. Type 0: a civilization that used only the raw materials of its home planet for energy. Coal, gas, oil. Earth was Type 0. Type I was a civilization that had colonized and explored its solar system and that could control the weather and earthquakes and mine the ocean floor. It would take probably another hundred years for earth to become a Type I. Another thousand years later it would become a Type II civilization, with so many energy needs people would have to mine the power of the sun. "Like a little binary star," William offered, "that sucks off the corona." Then, several thousand years later, it would become a Type III civilization, capable of harnessing the energy of every star in its home galaxy as well as the black hole at the galactic center, and probably capable of manipulating space-time too.

"So like anything becomes possible," Darren said. "We could like travel in time and everything."

"But if there's time travelers," William asked, the hospital paging system bonging behind him, "how come we don't see them right now?"

"They're probably instructed to stay out of human affairs." *Bong, bong, bong. Then what good are they?* was the unasked question. Silence. Silence. To break it, he thought it would be a good idea to tell a joke, one he had heard years ago from his father. "It's pretty stupid, okay?"

"Okay."

"Okay. It's stupid! Okay. There's this church minister and he's looking for a guy to ring his bell. And so he interviews a bunch of people and he takes them up into the bell tower and he tells them to ring the bell, and they all take this like big old sledgehammer and they wham it into the bell and they see how loud they can ring it, and he goes, Good, good, good, and then this one guy comes along and he says, I don't need the sledgehammer, man, and he backs up and then he runs as fast as he can and he whams his face into it and it goes *bo-o-o-o-o-ng,* and the minister goes, Okay, you're hired, because he rang it the loudest. Okay. Well, so one day he was running at the bell and he like missed and he went *wooooo* sailing out the window and he goes splat on the ground and everybody's looking around and somebody says to the minister, Do you know who it is? and the minister goes, No, but his face sure rings a bell!

"Ha!" said William creakily. "That's good."

"Wait, it's not over! Okay, so the next week the minister needs another guy to ring it, so he hires another guy who's like the other guy's brother. And so he does the same thing, he runs up and hits the bell with his face and it goes *b-o-o-o-ong* and so the minister says, Okay, you got the job, just watch out for the window, but this guy does it too, he misses and he falls out the window and goes splat on the ground and everybody comes around and looks down and says, Do you know who this guy is? and the minister goes, No, but he sure is a dead ringer for that other guy!"

From the other end of the line came a dry, sniffy, cackling sound: William laughing. "That's *so* stupid."

"I warned you," Darren said.

"Tell me another."

"I only know like a million jokes, though."

"Tell me the good ones."

"Uh, okay. Why is it good to have a hole in your pocket?"

"Why?"

"Because you feel cocky all day."

William snorted. "That's stupid."

"Why shouldn't you fart in church?"

"Why?"

"Because you have to sit in your own pew."

A mild cackling. "Pew," William said. "That's pretty good."

"Where are you going if you walk through the airport door sideways?"

"Where?"

"Bangkok."

"Ow," he said, wheezing. "That's funny."

"Okay, there's this whorehouse. There's one guy going in, one guy coming out, and one guy inside having sex. Where are they from?"

"Where?"

"The guy going in is Russian. The guy coming out is Finnish. And the guy inside is Himalayan."

A long dry wheeze and a coughing cackle. "These are the worst jokes I've ever heard in my life."

"You hear about the Polack who bought four snow tires?"

"No."

"They melted on the way home. What do you call a cow with no legs?"

"I don't know."

"Ground beef. Okay, what did the cannibal do after he dumped his girlfriend?"

"What."

"Wiped his butt." He had a million of them, it was true. "What's brown and found in second-graders' underwear?"

"What."

"Michael Jackson."

"That's disgusting!" William said, but he was cackling again, a weak, breathless, desperate sound.

Not totally pleasant, actually. But it was sort of cool. "Okay," Darren said, "three strings walk into a bar."

After talking to William, Darren was always a little proud of himself and also a little freaked out. And guilty: he shouldn't be doing it, probably. He should at least tell his dad. But no way would he ever do that. Not that his dad would be angry. Still. It was weird, a weird thing for him to be doing.

Down the hall Sandra was banging her barbells. He knocked, opened her door. She was on her back, on the padded maroon weight bench, hoisting the metal bar. "What," she said.

Yeah, what? Nothing. He was fizzing with nerves. He could run a mile, lift a car. "Can I try that?"

"I'm in the middle of a set." She lifted again, again, again, and finally settled the bar on its rack and dropped her arms to her sides. Her flat chest heaved.

"How much is that?"

"It's not the weight, it's the reps."

"How much do you think I could lift?"

She tipped her head to the side, eyed him. "Probably about sixty pounds." Her gaze lingered, then flicked away from him. "Most I've ever done is one ninety-five."

"A hundred ninety-five *pounds*?"

"No," she answered, "dollars. Duh, pounds."

"What's on there now?"

"One fifty."

She lay back and began again. She wore cut-off sweat shorts and big puffy basketball shoes. Every time the bar topped out she made a little huffing sound, which he liked; it sounded serious and full of effort. He watched her. *Guy walks into a bar with an octopus, says it can play any instrument in the house. It plays a guitar, a flute, a mandolin. Finally somebody brings it some bagpipes and the octopus rolls up and down the bar with it, not a sound coming out. "Don't worry," the guy says, "he'll play it once he figures out he can't fuck it."*

When his sister finally peeled herself up and stepped aside, a long dampness had darkened the vinyl. "Gross," he said. She rolled her eyes and threw him, from her dresser, a clean towel, which he laid across the bench. The bar was ridged, warm where she had gripped it.

"Don't start yet," she said, then came to stand behind him. "Let me spot you." She helped him lift the bar up and out of its cradle. "This is one fifty," she said.

"I can lift that easy."

"Okay," she said.

"I think."

"Sure," his sister said, "no problem."

But it was heavy. Then suddenly very heavy. "Oh, shit," he said, laughing, and his arms buckled. Too much. "Help," he said as the bar began to sink toward his nose. A single quick stroke of fear went through him: he would be crushed. "Help!"

She clutched at the bar, pulled it up. Together they reseated it in its metal rest. The effect, of borrowed strength, was strange. Intimate. The metal disks on either end of the bar clunked solidly together.

"That's like a thousand pounds!"

"I could help you start off lighter."

"Like *five* pounds."

"No, you could probably do sixty." She stood above him, peering into his face upside down. "Impress that telegirlfriend of yours, whatever her name is."

"Tanya."

"You should ask her out."

"But I do," he said. "Like all the time."

"You need bigger arms," she said, and flexed her two huge biceps above him. "Here you go. Like this. Check the guns."

Huge. Huge wasn't the word. *Crazy* huge. "That's so scary. Oh my god."

She bared her teeth at him. "I could lift *two* of you," she said, upside down, "ya little weed."

He and Sandra weren't close, exactly. They sat in separate seats on the banging, exhaust-smelling school bus. Teachers recognized him with a long *ah-ha* kind of nod, Sandra's little brother, *Sure, I can see it now.* But she turned out to be a tough act to follow. Mr. Ginns yelled at him, *Your sister ran a six-minute mile, boy!* And Mr. Cartigan kept calling on him in algebra class even after it was obvious he was just basically average at math. So it would have been easy, he suspected, for her to ignore him completely. Little brother, ruining her reputation. But when he encountered her in the halls of Garfield, she always acknowledged him somehow. Shoved him, usually — shoved him with a slow forearm that had behind it an unanswerable strength, so he couldn't help it, he laughed while she mashed him, slow motion, into a row of lockers. "Gah, stop, you tard!" he would cry, smiling like a moron, unable to conceal his happiness. Totally, totally not cool. Everybody watching him get crushed. His face against the metal, his chest pinned to the locker. Laughing his ass off. What a doofus. Oh well.

8

BERNIE DURBIN'S FIRM, Garhart, Yarrow, and Mercer, had its offices downtown, on the thirty-fifth and thirty-sixth floors of a blue glass skyscraper with views that took in the white-capped water of the sound and the rolling domesticated hills of the city to the east and, to the south, the low concrete grid of the industrial district. It was a view Henry didn't see often — he did not have much occasion to spend time in the downtown high-rises — and he found himself staring, foolishly, maybe, at the view for long minutes while Bernie and a series of other very well dressed people came and went, bringing him coffee and a little pad of smooth blue paper in case he wanted to take notes, and a bottle of very cold water. Finally he was left alone in a conference room with a short young black woman, Justine Jones, thirty-five at the outside and with her hair tightly arranged in a field of beaded cornrows that tumbled this way and that as she tipped her head. She was in charge, it seemed, of the bioscience patents, and Bernie left them alone with a handshake. "Relax," Bernie told him. "She's the best in the city."

"Yes, I am," said Justine. She was pretty, with large intelligent eyes and a jutting chin that seemed to seek Henry out across the table, though she did not meet his eyes all that often. "And still underpaid."

Henry sat with his back to the window; Justine was brilliantly illuminated, and now and then he had the uneasy sensation of falling backward out of the room and into the air, and at this he would grab at the table to catch himself. The papers before him, prepared in advance, made a tidy stack a quarter-inch thick on the polished surface. "Looks complicated," he said as she slid the stack across to him.

"We've done this before, believe me." Reassuringly, she clicked her ballpoint open and shut. Her voice was rich and throaty, with an anchorwoman's unaccented cadence. "It's not really as complicated as it looks. Most of this has to do with limiting our liability in representing you. It's the agreement between the two of us that takes up all the space."

"I can really just do this."

"As far as we can tell, you can. Your contract does not disallow it. The published guidelines you've made available to us do not disallow it. You've given us everything you can find."

"Yeah."

"So I think we're okay," Justine said. "We've done our research, and you've done yours, and judging by the materials you've provided, we're entirely on the up-and-up. This whole stack represents our due diligence, yours and ours. Nowhere in here does it indicate that you need to tell anyone what you're doing."

"But it doesn't say I can do it."

She shrugged. "You know what? This is a new area of law. This is a new field. This is how law develops. People do what they do, and society comes along behind them and cleans up the worst of the messes while trying not to get in anyone's way. Ideally, anyway."

"And institutionally I'm okay?"

"As far as you've given us an understanding of the procedures, and as far as we've been able to determine, you're okay. There's no reason you can't work on something like this even if eventually you intend to auction it off to the highest bidder, as you say you do." Without meeting his eye, she said, "If it were me, I'd tell somebody. If only to make sure I'm not making any mistakes."

"You would."

"Sure. If it's all on the up-and-up, why not?" She picked up the stack of papers, squared it on the table, and laid it down again. Tidily she pinched the corners. "But as far as we can tell, you're all right even if you don't say a word."

"Then that's all I need."

Across the table from him Justine tipped her head again, and the white beads in her hair moved in unison down their strands. "Now, let me tell you this," she said. "We're covered. By *we* I mean Garhart, Yarrow, and Mercer. Which is important to us. As far as we're concerned, we have zero exposure on this thing. That's our job, and we've done our job, and we're okay, and as far as our understanding reaches, you're okay. But if you start to do something that's out of bounds, Dr. Moss, you're on your own again. Not that you would? Of course. But just so we understand one another."

"We do."

"Mr. Durbin gave us an indication of your, you know . . ." She searched. "Reputation."

"Good old Bernie."

"I know he has an affected child."

"That's right."

"You know he speaks very highly of you. He and Mrs. Durbin both do."

This seemed a sort of warning, though her expression was neutral.

"They're a wonderful family," he said. "They're three of my favorite people in the world."

For a second she examined him from across the table. Her eyes were dark and frank, deep in their sculpted sockets, and in the bright room her cheeks showed a glossy, flawless regularity. She was visibly considering her next sentence, and taking her time doing it. "All right," she said, breaking her gaze. "As far as we can determine, the work you're doing with the Benhamoudas is entirely on the level."

So there it was, the unsaid warning: any experimentation on William was absolutely forbidden. And the rules of the university were stark and clear. Utterly and totally immoral, as far beyond the bounds of acceptable scientific and medical practice as he could go. Not that it didn't happen, and not that people didn't get away with it sometimes. But if he was discovered, he'd be fired, and he'd never get a grant again. Never get a job as an active academic researcher. Not in this country.

"This whole thing just came out of the blue," Henry said, by way of defense. "It just showed up one day."

"That's how these things tend to happen."

"I'd be stupid not to take advantage of it."

She spread her steepled hands, closed them again. "I do think the fact that the guidelines were composed twelve years ago is in your favor."

"They keep talking about revising them, but they've been in committee for years."

"Let's hope they stay there a few more days," she said, nodding at the stack of papers, which without fanfare he signed now, serially, his big blue signature shrinking through its half-dozen successive incarnations as though in fear of discovery. And he had good reason to fear. As Henry figured it, this was the most damning part of what he was going to do. These signatures not only swore he'd discovered the new insertion on the third exon of the Hickman gene but also attested to the fact — the true fact — that he and his lawyers had scoured the seventy-page ethics guidebook and that he was swearing to follow those guidelines to the letter in establishing his contract with the Benhamoudas. Which meant that he'd read and understood the paragraph prohibiting experimental treatments without proper protocols — the paragraph lifted directly from the latest version of the Helsinki Declaration: *The design and performance of each experimental procedure involving human subjects should be clearly formulated in an experimental protocol. This protocol should be submitted for consideration, comment, guidance, and where appropriate, approval to a specially appointed ethical review committee, which must be independent of the investigator, the sponsor or any other kind of undue influence.*

So it could not be clearer. In signing the papers, he was taking the biggest gamble of his life. He was betting no one would discover him. And betting further that if he was discovered and busted, he'd be able to make up the loss of income by selling the mutation to one of the bioengineering firms. But his hand, as he signed, was steady. Nothing had been decided, not yet. Not really. He would have to talk to Ilse before he did anything, of course, and he was dreading that conversation, dreading it terribly.

"So that's all you need?" he asked, returning the pen to his shirt pocket.

"It is." Justine was signing the papers as well, in a round, legible hand. "Patenting a sequence like this? Easiest thing in the world, once you prove you were the one who discovered it. You don't have to show originality, because originality's built in. You don't have to show reasonable differentiation from previous inventions, because there aren't any. You don't even have to know what it does. Or if it even does anything. You just have to show that it exists somewhere in the real world. You know Gunnar Peterson?"

"Sure."

"Allied Genomic. They've got five or six lawyers working full-time. This is all they do. He sees anything strange show up, he patents it automatically. Saves him the trouble of having to check out everything ahead of time. When something starts to look promising, he's got it tied up already. When he does acquisitions of things like this, there's usually a royalty agreement between him and the original patent-holder, so nobody ends up just giving away the next Taxol. Everybody wins. People like you do the fieldwork, he does the development, everybody gets a cut." Her words were a tiny bit slurred, held forward in the mouth, as though being given a last examination before their release. He liked her: the swift competence, the way she straightened the papers again with her dark hands and tucked the stack into a folder.

"It's funny," he felt compelled to say as she walked him out, "that this is how it works."

"As you probably know, the laws have largely been derived from the pharmaceutical model. Which makes sense, if you think about it. The first-dose model, where the issue is the capital invested to get the drug in the first place. But yes, you own it, which is strange to think of. Or you will once we file."

"That's the strange part."

"The ownership," she agreed. "Get it while you can, I say."

Downstairs, in the bright ferny public thoroughfare of the lobby, she met his eyes directly, her face turned up to his. "Congratulations," she told him.

"You don't think splitting the profits fifty-fifty is a bad idea?"

Her uplifted expression, friendly in her readiness to leave him, became professionally neutral again. "Whatever makes you happy. It's your decision. Buyouts can make you quick money sometimes. Otherwise, profits can be decades away, so if the family's looking for any kind of quick return, they're going to be disappointed. Usually in these cases the family isn't even informed, because it's such a long shot. And the way the law's written you don't have to tell them."

"Would you?"

"No. And no, fifty-fifty's not too much."

"But I could legally keep it all."

"Legally? It's all yours. But personally I think you've designed a nice agreement." Blinking slowly in the lobby's bright light, she turned to the bank of elevators. "You should feel good about it."

The deal was: expenses came off the top, not including his labor but including some laboratory odds and ends, plus whatever Garhart, Yarrow, and Mercer ended up charging for the patent, which Bernie was underwriting with the understanding that he'd be paid back if things worked out. From that point, all net profits — in the event that Henry sold the patent or, less likely, began to manufacture and distribute it himself somehow — would be divided evenly with the Benhamoudas, right down the middle. With the papers signed, it was done. The Benhamoudas wouldn't know until something eventually came of it, if it ever did. It was, after all, a long shot. But it was done. He'd signed away half his fortune, whatever that fortune turned out to be. It felt, at that moment, in that sunlit, murmuring space, like a cleaving, a pure dividing gesture that lightened and exalted him. It left him breathless, in the way that stepping outside on a bright, freezing day can. Taking himself out through the revolving glass doors, Henry — still by his own definition an innocent man — felt it had been the right thing to do.

Beginning the patent process was step one. Step two involved acquiring a delivery system — the means to transport Thomas's mutation from Thomas's cells into someone else's cells in a usable form. To that end Henry approached Carrier BioMed in San Francisco and asked for a supply of their adeno-associated virus, widely used in experimental gene therapy. He'd never dealt with Carrier before, but the people there knew his name and were happy to oblige; an otherwise lengthy security clearance, designed to forestall bioterrorists, was bypassed on the credit of his reputation. A week later a shipment of the AAV arrived with a creamy ink-smelling letter that confirmed that Carrier was charging only ten thousand dollars plus five percent of eventual gross profit, should such an eventuality arise. Bernie Durbin paid Carrier the up-front fee and negotiated the cut, which Justine told him was a standard one.

Henry felt he was in no position to argue; he needed the AAV to continue his work. That five percent, he supposed, would come off the top too.

Carrier's modified virus would act as a courier. After obligingly accepting the new sequence of nucleotides into its own code, it would transport that sequence through the cell membranes of any targeted organism; then the gene sequence would be made into mRNA, which would find its way through the ribosomes, and the ribosomes, after reading the mRNA, would produce the enzyme encoded there — in this case, the enzyme that was keeping Thomas Benhamouda alive. Henry, granted the license by Carrier, could produce in his own laboratory as much of the AAV as he needed, beginning at noon on April 17, 1999, and ending at noon exactly three years later, when his license would expire.

So the vast, sincere, exacting machinery of medical commerce had begun to move, and Henry, in his office with the two pink vials of live AAV before him on the desk, felt it: a little shuddering, his ship embarking. He was going out to sea to save William, who was already half under water. *Hold on, old buddy,* he thought, and the image of William drowning — disappearing forever — struck him with a sudden terrible vividness. *Hold on.*

The arrival of Carrier's small Styrofoam shipping container was also the beginning of a paper trail, although not a particularly damaging one. Carrier's AAV was designed to work in a wide range of mammals — rats, dogs, pigs, and primates, including humans — and because of its flexibility and reliability, it was used by most researchers who found themselves in need of a transmembrane courier. Anyone who wondered what Henry Moss was doing with Carrier's AAV would assume he was using it to conduct rodent studies — which he would be, on the side, with Gretl's help. So it was all plausible. Henry himself felt fairly reckless — surely someone would begin to wonder what he was up to — but objectively he had no reason to worry. This sort of work went on all the time. To study the enzyme itself he could use the Pathology Department's sterile bioreactors, which would attach Thomas's enzyme to a structured resin and filter out the garbage, then buffer it, mix it in a water vat, filter out the impurities again. All the facilities existed down the hall. Gretl could do all of it without arousing attention, and as long as no one got too curious, it was fail-safe. And though he was taking a gamble, he knew it was a fairly safe one. Only William, Lillian, and Bernie would know he was doing human experimentation. And Gretl, of course. And Ilse. No one in that group would think to betray him. All he needed was for William to keep his nose above water while they did what they needed to do. *Hold on,* he thought.

As the wet spring days lengthened and the evenings grew longer and warmer, his wife took up jogging. "Don't call it running," she insisted, pulling on her shoes, "because I don't go that fast. You can't look!" She faced him down in the front hallway. "You can't watch me, you make me feel like a buffoon."

Buffoon — she had always loved that word, Henry knew, a combination of *buffalo* and *balloon*. "I can't watch?"

"You want to, so you can make fun of me."

"I like the idea. I approve."

"Don't you think," she asked, looking at him narrowly, "it's ridiculous, for a woman my age?"

He didn't. But he knew better than to answer such a question at all. She returned with her face crimson, as though she had been in a violent argument with herself, but after dinner she glided around the house with an uncharacteristic calm. The local streets, seen anew at five miles an hour, turned out to hold a number of secrets. "I found a tiny little precious house," she told him in bed, "with two tiny little diamond windows upstairs, and this beautiful maybe *plum* tree? Frilly and green, and a fence in the front. It's a perfect little house, and I'd never seen it before tonight!" This was a rebuke of both of them. "There are also," she added darkly, into the motionless air of the bedroom, "a lot of houses suddenly for sale."

At night now Ilse smelled clean and damp from the shower, and the closet where the wicker hamper lived had taken on a new odor: the not unpleasant, sweaty smell of her discarded T-shirts and socks. But in the mornings her hair stood on end and her face was back to its pinched private agitation, a sight that pressed itself like a hand on Henry's married heart. His own peace of mind was iffy, and now he would have to tell Ilse his plans for William, and soon. And though he had been with her long enough to know that she was at root fearless, he was not sure how she would react. He was afraid of disappointing her with what he wanted to do. The world, in his wife's eyes, had plenty of disappointments already, and Henry sometimes felt vaguely at fault in this, having removed her not only from the continent of her birth but from a life she had described, at the time, with such fondness. The white apartment, the iron stairs to nowhere, the rich weighty density of that city, its windows and unlit back corridors and centuries upon centuries of paint, the green tint to her bedroom ceiling in the mornings — all of it gone in exchange for this unbeautiful house with the leaky porch and yard they rarely used, the basement with its wearying accumulation of clutter. Henry had lured her here, and still half consciously he felt obliged to make her life here a good one. Surely she deserved that. In youth, Henry thought, we learn to see. His wife had grown up in another world, and nothing in America looked right to her, even all these years later. And what would she think, now that he was planning to treat William illegally — not just talking about it, but really doing it? This was not what she had bargained for either.

His wife's runs grew longer, and on Sunday mornings she inspected the local real estate section with a practiced eye, and eventually she suggested they actually get into the Honda and drive around to open houses. "You don't have to come if you don't want to," she told him. "I'm really just doing this because I can't believe what these places are selling for."

"I'll come," he said.

"You really don't have to."

"But you don't mind?"

She flashed him a quick, hopeful smile. "I'd love it," she said. "We could pretend we're shopping."

He had never been much of a shopper, but as it turned out his wife in a stranger's house was a newly erotic object for him. Their presence together in these unfamiliar rooms was suggestive of an affair, of stolen time, and alone with her in the vicinity of someone else's naked bed, Henry's blood leapt. Meanwhile Ilse seemed on a mission of her own, a mission of comparison. "They have no *pictures*," she would remark. Or, in a sun porch with honeysuckle winding on a lattice outside, "Oh, this is superb." She was drawn, he noticed, to upper windows with their various views, and to basements, where the primitive original workings of a house were laid bare and where families allowed their least prepossessing belongings to collect. Often one basement room was made over for teenagers, with posters tacked to the paneled walls. "Whew," Ilse would say, "at least our guys don't smell like that."

These houses, abandoned between householders, gave up their contents freely to the eye, as though in appeal; the oddball candy dishes and dirty pink carpeting seemed to Henry as vivid and fraught with meaning as the objects in dreams. And after he had seen so many of them, the houses blended into one another, and so were further dreamlike. His wife in the car going home was sated and quiet, the newspaper folded on the floor in front of her. For Ilse, Henry saw, this activity was another form of exercise: the imaginary construction of a series of alternate lives. It gave her brain something to do. It was a weight against which she could use-fully push for a few hours a week: *At least I'm not like that.*

On one of these becalmed Sunday nights, Henry finally con-fessed his plans to her. In bed, she regarded him with a look of such benign surprise that he thought he must have misspoken.

"I sort of thought you wouldn't," she said at last. "What if someone finds out?"

"If no one tells," he explained, "no one finds out."

"Someone could still find out."

"How?"

"Someone could tell."

"Who?"

She opened her mouth to pronounce a name, but did not. "I don't know," she admitted.

"It's in nobody's interest to tell. Everybody wants to try it."

She considered this. "What about Charlie Calens?"

This was a weak link, he knew. "I can talk to Charlie."

"Maybe." But only a flicker of surprise, not the storm he had ex-pected. "But will it help him?" she asked finally.

"I don't see why it wouldn't," he said. "It's exactly what he needs to get better. It's like a marrow transplant, but it's every-where in his body. And there's no time to go through channels."

"But you haven't tried."

"There's no time. He's still in the hospital."

"But isn't that an argument in your favor?"

"It's Larry Rich and Stephan Wernerheit. They'd squash me. They'd have us going at the rodents for two years minimum."

"You're not just thinking it'll work because you like him so much?"

"I thought about that," Henry said.

"You couldn't live with yourself if you didn't do it, possibly," she provided.

"I think I would always wonder."

"But you do think it would work?"

"I think so."

"Do you really want to prolong his life? Barney Clarke regretted it."

"I know," he said.

His wife, in the side-skimming light of her lamp, cast a tall upright shadow on the bookshelf. "How much does a thing like that sell for?" she asked.

He shrugged. "It depends on what it does."

"You think it might work on healthy people?"

"Yeah, I think it might."

"Oh." She looked into the middle distance, her hands stilled on the quilt. "I can see that," she said, "if it's really a hypercatalysis of some kind. But you're really sure of this, Henry?" She was calm. "You're sure?"

"I think so."

"The risks are terrible, aren't they?"

"They could be. I think it's worth it."

"For whom?"

"For everybody." It was frightening, suddenly, that he might be able to convince her. He had expected her to resist. To talk him out of it. In fact he'd half hoped she would. But she wasn't even trying. "You want to take it yourself?" he asked her.

"Not if I have to live forever, no. I couldn't stand it. Not like you. You still want to be an astronaut."

"John Glenn did it at seventy," he said. But the truth was, he was intrigued by the idea. Who would be a better subject than himself? He felt in the longer late-spring evenings the blossoming breath of possibility, as the breeze through the open window brought with it the warming smell of the nighttime earth: the alyssum in the flowerbed, the acidic odor of the multiplying weeds. Never die. Live forever in a dark fruitful gust from the window. To his surprise, Ilse had apparently given him the go-ahead. She trusted him. And, as was often the case, he felt he was an insufficiently serious man to be trusted.

*   *   *

The third week in May they discovered that the new sequence produced just a single enzyme, a small thing, a compact little bow-tie protein that did — well, what? Locked on to some cellular receptor, piggybacked on an mRNA replication editor? It was impossible to tell.

But in a sense it did not matter, not right away; that same week Gretl used the AAV to produce a therapeutic copy for William. She brought it to Henry's door in its little foil-capped vial, a few milliliters of clear fluid swimming within. The anomalous helicase had been fitted within the refashioned virus shell and suspended in a sterile water solution. Infect the kid with health. "Made to order," she said, tossing it from the doorway. "We can probably have ten more in a day or two."

He caught it. "That should be plenty for a while."

"It's so slow with this equipment. If I had the big bioreactors, I could fill a wading pool. And we're getting the mice this week," she reminded him. "We'll need some for those guys."

Held to the light, the fluid was just perceptibly cloudy: he thought of the old tonics full of laudanum and gold flake, now just empty brown bottles from an age of faith and cupidity. As if this were any other sort of age. "They're ready for us up there, you know."

"I know."

"I keep thinking maybe he's too far gone for this to make a difference."

"He might be," she said.

He felt a weight dropping through his guts. "Or, you know, we could end up killing him outright. Even if it starts to work, it could kill him by speeding up his heart rate before it repairs his aorta, or it could bump his insulin up again without touching his kidneys, so he comes down with acidosis, or it could improve the hemoglobin count without actually improving the carrying capacity, so he basically suffocates. His heart's still a mess anyway. I mean if it doesn't fall over him like a magic cloak, it's going to do some kind of damage, isn't it? And probably something we won't even see until it's too late."

"I think," Gretl ventured, "they'd give you a break. Wernerheit would, anyway."

"No, they'd kick me out."

"Under these circumstances, I'm not so sure." She buried her red hands in the pockets of her lab coat. "But I can't tell you what I would do in your position."

"I think I've got my bases covered."

"I think so. They're my bases too," she said.

"I know. I'll tell them you had no idea."

"You'd better," she said, and leaned forward, as though to get a closer look at her shoes. Her straight white hair fell heavily around her face. "I don't have a lot of dough saved up."

"As far as I'm concerned, you're just in charge of the mice."

"Sounds like my life, all right."

"You still think it's a good idea? Medically, I mean."

"Medically?" She looked up, her face bright beneath its white cap of hair. "I think it's a wonderful thing. He's not going to live much longer anyway. There's nothing else we can do. He didn't even remember me the last time I was up there." Her mouth sloped into a froggy frown, and her lips began to tremble. "Of course it's marvelous, Henry, it's the most marvelous thing that's ever happened here, even if it doesn't work at all. It's a chance. He's so scared, Henry. I just think, what if two months from now he does die and we sit and wonder what might have happened if we'd gone ahead and tried it? And what if it *works*?" She came up with a brave, grandmotherly smile. She had two children, now long grown — son and daughter — and four grandchildren, two boys, two girls, as neat a family tree as could be drawn. "What if he gets better? What if he gets up and walks around? Even if it only puts things off five years or so, wouldn't that be something worth doing? When they started on CF they only added a couple months at a time, and now they've got them up to forty-five."

"That's how I've been justifying it to myself. But it still feels like I'm justifying it."

"Well," she said firmly, "you are. It's a risk."

"Chin can't know."

"Of course not, it's not fair to him if he does."

"And Victoria absolutely cannot know. I've told my wife."

"I'm not telling Tom."

He set the vial upright on his desk. "I might be chicken," he said.

"That's all right. They'd understand."

"You won't tell anybody. I won't tell anybody. Ilse won't. The Durbins won't. And that's everybody."

"You told me," Gretl said, "that it's human growth compound."

"Yeah. Again?"

"You're trying it again," she told him, with a look of encouragement, "because you thought it might help him keep some weight on."

Still he didn't move. He was savoring, he supposed, this last moment of innocence. It was an old, familiar sensation for him, one he had enjoyed long ago, in the moments before seducing some woman in his youth, before swallowing the phenobarbs that had gone from hand to hand in his internship — the hovering, weightless moment before he did something daring. And then the plunge. How long had it been since the last time? Since that breakfast with Ilse, so long ago, in that glassy interior with the grapefruit trees and the doorway onto the courtyard? That light.

He stood. It might actually work. And he trusted people to keep quiet. And he could not stand to think of William withering away upstairs while he sat in safety two floors below and let him die. "You want to come?" he asked.

"Oh, I guess," Gretl told him. But she would never have missed it, he knew. "Let me just wash my little handy-poos."

William had been in the hospital for almost a month now, with improvement coming only slowly. The heart was what killed most Hickman patients in the end. What killed most old people, in fact. Even after several weeks there was fluid in his lungs and he was dizzy when he sat up. Still, he wanted to walk; usually he could make it by himself to the bathroom, but not always. He had to be watched all the time. As his heart failed he was more prone to fainting, and a fall could be deadly. Now that time had weakened him, even gravity was a strain.

But he was alert. His mother sat in a chair beside him with a box of Trivial Pursuit cards, reading aloud. "What is the deepest lake in the world?" she asked. "Lake Baikal," said William, as if by rote. Bernie was standing at the window, looking down the seven stories into the courtyard. "Bingo," said Bernie.

William's head, even at rest on the pillow, seemed an enormous vulnerable burden he had been assigned to carry on too fragile a pedestal, and his eyes looked out listlessly beneath his sagging lids. But when he saw Henry, his face brightened. The boy loved him, for whatever reason, and Henry loved him back. That Henry could do nothing for William had for years stood as a guilty constant between them, but William in his wordless way had forgiven him for it every time they met. Because of this Henry loved him all the more. Now maybe he could pay him back.

Lillian looked up, her pretty mouth opening. "Is that it?" she asked.

"For what it's worth."

"So." She stood, shook down her skirt. "I wasn't sure we'd actually go through with it."

She was giving him an out. But he didn't want it. "I think we're doing it," he said, more abruptly than he meant to. He exchanged a look with Bernie, then greeted William: "Hey, buddy."

"Hey, we were watching this cool show this morning," William said breathlessly, "about solar sailing. I guess there's this . . . idea for a new sort of polymer that you can build in space that's super, super thin, three . . . molecules thick, so you can take up like a couple big canisters of this stuff and disperse . . . it in the right way, and it just self-assembles in this big sheet? And the only problem turns out to be how to keep it from sailing . . . right away before they attach it to anything. Like one of those ghost nets in the Pacific they were . . . talking about a couple years ago? That're like catching sharks and porpoises and everything, miles . . . long and you can't see them? You'd have them in space instead. Although with the" — his eyes were reddening with the effort of speech — "volume of space you don't worry about it so much, the chances are so slim you'd run into it ever are just about zero."

"Easy," said Bernie, coming to put a hand on his shoulder.

Henry said, "I was just thinking of going to Mars."

"You wouldn't use these for . . . interplanetary travel," William said quickly. "They're long-distance machines. Mars is just next door."

"Relatively speaking."

"It's true. Chemical rockets'll do fine for now, although I think the" — he inhaled deeply — "Orion model'll eventually be what we use, once the politics of it get cleared up, which I think should happen in a couple . . . hundred years." He shut his eyes. Put a hand on Bernie's, let go.

Henry took the chart, looked it over. The same ragged decline of blood sugar levels and blood oxygen levels, and a long, sloppy EKG folded accordion-style into the day's chart. The heavy, labored heart doing what it could.

Lillian nodded to Gretl. "You look eager."

"Oh, I am," said Gretl. "I think this is a *very* exciting thing."

"Another needle, Willie," Bernie said. "You up for it?"

"That's the" — he gestured with a bony hand — "thing?"

Henry rolled the vial, warm from his pocket, into William Durbin's cavernously wrinkled palm. An old man's pachydermal crevices, deep enough to lose a dime in. "That other kid's magic potion. In a saline solution. Like the stem cells were."

"What'll it do?"

"We don't know exactly. Maybe nothing. Maybe something."

"Could it kill me?"

"No," he lied, and then abruptly did not. That solar sailer — the boy would appreciate a little adventure, he reasoned. "We don't think so. We don't know anything about it. We don't know how it works. It could do anything. If it does what it does for this other boy, it might help you."

"How old is he again? Seventeen?"

"Seventeen."

An unimaginable country, those upper teen years. Other galaxies, the twenties and thirties. "Could that happen to me?"

"We don't know." Henry's glance flicked to Lillian, who had taken a big Nikon from her bag. "Your parents told you about all this. And that it's a secret."

"Yes, of course we did, Henry, he just likes to hear it from you." Beside him she was carefully adjusting her lens. "He wants to make sure he's getting the real scoop."

"We really don't know what'll happen, Willie. I don't want you to get your hopes up too much, okay?"

"Why not?"

Why not, indeed. He shrugged. "Just because we don't know. We're flying blind."

"I get to be a guinea pig."

"If anyone asks, including Charlie, this is just more HCG," Henry said, glancing at Gretl, Bernie, Lillian. "But you don't say anything unless someone brings it up."

William collusively nodded. "I get it."

"Okay?" Gretl asked.

"Okay." Henry looked around the room. "So," he said, with finality.

A frightful silence descended as Gretl handed him a paper-wrapped syringe from a drawer. Henry, his hands shaking, tore the paper and handed the wrapper to Gretl. Then he delicately filled the syringe. But no: he shouldn't do it himself. "I'm guessing you'd like to do this," he said to Lillian.

"As a matter of fact," she replied, nodding, "I would."

Lillian gave Gretl the camera and took the syringe expertly in her gold-ringed fingers. Tossing back her hair, she injected her son in the sagging, wrinkled skin of his forearm, beneath his rolled-up green sweater.

The fountain of youth, Henry thought. Applied intravenously, the AAV would travel through the bloodstream and find its way to the lungs; what happened from there was anyone's guess. It would multiply, possibly. It would have an effect, or it wouldn't. Together they were conspiring to send William on a trip into the unknown, and Henry, looking on, had the urge to call to the boy in the bed, to wish him well. *Safe journey. Navigate by the stars. Head north to home.* But he said nothing.

William reclined on his pillow and closed his eyes as the needle went in. Gretl, her professionally steady hands unfailing, aimed the lens. There came a great silky mechanical gulping as the expensive camera opened its intricate interior for a millisecond and swallowed a moment of light. Gretl looked up, surprised. "For the album," she said, apologizing.

Henry exhaled. It was done. He felt — oh, Christ almighty — he felt wonderful.

9

THEY HAD CLONED Thomas's new sequence into a colony of *E. coli* in order to have a permanent stock of the mutant gene on hand — that had been easy, a matter of routine for Chin. In this way they could produce as much of the mutated sequence as they needed and introduce it into the AAV as they went. It amounted to five milliliters of virus a week, plenty for therapeutic purposes, especially when there were only two Hickman patients within a thousand miles of the laboratory. A weekly dose, for now, was two milliliters. A heavy dose, probably, but the signposts out this far were hard to read. Who knew what William could tolerate? The glass vials glittered in the laboratory refrigerator, row after accumulating row of them on the wire rack. Every now and then Henry would get up from his desk, walk through the lab, and look through the glass door of the specimen refrigerator at them. In each, a single clear droplet.

The bow-tie enzyme produced by Thomas's mutation obviously did something, but what? There were a few tools they could use to begin to narrow the field of inquiry, including the Basic Local Alignment Search Tool program down the hall. What, they asked, does this peculiar new strand resemble? The BLAST blinked and thought for a long moment, rummaging through its incomplete segments of genome, and then, with the obliging near-immediacy of an online shoe store, identified a seventy-two-nucleotide segment that was believed to be at least in part responsible for recognition of DNA replication errors. This seventy-two-nucleotide segment on the eleventh chromosome built a protein that was not a bow tie but a sort of broken box kite, much larger than Thomas's enzyme, with a pair of what looked like antennae on the side. A strange, awkward-looking protein. Not unlike the Hickman protein, in fact. Even that much information was exciting. Intriguing. Maybe Thomas's enzyme attached more easily to whatever receptors the broken box kite currently attached to — and if it did so more snugly, the catalysis it induced would be more efficient. Cells would be more actively, more perfectly maintained, in a way they'd never been maintained before. And that was definitely congruent with what they saw in Thomas.

But it was impossible to tell for sure. Releasing the virus into William Durbin's body to produce its anomalous enzyme was like releasing a butterfly in Alberta and trying to imagine which tree in the Yucután it would eventually descend upon. Somewhere out there in the wilds of William Durbin's endocrine system the enzyme was probably landing, but where, and to what effect, they didn't know. After a week, then two, they could not detect any of Thomas's enzyme in his blood, but that might just mean it was still at low levels. Or it might mean it wasn't there at all. Or that it was being destroyed somehow by the Hickman enzyme, which was still everywhere.

So they knew nothing, really. What other enzymes would the viral implant interact with? What oxygen was it removing or adding as it landed? What complex of interrelationships was it affecting, if it was doing anything at all? The study of how proteins folded and unfolded and why they worked and stopped working would occupy geneticists for decades into the future — that was the real work that would be waiting for them all after the fanfare of the genome project had faded, the work of taking the completed genetic map of the human organism and walking into the body itself to discover exactly what happened, moment by moment, inside the human cell. Lewis and Clark. Thousands of Lewises and Clarks, really, and all of them prospectors in the biggest gold rush in history. Still, it would be the work of many years. Even now, the normal human body was an almost total mystery at the molecular level. And someone like William was an utter wilderness.

The lab had only so much money to expend on experimentation, with just Gretl and Henry to do the work and Chin allowed to do nothing but the aboveboard cloning and storage and kept in the dark about William's treatment. Henry was reluctant to dun the Hickman Foundation for more operating funds, not only because he'd just asked them for six thousand dollars to move the Benhamoudas but because he intended to profit from whatever he discovered, and in order to get more money out of them he would have to write a grant describing exactly what he was doing, and he wasn't about to do that, not yet, and he didn't want to lie to them.

On the other hand, Henry's laboratory functioned for the most part as an individual medical clinic within the larger institution of the university; and because he was the head of his own one-man Department of Geriatric Genetics, he had no one to answer to except the dean of medicine — and even the dean had no real say in how Henry conducted the business of his office, and was more interested in how his fund-raising was going than in anything else. The cancer labs got most of the attention parceled out to the research sector, and now, after the tobacco settlement, they also got most of the money. Henry's lab was very much out of the way. So he was on his own, left to pursue whatever avenues he could afford.

The rodent studies were cheap, easy to run, and easy to keep secret. Fifty mice, half artificially progeroid and half normal, were injected with varying amounts of the virus and monitored for overall health and cellular mutation rate. The rodent lab was two hundred yards down the hall and was run in common with about thirty other laboratories on Henry's floor, so dozens of studies were conducted there at once, and even the technicians injecting the mice or rubbing a compound on their shaved bellies had no idea what sort of toxin or medicine or bioengineered material they were administering, not just for secrecy's sake but for the integrity of the double-blind. The rodent lab was big, well lit, with hundreds of plastic cages on shelves, and had the funky, grain-infused, pet-food smell of a veterinarian's. Henry liked spending time here, trying to guess what the bald or grotesquely fat mice were having done to them, watching them go about the business of their lives, unknowing, not altogether uncomfortable. And his own mice he had a special fondness for. *Good work,* he would think, watching them build their paper nests. *Keep on living.*

Determining what the enzyme did — how it worked, where it landed, what its long-term effects were — was, to say the least, problematic. All they could do was observe results as they went. Week after week Gretl scraped out a sample of Thomas's buccal cells and ran them through the compact black PCR machine just inside the laboratory door, and week after week the boy's mutation rate — against all logic — was almost zero. Every normal cell in a normal body mutated at least a little bit every ninth generation or so, with a generation coming every ten days, the mutations usually occurring in the vast dark unread spaces between genes. But Thomas's hardly mutated at all.

"Man," Henry said. "Look at that. That looks like a mistake."

She whistled. "Holy spumoni. It's working fine for Chin's AIDS work."

"What's the AIDS mutation rate, something like one in every ten to the fourth?"

"Harmon's got it down to ten to the sixth."

"So what's this, then? Ten to the zillionth."

"It's practically zero. Nothing. Which should be impossible." Gretl's disputatious forehead furrowed as she scowled again at the ticking machine. "But it keeps coming up like that."

"The kid's a time capsule."

"He really is a rude little thing, isn't he? He said I was an old goat the other day. And the insult to him was that I was *old*," she said. "That was as bad as *goat*."

In the office the thick stack of Thomas's lab results kept growing. Twenty sheets a week, each showing exactly what it shouldn't — a boy in full health, health duplicated over and over again on pink carbons affixed with double prongs to the green folder. "That's me?" Thomas would ask, eyeing the reports warily. "Something wrong with me?"

"No," Henry said, "there's *nothing* wrong with you, for some reason."

"Nothing secret you're discovering and not like telling me?"

"No."

"My mom thinks I should be getting some money for all this. For the hassle."

A purl of alarm rose in Henry, fell back again. But no, Thomas was under patent. He was Henry's. "If your mom thinks that, then your mom should let me know," Henry said smoothly, and nudged away a little bubble of guilt.

*   *   *

Upstairs, as the weeks passed, William was still a patient. Henry went up to see him twice a day, and every third day he carried a vial of the virus — through the gift shop, up the elevator, through the sad pediatrics ward. By the first week of June William was able to sit up in bed most of the day, though his chart at the end of the bed showed no real improvement: temperature, blood pressure, urea clearance, bowel movements. "I see you crapped this morning," Henry said. "Congratulations. And how many children exactly did you drop off at the pool?"

"Just one really long smelly one." William's sunken mouth twisted into a tiny smile: a small, tentative, shy expression. Boyish. He slapped both hands weakly on the white cotton blanket. "Guess what."

"You spill the beans?"

"No! I have a question."

"Okay."

"So is that actually cocaine you're giving me?"

"Well," Henry said, "not exactly."

"Because it sort of feels really weird."

"It does?"

"Really weird. Like morphine or something."

"It's not."

"It's not, right?" The smile was gone. "You'd tell me if you were doing the morphine thing?"

"It's not morphine. Really."

"Okay," the boy said. "I believe you."

"But it feels like something?"

"It feels nice," William said. "It's peaceful."

Bernie entered the room backward, carrying a wrapped sandwich and a cardboard cup of coffee from the hospital's espresso stand. His eyebrows shot up when he saw Henry. "Doc," he said. "How's business? You hear from Justine?"

"Nothing yet."

"Yeah, well, thank god you're not trying to buy a house, that's all I've got to say. Neighbors just sold for eight hundred forty-five thousand dollars. Went on the market at six hundred. Monopoly money, as far as I'm concerned, and you and me start to feel poor all of a sudden. What's the world coming to? But it won't last. Right, Willie?" Bernie lowered his solid frame onto the padded chair, eyed Henry. "I see it out there, people are edgy already. People are calling their notes in. Still, you can't help feeling you're missing the boat. You know what? I could have signed up with Amazon two years ago."

"Don't look back."

"Tell me about it. They were desperate for decent counsel. Last couple years we've been having trouble keeping the good associates, if we even get them in the first place. The minute somebody hits town they're snapped up. We can't match the offers. Not even close."

"You should do it. Jump ship."

"Nope. Too late. Ground floor's filled up in all these places, now it's just another corporate environment. Same long hours, same bullshit. Except everybody's younger than you are. Yeah, no thanks. We'll plug along."

"You should have taken that job, Dad," William said. "You'd be a multimillionaire right now."

"Yeah, well, we're not doing so bad, pal."

"You should have," the boy repeated. "It was stupid not to. I told you to do it about a hundred thousand times."

"We discussed it."

With rising heat William said, "It was the one chance you had."

"Hey, like I say, I missed the boat." Smiling, Bernie turned to Henry. "It's true. He was all over me about it. Seems funny now. The kid reads the papers, though. As you know. He's got an eye."

"It's not funny."

"Next time," Bernie said, gently now, "I'll pay attention."

Stonily, William croaked, "There is no next time."

In the pause that followed Henry looked away. No one spoke. The weather beyond the windows was cloudy and mild. The morning's haze hung over the dark water of the lake, and the nameless populated hills, green with spring growth, rolled away to the south. After a minute Henry took a syringe from the drawer and drew a vial of William's blood. Then he took out another syringe, and as the other two watched he filled it with the AAV.

Silently William offered his arm again. A conspiratorial feeling settled over the room. A spell being cast. And there *was* something magical, Henry thought, in the brilliant needle and the perfectly balanced plastic syringe swimming with cloudy fluid — this nameless protein, an unread sentence in a foreign language. His fingers were steady as he ran the sharp point into William's tired vein. The fluid expelled itself steadily, another held breath released. To be safe, he took the empty glass vial and dropped it in the orange plastic biohazard jug. The jugs were emptied and the contents destroyed every day. He would leave no evidence.

Afterward, Bernie followed him into the hallway. "Listen," he said, taking Henry's arm. "He really does seem a little bit — up. Or something. Awake. You see how pissed off he was in there?"

"I did."

"Charlie thinks so too. I think he suspects there's something going on." At the far end of the hallway a boy was laughing by himself, sitting alone in a wheelchair, as nurses swirled around him without stopping. "But you still don't want to tell him."

"Charlie? Not yet."

"You want to wait till William's really better? I think he's better."

"He's talking a lot. I think mostly he's feeling better because he can breathe again." Henry paused. Bernie was waiting, his tanned, patient face turned up. "And he likes me, you know. He's a nice kid. He wants to please us."

"You don't think it's anything more than that."

"There's a chance. The enzyme's probably doing something. Maybe. We can't find it yet, but it's probably in there somewhere."

"So you think there's a possibility."

"We wouldn't be doing it otherwise."

"He's starting to forget things all the time now," Bernie said, grimacing. "Like my old man did."

"I know."

"Anything you've got," he said. A look of frightened pleading crossed Bernie's features. "You know. Carte blanche, Henry. Whatever you need to do. It's getting pretty close, I think. So," he whispered. "Listen, thank you, you know? I'm sorry I yelled at you before. In the cafeteria."

"He's a great kid, Bernie."

"He's so fucking brave it kills me."

"You know why I'm doing this? Because he's so fucking great, okay?"

Suddenly they were both crying — holding it in, letting it out — and then abruptly they were embracing again, Bernie's jacket bunching around his shoulders. Down the hall the laughing boy had vanished — wheeled away in a bustle — and when Henry made his way to the elevator, the hall was silent again. He shivered. Descended alone in the oversized cab. Room for a gurney, a stretcher, a body. Downstairs, William's blood in the PCR machine showed no change — no improvement at all. *Not yet,* Henry made himself think.

It had rained most of the day, but by late afternoon the air hung fertile and rich in the ferns and rhododendrons, and despite everything, as he walked up from the bus stop, the sidewalk curving along under the hemlocks, Henry felt an unexpected spurt of contentment. Did he? He checked himself. He did. He was doing a brave thing at work, a decent thing, and why shouldn't this make him happy?

In this spirit he encountered his neighbor Saul Harstein at the curb, unloading cardboard boxes from a white-sided panel truck: Meyer Brothers Specialized Delivery. The boxes were big, unwieldy things, and Saul was alone, sweating into his blue button-down shirt. Half the boxes had made it to the sidewalk; the other half — there were twenty or so in all — remained in the aluminum-lined interior of the truck, stacked neatly, heavily bound with brown shipping tape. It was a long step down from the van. Saul — stocky, balding, heavily tanned, his scalp strewn with tawny brown spots — was breathing hard.

"My god, what women won't do," Saul said.

"Need a hand?"

He shook his head, not looking Henry in the eye. "You don't want any part of this. This isn't even my project, and I end up holding the bag again."

"What's in those?"

"You don't want to know."

"Okay."

"Yeah, it's an auction," he said, stepping heavily onto the asphalt. "I get to keep all the crap for the next week and a half. I've got room for this? I don't know what I'm thinking. Rent a storage unit, I tell myself. Get somebody to do some dirty work for you. But it always falls to me. Then the driver gets here, he says he doesn't do unloads. So I say, Here's fifty bucks, he says he's got union rules to worry about. I say, You're seventeen, you're in no goddamned union, let me see your card. He says, Seventy-five. I say, You've got to be kidding me. So he's sitting there. In the truck. Listening to the radio. You don't believe me, go look for yourself. How's the family?"

"Good. Fine. Everybody's fine."

"You looked worried, coming up the hill. Like something was bothering you."

He'd forgotten this about Saul: he noticed, he commented. A smart man, a rich one. "Ilse just bought a motor scooter."

"A midlife crisis? Not for Ilse."

"She's a little at loose ends. I've been working a lot."

"She has her own work still?"

"Yeah, she's still up at Kreutznaer."

Saul heaved a deep breath, his wide chest rising and falling. He wiped his hands on a handkerchief, looked up into the trees. "Good place," he said. A shiny brown face and tidy round lips and a big hooked nose that Henry envied — a great schnozz, manly and well shaped, with an antique grandeur to it. The nose of a people. Not like his own blob of dough. "That's what this friend of mine should do. Stop with the goody-goody stuff and get a job. Get her feet back on the ground. But I'm not the one to tell her."

"Who is she?"

"Don't ask. A friend," said Saul, and swung himself up into the truck. He hitched up his pants and lifted another box. "This? This is who she is. You want an antique cuckoo clock?"

"Hell no." But this was too firm a note, Henry saw immediately; Saul frowned, a little hurt, and looked away. The clock had been his, Henry intuited, or hers, whoever she was — Saul had never been married, as far as Henry knew. It was a misstep, anyway. "I've got enough racket up at my place."

This was transparent, but Saul held up a hand to let him go. "Yeah, maybe. You can't make everybody happy."

Henry went off toward his house. The truck remained for another fifteen minutes, then pulled away.

When Ilse returned from her run she shut the door too firmly, making the wineglasses shiver on their shelf. In white shorts and dark blue T-shirt she stood steaming in the kitchen before him. "Just FYI," she said, and pulled from the front of her shorts a sheaf of real estate flyers, which she smoothed on the counter. "Things are still going up." In her eyes he saw her meaning: *Should we get out now, while the getting's good?* She eyed him for a sign. "If we did it, though, I think we'd have to buy another house."

"Unless we went to live with your mother."

"And we'd have to stay in the same school district, for basketball." Little wicks of hair clung in dark blond rings to the sides of her neck. "Should I just forget it?"

"I don't know."

"You're probably right," she said. But she stood there, considering the flyers.

"Do you want to know one bad thing about running so much?" she asked.

"Bugs," he said.

"There is a lot of time to think about things. Do you know who I was thinking about tonight?"

The hair began to rise on the back of his neck. "No," he said.

"Gregor," she said.

"Gregor Hals?"

"Gregor Hals," she said.

"Sex?" he asked, after a moment.

"Yes. Which is odd, because we didn't have much sex at all, the two of us. He liked other women. But when I could get him going," she said consideringly, "he was very good in bed, Henry. Not as good as you. But he had a different style, which I'd forgotten about, very sinister, a big, mean jaguar. Do you know when I met him I sold my motor scooter because he was afraid it would kill me? Plus he didn't like the idea of his wife riding around on it like a schoolgirl."

"I think you're cute on it."

"Yes, cute," she said, pained. Saddened, embarrassed, she shut her eyes. "I've been thinking about my papa lately too. All these things are coming up — do you think I'm going crazy?"

A midlife crisis? Not for Ilse. "No," he said.

"Tonight I was thinking, all the way up the stupid hill, how Mama was so awful to him for so many years. Decades, *decades* of his life were spent with that terrible woman scraping away at him. You know, saying how pretentious he was, stupid old Leopold, you know nothing about art or anything, you can count the pills, one, two, you were always good at math at least. You know. And I'm like that, aren't I?"

"Like him?"

"No," she cried, "like *her!* Like *Mama!*"

"Hell no you're not."

"But what about Jackie? What business is it of mine what car she has? She's not the only one in the world who has one, I just choose her because she's convenient and nearby, she's a target, and that's what Mama did to *him* forever, she scraped and scraped at him and she wasn't angry at *him,* really, she was just angry at the *world,* and he happened to *be* there," she said desperately, "*like Jackie is!*"

"Jackie deserves a little poke now and then."

"Who says?" Flaring, she stood before him. "I say?"

"You always have before."

"I have?"

"That's what I like about you," he said. "You're so firm."

"I'm firm?"

"Aren't you?"

"That sounds *awful!*" she cried. She inhaled and without warning began to cry, then took his hand and led him upstairs to the bedroom. Before the windows she pulled off her sweaty clothes. She was forty-seven, and in her nakedness she was, he observed for the thousandth time, his wife, his companion, the fellow-goer of his days. The Turgersons would see, if they cared to look, her long white hippy body, with its heavy thighs and long feet, and her graying blond bush, and her scarred flaccid pink belly, smaller now that she had been running, and nice round downturned breasts — his big woman, padding across the room to him in mysterious tears to embrace him. He pulled down the shades and locked the door. She clung to him roughly. Her face, when she came in silence, was pained, and she didn't look at him afterward, just turned away while the ash tree dripped outside, dropping its browning blooms onto the roof of the garage. His wife had never been like this: never been so on edge in the world. It upset him: he had done this to her, he could not help thinking. Something, he feared, was about to break.

Still, he was surprised eighteen hours later — he was at work, reading a series of Thomas's glucose uptake tests — when Ilse telephoned him to say, Oh, it was horrible, Henry, it was hard to imagine, but Saul Harstein, the nice guy across the street, had shot himself in the head. Shot and killed himself. No one knew why he had done it, and he had left no one behind to ask.

TWO

10

H E *SHOT* HIMSELF? Saul did? Why?"

"Well, Henry, who knows?" His wife's voice over the telephone was stern: it meant she was mastering herself. Outside, rain was falling onto the brick plaza below. "I have no idea."

"Who found him?"

"His cleaning lady. This morning."

"Saul Harstein — you mean the guy across the street? I just talked to him last night. Just —" It didn't seem possible. "He *shot* himself?"

"Jackie called."

"What'd she say?"

"She said the cleaning lady found him, that he'd shot himself, and that there are police everywhere, sweetheart. I don't know. The end."

"You think he was sick?"

"I don't know. He lived all by himself, maybe he was lonely."

"He looked fine yesterday."

"I need to pick up the children. I know Jackie exaggerates, but I don't want them coming home to that, if there really are police everywhere."

"Does he have any family? Somehow I don't think he does."

"I've got to go, darling."

"Whose gun was it?"

"I don't know, darling, I guess he had a gun. He had everything else. I'm sorry, I need to go if I'm going to get them before they leave."

"He shot himself in the head?"

"That's what she says. I'll see you at home, Henry."

But no, Saul had been fine, fine, unloading those huge boxes, he'd been fine. It couldn't be right. It was too normal a day, too rainy, too gray, for such a thing to happen. Wasn't it? The rhododendrons below his office window were nodding their heads in the wind. Traffic on the bridge was slow; he could see trucks creeping along into downtown, their headlights on, and the Ship Canal was empty of boats.

He drove home through the rain, the wipers chattering on the windshield. Shot in the head: the bone, the filmy arachnoid membrane, the rubbery arterial walls, the soft, greasy, complex stuff of the brain itself. And then the blood, the blood of the body would empty through the head. A mess — that beautiful house of his stained and stinking of iron. Why? Stocky, balding, his round, ponderous face swinging to consider one thing, then another — all of it stilled forever, that big tough tradesman's head of his blown open. Jesus Christ. It couldn't be right.

But the street was full of cops, the blue-and-red lights flickering, flickering, in the gloom under the hemlocks. Oh — it was true. Henry's heart sank. He left the car around the corner, in front of Ted Bell's house. An ambulance waited silently at the curb, and the door to Saul's big timbered house hung open in the rain. Two men in suits stood on the porch, wearing latex gloves. Jesus Christ. Poor Saul. And poor Darren, poor Sandra — how the hell was he going to explain this to them? What the hell could he say?

He went across the street to the yellow tape and got the attention of one of the men standing on the porch. He was a neighbor, he said, and he'd talked to Saul the night before. Dr. Henry Moss, he said, introducing himself.

"You live where?"

"Right there."

The man cast an estimating gaze at Henry's porch. "You knew him?"

"A little." He was not the only neighbor out, he saw; up and down the block, people were standing on their porches or drifting down the sidewalk with coffee in hand. He saw Jackie White consulting with the Turgersons.

"You a friend of his?"

"No, just — neighbors." But also — it was strange to remember it suddenly like this — ten years ago his family had stayed with Saul for three days while their floors were being refinished. A little interlude in their lives: Saul had cooked them dinner, entertained them around the table with stories of buying and selling, the problems of being a landlord, and then they had hardly ever spoken to him again. Neighbors, doing what neighbors do. "I mean, we were friendly."

"You talked to him yesterday?"

"Just for a second."

"You got a card?"

Henry took one from his wallet and handed it over. The man — a detective, he assumed — walked off to consult with the other detective on the porch, then came back. "You're a doctor?"

"Yeah."

"Sundstrom. Steve." Sundstrom inhaled and said suddenly, half under his breath, "Listen, could you possibly do us a favor and come up and identify him quickly?"

"Me?"

"You think you'd recognize him?"

"What about the cleaning lady?"

"She doesn't really speak a lot of English, and frankly she's sort of freaked out."

"Can't you get a translator?"

"You're a doctor."

"Yeah, but —"

"We'd really appreciate it," said Sundstrom.

"I don't see a lot of blood in my line of work. Just, you know, little vials of it at a time." The urge to be comic came on him like an urgent need to shit. "Not gallons of it."

"Do us a favor?" Sundstrom touched him lightly on the shoulder. "It'd help us to be absolutely sure. He lived alone?"

"Aren't there pictures you can use?" He had seen bodies before, of course, but he didn't want to see Saul's, not now. Not with a bullet hole in his head. "I don't think you actually need me, do you?"

Sundstrom leaned toward him. "It's a difficult thing for a relative to have to do. It'd be a charitable thing. It'll just take a minute." Sundstrom lifted the tape with one hand, put his other hand on Henry's elbow, and led him, a little too firmly, toward the house. Henry allowed himself to be directed along the sidewalk, up onto the porch, and inside, where the wood floor of the foyer was patterned with wet shoeprints. The smell of Saul's house was the same as it had been years ago: warm, spicy, not entirely pleasant, like a boy's room that hadn't been aired out. Mixed with this was the complicated scent of the outdoors, the wet leaves of the camellia and the damp carpet of short needles that collected under the yew trees beside the cement walk, and the medicinal smell of the junipers near the porch, and the rain of this endlessly rainy June, all of it brought inside, as though Saul had wounded his house as well, left it open to the elements.

Two cops were standing in the living room and nodded to Sundstrom as he went by. He led Henry to the bottom of the staircase. It was a grand, wide-gauged staircase, the old oak shining. Stained glass at the landing — green and gold, the watery light of the day giving the colors a dim, glowing intensity. Upstairs, the body. Henry felt a wiggle of unease. Shot himself in the head.

"Is it bad?"

"It's what it is," Sundstrom said.

The upstairs was empty. A long hallway. A soapy perfume from the bathroom. Dark.

And blood too — he could smell it, its sweetish, metallic stink, mixed with shit, the bowels letting loose at death. The hall was windowless, its only illumination coming from the open doors along its length: eight doors. The layout of the house rose in his mind, ghostly, familiar, though it had been years since he had been here. On a table, a lopsided green bowl was rocking, rocking, with the rhythm of their footsteps. Sundstrom reached out with his sleeve to quiet it.

"Okay," said Sundstrom, stopping him. "You ready? We'll make it quick."

"Okay."

"Don't touch anything." He pushed the door aside with the tip of a gloved finger.

The master bedroom: a large rectangular space with four windows. Saul was in bed, beneath the covers, both arms exposed above the quilt, his right hand contracted and empty. The bed was

[146]

large, very beautiful, made of polished dark wood, a baronial piece of furniture. The rug on the floor was a rich red, with a complicated floral pattern that began at Henry's feet and rushed in a swirling wave across the room.

"You all right?" Sundstrom asked.

"I can't really see him from here."

"I'm asking if you're all right."

"I'm fine." He was. The smell was stronger here, and he caught a whiff of something sharp and incendiary. Gunpowder, he imagined.

"You ready?"

"Sure."

"Don't step in the blood."

They walked forward together. Saul was lying on his back, his head on a pillow. He had shot himself in the right side of the forehead and blown off the back of his head. Blood had spattered the wall behind the bed, but most of it had soaked the mattress and then leaked, Henry could see, into the carpet. Once the carpet was saturated, the blood had run two feet sideways across the floor to the baseboard, then followed the baseboard along the length of the room, where it snaked down a heating vent. Saul's eyes were open, his mouth agape. That big capable easy hucksterish way he had had just a few hours ago was still evident in his face, his eyebrows lifted in a question, his eyes about to propose something at the last minute. A deal-clincher. He had been a dealer, a guy who made arrangements. Liver spots were scattered across his scalp. A well-used, well-kept man of about sixty, with a sickening hole in his forehead, a neat surgical entrance. Jesus. Poor Saul.

"That's him," Henry said.

"Thank you very much," said Sundstrom, and led him from the room and pulled the door delicately shut behind him. In the hall he asked, "Did you know he owned a weapon?"

"No."

"You said you spoke to him recently?"

"Last night."

Sundstrom glanced up and down the empty corridor. "Would you mind telling me what you discussed?"

"Nothing, really. We just . . . passed the time of day. He said he was getting ready for an auction. He was unloading a bunch of boxes."

"We'd like you to make a statement about what you talked about. Can you do that?"

"Sure. Right now? Why?"

"It would be at the precinct."

"Today?"

"If you don't mind."

"All right." In the dark hallway Henry felt a professional competence rising in him — the doctor at the crime scene — and at the same time a terrible sad revulsion was entering him too. The stink of blood and shit filled the air, and he swallowed. Poor Saul, Jesus. Oh, Jesus, it was all hitting him at once. The sadness of it, the bitter metallic stink, the soundless, empty house. God, why? "Did he leave a note?" he managed.

"You understand we're going to withhold a lot of information for a while."

"Okay."

"But you want to know something?" Sundstrom asked, a grave hurry to his voice. "A lot of times, what it looks like to us? Is that this kind of thing happens on a whim. At least, that's what it looks like from the outside. You can go along for months without doing it, and then one day it just seems like the right thing to do, and bang, you do it. I've been working these for years. I'm telling you, a man can be sitting with his wife watching television and he gets up and goes into the next room and shoots himself in the head. It happens," Sundstrom continued, in a low murmur that was not quite a whisper, "all the time. No note, nothing. Half the car crashes in the world are suicides."

"Not half."

Sundstrom's blue eyes settled on him. "I imagine it'd surprise you."

But there in the big quiet house with the wet late-afternoon light trying to break into summer through the windows, it seemed impossible that anyone would do that, would voluntarily step aside from things. Henry wanted out of that house, fast, and downstairs and outside he felt a dizzying rush of nausea. Saul, dead. That hole in his head. Of course in medical school they'd carved up corpses: his had been a black man, forty-five; they'd lifted out the organs one by one, the pale leathery lobes of the liver, the wet slippery lengths of the lungs like fish from their underwater element, and the hard heaviness of the fleshy heart, five pounds, as weighty as a small cat and possessed of a cat's dense wriggliness when you held it in your two hands, cut out of its sac and stripped of its arteries, as though you had just birthed it. The only heart he had ever held, that dead man's; they had called him Richard, after the president.

"So could you go downtown with someone?" asked Sundstrom under his breath, on the sidewalk. "I don't want to inconvenience you. But it'd be a help."

Could he? He swallowed. "Let me go leave a note for my wife," he said.

The trip downtown was fast and almost wordless in the company of a woman cop, *Cruz* on her nameplate, though she looked Hawaiian. Lots of dark brown shiny hair. "Hey," he said, leaning forward, "you ever seen anything like that?"

"One or two."

"He was my neighbor."

Cruz nodded. She knew. But what kind of credit could he take for knowing Saul? None at all, really. Encased in the back of the patrol car, on its soft beige seat, Henry allowed himself to be taken out of his neighborhood, driven up over the hill and down again to the police station. That single hollow spot in the forehead, the flesh burned and blackened around the edges, a crater, and the dark stink beneath the big duvet — poor Saul, he'd put the muzzle exactly where it needed to be. The bullet had passed through the right frontal lobe at an oblique angle and probably right through the corpus callosum, through the vision centers in the back of the brain and out the occiput, bang. How fast would it be? His strong hairy hand resting clenched on the quilt, the gun obviously removed from its grasp. What would you see in that last second? Nothing, of course; nothing.

When her mother arrived with Darren to get her out of English class, Sandra's first thought was that her grandmother Freda had died. Why else would her mother be here, standing like a ghost at the classroom door? Following her into the hall, she felt suddenly frightened, a swift emptying of her heart that left her ready for anything, any kind of news. But no, that wasn't it. "Everyone's fine," said her mother, big, blond, tall in her white pants. "But there's been some bad news in the neighborhood. We wanted to come and get you to tell you first."

"That guy across the street," said Darren.

"Saul Harstein," said her mother quietly as they walked down the hall toward the door to the parking lot, "killed himself last night. We didn't want you to come home and see a hundred police on the street and think something was wrong with us. It's okay to take you home?"

"I've got practice." But they were already going. "What happened?"

"He shot himself, sweetheart. The police are all over the place."

"He shot himself?"

"Pah!" said Darren explosively. He sounded — excited, was that it? No. But eager to pass on the news. She hated to hear it in his voice, that excitement; it made her hate him, temporarily.

"Why?" she asked.

Her mother had quickened her step and brought them to the big scarred purple doors, with their brass crash bars and wire-enforced glass. She slammed her way through them without slowing down. "No one knows, honey."

"Oh my god," Sandra said as it hit her. Dead? Not that she'd ever really spoken to the man since that one time years ago when they'd all stayed there while their floors were being sanded. Why had they stayed there instead of with the Turgersons or the Whites or someone they actually knew? She couldn't remember. That big house, with its airy upstairs hallway that seemed to go on forever, that's what she remembered, and Mr. Harstein cooking at an enormous steel stove with flames shooting up from a pan: she had worried that he might burn his house down, the violent sizzling sounds and the way he kept shaking the pan. "Doing it on purpose," he'd said, smiling down at her. Weird. But nice. And she'd discovered, in the bedroom she slept in, a row of three black metal boxes on a shelf, each about the size of a paperback book and containing, in turn, a red plastic boat, a little green alligator, and a tiny gold pencil, all hers to keep. "Of course they're for you," he'd said when she'd dared mention them, "not the boxes, but the toys," and she had accepted that. It had seemed enough.

Darren, in the front seat, turned around and said, "Isn't it weird? Just like right across the street?"

"Yeah," said Sandra, as noncommittally as she could. But the thought filled her with sadness. The poor man! "He wasn't married or anything?" No, she knew he hadn't been. In all these years she hadn't talked to him either, though he drove his Mercedes around and you saw him on the street now and then, sometimes in his yard, not mowing it or anything but signing for packages or getting his mail or taking a bunch of boxes out of the trunk of his car, for example. Not somebody to talk to, exactly, but not somebody you expected to kill himself either. It made you instantly guilty for not knowing him better, for not being able to see that something was wrong. Being a normal grownup had been too hard for him, but no one had seen it. "I like him," she said. Those things he had given her had all disappeared — disappeared in the way objects from early childhood do, without a trace. "Liked," she amended. Admitting it to disarm her brother mostly. But also to say it aloud: it seemed a decent thing to do.

"It's a very sad thing," her mother said. "I'm sorry, sweetheart."

"It's okay." But her voice was breaking.

Without a word her mother sent a long arm over the seat, and when Sandra reached up to grasp her hand, it was wet. Her mother had been crying too, and at this Sandra couldn't hold it in anymore. Darren looked out the window at the road.

A television camera was propped up beneath the hemlocks, and its light illuminated the shadows beneath the trees. Ilse parked around the corner and walked down the hill, holding her children's hands. "Oh, no," she said, seeing Saul's door wide open and the yellow tape in the trees. It was true.

Jackie White was on her porch. "Darling, your husband has gone and done something very brave," she told Ilse, and explained.

"Oh, no, poor Henry," Ilse said, and over the next few hours, as she sat in front of the television with her children and Jackie, her sorrow was replaced, slowly, with anger — anger at this brutal, violent country with its guns wherever you wanted them, thanks to Charlton Heston and the rest of the Republicans, Jackie included, people who wanted to drive stupid Suburbans that blocked the road and ruined the planet, who wanted to smoke cigars and eat a big steak and watch baseball on television and remodel their houses and go to a restaurant called Hooters and buy books with silvery embossed covers. Morons. It was still an uncivilized country, particularly the West, where there were cities but it was every man for himself. And now, what a horrible waste! That poor sad man, lonely all his life and now dead.

On the couch watching the television — the local cable news channel was showing the house in the half-hour headlines; he had been that important, a *prominent local real estate figure,* they called him — she put her arms around both her children, who were nice enough to sit and let her do it. Even Darren didn't mind. In front of the television he was silent, wordless, pretending to be tough while Sandra sat beside him and cried, big girl. A woman, really, in any other era, but in this age permitted to have a purple frilly bedspread and to moon around with boys. Her big face got swollen and her bottom lip pushed itself out and the tears came down, one after the other. But she was quiet.

"I'm sorry, sweetheart," said Ilse.

"When's Dad coming home?" Sandra asked.

"I don't know. Soon, I guess."

"He's being very brave," Jackie said.

Sandra edged away. "I think it's stupid that he's down there. That's not his job."

"You ought to be proud of him." Jackie wore a white silk blouse and beneath it a bra that everyone could plainly see, and a yellow linen skirt with an attractive weave, and a pair of gold bracelets that kept sliding up and down her arm, up and down, as though the woman never had to do anything practical, never had to make herself useful in any way except to look pretty, which she was not, particularly. Jackie's tears were few, and when they squeezed out she wiped them from under her eye with one finger and then rubbed her fingertip and thumb together to make the makeup disappear. Occasionally she used a Kleenex.

"It's just awful," she said. "I keep wanting to go over there and comfort someone! And then I remember, there's no one left over there. And then I want to blame someone, and I just end up blaming myself for not knowing, or noticing!"

"Republicans," Ilse said darkly.

"Oh, really, I'd like to see how you can blame this on Republicans."

"People who don't like to spend their money on the public good, they own all the insurance companies and the drug companies so no one has health care."

"Mom, that's crazy," Darren said.

But she was furious, furious at them all for not having noticed he was in trouble. What had been so important? She patted Darren's hair, felt him duck. "At most it's only half crazy, sweetheart."

"I imagine he had fairly good health care," Jackie guessed. "And frankly I'd rather spend my money the way I want to. Do you want to know what our tax bill was this year?"

Ilse waved her away. "If you spent more or were a more socially conscious person, then Saul would be alive and none of us would be sitting and crying at the television like this."

"That *is* crazy, honey. And don't blame *me* for not being social, neither were you. None of us were. And it's not the spending I object to, it's the waste. That's what gets me. I don't mind spending it if I know what I'm getting back. Not like a six-hundred-dollar screwdriver. Or some big fat black welfare queen with her six kids." Jackie's voice dropped on *black*. "Although I guess that's not happening so much anymore, supposedly, although Clinton'd just love to see everybody get a check if it made them happy."

"You get the waste if you don't vote, if you don't write letters and annoy people."

"I vote, honey," Jackie White told her. "Believe me, I vote."

"Who did you vote for on the city council this time?"

"Cheryl Chow."

"Cheryl Chow," said Ilse. "So did I."

"I voted for her even though she's a Democrat. I think it's good that the Asians are getting into politics," said Jackie. "They've got such high morals."

"They're almost all Democrats."

"So far. The next generation won't be, though."

"You mean once they get rich and comfortable and sleazy?"

Sandra said, "Could you guys like be quiet, please?"

"Oh, look," said Jackie, gripping Ilse's arm, "there we are again."

Another little report came on, just thirty seconds of Saul Harstein's huge, well-tended house, the yew hedges in front and the junipers stiff to one side and the police cars sitting in the street. Just a blip in things because he was a rich man, well known as an owner of a good bit of real estate in the International District, understood to be a figure in the civic landscape and one who would be missed. The reporter, a black man with a very short haircut, shorter even than Henry's, pronounced his words into the air, and that was that. Ilse found herself straining to see around the edges of the screen, to see their own stairway, their own porch, their house, to see it safe and sound. It bothered her that she had not heard the shot. But no one had, according to Jackie.

The East Precinct, at the corner of Pike and Twelfth, had been re-modeled in its old brick building sometime in the last two or three years, unnoticed by Henry, who had no reason until now to know where on earth the police stations were. Inside, the carpet still smelled chemically of its manufacture, and the forest-green trim on the beige doors was still, to Henry's eye, stylish and new. Little round coffeehouse lights hung from the lobby ceiling. He was shown along a pleasant hallway, past an exercise room full of sta-tionary bicycles, up an escalator, following this woman named Cruz into a bright, glass-walled, second-story conference room. Three big comfortable chairs; he lowered himself into one of them. "Someone will be with you in a sec," said Cruz, and left him alone. No magazines; no coffee in a Styrofoam cup. Traffic passed lazily below, past the liquor store across the street.

At length he was taken into a room of cubicles. There was no tape recorder or typewriter but a man named Dennis Hale running a bulbous green iMac, a tall, sandy-haired, loose-jointed gay man, who looked to Henry as though he had just come in from the bar-ber, his blond goatee was so perfectly trimmed. Over the course of fifteen minutes Henry described his conversation with Saul, and Dennis Hale typed a statement, his blue eyes flitting from the screen to Henry and back again while his head remained perfectly still. The top of his head was flat, and his kindly eyes drooped a lit-tle at the outer corners.

"Okay," Hale said finally. "That should about do it. I'll just print this out so you can sign it, and then we'll be finished with you."

"Then what happens?"

"Nothing, as far as I know. This is" — he took the paper from its tray — "the end of it."

"He didn't seem depressed at all."

"People kill themselves for all kinds of reasons," Hale told him, hesitating a little as he looked over the form before handing it to Henry. "Especially older people."

"He was probably sixty."

"I mean, once you get past the teenage years. For them it's mostly girls, or boys, or deciding that everyone hates you, or, you know, realizing that everybody actually *does* hate you, or that you're a homosexual, for example," he confided briskly, "which is very sad. A lot of young people kill themselves because of that. But once you get older it gets more complicated. Mostly, in my opinion, people kill themselves because they're ashamed of something. Unless they're just insane," he finished. "Then you can't blame them for anything."

"He seemed happy, though."

"But it's sort of easy to seem happy, isn't it?" Hale sighed and looked Henry in the eye. Was Henry imagining it, or did a little shadow pass across the other man's slender frame, a shudder from top to bottom as he extended his hand to shake? "This was a sad thing," he said, "for you to have to do." With his left hand he patted him, a gentle touch on Henry's forearm. A long, curved, hairy hand, ringless, bony. "But it was a big help."

Henry, in the large, well-lit room, caught his breath. Hale, sighing again, handed him a Kleenex. "Sorry," Henry said, sniffing.

"Oh, that's okay. We see people bawling in here every single day, believe me."

"It was such a surprise."

"I know it was. There's no way you can prepare for something like that, is there?"

"What the hell was that asshole thinking, making me go in there?"

"Oh, you helped. Everything gets finished up much more quickly this way."

He was not crying, exactly, but a great squeezing hand was constricting his chest rhythmically, expelling a little *hoop-hoop-hoop*. He had been crying a lot lately, it seemed, and he was aware of the noise he was making, but the other people in the room, scattered at the other desks, did not seem to care. A breath, then two, and he buried his face in his palms. There was no solace there, but his hands smelled good: like coffee, flesh, and the city's dirt. Poor Saul. Poor Henry.

He stood to go, but a witless black terror fluttered within his ribcage, and it remained there, twitching against his heart and lungs, as he put himself into his blue Gore-Tex jacket and, as an afterthought, affixed his big blue signature to the statement. "I'll need a ride home," he said, rising, and Dennis Hale, shaking his hand, thanked him.

Together they went down to the green-glass lobby. "I'll arrange to get you a car," Hale said, and left him standing there alone. The rain had resumed, and the concrete sidewalks had darkened outside. The wind was pushing the traffic light gently back and forth above the intersection, and it swung in and out of Henry's line of vision, winking out, winking on, winking out again.

Back home, yellow tape ran around the perimeter of Saul Harstein's yard. A single cruiser remained out front, but the police had closed Saul's door, finally. Up and down the street, houses were illuminated: the Gerhardts, the Whites, the Bells, the Turgersons. Henry began to mount his stairs, past the mailbox. Was he being watched? No. Just the empty cruiser, the gloomy street, and the timbered depth of Saul Harstein's house fifty feet away through its yews and junipers. No one was watching him. But when he turned his back again, he felt himself observed. The house itself, he imagined, was watching him go, with its silent, stinking corridor and the yellow tape everywhere, like the remnants of a party. Shadows moved in the upper rooms, and twice he saw the electric flash of a police camera at work.

Inside, his wife was in front of the television with Jackie and Sandra.

"Where's Darren?"

"Upstairs," said Ilse. "He says it's no big deal. You were *in* there, Henry!"

"Yeah."

She stood, embraced him. His warm wife, his life. "Poor sweetheart," she said.

"Henry, you look absolutely exhausted — you've obviously been very brave." Jackie lifted herself from the sofa and shook down her bracelets. "I can't think what they were doing, making you go in there. I hope you call the newspapers and let them know. If they're going to use you as a forensic scientist, they could at least put you on the payroll." She too embraced him; she smelled damply of foundation. "I'll go and leave you all alone. I'm sure there's all sorts of things you want to talk about, and you must have all kinds of things to process. Men do this very differently from women," she added to Ilse, "so don't worry if he seems standoffish for a while. We've all been touched by this. The police don't understand that, it's very clear. They were very businesslike when I talked to them."

"You talked to them?"

"Well, I saw a few things," said Jackie. "But they asked me not to say."

"What'd you see?"

"A few things." She leaned forward and kissed Ilse on the cheek. Surprisingly, Ilse allowed it without much show of displeasure. Then Jackie went out through the living room and the front hall in her low, flat canvas shoes and shut the door too sharply behind her.

When she was gone, Ilse said, "It was awful, wasn't it?"

"It was awful."

"What'd the police say?" asked Sandra.

"They said it happens all the time." This wasn't quite right; he softened it with, "They asked if he had any family."

"Was it like really . . . disgusting?"

"It wasn't too bad."

"Why'd they make you do it?"

"They knew I'd recognize him. They thought I was a doctor. You know, a doctor doctor."

"He shot himself right in the head?" his daughter asked.

"Right here." He lifted a pinky to his own forehead. "He didn't feel anything, honey."

"Why'd he do it?"

"That's what she keeps asking, Henry. She keeps asking why he did it, as if anybody could know."

"It's a reasonable question."

"I just *wondered,* Mom." Sandra looked at Henry, a hand to her forehead. "Did he like have any head left?"

"Honey —" Ilse began.

"Really, baby, he just looked like Saul."

"Did he look sad?"

"No, honey."

But a quivering had begun in the lower part of her face, and Henry moved forward awkwardly to embrace her. Her unfamiliar womanly head against his stomach felt larger than expected, the sandy blond hair under his hand finer than his wife's. Saul's broad dark forehead marred with that neat hole, the clean watery smell of brain and the fetid, sweet stink of bone exposed to the air — what could he tell her? "No," he said, "he looked fine. He looked just like he always did."

"Then why'd he do it?"

"I don't know."

"Did it hurt?"

"No."

Ilse said, "He never felt anything, sweetheart. Really."

"How do *you* know?"

"I'm a doctor."

"You are not."

"I went to medical school," said Ilse, "just like your father."

"I think he was killed by somebody else," said Sandra, standing. "I think somebody broke in and killed him when he was asleep."

"Honey —" Henry started.

"He probably tried to get away, and whoever it was put him back in bed to make it look like a suicide," said Sandra determinedly, and then she left the room.

The phone rang all evening, neighbors checking up on one another. Henry hadn't talked to the Turgersons next door in months. "Isn't it awful," said Millie scoldingly. "All that time he was over there by himself and said *nothing*." Henry kept his mouth shut. Lars Nilsson telephoned from across the back fence, sounding strange and hollow. "I thought I recognized that street on the tube, and then I realized it was just around the corner," he said. "I couldn't believe it. I mean, Jesus." Kevin White said, "I came back to check on the new bathroom this morning and I saw his car still in the driveway, but I didn't think anything of it, you know? I mean what the hell business is it of mine?"

Everybody knew Henry had been through the house — Jackie White had spread the news — but Henry didn't gossip. "It was very sad" was all he allowed himself to say. Nobody could ever tell that he was flush with all kinds of contradictory feelings; that he was just as sad and guilty as all his neighbors were, and maybe in a kind of shock besides, and also proud of what he'd done, and happy to be part of the flurry of concern, and also — was it true? — darkly, unforgivably excited by what had happened, by the sudden inexplicable death that had come out of the sky and so narrowly missed his family. No; he sounded reasonable, sedate, sorrowful. A good man, he supposed.

Darren was doing pushups on the white carpet of his bedroom. This is what he did now, every day, working on himself, as boys do. His shoulders labored under the overhead light, and his graph-paper chart was tacked without shame to the wall above the bed, marked with almost a month's worth of pushups and sit-ups, plus the weight he was able to manage at Sandra's bench press. As a boy Henry would have never allowed himself to be seen paying such careful attention to his body; his parents, in their gentle other-worldliness, would have seen in it a moral failing, a neglect of the serious business of life, whatever that was — certainly it had nothing to do with pecs and abs. So at least Henry had done this right, raised his son differently, to be unashamed of himself. Still, it had ended up making the boy a kind of foreigner.

"You all right?" Henry asked.

Darren, for show, held himself halfway down, his triceps shaking, then let himself slowly down onto the carpet. Shirtless, he rolled over on his back, faced his father upside down. "What was it like?"

"Oh . . ." Henry sat in Darren's desk chair. "Sad."

"What'd he look like?"

"Like a guy with a hole in his head."

"Like blood and stuff?"

"A little. Not much." A wounded look on his son's face made him say, "I'm really sorry."

"It's not your fault," said Darren wryly, "it's the Republicans." He smiled. "Hey, I have a question, though. Why'd we go over there and stay that time?"

"We were getting our floors done."

"Yeah, but why there?"

"Well, it was a long time ago," Henry said. "I think it was just that he had the most room."

"You know what I was thinking about? That he had a burglar alarm. That's like all I remember from going there. It's the first time I saw a burglar alarm. And the password was *hell*, upside down. Like on a calculator, 7734? Upside down. And you turned me upside down to read it, you remember? Right in the front hall." He pointed a finger at an imaginary wall, tipped his head over. "So was it like totally bloody and nasty?"

"Mostly it was just very sad and" — he searched for the word — "disappointing or something." That wasn't it. "I don't know. To think he'd been over there all that time working up to it." *How awful,* as Millie Turgerson had said, but he wasn't scolding anybody. "Makes you feel inadequate as a neighbor."

"Seriously, was there lots of blood?"

"No," he said, "it had mostly soaked into the mattress."

This was maybe too much; it silenced his son for a long minute. Finally Darren asked, "So was he like depressed or something?"

"I don't know, hon. It didn't seem like it, but you never know."

"I wish we had a gun."

"We're not getting a gun."

"People are crazy. I mean if he can go like totally insane or something across the street without even anybody knowing or anything, then we need a gun. I mean what if he'd decided to come over here instead and shoot everybody to death? Then we'd be all dead and we couldn't do anything about it."

"We're not getting a gun."

"Dad!" But Darren was smiling at him. "We could go practice, like at a range or something, wouldn't that be cool?"

He was joking, but not entirely, and the evening went on darkening outside. And then what was there to do except eat and put the dishes away as normal and take out the trash and stack the newspapers in the rubber recycling bin? In the back yard, when Henry went out to wind up the hose, the ash tree was dancing in a little breeze, its branches bobbing in all different directions, a few more of its spoiled brown blossoms tumbling off into the garden. Above him, his house — lit up defensively, as were all the other houses on the block, as though a giant party were in progress — loomed friendly against the deepening blue of the sky. Would he ever move again? If he made a million dollars from Thomas's enzyme, would he move? He probably wouldn't be able to afford to even then, and why bother, after all? It was a good old place, with this nice secret yard out back, framed with the ash and the hemlocks overhead. In the driveway the cracked concrete held its half-dozen frogs, each a quick-breathing cubic inch of vulnerable flesh and membrane. *Move, you dumb guys,* he thought, and shuffled his feet. They leapt away into the grass with a flat amphibian stare. Maybe if you were such a porous creature, you weren't distinct from the world, just staring indiscriminate matter, not entirely differentiated from mud and water. Fish in the sea.

Saul had looked so hopeful: almost happy. Oh, poor Sandra, poor Darren — how Henry wished for their sake this had never happened! When his parents had died, he'd been in Ann Arbor in medical school, and somehow he hadn't veered off into squalor and desperation. He'd gone back every night to Golden Avenue and put his books away on the shelf and collapsed onto his mattress on the floor. He had been just seven years older than Sandra was now. He shuddered. His poor old self, orphaned so abruptly. He thought of that time as a demarcation in his life, a hidden dark ring in a tree burned but not destroyed by fire. He had survived, but it had marked him.

When he looked down at his feet again, the frogs were back.

That night the house enclosed in its circle of trees creaked and popped; the ninety-year-old beams emitted their usual oceangoing groans, and the squirrels scrambled up the roof like sailors on the netting while Henry, on his back in bed, watched his wife turn out the lights.

"You could leave them on," he suggested. "For the kids. Leave the hall light on. Look at the Turgersons'." Next door the Turgersons' front porch was illuminated, and upstairs a tall, beautiful brown armoire shone beneath a pink chandelier that Henry had never seen from any but this angle: secret lives and arrangements, other people's houses. That rotating bowl in Saul's upstairs hallway — what purpose had it served? Who had given it to him? That woman, maybe, the woman with the boxes, whoever she was. Had she heard about it? Who was going to tell her? "*They've* got the lights on."

"Henry, they're old. They never sleep." Mercilessly Ilse sank the room into darkness. Approaching across the bedroom, she was first a shape and then a smell, the flat floral grease of her lotion.

"Ils," he said, burying his nose in her, "it was so *awful*."

"You looked very strange when you came in the door."

"Did I?" He was glad she'd noticed. "I was trying to play it cool. I didn't want Sandra to lose it."

"You were just fine." Turning in her lotioned grandeur, she embraced him. "Nobody noticed but me."

"His house was so *neat*," he told her. "He had this enormous big bed and all his diplomas on the wall in the upstairs hallway, and nobody there. The guy at the police station said they were looking for his family, but I don't know if he even has any."

"He doesn't. I remember him telling me he hasn't got any, years ago. I said, *No one?* and he said, *Nobody.* I remember distinctly."

"Poor Saul."

Her voice rose plummily into the darkened room: "I'm sure he has plenty of friends, though, or a business partner. Think how much worse it would be if he did have a family. It's all right, Henry. It's not *you* — *you* didn't do anything wrong."

"I know."

"Yesterday he was no one to you."

It was true. Ilse breathed against him, broadcasting a serene warm rumbling pulse from deep within her chest, like an ocean liner heard through miles of water, while Henry lay in bed with his glasses on. Next door the Turgersons' lights went out, extinguishing the bright panes of illumination that had lain on the lawn. Ilse stirred and rolled away. The darkness had pockets in it that seemed to swell and shrink, phantoms created by the vitreous fluid shifting within his eye; shadows loomed and vanished against the wall. That funny scraping against the bottom of his stomach had continued all evening; now it was a kind of gnawing, a chewing on the tender underswing of his gut. Midnight. His children had turned off their lights. Only he was awake and unnerved. Childish, was he? But only he had been in that house. That silver muzzle on your skin, its dark purposeful glint, that breathless moment when the looping dread cinched and caught, the flickering second when you decided to do it, before you actually did. Your arm would rise on its own, you would clench your teeth. You would leap from the terrace, drink the drain fluid, plunge the knife into your heart, drive the car through the rail. The paper carrier came and went, but Henry didn't sleep until first light began to show through the windows and the robins, or whatever the hell they were, began to trill in the ash tree, their songs sounding huge and echoing, as if the house and lawn and neighborhood were contained — as he saw it, plummeting down to sleep at last — in a vast high enclosure, a protective shelter, whose walls were just visible in the distance, bright, immense, and inviolable, and unreally shimmering.

11

THEN THERE WAS NOTHING to do but go off to work, and arriving there he found that the world had not changed in the slightest. The corridors hummed with their early stirrings, the mechanisms of the elevator churned in their hollow shaft, and Victoria had made a pot of coffee and was chewing the day's first stick of cinnamon gum. While driving in he had resolved not to tell the story, but he told Victoria the whole thing right away, watching her jaw become still and then begin to move again, and when Gretl and Chin arrived together twenty minutes later he told it to them too, leaving out nothing.

"What a day," said Gretl, grasping his shoulders in concern. "You look like you've seen a ghost."

Chin's dark friendly eyes traveled over his drafting table, his computer. "Did he leave a note?"

"No. Just —" Involuntarily Henry lifted his finger to his forehead again.

"Bang," Chin supplied.

"And how about Ilse?"

"She's fine. I mean, we're all fine," he said. They were, after all.

But it grew harder, as word spread that morning, to get any work done. He didn't mind. In fact he felt tender and bruised and in need of a little gentle handling. Old Larry DeBuske and ancient Kensington Fatunde appeared with grave faces and shook his hand, which they never did. Danny Rosselli exhaled noisily and said, "You ought to write a letter or something, you know? That's not your job, buddy." Henry, in this embrace of fellows, felt buffered and contained. Those shimmery walls. Good people all.

Lisa Tung rushed into his office and embraced him, her ninety-pound frame brittle against his own. "Henry!" she cried. "I heard from Kenny, how awful! Oh, you're *pale,* you know? You're actually pale. Did they make you take him down and put him in the hearse too?"

"They were about to."

"He shot himself? Did you know him?"

"We didn't know him well," Henry said. "Which makes it strange."

"Because you could have saved him, of course."

"Something like that."

"Well, I'm sure he had all sorts of friends, Henry. Everyone does."

"It doesn't look like he had any family," he said. The sadness of this struck him again, caused another dark motion beneath his ribs. "There wasn't even a note."

"I personally think it's outlandish you were ever in there. That is absolutely not your responsibility. Are they just lazy or what?"

"They said the cleaning lady didn't speak enough English."

"That's ridiculous. All she has to do is point at him and nod." Her gaze flicked back and forth across his face, examining him. "Was it awful and gory?"

"What the hell do you think? He shot himself in the head."

"No, it couldn't have been pretty," she agreed. "How are your children, Henry?"

"They're fine."

"Sandra," she prompted herself, "and Darren. She must be in high school now."

"She's a junior."

"No!"

"Yeah."

"That means *Darren's* in high school!" She pressed her hand to her chest. "Can it be?"

"Believe it or not."

"I don't," she insisted. "I don't for a second." Then her expression changed, grew circumspect and collegial. Her little tongue darted out and moistened her lips. "Henry, not to change the subject, but I notice you've been a little bit busy lately, is that right? Are you maybe sitting on something big?"

Startled, Henry said nothing for a second. "Are you hearing rumors?"

"I wouldn't call them rumors," she said. "It's more like informed conjecture. Mostly mine."

"Chin?" said Henry. "He spilling the beans?"

"No, I swear, Henry, I can't get a word out of him sideways. It's very Korean, he refuses to say anything. No, actually I'm just connecting the dots myself. Is this absolutely inappropriate of me to ask? You can tell me to go jump in the lake if you want. It's probably not the sort of thing you're exactly eager to talk about, especially today. Poor Henry! You look stricken. Oh, you do. You should see it. That expression of yours." She put her tiny hand against her sternum. "You must be in shock."

"I'm fine," he said. "Seriously."

"Maybe. Well, Henry, I hear you've maybe been talking to lawyers." Sitting opposite him in a steel chair, she eyed him closely. "And you've got that new family in town now. How'd you manage that?"

"Who?"

"Whoever they are. I don't know their name."

"They wanted to move. We had a little foundation money for relocation. It happens."

"Everybody thinks you're sitting on something."

"Who's everybody?"

"Oh," she said, shrugging, "I don't know. Just me, mostly. I'm the only one who cares, I think."

"Everybody's got something going on these days. You see what Kenny Fatunde's guys are doing with Ehlers-Danlos now? They finally excised the promoter."

"And it won't do them any good at all, will it?"

"Not for a while, maybe."

"Besides, they had the genome there ahead of them. Kenny's good, but he's not like you. You're sneaky, Henry. I remember hearing about you from Gary, how you withheld until the last minute. You had the gene pegged for a month before you announced."

"I like to be sure."

"Mmm, you like to withhold."

"I didn't want to pull a Pons and Fleischmann. Besides, I like the low profile. It lets me get away with things."

"Like what?"

A beat. "Like mistakes," he said.

Lisa crept forward on her seat until she was poised on its edge, her small feet in their black shoes propped on a rung of the chair. She wore a black turtleneck, which held her square, pale face high. Her slip of a body was tensed. "Henry, I think you've found an asymptomatic positive."

"Now, wouldn't that be something."

"Wouldn't it. You moved that family out here so fast. That's not how you usually do things. It's usually wait, wait, wait. So it's one of the four of them, isn't it? I think it's the older boy. I understand there's an older boy?" She smiled. "Now you talk."

"The family has some relatives out here. They were moving anyway. They didn't want to go to Berkeley. I told them about Gary. There's nothing funny going on."

"You've seen a lot of William Durbin lately."

A chill. "I have?"

"Haven't you?"

"Yeah, well, I'm his doctor. Why don't you go bug Charlie Calens and leave me alone? I'm poor traumatized Henry."

"I'm not so sure. Anyway, it's not fair — you get all the interesting patients, all I get is one ichthyosis after another." Lisa clamped her lips together, leaned forward, and kissed him briefly on the cheek. "We love you, Henry," she said. "I'm so sorry for what's happened."

"I'm okay."

"I hope so," she said, and left.

It was a warning, he felt. But Chin knew nothing, Gretl was above suspicion, and Victoria hadn't been told anything at all, and while she knew enough about medicine to be useful, she was by no means in a position to betray him. Charlie Calens hadn't been told yet. Lisa was smart and had a nose for the unusual, and she could well have come by her conclusions honestly. When he heard no more from her the next day, Henry decided that this was the case. If she did suspect him of dosing William, she would warn him, he believed. They had known each other for a long time, and there was no malice between them. With an effort, he put her visit out of his mind.

Whether it was because of the treatment or not was impossible to say, but two days after Saul shot himself, William was well enough to walk up and down the hospital hallway, followed by Henry, Charlie Calens, and Lillian. It wasn't a long walk, forty feet, but the boy's heart was stronger, and his lungs had finally cleared themselves of their fluid, and he looked a little less wooden. His kidneys were still feeble, and the computed tomography scan showed a new collection of pseudocysts in the pancreas, which hurt. "Feels like somebody punched me," William said. But he seemed better, more alert, and with this alertness a kind of caution had entered his voice, as though he suspected something good was happening and didn't want to jinx it. All these things might have happened anyway, but now there was doubt. Was it something else, something beyond the normal?

"Not bad, kid," Henry said at the end of the hall.

"I used to be able to do that all the time," William said, and lowered himself into his wheelchair.

So it was good to see. But these kinds of ups and downs were common in Hickman patients at the end of their lives, as the body fought and failed, fought and failed. Charlie Calens knew it too.

"His GI's what's starting to worry me most," Charlie said in his office. "The heart, if it goes, goes quick. His GI shuts down and it'd be slow. That's what I'm afraid of now, a slow end. I think he's scared too. He talk to you about it?"

"No."

"Me neither," Charlie said, steepling his fingers. Behind his hands he wore a curious, speculative expression, and it made Henry nervous. "He talks a lot about business to me," Charlie offered.

"Same here. Or science, sometimes."

"They're never going to have any more kids, are they?"

"I doubt it."

"She's getting up there anyway, I guess," Charlie said. "So you still think we're looking at another six months, probably, at the outside."

"That's about right."

"I've been talking to them about hospice care. But they don't really want to hear it. I guess they've got the nurse at home already, so —" he shrugged. "Is that what happens now? Do we wait and see if he has another MI? I was looking it up the other day, you can do bypasses on these guys sometimes."

Henry hesitated. Should he say anything? It seemed the place. "I'm going to tell you something," he said, clearing his throat. "Which you can't tell anyone."

"Oh yeah?" Charlie nodded, and leaned back. "Well, okay, I was sort of wondering."

"It's something new."

"What is it?"

"It's a new sequence," Henry said. "We found an asymptomatic positive. A new mutation."

"Jesus Christ, really? Why haven't you published?"

"It was only a few weeks ago."

Charlie inhaled. "Oh, Jesus."

"I didn't take it through the IRB."

"Oh, Jesus. Okay, I have no idea what you're talking about, and you never told me" — Charlie's voice dropped — "and we're actually just sitting here talking about politics. Oh, my god, Henry. You're not doing this."

"The heart failure's just going to get worse. Look, the kid with this mutation just showed up out of the blue." His heart felt feathery and light as he spoke: everyone who knew this could ruin him. But he had to tell Charlie; Charlie would be administering drugs and listening to William's heart and keeping records, and the ethics of the situation demanded that Henry tell him what was going on. And they had known each other for years, and Henry trusted him. "He's asymptomatic. We isolated the product. I wouldn't have done it if I didn't know the family and if William hadn't been so close to dying anyway."

"You're keeping records, though."

"Yeah. Sure. Stacks."

"Well, shit, you know someone's going to find out." Charlie's expression had gone from surprise to anger. His jaw had set. "I wish the fuck you'd told me before you started."

"Maybe I should have."

"I do *not* know about this. You never told me, okay? You never even hinted."

"You wouldn't have done it?"

"Hell no, Henry. Jesus Christ. There's a reason we've got an experimental protocol set up and there's a reason the consequences are so dire — it's because you don't have the slightest idea what you're giving this poor kid, and the parents don't know shit either, except for what you tell them. You're putting your ass way out on a limb without anything backing you up, and if it goes wrong there's no one to blame except yourself. You think the university can afford to just lose you like that? They've given you a lab and a place to work and they've lent you their name for twenty years or whatever it is, and they expect you to stick around."

"I know all that."

"Maybe you don't." Charlie looked at him now with open disgust, which on his usually comical face seemed an expression of great severity. It was frightening. Henry had never seen the man's temper before, and he feared that he had miscalculated badly. "You don't think William's going to die anyway? You don't think he's going to be seduced into who knows what kind of hope? And the parents? It's cruel. I mean it, Henry, it's cruel."

"It's not cruel. It was their idea, mostly."

"Oh, bullshit, their idea. Come on." He lifted his hands into the air and let them fall to his lap. "You know better than that. It was as least as much your idea. How'd they find out about it if you didn't tell them?"

Yes, of course it had been his idea, but he didn't regret it. Charlie's anger was justified but beside the point. Saul's broad ruined forehead rose suddenly in his vision. What would Saul have said?

"I made a decision," Henry said, trying on Saul's voice. "I thought about it for a while, and I talked to the family about it, and then I made a decision. I didn't think I could stand to sit here and do nothing."

Charlie put his fingertips together again and exhaled through his chipped teeth, then threw his head back and looked at the ceiling. Henry knew his position was perilous, so he said nothing until Charlie dropped his head again and said, "I think it's a terrible mistake."

"He's such a great kid."

"Oh, Jesus, Henry, they all are, that's the thing," said Charlie, but there was less venom in his voice.

"But he is."

Charlie's office was full of toys. A little round rag rug had been placed in the corner, and on it sat a dozen stuffed animals that all shared Charlie's bright, jewel-eyed stare. He was a kind man, really. "Listen," he said, "I think it's a terrible idea, just terrible." He dropped William's file in Henry's lap. "And we were only talking about politics."

A terrible idea, but the man wasn't going to tell anyone. Henry stood, relieved. It was another obstacle behind him — the last one, maybe. "Thank you," he said.

Henry had never been depressed, not in the clinical sense anyway, but he knew that suicide was an irrational, private act of passion, and that while you could construct a kind of logical argument for doing it, it would necessarily be an argument based on a mistaken premise. But any kind of passion was like that, he knew; and he knew too that most passionate acts required something else, a kind of courage, or at least the despair produced by extremity.

Somehow, though no one had seen it, Saul must have known these things. It was hard to picture. His house was lovely, large, and valuable. His business was thriving, as far as Henry knew. Up and down the block the neighbors described his charity, his industry, his friendliness.

"It just doesn't make sense to me at all," Jackie White said, standing on their front porch. "I know you deal with all kinds of awful things, Henry, and I think, just theoretically, if someone were to do it, we would at least be able to understand if *you* ended up, you know . . ." She looked away vaguely in the direction of his wisteria. "But Saul is just a mystery. Anyway, we're trying to think of something we can do. I mean, you know, *us*, everyone on the block. We were thinking some sort of sign or announcement, possibly? Will you come to a meeting? Millie has agreed it can be at their house, although she hardly knew him at all. I guess none of us did."

"Who's coming?" Henry asked.

"Anyone we can convince to come. He didn't have any family, as I guess you know, and someone has to write his obituary, for example, and someone has to watch the house. But we just wanted to do something *for* him too."

Ilse appeared at the door beside him. "When is it?" she asked.

"Next week."

"Of course we'll come," she said.

"You will? Well, that's wonderful. I must say, you did everyone a wonderful service, Henry, by going in there. Or at least you did *me* a wonderful service, because I suppose the next person they would have asked would have been me." Under the porch light Jackie looked at them worriedly. "Which, as you probably can guess, would have been very, very difficult. My uncle shot himself," she said.

"I'm sorry," said Ilse.

"Oh, you know, when I was a girl. It's still a very vivid memory, even though I was only four years old. I remember my mother answering the telephone and then just sitting down on the floor, which is something she never did. The only time I ever saw her cry besides that was when Ruby shot Oswald. I think it's why I became a therapist, in fact. I wanted to help her, but I didn't know how."

The Turgersons had lived in their house for the fifty-two years of their marriage. The house, on the Mosses' side of the street, was small and full of lacquered Japanese screens, tiny clay teapots, and bonsai trees on the living room windowsills. Years ago, when Henry and Ilse had moved into the neighborhood, the Turgersons, then in their sixties, had seemed the perfect picture of elderly manners, and on the night of the neighborhood meeting they seemed not to have changed much except to have grown thinner and more brittle. Millie Turgerson's hair was restrained in a bun at the back of her head and Gerald had grown a stiff white mustache, but other than this they were as they had always been. Their lives, seen at a remove, seemed orderly and rewarding, and Henry inhaled the fine air of their living room with pleasure. The neighbors all came, every last one of them from both sides of the street, and arranged themselves on the golden sofas and green armchairs. The air of orderly quiet seemed to affect them all. Conversations were subdued.

"I think," Jackie White said, "we were all very surprised by what Saul did, and although it's too bad it has to be something like this that brings us all together, I'm glad it was something." She looked down at her clipboard. "So there is a question of what we ought to do."

"If anyone wants a drink, you should all help yourselves," said Millie. "I'm not getting up a million times."

"The booze's in the cabinet," said Gerald. "I guess that's a good idea."

The cabinet was inspected and a rack of bottles brought out and put on the table. Henry watched his wife set out a series of tumblers. "Your wife has a nose for nice things," Millie remarked, watching the glasses go on the table.

"Are they too nice?" Ilse asked, turning.

"Nooo," said Millie. "Just as long as nothing ends up in the fireplace."

Drinks were poured and Henry accepted a glass of beer, which he balanced on his knee. The group of neighbors had never, in his memory, collected like this in a room, and it interested him to see them all together. They were all white, most of them older than Henry and Ilse, and half of them were rich — the half that lived on Saul's side of the street, including Jackie White. As a group they gave the impression of lives passed in comfort and sobriety, and in the calm pursuit of good works. Among them he felt, as he still did among his elders sometimes, an imposter, a poor orphan who had made his way in the world on his wits and his striving but who was, at his core, lacking some polish and sophistication that the others, including his wife, had been born to. Charlie Calens belonged more rightly to this crowd, and his surprising disgust at Henry's adventure was in part, Henry sensed, a reaction to that thing in Henry that was missing — a sense of decency that would have kept him from making such a decision. But hadn't it been the right thing to do, really? Yes.

Saul had lain dead in his house only a few hours, according to his neighbors. His cleaning lady had a standing appointment, which meant the timing of his death could have been calculated. "He obviously didn't want to lie there forever," said Ted Bell. "He knew she'd be coming."

"Yes, that's possible. But you can't always plan it that way," said Jackie. "I think it's something that just overcomes you. I know for a fact, being in my line of work, that suicide isn't a *decision*, it's a physical act. There has to be something that moves you past just making the decision to do it and makes you actually, finally" — she mimed pointing a gun — "do the thing."

"Saul was a rational guy," said Ted.

"Not entirely, apparently," said Jackie.

"It could have been a rational act," said Ted. "He could have had some reason we don't know about. Does anyone here know what his business was?"

Gerald Turgerson said, "He was some sort of real estate broker."

"God knows there's enough money there."

"And he was a Jew," said Millie.

A ghostly silence descended, and Ilse, sitting beside Henry on a little lacquered stool, put in: "It was my understanding he owned quite a lot."

"Owned or managed, I was never sure. Both, I imagine," said Millie.

"I don't think his being a Jew has anything to do with this," said Jenny Gerhardt. She had a long face on which a collection of faint wrinkles had been drawn, and her blond hair was piled on top of her head. "I think he was probably just a lonely man who was depressed."

"I didn't say being a Jew had anything to do with it. I was adding that fact to the other facts we happen to know about him, which don't add up to much."

"I still think he was lonely."

"Did he have a girlfriend?" Ilse asked.

"Not that I saw," said Jenny Gerhardt. Others shook their heads.

"And he doesn't have any family," Ilse said.

"Apparently not."

Ilse asked, "So who exactly are we doing this for, if that isn't an awkward question?"

"We still don't know *what* we're doing, honey."

"But who are we doing it *for*, Jackie, is my question."

"For Saul, I think."

"And what would he like us to do, wherever he is?"

"Well, that is the question I was hoping we could address," said Jackie with satisfaction. "Anyone have any ideas?"

"I think you knew him the best, Henry," said Ted Bell.

"Me?" Henry sat up straighter. "I don't think so."

"You had a conversation with him the other day, didn't you? Personally, I can't remember the last time I actually talked to him."

"He did keep to himself," Nora Bell reminded them.

"I know he kept to himself, which is why it was surprising to hear that Henry had actually talked to him."

"But I didn't really talk to him."

"And then you went inside," Ted continued, "which is interesting to me, frankly, because I've never even seen the inside of his house."

"I didn't go inside until he was dead."

"Even so," said Ted.

"He used to let me into the front hall," said Jackie, "when I was collecting for the Diabetes Association. It's just beautiful. It's very Old World Charm."

"I need a drink," said Gerald Turgerson. "No, don't get up, I can get it myself."

Kevin White said, "Technically it's Arts and Crafts."

"I know what it is," Jackie said.

"Maybe he would have liked some sort of donation in his name to the Historic Preservation Society," Kevin suggested.

"There is no such thing here, darling, there's hardly any history to preserve."

"Of course there's such a thing here, Jackie," said Millie. "Don't be ridiculous."

"Well, I don't think that's a very appropriate memorial for a real estate developer."

"He wasn't a developer," said Gerald, "he was a broker. In fact, I think he owned an interest in some of the old buildings in the International District."

"You mean Chinatown."

"I think I'll call it," said Gerald, "whatever they want me to call it."

"Well, Gerald, I think I'll call it Chinatown," said Jackie, "until they put the signs in English and I can read what they're supposed to say."

"The signs all say WELCOME TO THE INTERNATIONAL DISTRICT," said Ilse.

"Those are *municipal* signs. I'm talking about the shops."

"What do you think, Henry?" asked Gerald. "Since you knew him so well."

"But I didn't," said Henry.

"Did you see a note when you were in there?" asked Millie. "I hate to think of him going out of this world without even a little explanation. It makes you feel so useless and unnecessary."

"No," he said. "There wasn't anything. It was just . . ." The room fell silent. Everyone looked at him, and he turned his beer uneasily on his knee. "It was awful," he said. He felt another dark gesture rising in his chest and swallowed it down. "No, there wasn't a note." The sadness threatened to erupt, here among his neighbors, and he looked out the Turgersons' window at the lawn that separated them from his own house. His bedroom window seemed suspended very high in the air, perilously so. The canted chimney seemed in danger of falling into the ivy, and the wisteria was working its damage on the siding, but the rooms within contained the memories of his daily life, and his children, and the air that had contributed to his happiness, and his heart lifted to see them there. He thought of William, laboring for breath. That painful walk down the corridor. Oh, of course he was doing the right thing.

"None of us knew him," he said finally, into the silence.

12

HER MOTHER, not surprisingly, was outraged by the whole thing. "A man like that living across the street from you and you don't even have an alarm! If I'm going to outlive one of my daughters, I don't want it to be you. I couldn't sleep if I lived there." Freda stared murderously at her. The taut elderly curls above her collar shivered. "This country is so violent! How anyone can stand it for a lifetime I don't know. Your decision to move was so rash, I didn't think it could possibly have lasted, and now you have children who don't know any better. Who are *Americans*!"

Ilse had come to tell her mother about Saul because — well, why? Because it was so horrible? Because it would satisfy her mother's sense of the awfulness of the world? "We're all just fine," she said.

"Just fine, she says!" Freda slapped her thighs. "A neighbor kills himself and you think this is just fine. You're happy about it."

"I certainly am not happy, Mama," Ilse protested. "You must really think I'm an animal."

"Well, you've never been a serious person, but now you look absolutely . . . absolutely . . ." Her mother searched her face. "Full of joy. You look as if you're about to fly away to the moon with joy. You think it's *exciting*. You think it's *interesting*. What you don't see is that it is very, very sad."

"Mama, of course I do. You're ridiculous. Of course I think it's very sad. Everybody liked him."

"Fff," said her mother, scowling. "You're rosy! You're pink with happiness! You and your children, you love this. Darren especially."

"Darren wants us to buy a gun," Ilse admitted. But in the face of her mother's automatic judgment she instinctively qualified this: "He's very sweet and protective."

Her mother snicked this away with her teeth. In the day's gray light her skin resembled the finely crumpled paper of an old grocery sack, woven with its crosshatch of wrinkles. But her sharp analyst's eyes, even sunk behind their sagging lids, flashed with their old hardness. "He's the sort of boy we used to have *before*. The suggestible boy. It's this place you live. This country. It's the air. This terrible air."

"You're here too."

"I'm too old and mean to change, as you have no doubt said a thousand times out of my hearing. Well, it happens to be true."

"I just wanted to tell you about it so you wouldn't hear it from someone else."

"Oh, I'd already read about him in the newspaper." Freda considered her saucer, turned it up to read the bottom. "I notice they don't say blacks are blacks or whites are whites anymore, and they didn't say he was a Jew, but of course he was."

"I don't think it was that important to him."

"Not important!"

"I don't think it was."

"What *is* important here? Nothing. And why? Because everyone is afraid of inciting something, and no one wants to say anything interesting or important. And why? Because the whole country is full of people ready to shoot their guns, and no one wants to be killed. Everyone is terrified of everyone else. You can't have a civilized public life when everyone is armed." But she drew a long conciliatory breath and tipped her head. "I have room for you all here, if you want. The door downstairs is coded. It's a bother, but it's worth it. If you can remember it. Half the time I end up calling the super anyway. Ha! That look of yours — you would never do it, I guess."

"It's not necessary."

"Possibly not. But you! Always keeping me away until something like this happens, when you want a little comfort. *Then* you're very happy to come see me." Freda waved her off. "Guilty, guilty, guilty, that's what you are. I don't want your kiss. You can't buy me so easily."

"I wouldn't pay two dollars for you, Mama."

"No, you wouldn't," Freda agreed. "That is the state of things exactly." Then she made a show of offering her cheek, and Ilse, suddenly teary, kissed it. Soft, a piece of leather meticulously worked, or a delicate piece of cloth, warm, just out of the dryer — her ancient, everlasting mama. "However, I am worth it," the woman said.

The Vespa had unexpectedly found its companions in the new Kozmo scooters that were popping up everywhere. Safety-cone orange, driven by young men in black jeans and boots, with grungy orange knapsacks slung over their shoulders. The scooters filled the streets between the house and Kreutznaer, and idling beside one of these boys at a light, Ilse's eyes would linger on the shoulders, the thighs, the carriage of the head. Clad in her usual white, her own rear end wide and a little ungainly on the padded vinyl seat, her big head encased in its white helmet, she felt ridiculous, like a snowman on a skateboard. The couriers were friendly, though. They waved at her.

"Hey," one had said, "nice ride."

"Thank you."

He smiled wickedly, his elfin face framed by the helmet. His accent was English. "You want a job?"

"Me?"

"Yeah, you want one?"

"I don't know." Funny, to be talking at a light like this. Like the old days in the Stadtpark, where the boys rode with beer between their thighs. "Do you get stock options?" she asked him.

"You know, everybody asks that."

"Do you?"

"Depends how long you stay, right?" His hair, blond and very clean-looking, wisped out around his shoulders. "You need a job?"

"Not really."

The boy shrugged. "You married?"

"What a place for a pickup!" she cried, flattered. "I'm old enough to be your mother."

"You know what they say," said the English boy mysteriously, and then the light changed, and he revved his scooter and pulled away from her, waving.

No — what *did* they say? In the mirror her face was enormous, her cheeks pinched by the helmet. The bunching of her skin gave her the fat-faced, helpless look of a girl. Not flattering.

To satisfy her curiosity, she looked up Saul Harstein's medical records to see if by chance he had ever encountered Kreutznaer General Hospital's all-seeing computerized eye. He had. Half a minute after she entered his name and address, an abbreviated medical history popped obligingly onto her screen.

It didn't amount to much. The last entry had been four years ago, 1995, when Dr. Carrie Gorton had seen him twice in three weeks. Carrie Gorton was in dermatology. Before that he had been only an occasional consumer of medical care, seeing Dr. Peter Nevis half a dozen times in the ten years up to 1991. Nothing remotely fatal on the radar. She could go ask Nevis and Gorton what they remembered; she didn't know exactly what this would prove, but it was something to do. She printed Saul's file, and it came to about half a page, the long lower part of the paper blank with the emptiness of an interrupted life.

The visit of an administrator to the working offices of a doctor was unusual, and Peter Nevis looked her over with a curiosity that Ilse felt as a tiny affront, one more indication of the distance that had grown between herself and what she once had been. Those old women in Paris who had come in with their thick hunchbacks to be studied were not ashamed of themselves or of the wattles that hung from their throats — they were women, they had seemed to say, and if not proud of their elderly decline, they had at least seen it as something ordinary, something natural to be borne. Despite their infirmities they went out shopping and bought new black shoes and argued with one another; they were still alive. It was that kind of thing Ilse missed the most about medicine — the rigor with which most people took their illnesses, the calm that most people were able to muster just when they felt their worst. Upstairs in her glassy aerie it all got translated into numbers and policies and positions, mergers and relationships. Her occasional presence on the rounds was a token idea, but all she could convince the doctors to allow.

Nevis knew her. He was older than she, with large, red, over-scrubbed hands and a face that looked raw, flushed with rude health. His hair was gray and lay heavily over his scalp.

"I remember him," Nevis told her. "What's this about?"

"He killed himself."

"No kidding. Okay, what, liability? I saw him a couple times. Years ago."

"Six times. No, this isn't about liability. He didn't have any family, for one thing."

Behind his desk, Nevis folded his hands, waiting. One good thing about being an administrator, at least the doctors knew they had to pay attention to you. But it was visibly difficult for him. "So . . . what?"

"Do you have his records?"

"Nope. Eight years the limit. You people are supposed to know all that."

"Not everyone follows the rules."

"If they're inactive as long as that, I actually chuck 'em a little before, usually. I've only got so much room. Before I do, I write people asking if they want 'em. If I hear back, I don't touch 'em. Otherwise, *pfft*." He unfolded his hands and put them behind his head. "What'd he do, shoot himself?"

"That's right." Could he see how sick this made her, how sad? She didn't think so.

"I remember he was a pretty nice guy. Healthy." Peter Nevis was staring over her head at the wall, thinking. "Nothing remarkable about him. Nice guy. Sort of quiet. Healthy," he repeated. He met her gaze again, querulous now. Squint-eyed, he asked, "What're you so interested for?"

"The police can't find any family," she said. "I thought I would see if I could help."

"Yeah. Well, he always seemed fine to me. Not visibly depressed or suicidal. I don't know. Long time ago." He trailed off and gave her another funny look. It was meant to make her sheepish, but back upstairs Ilse had the unmistakable feeling that it was better for someone to care about the dead man than not.

Carrie Gorton, said a voice on the other end of the telephone, was on vacation, but she was welcome to make an appointment. With practiced smoothness she requested that Saul Harstein's records be sent upstairs — was that possible, please? It was. *Right away, Ms. Moss,* came the answer.

Five minutes later her secretary, Miriam, appeared at the doorway and gave Ilse a dark look. "What on earth is this about?" she asked, handing the folder over.

"Nothing at all." Innocently Ilse opened it on her desk and paged through it. Saul had been treated for a fungal infection in his left ear: a tiny thing, unthreatening, just irritating and itchy. It would drive you to the doctor only after months of putting up with it. Dr. Gorton had prescribed econazole nitrate.

A very slender folder it was. His admissions sheet; his medical history, full of negative answers to all the intrusive Xeroxed questions: *Have you ever been treated for (check all that apply) angina arteriosclerosis bladder disorders cancer diabetes emphysema endometriosis gallstones hepatic disorders (liver) intestinal disorders jaundice lung disorders multiple sclerosis,* on and on through the alphabet. Take your pick: he had chosen the most benign in the bunch, *allergies.*

In the blank for next of kin he had written nothing. He had left the empty box empty.

And all at once what had felt like a mild adventure struck Ilse as insinuating and indecent, like a rat scratching after something worthless in the walls. Saul Harstein had had nobody to go home to. She closed the folder and stood and took it out to Miriam. "Nothing," she told the other woman, handing it back, and then she admitted, as a filmy veil of shame dropped in front of her eyes, "I was just curious."

The afternoon ride home on her Vespa took her up and over the hill. Union Street was broad all the way, a fat arterial lined at first with slummy houses and two or three shabby convenience stores with bars on the windows, gas stations and fast-food franchises; then past the Green Party headquarters and a quaint intriguing run of storefronts where hair was done and barbecue was sold, then down again into the little modest valley near where the Benhamoudas lived and up again into her own neighborhood, with its bigger houses and views of the lake and shameful monochromatic prosperity. She was entirely used to living in this city but believed she saw its flaws more clearly than most people did; the newspapers were full of a constant old-fashioned boosterism, hooray for Boeing and Microsoft and Amazon, hooray for all of us. But you couldn't ride a subway anywhere because there was no subway, and the museum was laughable, a narrow afterthought that seemed the lobby of a much larger museum you could never quite find the entrance to. And everyone, including herself, was now obsessed with money in a very unflattering way. Even Jackie White had been nothing worse than a little boring before Kevin had retired at forty-five. Now rich, Jackie was an active threat to Ilse's well-being, because she could do what she wanted; Jackie had been delivered by kindly fate from the hateful necessity of earning a living, and, what was worse, believed she deserved it. But the whole city was like that now, Calvinist, believing that its high opinion had been fully ratified by this enormous accidental success. This *froth*.

Still, it was pretty. And quiet. In the driveway, after she silenced the scooter, the city seemed vacant, a provincial town on the edge of the empire. The yard was rustling, alive with cloistered water, which took days, she had read somewhere — or had Henry told her? — to trickle from treetop to roots. The rhododendrons had cast aside their fleshy flowers and were left with their naked spidery stamens. June. Idle in the side yard, still wearing her helmet, Ilse broke the deadheads crisply from the leaf clusters and cast them into the grass. Maintenance. Their little gray house, sitting on its patch of lawn, badly needed paint. One breath, two, three, four. Was she all right? Poor Saul. She was, mostly.

But *was* she secretly, unknowingly, happy about his death? Like everything her mother said, this was wrong in every detail but contained some uncomfortable, bothersome seed of truth. Did she in fact enjoy some schadenfreude knowing that while Saul Harstein had succumbed to his sadness, she had so far survived? Did this strike her as satisfying? As proof of her own sturdiness? How terrible that would be! And how absurd it was to be so old, nearly fifty, and still find the inside of her own mind such a wilderness! And how American, to be so lost in herself! She felt she owed Saul an apology for her prying, but who could she apologize to? No one. Well, Jackie, maybe. She could apologize for going on like that about the Republicans. It had been unreasonable of her, she knew. Worse, it had been unfriendly.

*   *   *

So that night after everyone was fed she made her way down the street and past the Suburban and the dumpster full of remodeling debris to Jackie Wright's porch and rang the bell. Jackie opened the door holding a single white tulip, cried in delight, grabbed Ilse's arm, and pulled her in abruptly.

"Oh, you have to see this," she cried. "They just brought the stove in today — it's *amazing!*" Jackie's front hallway was lined with cardboard matting, and plastic sheets hung in all the doorways. The smell of sanded plaster was in the air. Down the hall, around the corner, there in the middle of the kitchen, sitting on the remains of its own cardboard box as if newly hatched, sat an enormous silver range. Six feet long, five feet deep. Shining.

"It's gigantic," Ilse could only say.

"I know, it's silly, but I looked at the four-burner model and then I decided, oh what the hell, you only live once, so I got the six-. You know I love to cook."

"You do?"

"Well, maybe I'll start to."

"What takes six burners?"

"Oh, nothing, probably. A pig roast or something, but I just love the look of it, don't you? It's so *big*. It cost five thousand dollars."

Ilse almost jumped at the figure. "But that's insane. For a stove?"

"Oh, I don't think it's so insane. It'll last at least twenty years, probably more like fifty, not that we exactly care about that. I think it weighs something like nine hundred pounds. Kevin and I tried to move it, but ha, ha, oh well."

Next door, in the dining room, the old walnut wainscoting had been pried off and the naked lath destroyed and replaced with drywall, whose seams were visible down the long unpainted room. Jackie gestured at it with the tulip. "And in here we got tired of how dark it was," she said, "and personally I just love how much light there is now. All that dark old wood's gone, thank god. Don't you think it's much lighter?"

"You ripped all the wood out?"

"It wasn't really an old house, you know, it wasn't built until 1920, it was really inferior work compared to some of the things around here. Saul's house, for example."

Ilse was stunned, stood gaping for a second. "You realize you just took about a hundred thousand dollars off the value."

"Oh, I don't think so."

"You certainly did. What awful person convinced you to do this?"

"We've replaced all the wiring and all the plumbing, sweetheart. People care about the *systems*."

"You'll regret it when you try to sell."

"I don't think so."

"You will. I've been looking around," Ilse told her.

"Oh? Are you thinking of moving? I hope you're not thinking of selling — we'd hate to lose you to, you know, Lynnwood or wherever you'd all end up." Jackie led her into the living room. "Sit down! Kevin's working late. Jonathan's upstairs doing his Doom or whatever it is. Have you seen these games? I don't even want to know anymore. I figure he's eleven and he can do what he wants, as long as I don't have to see it. There's a block on his machine so he can't see pornography, but I imagine he sees enough of that at his friends' houses that it doesn't make any difference. Did you come to tell me you had an idea for Saul's memorial?"

She had not, of course, she had come here on a guilty impulse, meaning to apologize. In view of that stove, though, how could she bring herself even to begin? "Actually, no," she said, but then a thought struck her. "Or maybe, possibly, we could possibly plant a tree."

"Oh, a tree!" Jackie nodded. "Well, but where?"

"I don't know," Ilse said, "but as none of us really knew him, it seems a nice neutral thing to do."

Jackie aimed a curious eye at her. "If you're planning on moving, what good would the tree do you?"

"We're not moving. I've just been collecting flyers."

"But where would it go — in the middle of the street? Everyone already has a yard. Maybe we could build a traffic island, but that doesn't seem like much of a memorial. Ted Bell called and suggested we put some kind of announcement in the newspaper." Jackie pointed down the street with the tulip. "And Millie Turgerson said we should contribute something to the Anti-Defamation League, although personally I don't think he cared about being Jewish — otherwise I think we would have heard from some of those people already. I don't remember seeing a menorah in his windows, do you? Is it a Jewish custom to plant a tree for the dead?"

"I don't know."

"We can think about it." Jackie put the tulip on the glass coffee table in front of her and sat back. "You know, I'm still so surprised by it. I don't even know if I'm even upset, exactly."

Jackie had been a therapist, supposedly, though it was difficult to picture. Ilse asked, "You're not?"

"I suppose I am a little," Jackie said. "But you know, I'm really very used to pain. You understand I used to deal with suicides all the time. It sounds funny, but I did, Ilse, I dealt with at least one a month. Even if it wasn't something that'd just happened, it'd be someone who came to my office and it turned out there was a suicide in their history that was still worrying them. Really, it's one of the worst things you can do to someone. It's very punitive. But that wasn't Saul at all, at least from what I knew of him. He was very kind. Which just makes me wonder if there's something nobody knows. I wonder if he was sick."

"He wasn't."

"How do you know?"

"I checked," Ilse said. "I was curious, and I checked."

"You did? How?"

"I've got ways."

"You do?" Jackie was alarmed. "Could you check on me if you wanted?"

"If I wanted. If you've been to Kreutznaer."

"Well, I haven't, thank god. I can't believe they let you just check on people without a reason. Isn't there some kind of confidentiality involved, or am I just being optimistic?"

"I wish I hadn't done it," Ilse admitted now. "I felt like I was prying, and now I feel very bad about it."

Jackie hesitated. "Oh, honey, don't."

"I do, I feel like a disgusting old snoop."

"A suicide has that effect," Jackie said. "It makes you do things you wouldn't do otherwise. It makes you nosy. I had a patient, who will be nameless but I think you've met her, who had an older sister kill herself. This is years ago. This woman was in high school and her sister was in college, and the sister jumped out of her dorm room window, if you can imagine, and she died. And then this patient of mine started to dress like her sister, and to take all her clothes and to move into her bedroom, and then she applied to the same college and made sure she got a room — can you believe this? — in the same dormitory. She said she just wanted to know what

[185]

her sister'd been thinking. In my experience, there's a very, very big difference between people who can kill themselves and people who never possibly could. Lots of people think about it, but not everybody can do it, even when they're depressed. And when somebody does it, you start to just *wonder* about them. You wonder how they got there."

"I think the same thing about people who own leaf blowers."

"I'm not kidding, there *is* a real divide. Personally I think it's a genetic thing, but you would know more about that than me. But that's my guess."

"You know, I have to tell you," Ilse said, "I went to see one of his old doctors."

"Nothing?"

"No." She had not come here to confess any of this, and Jackie was the least likely confessor Ilse could imagine. But the woman was safe, somehow — someone whose judgment she didn't care about at all. "It just made me feel worse. I felt like I was pointing out somehow that he didn't have anyone who cared about him."

"Oh, I know. And then you feel ridiculous, don't you, for caring so much about a man you never really knew! I know. Well, that's how it goes. How's Henry doing? At the Turgersons' he looked like he'd lost his best friend."

"He's upset."

"I would think so. He's such an admirable man," Jackie said with feeling. "I know how you feel about me and Kevin, but I really think Henry's a wonderful man. He's doing something worthwhile, isn't he?"

"I like you, Jackie," Ilse was forced to say.

"Oh, not really you don't. But it's all right."

"I do think you're wrong about almost everything," she offered.

"I know! The feeling is mutual, believe me."

"You *are* a Republican, aren't you?"

"I'm not a Republican, I'm a conservative."

"You don't like black people, do you? You don't like Chinese people."

"Oh, I don't want to get into it," Jackie said. She crossed her legs at the knee, and one sandal hung suspended from her toes. "You live in this neighborhood just like I do. There isn't a black family for blocks in any direction, and you know it, and the only Asians are doctors and lawyers. But for some reason you look at those little Chink markets on Jackson and you think, How wonderful and lively and diverse, and I look at them and I just go Yuck, the idea. But I'm honest about it, at least, while people like you think you're very special for having certain thoughts, but you aren't exactly known for acting on them."

"That's completely untrue. You don't know the first thing about my work."

"No, I don't." The sandal dangled, dangled. "I don't. But the thing is, I'm happy being who I am."

"Which is a terrible thing to admit, Jackie, really."

"Is it?" Jackie extended a hand to the room, the house beyond. "What problems do I have? I don't think you really like me at all, by the way."

"Maybe *like* isn't the word."

Jackie laughed. "Which is fine! We don't have to like each other. I like talking with you, I think you're very interesting. I heard you talking about my car, by the way."

She froze. "Your car?"

"My new Suburban, which apparently you have opinions about. Outside my window."

"I don't know what you're talking about."

Jackie fixed her with a long look and was about to say something else when Jonathan descended from the upper reaches of the house, wearing sweat pants and a T-shirt, his slippers making a swishing sound on the cardboard floor. He was very small at ten, smaller than he should have been, and to Ilse's eye he looked so forlorn in the dust and disorder of the remodeling that he could have wandered in by accident.

"You remember Mrs. Moss," Jackie prompted, and Jonathan approached and extended a skinny arm and hand.

"Pleased to meet you again, Mrs. Moss," he said with a practiced smile.

This seemed to Ilse obviously the result of endless badgering, but she managed to say, "Hello, Jonathan," without malice. Children were not to be blamed for their terrible parents, were they? She hoped not.

Henry was asleep when she got home, but she woke him getting into bed. "She suspects us," she whispered in his ear.

"Who does?"

"Jackie. She suspects us."

"Of what?" he mumbled.

"Hating her car." Henry's shape was soft, and she applied herself to him beneath the covers. "She's hot on our trail."

"What'd she say?"

"She just hinted. Oh, you should see what they're doing to that house. It's a crime. You should have to get a license before you can own something nice like that. And poor little Jonathan hasn't had anything decent to eat in about a year."

"Is he okay?"

She moved closer to him. "I'm only joking. Go to sleep."

"I am asleep."

"Jackie's just awful, isn't she? Just being over there makes me feel dirty. But," she whispered, "you realize we don't really have any black friends? Even Kenny Fatunde's African, which isn't the same. And he's someone you work with. Even Darren has black friends, half the people at his birthday party were black or Chinese."

But her husband was asleep again. Across the street the dead man's house was empty, empty. She covered Henry's stomach with her hand. Her husband's recent adventures had left him exhausted, and she felt toward him a tender protectiveness. Jackie could spit venom but had her money to hide in, and her mother could throw cups off all the balconies she wanted but she was alone in the world and could afford that sort of reckless gesture, with no one to be accountable to. Ilse and Henry were together in the middle of their lives and had only each other to rely on, and tonight Ilse felt this very keenly. He loved her, and she loved him, his great eternal calm, his unflappability, his even temper; he was a cushion for her, a soft wall against which she could occasionally, harmlessly, hurl herself. He was still moaning in his sleep, and recently he had begun to talk, long strings of nonsense syllables. "Be zee be zee be zee," he said tonight, into her neck.

"What, sweetheart?"

"Dodee," he said.

"You're asleep, darling."

A long considering pause. "Fing," he said thoughtfully. It was his voice, his intonation, but with an extra, negotiator's note. "Sun dun dun dun."

"Would you like some apple crisp?"

"Singanun," he said.

"Do you have any shoes?"

"Pinto," he said.

"Do you love me, darling?" she asked, into the air. And as soon as the words were out she wanted to call them back; he could say anything, she realized.

"Boosh," he answered emphatically, and embraced her with feeling.

With a rush of relief she returned the embrace; for a moment she had teetered on the edge of a canyon, but he had pulled her back. When she tried to explain her gratitude the next morning, he just looked a little hurt. "You asked me questions?"

But she hadn't meant anything by it. And by the tone of his unconscious voice he had obviously meant to say something like *Of course I do,* and how happy that had made her! Still, the flush of shame she had felt in the office was back again. So much of what she did was terribly wrong, terribly careless. He couldn't have helped what he might have said; he could have said anything to her, not meaning it, and then how would they have felt? And she should never have gone snooping into Saul Harstein's records like that, and she should never have confessed her snooping to Jackie. Of all people! Across the street the yellow police tape still hung in Saul's yard, and in the morning light it was illuminated, a twisted golden thread sewn through the green fabric of yew and juniper, a black seven-note chorus sounding CAUTION — CAUTION — CAUTION. It seemed a warning from Saul to the world, aimed at anyone who would listen. Aimed, she felt, at her. "I'm sorry," she told her husband, and kissed him.

13

H E STILL DIDN'T HAVE any friends, as far as Sandra could tell. He was weird. He had a way of calling things out to nobody in particular. *What's that about?* he might shout in the hall, or *That's not right!* and they would all turn and shake their heads. He shouted, he grabbed his crotch, he performed his tricks: pulled fluttering pieces of paper out of the air, read books from fifteen feet away — dumb stunts that nobody else could do but that only Sandra knew the significance of. He would stand there at his locker with his eyes closed, balancing a ruler on his fingertip, motionless, as if it were glued to him, while a couple people watched politely from a few lockers over, and when Sandra saw this she felt a little spurt of jealousy. But his tricks never got him anywhere. Everyone had his or her own group, and even the cutest boy needed to be a little bit friendly to have hope of breaking in. And she had no reason to go up to him, did she? So she stayed away.

She didn't talk to Thomas again until the day he surprised her at her locker before school. It was June, another rainy day, the smell of mildew was everywhere, and Mr. Garr had put the usual green wastebasket just outside his door. Drop after drop was pinging into its rusty bottom, and then something was poking her spine, a rod or pole or something, and she turned around and it was Thomas, with a little black truncheon. A billy club. "I stole this," he said. "You want it?"

Wordlessly she took it. Firm and flexible. She handed it back. "No."

"I beat up this cop? He was all asking me where I'm from, and I just popped him." Thomas made a sudden violent quarter-swing with the club. "Pah!"

She flinched, and to cover it up she swung out her right hand and hit him, not hard, on the shoulder, knocking him back a step. A lightweight. She hadn't meant to move him.

He smiled, showing his perfect teeth. The locker gave off its odor of steel, a bloody scent that came off on her hands. Thomas watched her gather her things.

"Almost summer," she offered, after a silence.

"Yeah."

"You doing anything?" she asked.

"No." He felt some insinuation in the question, Sandra saw; he stepped back scornfully. "What're you, like going to horse camp or something?"

"Basketball camp. Or not really a camp. Like an academy. In Oregon."

He put the truncheon into his back pocket. "All girls?"

"No, it's coed. Two weeks."

"How much that cost?"

"I don't know." Eighteen hundred dollars — she knew it exactly.

He was so pretty, that was the funny thing: pretty in a masculine way, with a face you couldn't stop looking at, all its planes and angles exactly right. His skin was a perfectly uniform light brown, almost artificial-looking, ideally surfaced and textureless, like a dark beach smoothed down by water. Like a blind person, you wanted to touch his face.

"I got a scholarship," she said, half apologizing.

"You get good grades?"

"Yeah."

"Straight A's?"

"Yeah."

He smirked. "You know what that is? Waste of time, man. The teachers don't know shit. If they knew anything, they'd be all like getting better jobs and making actual money, working in computers and whatever. Like Mr. Jensen — dude can barely even read, he was trying to read this thing out loud yesterday and it just took him forever."

"I think he's got this problem with his eyes."

"Sha, with his *brain*."

"So you don't study because the teachers are stupid, so *you* end up stupid. That makes a lot of sense."

"It's about respect," he said. "They don't respect the fact that we're sitting here in a classroom with people who don't know shit. So I don't respect the things they tell us to do."

"That's dumb."

"Sha, you know what?"

"What."

"You're all staring at me all the time."

Caught, she said heatedly, "I am not. That's a vain thing to say."

"Everybody wants a piece of my ass. You know who really does? Faggots." Abruptly he drew close. He was five inches shorter and had to tip his head back to look up at her. He kissed the air a foot in front of her face, his eyes closed. "Hey," he said, "I like big girls."

Her heart, despite itself, was racing. "Yeah? Good for you."

"Good for *you*," he said. "You want to meet me after school?"

"No."

"You got practice today?"

"Maybe."

"You're sweating."

"No I'm not."

"Yeah you are." His eyes traveled over her face; his breath was hot and odorless. "You know something?"

"What."

"You look like your dad."

"No I don't."

"Yeah you do." Whispering, he said, "You got a brother."

"Yeah."

"What is he, fourteen?"

"That's right," she said.

"You know what else? My brother can't even take a shit by himself."

She said nothing to this.

"You think that's funny?"

"No."

"You don't?"

"I think it's sad," she said, composing herself. "It's not funny at all. It's sad."

"You think you know something? You don't know *nothing*," he said. Then, as though feeling it was the dramatic moment to do so, he turned and walked off, the black truncheon waggling in his back pocket. As he went he glanced over his shoulder. Lifted one arm dismissively into the air, turned the corner. Gone.

She *was* sweating, actually. Her palms were damp against her books. She wiped them on her pants. She hadn't meant to talk to him. Hadn't meant to be interested in him at all. But she was. Alight, aloft, she went off to class, feeling good. He was gorgeous, after all, and that made up for a lot.

Thomas did appear halfway through practice, creeping through a side door and loping to the top of the bleachers. His skinny legs in black jeans gave him a weird spidery look, and from a distance his perfect features coalesced, became somehow frozen and motionless, so that he seemed to be a very realistic mannequin sitting quietly near the ceiling, looking down on them all from a high corner of the room. When she emerged after showering he was there, outside, under the overhang. The rain had stopped and the air was warm and fragrant.

"You got a car?" he asked.

"No."

"You want to come to my house? We can walk."

"Okay."

"You don't have to if you're nervous or whatever."

"Nervous about what?"

"I don't know. Whatever." Thomas looked up at her blankly.

"No," she said, "I'm not nervous."

He turned without a word. She followed him, feeling her bulk, as though she were a barge that Thomas was towing. Together they moved out through the student parking lot. Through the neighborhood. Little houses fenced in with chain link, the yards gone weedy or worn to mud. Wet, damp. Dead cars everywhere. Dogs tied up. Black people, old women mostly, and also children now that school had let out for the day. And here and there, maybe once a block, the brightly painted house of a gentrifier: the yard filled with flowers, the trim picked out in forest green.

"Faggot house," said Thomas.

"I think it's nice."

"Seriously, they're mostly faggots. Where we used to live, we had this apartment. This is the first time I've ever lived in a house."

They were walking along the cracked pavement of the sidewalk, not touching. Low-riding cars went sliding by, bass thumping behind their darkened windows. Black men seemed to like her more than white men did, in general: they whistled and yelled more. She wasn't supposed to think that sort of thing, probably, but over the past two or three years she had found it to be true. But no one yelled at her here, with Thomas. She was spoken for.

Thomas's house was behind chain link, a small brown house that the Benhamoudas had obviously tried to improve. New marigolds, dark crimson, lined the front walkway. The shrubbery, whatever it was, had been clipped back recently — it still had that fresh-haircut look to it — and the little lawn was mowed and edged. A one-story house, with a big picture window looking over the sunken driveway, which sloped down to the garage beneath the house. A porch shaded by some kind of flowering tree, its plastic-looking leaves holding some rotten red blossoms.

"My mom's here," Thomas said.

"Okay."

"My brother's probably asleep." He stepped into the hallway and, looking around furtively, motioned her into the house.

She was not, she told herself, going to have sex with anybody. She might do some kissing. But a blush of excitement was blooming in her chest. His slender back, wrapped in its black T-shirt, seemed to draw her hands: she could put her hands under his shirt, could slide them up his back, to the shoulder blades.

"You hungry?" he asked.

"No."

"You want a Coke?"

"Whatever."

The house smelled good. Warm. Full of cooking spices. Somewhere music was playing, African-sounding or something, Arabic maybe? Something strange. Through a little archway she could see the living room. A new blue sofa sat alone at the end of the room.

There was a gold fireplace with a glassed-in front. She followed him into the kitchen. A woman was at the sink, her dark hair up on her head. Skinny, like Thomas, and with his dark, pretty eyes.

"This is my mother," said Thomas. "This is Sandra. It's Dr. Moss's daughter."

"Oh!" His mother looked her up and down, surprised. "I didn't know he had a daughter."

"Just one," Sandra said, nonsensically. Both Thomas and his mother had this weird intense stare that made you feel you'd screwed up somehow. "Just me and my brother."

"You must be hungry." The woman began opening cupboards. "I'll make you something to eat."

"She said she's thirsty."

"Just thirsty?"

Sandra shrugged. The kitchen smelled good and she was hungry, but she didn't want to be any trouble. "I don't usually eat after practice."

"You play a sport?"

"Basketball."

"Ah! So that's why you're taller than him."

"Shut up, Ma."

"Oh, you're still just a *little* man," said his mother, turning back around. "Like your grandfather — he could fit in a cupboard and keep the pots in."

The basement stairs, covered with a rubber tread, led to a large, nearly empty room, which smelled of gasoline and paint. Thin brown carpet covered the floor, and the television — gigantic — was against one concrete wall, beneath a tangle of pipes and wires that ran through the exposed ceiling beams. Facing the television was a brown plaid sofa, its foam leaking out. Sandra and Thomas sat, and Thomas turned on the television: MTV. Destiny's Child.

"You ever seen this one before?" he asked.

"We don't have cable," she said, lying.

"Serious? So what do you do?"

"What do you mean?"

"Like you just listen to the radio, or what?"

"And we read," she said piously.

At this he leaned over and began kissing her. Automatically she began kissing back. His lips were narrow — skinny and hard — and his tongue was long and seemed to have a point at the end. His hand grasped her thigh — her leg was much too big for his hand to encompass, but his fingers moved up the inside seam of her jeans, an inch at a time; her legs were a little bit open, but should she close them? She didn't want to, exactly, but she knew she should. Blocked, his hand moved up her leg, up her belly, then onto her left breast, which he had a little trouble finding, she could tell, beneath the sweatshirt and T-shirt and sports bra. "Sorry," she said, and lifted her sweatshirt.

Like a bird diving for cover, his hand darted beneath it, beneath her T-shirt and to her bra, which he pushed up, his long slender digits active and grasping. He pinched her nipple, first softly, then harder.

"Ow," she whispered. "Not like that."

"You like it?"

"It hurts." She reached under his shirt — she didn't think about it — and pinched him back.

"Sha, don't!"

"Gently."

"Yeah. You like it gentle?"

"All girls do. They just don't want to tell you," she said.

Was this going too fast? Obviously. But she didn't care. They kissed, and the television flashed at the end of the dim room, and Thomas's mother walked overhead in the kitchen, her heels *tock-tocking* on the ceiling. His hand went from one breast to the other, and hers remained on his slender chest, flattened like a spider on a wall, feeling his sternum rise and settle. She had been kissed before, and had had her breasts felt a couple times, at parties and after dances, but she wanted to rip his clothes off right there on the sofa, with a choking lust that sickened her a little. She restrained herself, but her underpants were wet and she was breathing hard, and her nipples were hard and twanged every time he touched them, and she was afraid she was being way too easy. But he was *beautiful,* and it made a difference, even though she knew it shouldn't, that he wasn't a serious sort of person and wasn't particularly nice either.

After a few minutes he stopped kissing her, pulled his hand out, and opened his Coke, and she did the same. She said nothing. Goo Goo Dolls, Britney Spears, Aaliyah. For a long while they sat and watched, in the cool industrial-smelling basement. Then she asked him, "Why don't you ever talk to anybody at school?"

He shrugged. "Nobody I want to talk to."

"How do you know, if you don't talk to anybody? People think it's weird that you don't really like bother to *talk* to anybody."

"People say I'm stuck up?"

"You should just talk to people."

He stood, took off his shirt, dropped to the carpet, and began doing pushups. Twenty in a row, quickly, his back writhing with a tangle of muscles. Then he leapt up and showed her his stomach. Flat. Then he was back down on the carpet, where he did twenty more pushups.

"I've been working out? In case I need to fight somebody," he said. "My mom says I should get a modeling contract."

"You should."

"My dad doesn't want me doing it, though. He says they're all a bunch of faggots and they'd want to like suck my dick or whatever and give me AIDS and everything."

"I guess," she said, trying for sarcasm, "that would be a danger."

"Especially if you wanted to like get ahead in the business. That's what he was saying, that you had to go down on all the hairdressers and whatever, and I just don't even want to think about that, it's disgusting. Plus my dad'd kill me. He's a hardass sometimes. I had a picture taken of me, though, like in secret. You want one?" Bouncing on his toes, he touched the beams. "Wait here." Shirtless, he raced up into the kitchen, was gone a minute, then returned and flopped down on the sofa beside her. From the front of his pants he pulled an eight-by-ten black-and-white studio shot — a sleazy cheapo picture printed by Madison Talent. Thomas, fully clothed, stared lustily from beneath his eyebrows. "You like it?"

"You look like a mental patient."

"Shut up. I look good, girl."

"Can I have this?"

"That's why I got it! For you. I got ten left." He looked around him at the concrete walls, the carpet, the washer-dryer. "You ever want to have kids?" he asked.

"Not right this second."

"Sha!" He pushed her shoulder, a feeble shove. "You're nasty."

"I guess I do," she said, "after I get through college, which is this like *school* you go to, you know? After you finish high school? I don't know if you've ever heard of it."

"Shut up. Get me a wife, make a bunch of little babies."

"Wonderful."

"Six," he said. "I don't know. I just want them. Maybe get a job as a pilot so I could make some money."

"A pilot."

"Cause I've got perfect vision!" he cried. "Better than perfect. I'm like an eagle. They don't let you fly planes unless you've got perfect eyes."

"I think that's the air force you're thinking about."

"Your dad tell you about my tests?"

"No."

"My reflexes?"

"He doesn't talk about that sort of thing."

"They're perfect," he said, with his eyes closed, his arms outstretched. "I test perfect on everything. That's what he told me."

"He did not."

"Yeah he did. He thinks I've got some mutation. Actually he showed me — he showed me this like code or whatever, and there's one thing wrong with it, which makes me not have the disease I'm supposed to, but he thinks it's some kind of magic thing."

"Not magic."

"Sha, you know what I mean."

From the kitchen she heard a high, reedy, strangled voice, like an old woman's. The little brother. She had heard other Hickman patients speaking, sometimes on the telephone or seen them on videos, fragile and strange-looking as aliens. "How old is he?"

"Three," said Thomas, putting his shirt back on, then coming to sit beside her again. "But he's a freak. You don't want to see that."

"I've seen it before." But he only shrugged, watching the TV screen. What did you say to a boy you hardly knew? "My mom's from Austria," she came up with after a minute.

"Crocodile Dundee," said Thomas.

"No, *Austria*. In Europe. She's a doctor too, like my dad? And her mom lives here now too, in Seattle. But her sister still lives in Vienna. Which is a city in Austria."

"Never heard of it."

"It's a country," she said impatiently. "Like France. You should like look at a map once in a while." There was another long silence. "What's your dad do?" she asked.

"Like construction and whatever, he's a kind of electrician, plumber, whatever guy. Like he'll work on a house. He works on like new houses or apartments, that kind of thing."

"That's a good job."

"I guess." Idly, he asked, "They don't talk about me? Not even a little bit, like once in a while?"

"No."

Another long silence fell. To break it, Sandra leaned over and kissed him. She put her hand on his leg. Quickly Thomas grabbed her wrist and pulled her hand into his crotch, where he was hard. Not her first but her third, this one just like the others except in the way he'd directed her to it so quickly, before she'd had a chance to think. She snatched her hand away, put it on the rough fabric of the sofa. The feel of his dick, the cylindrical shape of it, stayed, but it was too soon. They kissed for a minute more, his hands on her breasts again. The afternoon, dim already, threatening rain again, grew dimmer here in the basement, and she began to relax a little: his tongue, her tongue, her nipples, his. He didn't try anything else. His tongue, in and out: one, two, one, two. So: he was dumb. He didn't know where Austria was. He didn't know *what* Austria was. But she was with him — it wasn't Jenny Glenn with her perfect face and big boobs, or Melissa McDowell, or Patty Silverman or Jenny Richland or Lisa Block, or any of the others.

Some minutes later she stood, rearranged herself. "I need to go home," she said.

"He's still up there." He wouldn't look at her.

"It's okay."

"You don't want to see it, believe me."

"I've got to get home."

He got up quickly and turned off the television. "Close your eyes," he said, and led her back up the rubber-treaded stairs, into the brightness of the kitchen. Mrs. Benhamouda was still at the sink. Giles — ghastly, egg-headed, fragile, pop-eyed, chicken-armed, tremulous — sat at the kitchen table. A tall red glass of cloudy juice was before him. He looked up at her, his elderly face regarding her calmly.

"Hello," he said.

"Shut up," said Thomas.

"No," said Giles.

The Hickman kids all looked alike, that was the bizarre thing. No matter what you started as, you ended up looking like this, like a kind of alien parrot. It was dumb to be afraid. It wasn't like he was going to infect you. But it was freaky. And of course she didn't want to show him that, because she didn't want to be impolite, even to a three-year-old. Giles. *Jeel* was how they said it. So she said hello to him while Thomas rushed ahead, through the kitchen and into the hall.

"This is Dr. Moss's daughter," said Mrs. Benhamouda. "Come to visit with Thomas."

"Pleased to meet you," Sandra said.

"Don't worry, so is he," said Mrs. Benhamouda. "Are you staying for dinner, or are you going?"

"I've got to go."

"Say goodbye, Giles."

"Adios," said Giles, squawking.

"Her father is your doctor. So what do you say?"

He shrugged. "Congratulations," he tried.

"No, you say thank you."

"Okay, thank you," he repeated.

Thomas was on the porch, pulling the rotting blossoms off the tree. A camellia, that's what it was. How the hell did she know this? Her mother. "It's okay," she told him, and kissed him once, chastely, on the cheek. He had a quick bright smell — perfectly clean, like the odor of air or wax. He said nothing, would not meet her eye, so she went off down the stairs, and when she looked back he was watching her with a complicated expression that reminded her of her father: as though he were putting something together in his brain. Trying to think of something to say. Or maybe he was just trying to remember what her name was.

Colleen had to be informed, and the next time they saw each other — at lunch the following day — Sandra told her everything. They sat on the sloping lawn overlooking the gym, in the sun. Colleen's expression was matter-of-fact but intent, and she shaded her eyes with her hand.

"You realize your parents are going to kill you," she said.

"They don't have to find out."

"Yeah, right. You went over to his house and met his mom! My god, of course they're going to find out."

"But it's not like *serious*," Sandra said. "He's totally stupid. He's not even like a stoner, he's just — he doesn't *know* anything. It's so completely the opposite from what I actually like. He's just cute."

"Uh, yeah," Colleen said. "Duh, he's only the one who looks like a movie star."

"They *are* going to kill me."

"Don't tell them, whatever you do." Colleen dropped her hand from her eyes and squinted. "They'll probably make you stop seeing him."

Across the street, Ezell's Fried Chicken was clotted with students. It was the second week of June, the school year was almost over, and after lunch the halls would be conspicuously quiet as the stoners and slackers leaked away into the neighborhood and disappeared for the afternoon. The air in the empty classrooms would be fresh, the huge purple windows open to the breeze, and Sandra felt a lightness in her bones; it was the lightness of the end of the school year, the rising loveliness of summer and its long days, days when Thomas would be with her, a cute guy who wanted her. This fact lifted her through the remainder of her classes, and during practice she looked for him again. But he did not appear. She thought of walking past his house but didn't want to venture into his neighborhood alone, so she took the bus home, and by the time she found her mother after dinner she was filled with a strange tumult. She wasn't in love, but what was this that drove her to her mother's side?

Her mother had come back from a run and was lying on the boards of the porch, sort of steaming, and seeing her there — her mileage times were hilarious; Sandra had to force herself not to laugh when she heard them and instead say, *That's cool, Mom* — Sandra sat down in her sweat pants and did exactly what Colleen had warned her not to do: she told her mother everything.

"Oh, dear," said her mother, still flat on her back. "Well, how interesting." The air was filled with gnats, which hovered and danced in a huge cloud over the lawn, visible in the declining light of evening. "Does your father know?"

"I didn't really mean to do it. I mean he's cute? But mostly I think I felt sorry for him or something. Or not *sorry?* But something like that."

"Not for boys, sweetheart. You don't feel sorry for boys, ever."

"But he doesn't have any friends."

"There's probably a reason for that. Can I ask, sweetheart, what you've done with him?"

"We just made out."

"Kissing?"

She nodded.

Her mother glanced at her upside down. "Does he want to have sex with you?"

"Would you?" Sandra asked. Her mother, still on her back, didn't blink. "I'm still a virgin," Sandra offered, her face going hot.

"Well, I should hope so, you're only seventeen. But do you really like him, or do you only pity him?"

"I don't know. I mean I think he's pretty dumb, and he's probably got like a sweet side but it's not the first thing you notice about him? He obviously thinks a lot of himself. He talked a lot about his — thing. His condition."

"That must be charming."

"He likes the way it makes him sort of important, sort of."

"Your father has high hopes."

"Don't tell Dad, okay?"

"Of course I will, honey, unless you do it yourself."

"Why?"

"Because you have to." Her mother's doughy face was a version of her own; Sandra recognized her own intensity, her ability to stare things down when she had to.

Ilse asked, "Do you have a picture of him?"

Sandra reached into her backpack. How stupid, that dumb glare of his! But with some pride she handed her mother the photograph.

"Madison Talent. What's that, his stage name?"

"Duh, Mom, it's an agency."

"Is he a model?"

"His dad won't let him. And he won't talk to anybody at school except me, and he only talks to me because he knows who I am. He was obviously embarrassed about his brother, so I don't think he has people over."

"But he had you over."

"Yeah." Safe. Everyone thought she was safe.

"Well," her mother said, heaving herself up, "please don't have sex with this boy. You can kiss and kiss all you want, and do whatever else, but don't have sex with him. He's very handsome. But it won't be very much fun. He'll just be out for himself." She handed the photograph back. "I thought Todd Grimm was very handsome too, and he was friendlier."

"He was *not* friendly, Mom, he like totally cheated on me with Lisa Block, plus he was a total geek besides."

"Well, some geeks are the best of all. Your father was a terrible geek, and still the women fell all over themselves for him, and do you know why? Because he was a nice man, very loving and kind and tender, and you could see that. You could watch him come into a room and see that he was a nice man. We met in Paris."

"I know."

"Lisa Block — isn't that the girl with the ponytails?"

"Yeah, and the big butt and the like crunchy granola wardrobe. The mirror skirt."

"Are they still together?"

"Sort of."

Her mother, the personnel manager, nodded. "I'm sure they deserve each other. The handsome ones are never really nice, honey, they don't have to be. It's the same with girls, of course. That's why we're both such nice people, sweetheart."

"So I'm ugly, is what you're saying."

"No." But her mother was caught. "I just want you to be happy," she said softly, into the yard.

The cloud of gnats had climbed into the air and could be seen drifting away across the grass, out over the street. Mr. Harstein's house stood dark and silent, the yellow tape still strung through the hedges. Poor Mr. Harstein. Well, it was true, she knew it: she wasn't Miss America. But happy?

"I am," Sandra said truthfully, "sometimes."

14

FROM THE HEIGHT of the Durbins' porch the city appeared flattened around the edge of the lake, and the hospital's winking light tower sent its everlasting signal over the water, *blink, blink, blink*. Like Justine Jones, that thoughtful, measured on-off. For the hundredth time it occurred to Henry that someone had to climb up into that light tower and change the bulb.

He was admitted to the house by Elaine O'Donnell. "He's waiting," she said soberly.

"How's he doing?"

"He'll be happy to see you."

"He seem any better?"

"Why don't you just go ahead on up?" Elaine closed the front door heavily behind him. "We've had a difficult morning."

This was not a good sign. The dark oak stairs creaked portentously underfoot. William was in his bedroom, sitting up in an armchair, his scalp illuminated by the light from the window. His blanket was spread over his lap. He put aside a magazine when Henry entered and said, "Boy am I glad to see you. All week long it's been Cameron Diaz, it's been Brandy Chastain, it's been Jennifer Lopez."

"The dames just won't leave you alone."

"How could they?" He lifted his arms from the blanket. "Who could resist?"

"Especially Elaine."

"Elaine," William said, scowling, "wants me to stay in that fucking bed all the time, even when I'm feeling fine."

"You feel fine?"

William let his arms fall. "Am I supposed to?"

"Probably not."

"Yeah, big surprise." The boy looked down at his roughened hands. His fingernails were split vertically and were as thick as Henry's toenails, yellow and hard. "To tell you the truth, I'm not sure I like being a guinea pig after all."

"Why's that?"

"I keep waiting for something to happen, but it never does. I just feel the same. And like today? I feel terrible. Right now I'm dizzy. And suddenly I forget your name. Dr. Something."

"Moss."

"Moss?" William gaped at him. "That doesn't even sound right."

"No," Henry said gently, "that's right."

"It's scary. You know? It's so scary. I can't remember who I am sometimes. I wake up in the middle of the night and I can't even breathe, and I think, *Is this when?* But I don't even know what it is I'm scared of. I can't even remember what's happening." He began to cry a little. "I *hate* that. I feel so stupid and scared and I just want it to go away. But it'll never go away. Even if that stuff works, it's just going to make me live longer, but not make me better."

Henry sat down on the bed. "We don't know what it's going to do."

"I'm still going to die, though."

"People with your condition," Henry said, though he knew it was something William had heard before, a fact that was a fixture of his world, the outer wall of possibility, "have lived to be almost twenty."

"*One* person — Hara Haraj. And she was blind and deaf and shitting all over herself, I bet."

"This other kid's seventeen." Thomas's sneering perfect face rose in his mind's eye. Upset, he thrust the picture away. "This kid, he's a lucky prick, okay? He's a lucky fucking prick."

William sniffed. His enormous head bobbled on his neck. "Can I meet him?"

The thought of the two of them in the same room made Henry

uneasy; Thomas's reaction could not be anticipated, and while he would probably be harmless and polite in his odd way, he would likely not forgive Henry for it — for making him feel uncomfortable. "He's not exactly a Boy Scout," he warned.

"I don't care." William extended his arm. "Go ahead," he said, and Henry, after locking the door against Elaine, gave him another injection, as if he were piercing a wilted balloon. The boy's skin was a delicate sac, too susceptible to time. "You know what I mostly want?" William said. "More than anything else?"

"Brandy Chastain."

"Ha, ha, and ha. What I want is to know how things end up. Like is the universe expanding or contracting? Because if it's contracting, then time will wind up running backward and causation will get reversed, so like two trillion years from now I'll wake up in some hospital and I'll know everything I know right now and then just get younger and younger," he said, working up to a smile. "And healthier."

"Is that how it works?"

"I think so. They haven't figured out all the details. But the Feynmann diagrams work equally well in both directions. If causation is reversed, then it'll seem logical to us and all the rules will just be backward. Or there's the many-worlds hypothesis, where each quantum event makes a new world. So maybe there's a world where I don't have this and we could somehow tunnel between universes." He stopped, inhaled roughly twice, swallowed, and went on. "It's a question of energy, just like for warp drives. You need negative energy. We don't know how to make it yet. But we will someday. Another thing I don't like is that people'll feel sorry for us. Like we feel sorry for people who died of smallpox. Or a broken leg in the Civil War or something, because they didn't have penicillin or Vancomycin. And eventually they'll figure out how to fix this and by then I'll be dead. Like what if you figure it out a month after I die?"

"There's going to be somebody who's first."

"I hope you've got a patent on it."

"We're getting there."

"I hope you make a fucking fortune."

"Hey, me too. Everybody else is doing it."

"That's the other thing." William slapped the blanket feebly. "I think Dad's right. I think the market's about to tank."

"Really?"

"You own a lot of stock?"

"No. Practically none."

"What about in your IRA?"

"Well, yeah. Now that you mention it."

"You should take it out of the market and put it into money markets. Not right away, but by next January." He swallowed. "This is about the peak. Or close enough. Everybody's coming to the end of their financing, and once the money's gone, it's gone. When the venture capital gets nervous, everybody else has to pay attention."

"Everybody says it's never going to end."

"That's a perfect sign it's almost over," William said, and he began to cry a little again. He licked his lips and stopped himself. "People are just trying to convince themselves it's not going to change."

William's eyes leaked constantly anyway, but he tended not to cry in Henry's presence. Henry had seen other Hickman patients in the last months of their decline, but he had never watched one die up close like this; like elephants, Hickman patients died in the secrecy of their family, burdened with their great sad weight, swinging their gigantic gray heads away. He was always contacted afterward, but he had never seen it happen himself, not in such detail. But if William had another heart attack or a stroke, or a fall getting out of his chair, he would be done for. It was as though they were standing on the edge of a cliff and William was losing his balance and Henry could do nothing but watch him flailing on the edge. It was almost too painful to think about — to think that tomorrow or the next day William might easily be gone forever. Gone.

Henry put the syringe on the bedside table. "So you still feel that funny feeling when I do this?"

"Yeah." William nodded. "Like there's no one else in the world. And I feel this weird feeling. It's like there's nothing out there? Or like everything's really *slow*." With an effort, he lifted his chin. "Empty. Calm. The first time I felt it I figured you were starting the morphine drip."

"I remember."

William said nothing for a long time. When he stirred, he said, "I'm sort of doing science right now, right?"

"Sure. Absolutely. Nobody's ever done any of this."

"I like that." He closed his eyes. "I like the empty feeling."

"Make you feel better?"

William said nothing. "Makes me feel like I'm dead," he managed finally.

Don't even say it, Henry pleaded silently. "But you're not, buddy."

"Yeah," he hissed, suddenly furious again, his eyes overflowing. "Not fucking yet."

William did seem a little livelier, Henry thought. The William of two months ago could never have stayed awake for a twenty-minute conversation. But there was no physical change in him that they could detect. When they ran his cheek cells through the PCR machine, they found the same incremental decline, and the urine osmolality test showed the boy's kidneys still struggling to filter poisons from his blood, and his atrial flutter was just as bad — the old heart valves doing their best to send the blood on its way, still failing. His heart was weak, weak, its arteries clogged and deteriorating, and really it could stop at any moment. If Thomas's enzyme was doing anything, it wasn't obvious. No: William — it grew clearer every day — was dying just as steadily as he had been before. If he kept on like this, he would be dead before Halloween.

But still Henry visited William twice a week, taking his blood, sampling his urine, leaving behind with Bernie and Lillian another rack of glittering vials, and afterward he drove himself home with a great tenderness: slow, slow, through the winding arboretum, across Madison toward the lake, the bright summer trees singing overhead in their green hilarity. In the rearview mirror his own old eyes looked back. No, it was not working. Charlie was right; it had been a cruel thing to do. It had been too much to hope for, and he had been foolishly hopeful. Time after time his wife shook him awake in the middle of the night. "You're talking again," she would say into his ear, and it would take him hours to sleep again. Saul was gone, William was going; soon only Henry would be left.

But what did he expect, exactly? Peace of mind? Ha, ha, and ha. He feared that Charlie Calens would change his mind and turn him in; he feared Lisa Tung's sharp eye; he was shaken by the death of Saul; and Thomas was as shifty as ever.

The boy's step was still doeishly light and his carriage perfectly upright, and when he entered the quiet of Henry's office, he made no sound at all. His delicate shoulders, and the perfect, unmarked face, with its pretty chin and enormous eyes, and the dark kinky hair, glistening — it all seemed the product of an unwavering attention and a final, meticulous editing, in which every tiny blemish had been excised. Nothing was out of place. Even his ears were delicate and seemed to sit lightly on his skull. He could high-jump nearly three feet from a standstill, Henry had discovered, and with a running start he could have bounded like a deer leaping a pasture fence. And what dainty inner ears he had! What tidy nostrils! How his heart resounded behind his ribs!

"You're still the healthiest kid I've ever seen," Henry told him.

Thomas rolled his shoulders. "You got to see more healthy people, man."

"Maybe you're right."

Thomas inhaled, exhaled on command. "So like I'm still not about to die for some reason?"

"Not unless you get hit by a bus."

"Sha, man, don't say that." Inhale, exhale. A moment of quiet. Thomas was visibly working up to a question, and then it came out: "Hey, you ever know a guy named Gary?"

"Gary?" Henry put down his stethoscope. "Gary what?"

Thomas wore a nervous, stricken expression. "This guy, man, he keeps like calling me. And I'm like, Man, I never even heard of you, how'd you get my number, and he keeps saying it's from you, and I'm like, Naw, that's not right."

"Gary what?"

"Hoffman or Harman or something."

"Gary Hauptmann. What's he want?"

Thomas exhaled noisily, rolled his eyes. "*You* know. He wants to check me out."

Lisa. Goddamn it. "What's he saying?"

"He's saying you all are making income from the products of my body," said Thomas. A whine, almost. "And I'm like, I don't know, man."

"What do you tell him?"

"Nothing." The boy was chastened, angry. "I don't know what to say. I mean he's like a nice guy and everything, he's just like making suggestions. Like, You sure you want to do what you're doing?

[209]

You know? You sure you're happy with that doctor? And I'm like, What's up with that, is he recruiting me or what?"

"I'll talk to him today."

"There's people that want to like . . . clone me, I guess, so they could get this stuff out of me that you get."

This was close enough. "There are probably some people who'd like to get their hands on you."

"This dude says you own me."

"We don't own you. We've patented some of your sequence, but we don't own you."

"See, you start talking like that and I get all like nervous. I don't know what you're talking about." He made a hopeless gesture with his hand, looked up at Henry pleadingly. "I just don't understand it."

"You want to know the truth?"

"I just sit there and I'm like, What the fuck is he talking about, man? You going to make money off me?"

"Eventually, maybe. Maybe we all will."

Thomas gave him a long, appraising look. "How much, you think?"

"I have no idea. It depends." With as much sincerity as he could, Henry said, "I'm new at this, all right? I mean I've been in the field my whole life, but the business side is mostly new to me. So we'll see."

"I get some of that?"

"You'll do fine, believe me." What would Saul have said at this point? What canny, reassuring thing would he have come up with? Henry, reaching into the back of his brain, said, "We know what we're doing." It seemed flimsy, and in fact it was not entirely true, and he offered it as if from behind a mask.

But it seemed to satisfy Thomas, at least partly. "Sha, right," the boy said, but he relaxed and extended his arm.

Gary — Henry would have to deal with him somehow. Crap. Gary. His friend, his rival, his telephonic companion, his fellow traveler in the country of Hickman. Gary was as tall as Lincoln, with Lincoln's long, somber face and thick bushy hair; at the annual Hickman picnics in San Francisco he would race in the eucalyptus with the kids, a giant among the fragile dwarves, carrying a Corona by its neck, but his marriage was infamously unstable and he was prone, as Henry well knew, to a catatonic gloominess that could suspend business in his Berkeley office for weeks. When he emerged he would be full of a sweet self-deprecating happiness that had something to do with the attentions of his loyal wife, who had badgered him out of a half-dozen depressions over the years. But it was a fragile peace and always vanished eventually. Gary.

With so much practice lately, Henry had become much abler with the syringe. The long point, the plastic vial that reddened so quickly, the featherweight of the instrument itself in his hand — like any skill mastered, it was pleasant to perform. While in the beginning Thomas had looked away, he had over the weeks become accustomed to the pinch, the hard insertion of the needle, and the disloyal leap of blood into the plastic; he now watched his skin separate around the steel with a tender fascination. His perfect body, marred, would show no evidence of the needle. His cells showed no evidence of anything: generation after generation they remained immaculate. Would he ever age? Would he ever die? If he never got any older, why should he ever die, unless he killed himself? Out came the needle, on went the gauze.

Thomas pressed the gauze to the crook of his elbow and said, "I got one more thing I need to tell you, man."

"You do?"

"But don't be freaked out, all right?" He pronounced it with a roll: *aaiight.* Did he sound blacker than he had before he moved out here? Henry thought he did. The Benhamoudas' new neighborhood was mostly black. But so was Detroit, after all. "It's nothing, all right?"

"All right." *All right.*

"Man, it's nothing, man, don't look so wiggy, all right? But I've got these like things going on I need to tell you."

Henry drew a yellow pad from a tray, uncapped a pen. "This has to do with Gary again?"

"You don't need the pad, man. I just don't want you to freak on me when I tell you."

He put the pad down. "You're worrying me."

"Don't get mad, all right? I'm like hanging out with that girl," he said. "Sandra."

No. Oh, shit. "Sandra my *daughter?* When? Tonight?"

"No, we've *been* doing it."

"Doing what?"

"Nah, nah, nah! Just hanging out. She comes over where I stay."

"Where you stay?"

"Where I *live*, man."

"Aren't they the same thing?"

He rolled his eyes. "Yeah they're the same thing! I'm saying we're like hanging out. Like after school."

"Which means what?"

"Nothing, man. Man, I knew you were going to freak out."

"I'm not freaking out." He had the sudden urge to strangle Thomas but instead clasped his hands together tightly. Why hadn't he heard about this from Sandra herself? Well, he knew why. "I'm not."

"Sha, look at you! You're all fucked up, man."

"I'm a little surprised. What did you think, I was going to say okay?"

"But she's all like friendly to me and nobody else at that school is."

"When does this happen?"

"After school. I told you."

"Is she skipping basketball practice?"

"No, man, after school, after practice, we like go over to my house and like hang out."

He shuddered, picturing it. "Which means what to you?"

"We go down in the basement and watch TV, man — it's nothing."

"Oh my god."

"Sha, but who else am I supposed to have over there with my brother all like sitting out in the middle of the kitchen, man? They'd be all like, What the fuck is that, man, and I'd be like, Sha, man, that's my brother, and they'd be like, Yaah, and gone." He said it with an extra syllable on the end: *guon-e*. Complacently, with his arm still crooked, he stirred his shoulders; his mother had that same sexy settling gesture. "I'm not like making her come over there, she wants to come."

"What else haven't you told me?"

"That's it, man. I just wanted to get straight with you."

But the idea of the two of them together was terrible. "Oh my god," Henry said again. "You have to stop it."

"It wasn't her idea, man, it was mine, all right? I recognized her from that picture." He nodded at the photograph on Henry's desk. Thomas was quiet now, almost cowering. And it did make sense in a way: he was afraid of what people would think of his brother, so he found someone who wouldn't be shocked by Giles. Thomas unbent his elbow and lifted the gauze away. No mark at all.

Henry couldn't help himself: he reached for Thomas's arm and with his fingertips brushed the point where the needle had entered. Nothing. As it always was, the boy's skin was a pleasure to touch — perfectly smooth and cool, unworn by time, as smooth as a baby's. Uneasily he thought of Sandra. Dropped the arm. His big girl, out in the world.

The boy glanced up. "I still got no bruise or anything," he said. "Giles, man, every time you touch him it's like somebody put a nail in his arm."

"I want you to stop seeing her," Henry said. But he could see the attraction, of course he could. "You have to stop."

"Sha, okay." Thomas shrugged, submissive. "All right," he said. *All right.*

As soon as Thomas was gone Henry picked up the phone. "Hey! It's *you,*" Gary cried. It was the happy, renewed Gary. That explained the call to Thomas, which was ethically a no-no but which Gary in his seasonal giddiness could have justified to himself. "Hey, listen, I hear all kinds of things. You're sitting on something, is what we hear down this way. There's some kid?"

"Yeah, there's a kid."

"Allied Genomics come to you? Don't wait, Henry. Boy, the facilities these people have. The bioreactors! It's like a hydroelectric plant. Like Celera but more targeted. Gunnar Peterson gets wind of something unusual, I'm telling you he'd be interested. He's out there collecting anomalies — I'm surprised you haven't heard from him already. He's got his fingers everywhere."

"How the hell would he have heard, by the way?"

"Oh, you know, people talk."

"Who is people, exactly?"

"I don't remember, to tell you the truth. People are always talking about something. But boy, you think Amazon's the place to put your money, baloney. They're just a big dumb Wal-Mart, same kind of mentality. But what are they actually? Warehousers. Peddlers. The same old low-overhead, won't-be-undersold blah blah blah. You want to hit the big time? Talk to Peterson. Maybe he's the devil, but the devil rules this world."

"I'm guessing you're not signing up."

"I would if I had anything he wanted. What do I have to offer? Nothing. Not like you do. So what is it, exactly? We all think you've got an asymptomatic positive."

"You've been talking to Lisa."

"It can't be true. What's he look like?"

"He's beautiful," Henry said. "He's perfect. I mean, he's an asshole and he's trying to have sex with my daughter, but physically he's perfect."

A second of silence filled the line. "It's true?" Gary's voice was suddenly soft. "Really?"

"He's seventeen. He's perfectly healthy."

"But he's really got it?"

"He's really got it, and he's got a corrective."

"How?"

Henry described it, loosely. "We're patenting," he said.

"I should hope so. Yeah, well, you know, asymptomatics, that's Peterson's favorite flavor, Henry. Walking drug factories." Gary, subdued, said, "I didn't think it was possible."

"You've been talking to him, though."

"Oh, I don't know. Yeah, I guess so. Listen, is he short?"

"He's small. Not short. He was just in here today. He's sort of like an airbrushed picture of himself."

"There's got to be something wrong with him."

"We can't find anything."

"Holy moly. Well, listen, I actually hate this whole commercial angle, it's not what we signed up for. But please just keep me in the loop. Otherwise I get jealous, Hen. You know how I get."

"Probably about six weeks from now we should know something, one way or another." William would be closer to death, or he wouldn't. Or dead. Or not.

"I'll remember that," Gary threatened. "Six weeks from now I'm going to want to see this kid myself. You can't keep him up there forever. You're thinking about a deal, aren't you?"

"Starting to."

Another sigh. "Yeah. Well, I'll tell Gunnar, if I ever see him again. You ever meet him?"

"No."

"Nice guy," Gary said. "Surprisingly, for such a moneybags."

No, he'd never met him, but he'd visited the Allied Genomics

Web site a dozen times and stared at the old man's pink face, trying to detect in it a strain of avarice or generosity, but it was blank, corporate, and inscrutable. Nice enough, he supposed. Henry suspected it was a matter of making one phone call — they'd know who he was — and he'd have in hand a check for — what, maybe fifty thousand dollars? Without a fuss. But then minus his costs, minus the Carrier fee, then half that for the Benhamoudas, minus whatever money he'd feel obliged to return to the Hickman Foundation — the six thousand dollars, certainly — leaving him with almost nothing. Before taxes.

But if he could prove that Thomas's enzyme really did something — that it stopped the progress of Hickman in progeroid mice, for example — he could hold out for more. And if it stopped the progress of aging in William Durbin? Even more. But he could never prove such a thing, and so he could never profit from it, because he would never be able to tell anyone.

However, if it worked on healthy mice, he might be able to bump the price up appreciably. And — even better — if it worked on healthy people, there was no telling what he could get for it. What would people pay to live another hundred years? Another thousand? If he could show Peterson something really remarkable, he could probably name his price. Of course for that he needed a healthy human specimen, and there was only one of those he could think of who wouldn't need to be convinced, cajoled, or paid: himself. It was not the first time he had considered the idea. But he had no idea what the enzyme was doing to William; he would have no idea what it would do to him either. For the possibility of ten million dollars, would he risk his life? He thought not. Darren, Sandra, and Ilse would never forgive him.

Still, the vials sat in the refrigerator, glinting — a temptation. "We're all nice guys," Henry told Gary finally, and promised he would call him in August.

Money, it seemed, was everywhere. His wife's adventures continued to fill the kitchen counters with real estate flyers, and prices were still climbing, and Henry felt himself in the middle of a quiet but very definite migration. The Nilssons across the back fence were rumored to be thinking of selling, and the Bells, on the corner, had just put their house on the market.

"Guess how much." Ilse clutched the flyer to her sweaty chest.

"How big is it?"

"Two bedrooms, Henry — you know, it's small. But it's got the corner lot."

"Four hundred."

"Higher."

"Four ten."

Her eyes gleamed. "Six forty-five."

"No."

"Yes!"

"They'll never get it."

"They've already had an offer." She laid the paper on the counter, evidence. "They're going to take it."

"We can't sell the house," he said.

"We could," she clarified, "but we're not going to."

"Because then we'd need another house to live in, and houses are expensive."

"I know all that," she said, "but somehow it feels like we're being very, very sluggish and stupid."

A troubling thought was twirling in his brain. "I've got a guess-what for you," he said. "Guess who Sandra's been seeing."

"Oh, that." Ilse rolled her eyes. "It won't last. Well, I'm sorry, I was going to tell you. Actually I told her to tell you, but I knew she wouldn't, so I was going to. I wanted to give her a little time. *He* told you? Thomas did?"

"Believe it or not."

"What on earth compelled him to confess?"

"I think he's frightened. Gary Hauptmann somehow got hold of him, and he was looking for somebody to talk to. You knew about this?"

"Gary. Oh, Gary. Word travels fast."

"What should we do?"

"She'll be all right," she assured him. "She knows what he is, Henry. She's not in love."

"He's really not a very pleasant person most of the time."

"That's what she thinks too."

"Then what's the attraction? Never mind, I don't want to know."

"But," she said cannily, "you do know." Flirting, she put the flyer to her chest again. "Guess how many bathrooms?"

"Five."

"One and a half!" she crowed, and kissed him on the mouth. "Leave her alone. She can handle herself. She came to me in the first place. I have no idea why. I think she was frightened too. She doesn't usually like those sorts of boys."

"He's attractive."

"He must be."

His wife's confidence was unsettling: what else didn't he know? The world seemed to have angles and corridors that he was missing; he was catching up, catching up, but he was never up to speed. It bugged him. Disturbed his sleep apparently too, because that night in bed Ilse shoved him again, saying, "That noise! You're talking again."

"I am?" He sat up. Remembered nothing. "Sorry."

She sat up in bed beside him, a ghostly shape in the faint orange glow of the streetlight. Beyond the window the neighborhood was silent. In half an hour or so the paper boy's car would come driving up. "Were you dreaming?"

"I don't know."

"Well, you sound like something terrible coming down the hallway. *Ho, ho, ho, ho, bi, bi, bi, bi.*"

"I'm not doing it on purpose."

"You're talking a mile a minute."

"I'm sorry."

"I know," she whispered. She turned, lifted the blind that hid them from the street. Dark, dark, the hemlocks stood silhouetted against the orange sky. What hour had it been, Henry wondered, when Saul had decided he had seen enough? What wind had been brushing his window? There had been no disorder in the man's house, and to Henry this seemed especially strange. Such a disintegration should have been visible, but Henry had sensed nothing, even talking to the man the night before. But then again, who would suspect Henry himself of so entirely disregarding the tenets of his profession? Who could see into his heart and see the greed, the disregard, all of it stained with a fearful love?

"I should go sleep upstairs if I'm bugging you," he suggested, and was not surprised when his wife did not object. There was a futon in the attic, and for ten minutes before dropping into unconsciousness he listened to the squirrels skittering across the shingles. They seemed to be playing a game, and certainly something hard was rolling up and down the roof, but then this became part of his dreaming too, and he woke when Ilse shook his shoulder in the daylight, saying, "Darling, it's morning," with her hair in its pins and her face bright and happy. She had slept well, and so had he. It seemed, even in the beautiful light through the ash tree, a terrible thing: he had slept soundly in a bed without his wife while William was dying across town. What sort of man was he? What right did he have to safety, to happiness?

15

FROM SIXTY POUNDS he had graduated to eighty, and pretty soon he no longer needed his sister to spot him. In his mirror he had gained maybe a millimeter of mass, but didn't his triceps seem made of harder stuff now? He felt them at every opportunity and could do his homework with his left hand clamped over his right bicep. A single faint blue vein had appeared on the underside of each forearm. The lever-and-pulley arrangement that moved his ring fingers was newly visible beneath the skin of each wrist, like the counterweight that moved in an elevator shaft, and he spent no little time watching it do its work. But how did a thought become an action? *Move your finger,* he thought. For that matter, how did the brain work? He knew that the neurons and axons were arranged in a kind of netting, and that chemicals were exchanged between the cells somehow, but how did a cell know what the color red was? Could you cut open a brain cell and somehow see the word *elephant* inside it, or was it more complicated than that? He could ask his dad, but he didn't. His dad had a way of giving him too much information, and he had the feeling nobody knew the answer anyway.

His own body was a territory that was familiar to him, but it had, in the last couple months, changed, like a neighborhood undergoing abrupt and uneven improvement. His balls were getting bigger. His dick was a little bigger, thank god. His breath was terrible, but his face had somehow widened so his jaw wasn't so strange and long, and if he squinted he could make himself look like Edward Burns in the mirror, sort of. He shaved twice a week, but suspected that only he could see the difference. The old childhood smell of his knees — if he pulled them to his mouth and breathed on them and inhaled — was still there, and this seemed the real smell of his body, a rustic, almost neutral smell of skin.

His toes were lengthening in their Tevas. He was a little taller, maybe half an inch, not enough to buy new pants. He could hold his breath for a minute and fifty-two seconds, and his longest sustained urination was a minute forty-five. He was five foot six and weighed 122 pounds. He had $413 to his name. He jacked off twice a day on average, had kissed exactly one girl, and had no idea what he would do with his life when it became his to do with as he wanted.

The end.

His conversations with William had continued undetected. Once a week or so, in the brightening evenings of the unfurling summer, they talked. And now and then the phone at his bedside would ring very late at night: two or three in the morning. *The bartender says, We don't serve string in here. So the three strings go out on the sidewalk. And the first string says, I bet I can get served, so he like rolls up in a ball and goes in and bounces up on a stool and says, Gimme a beer! And the bartender says, You're a string, and the string goes, No, I'm a ball of twine, and the bartender says, Get outta here! And the second string says Okay and rolls himself up in a loop and goes in and says, Gimme a beer! And the bartender says, You're a string! And the string goes, No, I'm not, I'm a lasso! And he goes, Get outta here! And then the third string ties himself up in a big mess and unravels both his ends, and he goes in and gets up on the stool and says, Gimme a beer! And the bartender looks at him and says, Aren't you a piece of string? And the string goes, No, I'm a frayed knot!* And then that raspy, withered laugh. *Ha, ha.*

"You sound different," Darren told him one night in a whisper.

"I do?"

"Yeah, you sound better. You're not like panting all over the place like some psycho."

"You're the psycho," said William.

Better. Definitely better. His voice was stronger. "I thought you were sick and whatever."

Between them the line seemed to open an electronic space; the sound of the wire had a breadth to it, a largeness. "I can't sleep," William said. "You watching TV?"

"I don't have one in my room. Wait a sec." Darren climbed out of bed, took the cordless with him downstairs, into the living room. Sat down on the sofa. "Okay," he said.

"Go to channel nineteen. You want some Maria Eau d'Essence Spray, only twenty-four fifty? Or Scarlet Caramel Topaz Camel Back Earrings, only twenty-eight bucks?"

"No thanks." He began to flip. Politicians, motorcycle races, ancient black-and-white cartoons. "There's like *nothing* on television at three in the morning, is there?"

"Hey," William said, "so I've got an idea."

"Okay."

"I think you should come visit me sometime."

"At your house?"

"Why not?"

He let the question hang. "I don't know."

"You afraid?"

"I don't know."

"I'm not contagious."

"Duh, I know."

"You're probably about the only person in the whole city who would actually understand why I look like this." The boy's high, reedy voice took on a genial, negotiating cant. He was bargaining. "We don't have to go outside, we can just hang out here."

"Yeah."

"Yeah what? Yeah you'll do it? Or yeah shut up?"

"I don't know. Both."

"You've never even seen me."

"I know what you look like."

"So what're you scared of?"

"I don't have a car or anything."

"There's a bus that goes right down Nineteenth, which is two blocks from here."

"Yeah." Why should he hesitate? "I don't know, man."

"Come on. There's only about ten people in the world I ever talk to, and they're either my parents or they're doctors, except for this one retard in Orlando who's got it, and he thinks going to Disneyland is the best thing in the world, even though he can't do anything, he just rolls around in his dumb wheelchair and gets stared at."

"Disney World is in Orlando. Disneyland's in California."

"See, I would come over there," William said, and then he inhaled heavily. "Wait a sec." The line hummed between them. Darren heard a swallowing sound, a muffled gasp, and then William continued. "I would come over there, but I don't have a car."

"I don't know if my dad wants me to do stuff like that," Darren ventured, and even as the words came out of his mouth he could feel the cowardice filling the room like a stink. God, he was a wuss. "He still doesn't even know I've been talking to you."

Another pause, a second swallow. "I really sound better?"

"You're breathing better."

"I guess I feel a little better." A rustling of sheets and blankets. "Go to channel seventy-five. You ever see this? It's live from the shuttle. No, now it's mission control. They're over the Indian Ocean." Another pause. "Now they're doing something with the arm," he said.

Darren was there now, on the channel. The white shuttle glowed brilliantly against the darkness of space, moving an inch at a time.

He could not picture himself at William's bedside or sitting with him in an overheated room playing chess or something, so he didn't mention William's idea to anyone. His dad was obviously busier than usual and had taken to sleeping on the attic futon — he was talking in his sleep — and Darren felt it would be pushy, and somehow not exactly polite, to suggest anything at the moment. And his dad these days spent a lot of time mumbling to himself at the window, and was now carrying a tiny blue spiral notebook with him everywhere, full of cramped and illegible notes to himself. He shouldn't interfere, Darren thought. He should just chill out and read Philip K. Dick and talk on the phone with William when he called, and that should be enough. But this was all bogus, and he knew it. He was still afraid of William, and like anyone else he could always find an excuse for not doing something he was afraid to do.

When the third week of June arrived, the mood around the big brick school building lightened, lightened, with the windows open, the posters shifting in the breezes that now traveled the long cluttered halls — ELECT SHAMEKA MCCOY — VOTE FOR BEN lifting heavily from the walls and sometimes coming loose and sliding to the floor with a rattle, to be trampled with muddy shoe prints. Lockers were open, empty, or the contents had been abandoned, so heaps of ink-stained, corner-worn, disregarded senior textbooks could be seen beneath Doritos bags and McDonald's wrappers, the owners having left school forever, never to look back. Teachers loaded odds and ends into the trunks of their cars, and Mr. Ginns dropped his terrarium in the parking lot and had to gather up his geckos in a cone of newspaper. The seniors TPed the trees one night, and for the rest of that week the disintegrating scraps of tissue floated over the hedges and down the sidewalks, gathered in drifts at the edge of the football field, sloped down the lawn to Ezell's, and lifted into the air to dance past the windows of Darren's algebra class before rising again, on a sudden updraft, out of sight.

He had not been out with Tanya since the disaster with the boob, but they had continued to talk on the phone (basically about nothing), and twice she had let him hold her hand in the halls, when no one else was around. But his position was not secure. She was pretty. She had other options. Jason Marcus, Ben Howard, Alex French, Sam Wasserman, just to name the guys in his algebra class he'd seen talking to her.

Determined to make his move, he asked her out again. "We could go see a movie," he suggested, taking a position beside her locker. It was tidy but not empty: a pink pencil box lay on the top shelf, a transparent plastic raincoat was hanging from the hook. "Not that original, I guess."

"The last time we went to a movie it was sort of weird."

"Yeah. Well, we could go hang out at GameWorks."

"Downtown?" Her brown eyes darted over his head. She was taller than he was, still. "I don't know."

"We could throw a baseball," he said. "I just figured, since you live right next to Montlake."

"I don't even know how to throw."

"I could teach you."

She didn't roll her eyes but came, he saw, perilously close. "That's okay."

"I looked up the Etruscans," he said. "Pretty cool." This caught her interest, minimally. "So, I'm trying to ask you out," he said, pressing, "and I'm obviously not getting anywhere. So maybe I'll just quit."

"No, don't quit! It's just" — she looked away — "it's the end of the year, and I don't know what I'm doing sometimes. I mean, sometimes I'm going out with friends, and, you know, it's hard to plan in advance." She shrugged.

"What about the Fourth of July?"

"We're going to Orcas Island," she said with distressing promptness. "My grandmother lives there, and we always go for the fireworks."

"What about Halloween? That's only like four months away."

She laughed, her head drooping, her shoulders slumping. It was killing him. "I'm sorry," she said.

"Thanksgiving?"

Her head tipped the other way. But he was winning: she was still smiling. "I'm going to see my other grandmother in Phoenix."

"Christmas?"

"Okay." She nodded.

"Christmas morning?"

She laughed again, sighed, seemed to consider. "My dad, okay, has this show going on? At the King County History Museum, which is like right by our house? It's this stupid show of this stupid stuff he collects, which is like stupid navy buttons and anchors and old like periscopes and dumb stuff like that?" Her mouth tightened. "And I have to go look at it on Saturday, he wants everybody to come, so I have to go anyway, so."

"I know where that is."

"It's like behind the bridge, sort of? You should come early in the morning, like ten." She looked over his head again. "I've got something I have to do that night, but you can hang out with me there during the day if you want. It's sort of boring, but we could walk out to Foster Island maybe, if he'll let me go."

It wasn't exactly the prom, but he would take it. The museum was a little one-story concrete building just across the drawbridge from the football stadium, so he cajoled his dad into driving him down that Saturday morning. Shaved, showered, with his crotch rubbed clean and smelling of his sister's lavender body wash, he ran the car window up and down nervously.

"This is a what, now?" his father asked.

"Some kind of show her dad's doing. He collects things."

"And the museum's putting them on display?" His father placed a hand over his mouth. "This is obviously very interesting to you."

"Yeah, not exactly."

"Is she going to be around this summer?"

Darren didn't know. "I just thought it'd be cool to hang out with her for a while."

"She's the one with the necklace?"

"Yeah."

"She's pretty."

"I guess." He buzzed the window up. He did not want to agree. That his father had noticed such a thing about Tanya was weird and produced beneath his diaphragm a bubble that threatened to rise into laughter. To talk with his father about girls had this effect: a good feeling that was almost too good, as when, while reading a magazine, the corner of a page would brush the edge of his lips and produce within the musculature of his face a hectic, almost pleasurable buzzing. Just thinking about it made his mouth itch. "Yeah, so I don't have a chance, is what I'm thinking."

"She invited you here, though."

"Yeah, exactly. She invited me *here*." They had arrived. A blue van, alone in the parking lot, sat with its side panel open. The museum ramp sloped up to a dim doorway, where a light burned. Beyond, the trail to Foster Island snaked out across the swampy lake; but the day was gray and cool, and even now raindrops were appearing on the windshield. Suddenly he was nervous. He could duck down in his seat and disappear, ask his father to take him home. But his cowardly impulses had to be fought eventually, so he unbuckled his seatbelt and stepped out. "I'll take the bus back," he said, leaning down.

"You've got money?"

"Yeah." He had eighty dollars in his pocket. Who knew where the day would lead, after all? "I'll be home this afternoon sometime."

The museum was dim and quiet, a big, low-ceilinged, open space under fluorescent lights. No one was visible, though he could hear a stirring through a distant doorway. He made his way into the room. Low glass display cases lined with black velvet held what appeared to be an infinite number of brass and silver buttons. Hello? Where was everybody? Some of the buttons — eagles, anchors, ships under sail — had corroded with time, or the finish had dulled. Others were shining under the lights of the display. *Water-bury Mark, c. 1874. Spanish Lancer Cavalry, c. 1898. U.S. Navy Seaman, c. 1905. Japanese Imperial Navy, c. 1937.* The room was full of cases. Around the edges of the room stood models of ships — battleships, submarines, older ships with sails and rigging.

Suddenly Darren was filled with a swooning despair. Where was everybody? What the hell was he doing here? What the hell kind of moron was he, to go on a date to a museum to look at a bunch of old buttons? His rubber soles squeaked on the floor: he had tracked in the rain.

Finally Tanya appeared from the distant doorway. Her hair was down, she was wearing glasses, and her boobs were hidden under a huge U.S. Navy Reserve sweatshirt. From across the room she called, "I thought I heard somebody." She came up to him, appeared to be about to hug him, changed her mind. "Can you believe all this stuff?"

"It's all your dad's?"

"This whole room is his. He's been working on this for like *months.*" Behind her glasses, her eyes rolled. Whereas he had spent the morning shaving his face and soaping himself raw, Tanya appeared to have climbed directly from bed into her clothes. Her skin had a greasy, unwashed sheen to it. "Thank god it's finally happening, we won't have to hear about it ever again."

"That's a lot of buttons."

"This is nothing. He's got like cases more of them in storage. This is just the good stuff."

"It's cool," he felt obliged to say.

"You really think so?"

"Um . . ." He calculated. "No."

They stood at an awkward distance, regarding each other. To be invited to such a strange and intimate affair as this — a family affair — seemed to Darren a gloomy and unpromising thing. It was a joke, maybe. Tanya would tell her girlfriends that he had come, washed and shaved, to look at her father's idiotic buttons. But she did not strike him as having a particularly malicious heart, and her untended appearance this morning could mean just the opposite — that she liked him, and trusted him, and was relaxed enough to allow herself to be seen in a sweatshirt, without her contacts in. He would be optimistic, he decided.

"They're also for sale," she said. "But you don't have to buy anything. They're really expensive."

"Is your dad here?"

"He's like printing out a bunch of labels." She gestured to the doorway. "He's freaking out, like anybody's actually going to come."

"I should say hi."

"No, he's freaking out. Let's just sort of walk around."

"This is a sale?"

"It's sort of a sale? And sort of a show. You want to look around? There's the whole rest of the museum."

"There's more?" No, it wasn't possible. "Is it all buttons?"

"No, thank god. At least, not *his* buttons." With a sudden decisive motion she took his hand, briefly, then changed her mind and dropped it. "He's crazy," she said.

There were other rooms full of other things. Indian things. Baskets. Harpoons with sharpened white seal teeth for the blades. A twenty-foot cedar canoe hollowed with fire and painted with black-and-red figures. They walked through this room, not touching. The dim light of Saturday morning filled the space with what felt like a terminal silence. A huge stuffed bear rearing on its haunches watched from a corner. Why was it so easy to talk to William and so hard to talk to Tanya?

"What would you do if you were stranded on a desert island?" he asked finally, standing in front of the canoe.

"What would I do?"

"You ever think about that?"

"Not exactly." She drifted away to a case of bone implements: combs, needles, more fucking buttons. "That's really cool," she said, jabbing a long finger at the glass, at a hairpin made of walrus tusk. He leaned over, peered at it. She was close: he could smell laundry detergent; she seemed to fill the air beside him with that dance of particles — a thick cloud of actuality, of presence — that he could sense with his skin. "I don't know, I'd try to find out where I was," she answered. "Would I know where I was to start with?"

"Let's say not."

"Okay, I don't know. I'd build a fire somehow. I don't know." She straightened, looked around at the dim room, and sighed. "I can't believe I'm here at ten o'clock in the morning," she said. "I can't believe you're here."

He thought it best not to respond to this. At the end of the central corridor was a flight of stairs, which led down to another dim, quiet floor. There they found old neon signs: BARTELL'S DRUG EMPORIUM, SEAFIRST BANK, IVAR'S ACRES OF CLAMS, SICK'S STADIUM. A long glass case was filled with a scale model of the Seattle Center, its white whalebone arches and boxy white buildings reduced here to a crushable size. Miniatures were usually fascinating to him, but he just glanced at the green plastic trees and mirrored ponds and walked on. Upstairs, her father could be heard pacing among display cabinets, back and forth. He sounded like a big guy, and not someone Darren was in a particular hurry to meet.

At the far end of the room, behind a red velvet rope, stood a white countertop and green vinyl stools from an old drugstore. *Woolworth's lunch counter circa 1935*, read the label. Farther on, a photograph: *Boeing's first commercial aircraft, the 1919 B-1 Floatplane.* Next: *Alki landing diorama, November 13, 1851.* Here were more miniatures — a clutch of men and women standing on a muddy shore, their ship moored in a blue-painted bay. The figures had been placed so no one faced anyone else; they seemed a sad and hapless landing party, with their meager plastic possessions piled beside them. A little lean-to of logs had been erected on the sand. "Stay dry," he told the tiny people.

"Come check this out." Tanya was leaning over a long dark case. Within, a lumpy shape was wrapped in a layer of disintegrating fabric: a mummy. "This is so weird."

"Is that your dad?"

"No, that's not my dad!" She shoved him. "My dad has like *way* more hair."

"Ask him if he has any buttons for sale."

"Do you have any buttons for sale?" Tanya asked the mummy. "He says no."

Why was there a mummy here, in the basement of this modest and undervisited museum? There was no card, no explanatory material at all. The case was half hidden beneath a back stairway and seemed to be on its way to somewhere else. Beneath the glass the mummy's skull was as brown and stubbly as a coconut, and a set of yellow teeth sat like candle stubs in the withered jaw. Gross. Long sinewy feet were held together by a stiff rind of skin, and the skeletal hands clutched at nothing above a sunken groin. "Weird," he said.

"Check out his tattoo."

On the mummy's varnished right foot were three parallel lines, each an inch long, etched a blurry black against the brown. "He shot down three enemy planes."

"No, he like killed three mammoths." Tanya's hands were leaving prints on the case. In her concentrated examination of the mummy her mouth had come ajar, showing her salmon-pink tongue clinging to her top teeth. "Or he had three wives? Or three sons or something."

"Maybe he had three balls."

"Gross!" She laughed and shoved him, elbow to elbow. "Isn't it weird? Like he probably had a name and everything, and there's probably people in the world who are actually descended from him."

"Like your dad."

"Like *your* dad."

"Like my grandmother," he said. "Actually, she probably met him once. I bet she'd know his name." He rapped on the glass. "Hey," he called, "you know an old lady named Freda?" The sound of his knuckles was loud and hollow; the glass was thick, but resounded when struck, and for an instant he had the image — it was odd, how it leapt into his brain — of the mummy turning its head and looking at him and trying to speak. Spooked, he straightened, turned to Tanya, and kissed her.

Her lips were dry but soft, and for a few seconds she kissed him back. Taller than he, she stooped to do it. Then she backed away, putting a flat hand on his chest. "That was fast," she said. Her expression was scrupulously neutral. "I have to tell you, though? I'm probably like dating about like ten guys right now."

"That's cool," he said.

"And I'm not like serious with any of them? But just so you know."

"That's because they're not like into buttons and everything." She didn't smile. "And I am *so* into buttons."

"And if I had to like rank you among the guys I'm dating?"

"You don't actually have to do that."

"You're not like top three? I mean, I like you, but." Now she smiled a little. "Just so you know."

"What about the horse?"

"The horse," she stated flatly. Then her memory caught and her eyes brightened. "The horse! Well, I had to give you something."

"I looked up the Etruscans, though."

"I liked the horse," she told him. "At least I didn't get you a pile of dog shit."

Not exactly, you didn't, he thought. The mummy hadn't moved. His three parallel tattoos remained where they had been for however many thousands of years. They had lost all their meaning in the intervening centuries and now were just empty marks — lines — signifying absolutely nothing. "I'm going to get a tattoo," he announced. "I'm going to get those three lines."

"They won't tattoo you without your parents' permission."

"I can do it myself."

"Oh my god, don't. You know Jeremy Cohen? He did that on his arm and it got totally infected and they had to scrape out a bunch of his skin and now he's got this big like scoop out of his arm — it's disgusting." She gave him a wary, distant look. "Don't do that."

"They do it in prison all the time."

"Oh, like you know. Plus, that's prison!" She tossed her head. "There's a reason people do dumb things in prison — it's because they're *dumb*. Which is how they got there in the first place. Don't."

He saw that he could do it, or at least say he would do it, and earn some points with her; she would pretend to see it as stupid, but in fact she would think it was wild and at least a little interesting. He would have to ponder this. Maybe he could move up from Position 7 or 8 to Position 4, and from there he could plan his further assault.

Back upstairs the rooms were as empty and quiet as before, and the buttons sat in their gleaming, horrible rows, hundreds of them, thousands, millions and millions of buttons. Mr. Schiffer was roaming among the cases, his hands in his jeans pockets, a huge mass of curly hair down to his shoulders. He gave Darren a bluff, eager, painful handshake. "Darren," he said. "You buying or browsing?"

"Browsing."

"We've got some things you could probably afford."

"Dad, oh my god. You *don't* have to buy anything. Seriously. He does this to everybody."

"What's a kid like you got on hand, maybe ten bucks?" Mr. Schiffer strolled over to a basket of loose buttons and began picking through them; falling against each other, they made a hollow clicking sound. Plastic. Or cheap metal. "You can get a pretty nice Vietnam-era button for, say, fifteen. I'd give it to you for ten. This is right off an aviator's uniform. That's the real deal." He handed it over. "That button probably flew three or four dozen missions over enemy territory."

"No thanks."

"You don't want it?"

"Not for ten bucks, jeez."

"You think I'm going to just give it to you?"

"Dad!"

"Okay." He put it back in the basket. "This one's Korean-era, but it's common. More like twenty for this one. I could go to fifteen." Mr. Schiffer was breathing heavily through his nose. "You know about the Polar Corps, right?"

"No."

"Polar Corps was an elite unit built to support troops that would participate in a northern invasion of the Soviet Union. Navy unit. Or this one? Grenada invasion button. It'd be ten bucks or so just on the age, but it's pretty rare, probably more like twenty-five."

"Yeah. Did you know there's a mummy downstairs?"

"Or if you're looking for something a little older, we've got all these Spanish buttons." He moved to a case, bent down, slid out a velvet tray. "You ever see anything so nice? These are solid brass. Feel it." The button he handed over was heavy, like a cool stone, with a loop on the back where it had been sewn to someone's tunic. "You like that? Forty bucks. I could go probably thirty on that."

"Dad! Stop trying to sell him your stupid buttons!"

"Thirty bucks is a good deal for that."

"No thanks."

"You don't want to go thirty bucks?" Mr. Schiffer's breathing had become louder, and his lips had begun to part. "Thirty's good for a Spanish button of that vintage. Good condition — look, there's no wear on the threader."

"Dad!"

"I'd go twenty," Darren said.

"Oh my god."

"I can't go twenty bucks on an artillery button."

Darren shrugged. From his pocket he extracted a single twenty-dollar bill, one of the new ones, with Jackson overlarge and off-center. "That's all I've got."

"Oh my god," Tanya said, and walked away. "I can't believe you're selling him a button."

"Twenty bucks is out of the question," said Mr. Schiffer, but he eyed the bill, which Darren had unfolded and laid on the glass case. "You don't know what you're asking."

But after another moment's pause the deal was struck, and Darren, feeling foolish but a little ecstatic, handed over his cash. Tanya laughed in disbelief, walked away a few more steps, then approached in a kind of humorous exasperation and asked to see what he had bought. He showed her. Imprinted with a raised shield, it was a humble thing, as dark as an old doorknob, heavy, as big as a quarter. It felt like something valuable in his hand. He hefted its weight in his palm. "What the hell are you going to do with it?" she asked him, and he said, "I'm going to pierce my eyebrow and stick it right in my forehead," and she laughed. He would, too, if it would help. *Up to Position 6,* he thought.

16

E'D LIT FIRES in his frying pans. What else? He'd owned an old printing press that she and Darren had taken turns on, lowering the giant iron plates and then raising them again while the iron machinery clanked and the intriguing geometry of the screw press did its work. The fireplace was big enough for Darren to stand up in, and he had done it, resting the top of his head against the hidden flue. At dinner, enormous flowers bent their petals over the polished table. Why did she remember all this suddenly? And those boxes in her room — Sandra had never asked, but she had assumed, in the way of children, that anything given to her in secret was meant to remain a secret, so she had hoarded the charm, the alligator, the tiny gold pencil. At night the alien bedroom had been darker than she liked, and she remembered the uneasy feeling that descended every night when her brother had been swallowed up in the darkness down the hall and her parents had hidden themselves behind one of the innumerable doors and she was left alone. It had been a feeling of abandonment she could almost, but not quite, ignore. Across the street the workmen had been given the run of the Mosses' house, and during the evenings they could be seen stepping out onto the porch and removing the masks they wore to protect themselves from the sanding dust.

Why had they all gone to Mr. Harstein's house? Money, probably. Convenience. But the whole episode was mysterious to her; she had never been inside the house again. And now she never would, she imagined. The yellow tape had been removed from his hedges, but a huge padlock was now affixed to the front door, and the lawn was growing weedy and tall. Cop cars came sliding down the street once in a while as though looking for something they'd lost, but no one ever got out.

Dead — it was hard to get her head around. How could someone just *die* like that? She wanted to see the house, see the place where he'd done it. Were there bloodstains on the walls? Her father, having seen the room firsthand, would tell her nothing more than he already had. She was old enough, she argued. Just: was there blood on the walls? Was it pouring down the stairs? He wouldn't say. From her bedroom window, the top of the house was visible; the valleys of the roof had begun to collect drifts of pine needles or whatever they were. In the past these had always been swept away by the Hispanic guy who did the lawns, but now that Mr. Harstein was dead, no one came by to clean the roof. It made her sad to look at it, and after a few weeks she drew the blind so she didn't have to look at it anymore.

But she was happy to plant a tree with her mother and half a dozen of the neighbors. No one knew what was going to happen to the house — they still hadn't found any family, and apparently he hadn't had a will, or at least that was the rumor. So they chose a spot on the Turgersons' parking strip. It was a Saturday, with spitting rain. Her brother was off at the museum on some supposed date and her father was at work again.

Mrs. White pulled the tree backward out of her new Suburban; it was tall and spindly, with a handful of budding leaves. "This is an idesia tree," she said, putting her hair behind her ears. "Also known as the wonder tree, it makes these very, very interesting orange and black berries. It can grow to a height of eighty feet and is very broad, with a potential span of at least a hundred feet, which means it could in theory shade some of his yard eventually."

"A hundred feet," said Mr. Turgerson.

"Eventually," said Mrs. White.

Together the eight of them wrestled the tree from its paper pot and lowered it into the earth. "I think it should go the other way," Sandra's mother said.

"You mean with the leaves in the ground?"

"That looks to be the strongest branch," said her mother, "and I think it ought to point at his house."

Wordlessly Mr. White turned the tree in its hole.

"Honey, it's not straight," said Mrs. White.

Mr. White said, "I know it's not straight. We haven't filled in the hole yet."

"And we can't start filling it in until it's straight."

Mr. White tipped the tree an inch to the left. "Presto," he said.

"A hundred feet is awfully big," said Mr. Turgerson.

"Gerald, you said you wanted something stately."

"That's more like a building."

"It grows very slowly," said Mrs. White.

"So I'll be dead, you mean."

"You and everybody else. We all will. Except Sandra." Mrs. White inhaled and folded her hands at her stomach and said, "We have come here as neighbors to mark the end of Saul Harstein, whom none of us knew very well but whom we all thought of as a very nice and pleasant man. Many of us feel guilty for neglecting him, though it was what he seemed to want most of the time, but little did we know he was in a condition where our company might have actually done him some good. In planting this tree, we hope to say to ourselves that company is always a good thing, no matter who we are, that it is no sin to talk to one another once in a while, or to say to one another that we love you, and that if we ask after you it is not out of nosiness necessarily but because we might be concerned about you, for whatever reason. Grow, tree, and remind us that we live our lives in sight of one another and that all of us need to be sheltered sometimes. There's a *beautiful* idesia," she said, "out at the locks — it's just beautiful. The leaves are very pale and the light that comes through them is just out of this world, it's absolutely *unearthly*. Gerald has agreed to water once a day for a week, once a week for a month, and once a month for a year, which is the schedule for watering transplanted trees, in case anyone thinks I made that up."

"I would like to say something," said Millie Turgerson. She wore a purple dress that went to her ankles, and her hair was gathered in its bun. "I knew Saul when he first moved in. He was very polite. But he made it clear to us that he was not to be bothered, and I for one don't feel guilty. We invited him over for dinner three times, but he didn't come. When I was out here I would wave to him, and the only time he waved back was when he saw me wearing a great big hat I used to have, and he was laughing at me and thought he should cover it up by waving. It happened more than once. I like this tree, but I hope it doesn't drop any berries on the sidewalk."

"Kevin will sweep them up," Mrs. White said swiftly.

They passed the shovel around. When it came to Sandra, she lifted a big scoop from the rocky pile and tossed it into the hole. But what about the little boxes? she wanted to ask. What about the printing press, with its smell of ancient oil? When they tamped the earth with their shoes, the tree shivered, its slender tip dancing back and forth, and Sandra felt she might cry again. Mr. Harstein had not been loved, she felt, by anyone but her, and even she hadn't spoken to him in years. Loved? Well, but what else was this feeling, this terrible clotted heat that threatened to explode from her throat? What else was this wish to see him again, to see him walk down the sidewalk and embrace them all?

She was continuing to see Thomas. She had not told her father and saw no reason to. Every now and then she would be on the receiving end of a funny look from him and wondered what it meant, but she didn't really want to know, so she never asked. She knew her father's work was a serious enterprise, and she was a little ashamed of meddling in it like this.

She wasn't in love with Thomas. In lust, maybe, but not love. She hadn't had sex with him, maybe because of some hovering sense of guilt at betraying her father, and also the mechanics of it were hard to imagine. Who would buy the condom? Where would they do it? Would Mrs. Benhamouda come downstairs at that point? No, no, no, she couldn't.

But it was nice to be wanted by such a cute guy, and he could be funny once in a while, though it wasn't always on purpose.

"Today they put me in this big-ass like X-ray machine?" he said in his basement. "Not X-ray, what's that called?"

"A CAT scan?"

"No."

"MRI?"

"Yeah. Something." Thomas glanced at her before continuing. "Then they took blood like ten times." He extended his arm, which bore no mark. "I'm on the hook. I'm making him pay me if he wants to do it anymore."

Long yellow rectangles of sunlight entered the high basement windows and angled to the floor. "You're making a contribution to science," she told him.

"Whatever. They should be making contributions to *me*."

She laughed. "You're so vain."

He smiled, looked away. "I got reason, man."

It was true: he was something to look at, especially close up. The apparent black of his irises was actually peppered with a gold glitter, like an art project, and his breath was clean and silvery, like bright water. It was strange. He didn't smell like anything, even when she plunged her nose into his armpit, making him yelp. Nothing. "You wear deodorant?" she asked. He did not. His long sculpted feet, divested of their white socks, showed the same marzipan uniformity as the rest of him — at least those parts she'd seen.

They fooled around a little, nothing too serious. But for at least an hour every afternoon she would insist on studying for her finals there in the basement. "I eventually have to go to college, actually," she told him.

"What about me? What'm I supposed to do?"

"Study with me." And chastely she would take out her books.

But they had no common classes. She was on the AP track, and he was not. All his classes had suspicious off-brand names like Computation and Writing English and Social Trends, while she was taking AP English 11B and AP U.S. History and Trigonometry. And his classes, it was impossible not to notice, were full of black students and thuggish-looking Asians and headbanger white kids. His classes were all like the health class she had taken last year, the one class everyone at Garfield had to sign up for, where they learned about The Penis and The Vagina, yawn. Taught by the tennis coach in a smelly corner classroom next to the cafeteria. A constant aluminum clatter had come through the doorway as huge trays of hamburger noodle and johnny tetrazzini slid into the industrial ovens. This was how the other half lived, taking classes from Mr. Vargas and reading, over the course of four months, a single slender booklet called *Your Body and You*. Depressing. That was Thomas's material, not worth mastering.

But after ten minutes or so Sandra would actually be reading her notes, and Thomas, after changing channels for a while, would wander off and return carrying his orange backpack. Making a great show of unzipping it and sighing as he leafed through his scattered, grubby papers, he would at last work something free from the mess — some dubious sheet of half-facts from Social Trends — and, shirtless, would sprawl belly-down on the warm carpet, propping himself on his elbows. "You see this?" he said once, and pulled out a folded, dirty printout of his DNA. "That's my mutation. People pay serious money for this kind of information, in case you don't know."

"Maybe you can buy yourself a brain."

"Sha, my brain's all right." Warily he looked up at her. "What's wrong with my brain?"

"Nothing. Or, no, wait — I mean *everything*."

He stared at her, exasperated. "Why the hell you want to say that kind of thing?"

"Where's Austria?"

"Man, I didn't hear what you said that time."

She doubted this. "The earth goes around the sun. True or false?"

"Shut up." He rolled onto his back. "People don't need to know that shit."

"Do you even know?"

"Yeah, I know! The earth goes around the sun."

"The moon goes around the earth. True or false?"

He hesitated. "True."

"The Civil War happened in 1945."

His silent glare took her in. He didn't know. Of course he didn't. Sandra at once felt a surge of guilt. Why should she hector him like this? He wasn't very smart, and she knew it. "That's false," she told him, abashed.

"Whatever," he said. Embarrassed.

But some of the time he actually studied, and she didn't want to interrupt the hush that fell over the basement, with Thomas, this beautiful guy, lying in front of her, his spine a series of gentle humps under his skin. Now and then Sandra caught him staring at her, sideways, with his head in his hands. Did he mean her well? Probably not. But he looked sort of harmless lying there, and his gaze had a perfect and total emptiness to it, which gave his face a brilliant, almost unnatural loveliness. It was hard to look away. Hard to keep from getting up from the sofa and kissing him ten thousand million billion times. But most of the time she managed. On her finals she got all A's, as she always did. And then school was out.

As she had done the previous summer, she worked behind the counter at the Miller Community Center. She answered phones, accepted checks from middle-aged men enrolling their teams in softball tournaments, checked out equipment. The supply of gray-white softballs in the cloth mailbag dwindled weekly, and those that came back showed up muddy, their threaded seams clotted with the orange dirt of the playfield. Each aluminum bat had *Miller Community Center* etched haphazardly into its barrel, the letters wandering in a maddening way far from level. Each basketball on the rack was known to her from last year, each owning its particular brownish tinge of leathery wear, each too smooth or too rubbery, none perfect, all nudging the mind in some unpleasant way when she handed them across the counter. She was becoming snobbish, she suspected, toward the imperfect world of objects; she was spending so much time around Thomas that she now expected everything to be as pleasing as he was.

It wasn't the worst job in the world, though. The pinging of basketballs and the echoing conversations of boys filled the corridors, and the big double doors crashed open every minute or two. Someone was always shouting, usually the black guys who came in from the neighborhood and dominated the courts in their mostly friendly, loose-jointed way. She basically just had to sit there, and she could shoot baskets on her breaks. For the first week of summer she worked on her baseline turnaround: back to the hoop, fake to the baseline with the left shoulder — it had to be quick — then pivot the other way and shoot the fade. She had trouble getting the lift off the pivot, but when she did the ball found its way as though guided on a string.

She had fifteen minutes of this twice a day, plus forty-five minutes for lunch, when she could usually get at least one game in with the black guys, who knew her. She stayed on the perimeter then and waited for the ball to find her, as it did once in a while, and since no black guy would deign to guard her, she usually made her shots. She didn't try to go inside against them; she took what they gave her. They didn't want to have to defend her, so she didn't make them. It was fair. She knew her place. She was actually better than most of them, but she didn't need to show off.

When Colleen wandered in, wearing her white cap and denim skirt, she attracted as much attention as she would have if she had been wearing a bikini. Maybe, Sandra guessed, that was part of the point. "You've got cars, right?" Colleen asked, leaning over the counter. "You got a motorcycle I can check out?"

"I wish."

"Shotgun? Vodka? Pornos?" She lowered her voice and held out her right hand to show a thin gold band on the ring finger. "You would not believe what they're making me do. You know what that is? You have to guess."

"They made you get married?"

"It's a chastity ring." Her hand was stubby and pale, and the ring pinched her flesh. "They made me take a vow not to have sex until I'm married."

"That'll work."

"Well, exactly. Because you know I take what they say very seriously."

"Don't they know they're morons?"

"They should? But guess what? They're morons! Which means they don't even know they're morons. It's just great being me sometimes. Next week? Bible camp. Everyone's favorite two weeks in Idaho."

"Two weeks?"

"Did I say two weeks? I meant ten years." Colleen muscled the ring off her finger. "You know what this makes me want to do — it makes me want to go sleep with somebody I've never even met. And they're so stupid they can't imagine that it might actually have that effect on a normal human being." She passed the ring across the counter. "You want it?"

"Nobody wants to have sex with me."

"What about Mr. Perfect?"

"It'd be too weird." Was that it? "*He's* too weird," Sandra said.

Thomas occasionally came by the gym too; it was only a mile from his house. As always, the sight of him struck contradictory chords in her heart. His jeans hung low on his hips, and his ribbed V-neck tank top showed the sweet hard boniness of his chest, and his puffy black jacket rustled as he leaned over the counter, bringing his breath, with its smell of water and wax. She wanted to leap on top of him, and she wanted to laugh at him.

"You got a basketball?" he asked.

The rack was three feet behind her, half full. "Wait," she said, "let me just check, okay?" She swiveled in her chair, waited, turned back. "No."

He rolled his eyes. "Can I get one, please?"

She turned again. "You have to sign for it."

He did. "You want to play?"

"I can't right now."

"Come on, I'll school you."

Through the wire window she could see a cluster of black guys milling around, shooting: Terrell, DeShawn, Om'ma, two others she didn't know. "Go run with those guys. They need someone for threes. You can school them."

"I want to play with you."

"I'm working."

He threw up his hands. She watched him saunter into the gym. He shed the jacket and hitched up his droopy jeans. With a sudden fluid gesture he lifted the ball into the air; it struck the side of the backboard and rebounded into his hands. She rapped on the window. *Nice shot,* she mouthed.

"Shut up!" he cried.

A game began. He was, Sandra was relieved to see, a terrible player. When the ball came to him he invariably shot, no matter where he was, and he always missed wildly. Soon DeShawn and Om'ma stopped passing to him and he was left to run aimlessly around the perimeter of the court, his hands in the air while he shouted *Here, here!* DeShawn gave her a look through the glass and saw her laughing and started laughing himself, with a secret little grin. Ridiculous. Thomas's signature on the form, she saw now, was cretinously huge, as though he had just learned it that morning. As he ran his pants kept sliding down, and twice he fell, tripping on his cuffs. Still, he moved with a notable grace, as though gravity had less of a claim on him than on most people, and once, when he happened to be under the basket and the ball fell to his left, he gathered it up with his left hand and took one big step and then, with a quickness that seemed superhuman, launched himself into the air and dunked the ball with two hands. Hanging on the rim, he looked around with surprise, and when he landed

[241]

again his pants fell all the way down, showing a long white pair of boxers. "How you like me now?" he shouted at her, pulling up his pants. "How you like me *now?*"

She couldn't dunk. She would never be able to. It wasn't fair, was it? Through the glass Sandra stuck out her tongue at him. DeShawn said, "That's some mad rise," and hopped up to straighten the net.

Afterward Thomas leaned against the counter again. The sweat was beaded on his forehead, his shirt was damp, but still he was almost odorless. "That's right," he said, "that's right, that's right, that's *right.*"

"You are like the worst basketball player I've ever seen."

"Sha, you see me out there!"

"So the only way you could possibly make a shot is to actually put it in the basket."

"Psh, you wish you could do that." He handed the basketball back across the counter. "How come you work here if you never play, man?"

"I play sometimes."

"What you get paid?"

"Eight bucks an hour." Did he think this was high or low? He didn't say. "Why, you want a job?"

"Sha, no." But in the heat of his accomplishment he took a long pink application from her and went over to a chair, where he worried over it with a ballpoint. He was not, Sandra knew, an ideal applicant.

That afternoon Norma came up to her desk, holding the form away from her by its corner. "Who *is* this?"

"A guy I know."

"He listed you as his reference." Norma, white, another lesbian, wore polo shirts fifteen years out of fashion. With the collar up, even. She was smart and goodhearted, not dumb, so why the Izod problem? "He's never had a job before, according to this."

Sandra shrugged. "Don't ask me."

"We don't even have any positions."

"I actually told him to apply."

"Oh, honey, why? Is this a boyfriend of yours?"

"Sort of," she acknowledged. "Yeah."

"Oh." Norma dropped the paper on Sandra's desk, then picked it up again. "Would he be a good substitute?"

"He's not like a criminal or anything. He just moved here."

"Would you vouch for him?" Norma's brown curls shivered; a thrill overtook her whenever some do-gooding came into view. She was known for handing out keys to untrustworthy boys who trashed the break room late at night and stole dumb things like boxes of candy bars. "We could try him out, if you think it'd be a nice thing for him."

"Sure."

"Let me think about it," Norma said. "We need more good subs, don't we? We do."

But Thomas, when called to come in, said he had found other work. Sandra doubted it. He was always home when she called, and he was always there when she went by to see him, so she assumed he was lying. And when she was honest with herself, she could admit that she didn't really want to see him playing basketball again. It was not just the unfairness of it, but the strange ease with which he had launched himself into the air, the lightness with which he had dropped again — it hadn't looked right. He had looked, in midair, as though he were rising on a wire, and the more she thought about it, the more it gave her the creeps. It was unnatural, the way he had moved. Alien.

Meanwhile her parents were acting very strange. Her mother was spending more and more time running, and would come home with her pants full of flyers and a strange, exhilarated strain in her voice. "Are we moving?" Sandra finally asked.

Her father said, "No," and her mother didn't say anything.

"Just in case I get a vote? I don't want to move."

"We're not," her mother said, and dropped the flyers in the recycling bin.

And every night her father mounted the stairs to the attic with his magazines and every morning he came down again, but this did not seem to indicate some separation between her parents; instead, the two of them seemed closer, and more demonstrative, than she remembered seeing them in a long time. Now and then her mother would give her father a glance of such encompassing fondness that Sandra felt compelled to look away, as though she had surprised them naked.

At the same time Sandra felt herself ballooning up — getting stronger, taller. She hadn't measured herself lately, but she was definitely six feet tall by now — or it felt like it, anyway; she felt as though she could see farther than she had been able to before. The police traffic in front of Mr. Harstein's house died down, and one day an empty moving truck appeared at the bottom of the street, and a crew of movers filled it with odds and ends from Mr. Harstein's house: a rolled-up carpet, a chair, a mattress, all of them wrapped in opaque white plastic. To hide the bloodstains, she imagined. Also a series of boxes, all identical, marked with the word AUCTION. Could they sell the man's belongings? Still no relatives had been found.

The idesia tree had settled into the earth; Mr. Turgerson came out in the evenings to water it, the green hose snaking across his sloping lawn. In his suit and tie he always seemed to be dressed for an event; Sandra, coming home from work, made it a point to wave at him. "I like your tie," she told him. Bowing, he answered, "And good evening to you, darling Sandra, good evening," and directed his hose at the tree again. It was such a small thing, so why did it make her feel so lovely, so at home? "Good evening," she would reply, and take herself up into the house.

THREE

17

YEARS AGO Henry had spent a long weekend stapling insulation between the attic rafters, old fir two-by-fours which, over the blind decades before he and Ilse had taken possession of them, had wept a beaded amber sap, so Henry had come down at night with the smell of that resinous liquor along with the chemically dusty Fiberglas on his hands. Then he'd hammered up the drywall, and the rafters were hidden forever. A shame. He still thought of them when he came up to the attic to sleep: his line of nail heads was not quite invisible beneath the drywall tape.

He had always liked half-finished houses; Wedgwood when he was growing up had been a neighborhood with occasional empty lots, and as they had filled with new framing, Henry had observed the walls and beams going in, defining — in the innocent space of an old weedy yard — a living room, a kitchen, a garage, where nothing had existed before. Those brief weeks when the structural wood was visible in the open air had seemed to Henry a glimpse into the heart of things, the secret, true ways of the world, and while the final houses, identical in their Norwegian brick and porthole windows, invariably disappointed, he would carry away the knowledge of the pure pine geometry that was the heart of these houses. His houses, in a way.

This attic had been the children's playroom for years, and it was only slowly occurring to him, now that he slept up here, that no one would ever use the NFL Electric Football again or the Malibu Barbie House, both stowed in the particleboard shelves against the far wall, or the SuperStar Slot Cars, which had never worked, and the Tinker Toys could probably go to Goodwill. Someday, maybe, when they had lost their sentimental appeal. But not yet.

Darren and Sandra crept up in the late evenings to see him. Could she borrow the car tomorrow night? Could he get a ride to Greenwood Lanes on Saturday? Calmly they looked him over for signs of trouble, which Henry, with concentrated blandness, refused to display. Everything was fine, he said. "I'm just talking in my sleep," he told them, "so I'm up here until I stop." A clock radio, a water glass, his white *Current Contents*. The futon. The secret sweet smell of the hidden rafters. The children investigated his magazines and his clock radio, peered at his wooly slippers, saw nothing unusual, and went away, it seemed, convinced.

From the attic windows he and Ilse could just barely see the frilly tops of the fireworks on Sunday night, the Fourth of July. The explosions, arriving seconds after the flashes of light, were filtered through the trees and shook the dried-out old putty in the windows. Henry had always loved fireworks, and it was nice to have his wife standing beside him at the glass.

"Happy Independence Day," she said, kissing him. "I miss you down there."

"Not exactly, you don't."

"But I do," she said. "I really should bring up your tape recorder — we could go to a linguist and see what you're saying."

"I used to sleepwalk," he told her. "I used to pee in my mom's grapefruit trees."

"Well, don't do that."

A wordless pause ensued. He snaked his arm around her waist. "Care to linger?" he asked.

"Henry," his wife said, reaching for him, "you become such a cornball when you're horny. I think all the blood leaves your brain."

"Some of it does." Sex against the attic windows, in the dark, while they watched the end of the fireworks, was a novelty. But his removal from the marital bed seemed to have enlivened his wife's interest in him; in his displacement, their sex life had revived. When they moved to the hard futon across the room, its slats were palpable beneath the cushion, reminding him of their earliest days together, in the apartment in Wallingford, and the sounds that carried up to their attic window now seemed to arrive from that other, lost world, where nothing too serious had been required of them. In the upward-slanting light from the street, Ilse's breasts cast shadows onto her shoulders, and her body shaded a looming double on the angled ceiling. When she left him he would sink effortlessly into sleep, as if he were being lowered into a well, but downstairs in the morning his children would greet him with gawking stares and half-smiles.

"You sound so weird when you do that talking thing," his son said, laughing. "It's hilarious."

"It really is, Henry."

"Still?"

"Oh, it's worse than ever."

"No."

"*Yes!*" they all cried.

Singled out, he had to play the boob. "I think you're all inventing this for some reason."

"Bo bo bo bo bo," Sandra began, and then was joined by Darren: "Bi bi bi bi bi."

"You're making it up."

"It's so fast, is the funny part," his daughter told him, delighted. Why delighted? Because he was showing himself to be ridiculous.

"You sound like an auctioneer," Ilse said.

"I do not."

But his family, in hysterics, nodded their heads in unison. "You do!" they cried. "You totally do," Darren added admiringly.

He remembered nothing. It was hard to worry about something he didn't remember doing, but he didn't think it was a good sign. "Whatever it is I'm talking about," he said, with as much dignity as he could, "I'm sure it's very important."

"Bo bo bo bo bo!" they said.

And then all at once — or so it seemed — William started getting better. His color began to brighten. His breathing became more regular. When Henry arrived one day halfway through July, William was bright-eyed in bed, smiling. Happy.

"If Jason looks into a mirror and touches his left ear, the image of Jason touches its right ear — true or false?" Henry asked.

"Duh. True."

"Okay. The third vowel that appears in this sentence is the letter *e*."

"No, it's *o*."

"Choose the word most nearly opposite in meaning to the word *fend: absorb, disperse, intensify, reflect, halt*."

"Absorb."

He looked at his wristwatch: six minutes, on a test designed to take ten. All the answers right. Well, William was a smart kid. But two weeks ago this sort of thing had taken him twenty minutes. What did it prove? Nothing, exactly.

Next was a reflexometer Henry had acquired from Edward Frost in neurology, a laptop device with an LCD screen and three large red buttons, on which William scored better than he had the week before; then a period when Henry read off a list of numbers and asked William to repeat them; then Henry peered with his otoscope into William's luminous ears and his pupils and affixed his stethoscope to his chest.

"Well, you seem pretty good, buddy," Henry said. He suppressed a rising leap in his chest.

"Yeah?"

"You're better than you've been in a while."

"I know. I can sort of feel it. It's like" — he took a breath — "it's filling in."

"What is?"

"I don't know. My body or something."

"Can you walk for me?"

He did. From beneath the sheets came an elderly smell, which William did not or appeared not to notice. He wore blue sweat pants and a heavy orange sweatshirt that hung in folds over his elbows. "Watch this," he said, and lifted his chicken-bone arms out, raised them slowly over his head. Concentrating, he lifted his right leg and stood on his left, his arms extended to either side. "You timing me? I got up to thirty-five seconds a couple days ago."

"Don't strain yourself."

"I'm not straining myself. This is actually pretty easy." He swallowed, swaying back and forth for thirty seconds or so, then lowered his foot shakily to the floor. "See? And watch, I'll go over to the door and back. Yesterday I did it in ten seconds." Barefoot, he began the long trip across the green carpet to the door with its glass knob. Five seconds out, five seconds back, leaning forward, shuffling more than walking. His arms worked feebly at his sides, and when he got back to the bed he leaned against it before climbing in and drawing the covers over him. "Okay," he said. "Now I'm a little tired."

"But that's pretty good." Henry felt the boy's pulse: elevated but not frantic. As though he'd climbed a flight of stairs at a good clip. "Enough for today, okay?"

"Tomorrow I think I'm going to try for the third floor. My room used to be up there. In the attic. With the Christmas decorations. And the . . . black-and-white TV. But no cable." William held out his arm. "You want to give me another?"

"How many is this for the week?"

"Just two. I'm being conservative," he said. "You do it better than my dad. It makes him nervous." With an avid eye William watched the injection, held the gauze against the loose skin of his forearm. "This whole thing," he announced after a minute, "makes them both really nervous."

"Just don't overdo it, okay? We don't know exactly what's supposed to happen to you right now."

"What's the worst that could? Happen." William licked his lips. "I die, right? So."

"Yeah, so relax. Don't try to do everything in a week and a half." Henry tossed the needle in the garbage, took William's pulse again. "Just take it easy."

"That other kid's alive."

"He's not you."

"But he's *alive*," William insisted. "It's working. You know the Parkinson's studies are all turning out okay."

"It's early days on those. And that's not a helicase disorder like yours is."

"The Langerhans trials are going well."

"That's not the same thing either."

"Feel my ankle." Shakily William withdrew his slender right foot from beneath the covers. "Feel that?"

Hickman patients developed calcium deposits in the soft tissues, and William had several, especially in the flesh of his right foot and calf. Henry felt for them now. Not marbles anymore: more like TicTacs. Holy shit, it *was* working. That kind of reabsorption shouldn't be happening; William's tissues shouldn't be capable of it.

"Okay, those do feel smaller," he said. "Boy, buddy, that's great."

"See?" William's eyes flashed. "See?"

"That's pretty promising" was all Henry would say aloud. Was it cruel to withhold optimism and celebration? He wasn't sure. There were no rules to follow, and there was no one he could ask. And the change seemed to be happening too suddenly. The mice were showing no effects — each of the fifty still sat black-eyed and incurious in its plastic cage, dutifully making its nest of paper and sawdust and eating the grain pellets and drinking from the plastic spout. The progeroid half were aging rapidly, as they should have been; the normal half were aging normally, as they should have been. To the mice, the injections seemed to make no difference. But it wouldn't be the first time a treatment like this did nothing much for rodents; genetic expression was a complicated affair, and any variation in the germ line could have cascading effects on the expression of every other gene in an organism. But in William, all at once, there were results to point to. Visual acuity, mental acuity, reflexes, urea clearance, those shrinking calci. He should call Charlie Calens, he thought. But no, he shouldn't. Charlie didn't want to know.

Downstairs he found Lillian and Bernie. "There are some interesting results," Henry told them in the kitchen, out of earshot of Elaine. "I'm going to tell you what they are, but I'm also going to tell you they don't mean anything, necessarily."

"Good results?" Lillian asked.

"They're good." He described them. "It could all be a coincidence. It could just be the normal ups and downs that he's going to experience from here on out."

"But you don't think so," Bernie said.

"No. I think it's starting to work." It wasn't false hope; he was almost sure of it. To be able to say these things was about the happiest thing he had ever done in his life. "I think he's improving."

"Oh my god," Lillian said, and a hand flew to Bernie's shoulder. "Really? Really actually improving?"

"A little bit."

"But really, really improving?"

"Yeah, a little." His eyes were wet, he discovered. "I don't know what it means for him in terms of longevity. But he's better. I mean, you guys can see he's better."

"He's walking." Bernie's voice was hoarse. "He's walking around."

"Keep him in bed as much as you can."

"He can do it now, though." Bernie was crying now. "I don't want to tell him not to do it."

"Have him go easy. We don't know what's going to happen next."

Henry left them with a hard embrace, Lillian pressing against him emphatically, her bracelets jingling in his ear, and Bernie's broad meatiness leaving an impression of heat and animal vigor.

At the office he filled Gretl in.

"Oh, Henry, it's *wonderful*." Her arctic eyes widened. "I can't believe it." She too hugged him. "Oh, I'm so happy," she said. "He's such a wonderful boy."

Henry was crying again — an old man, leaking tears everywhere he went. Well, as long as Lisa didn't see him, it was okay. "Yeah," he croaked. "Keep your fingers crossed."

They did, all afternoon, while William's blood swirled in the centrifuges and the bioreactors and was broken down in the PCR, and when the figures finally came back they showed what Henry and Gretl had already decided was true: the enzyme was present. His mutation rate was slowing. He was getting better.

Ilse's runs now took her miles from home. She ran down Union to Yesler, down Yesler to the International District, then into the warehouse district that began at the Kingdome and extended south along the water. "Eight miles," she said, hands on her hips, pacing, exhausted, on the driveway. Her T-shirt clung to her shoulders. "You would not believe what they're doing down there! It's all suddenly *glass*. And is it my imagination, or do all these companies do nothing? I see people in there sitting at desks, but I can't tell what they're making. Forget making, I can't even tell what they're *doing*."

"I think they mostly do nothing."

"But then where do they get the money they're spending?" She pushed sweaty tendrils of hair from her forehead. "Somehow I suspect it's my money they've got their hands on. Is it mine?"

"Are we missing any?"

"Every time I go on the Internet, everything is free. But if everything is free, how can they be making any money?"

"I don't know. Advertising."

"Can it really be advertising? But it's not like television, Henry, where you have to sit and watch the commercials — it's like a newspaper, you just keep going. I'm suspicious."

"Eight miles."

"Not bad." She daubed her nose with her shirt. "For an old, old, old lady. You know what I was thinking? We should probably buy a Humvee, don't you think? I saw four of them today. *Four.* That neighborhood used to be just carpet stores. Oh, don't, I'm too smelly."

"You're sexy."

"I won't have sex with you again until you buy me a military vehicle."

"I've got a military vehicle for you."

"There you go again!" She embraced him. "You look happy."

"William's getting better."

"Really?" She held him away, her eyes bright. "That's *wonderful.* Lillian and Bernie must be ecstatic."

"They are. We're taking it slow, but we're definitely getting results."

"I can't tell anyone, of course."

"No."

"I wonder," she mused, "if I have an ethical obligation to rat you out, dear husband."

"You wouldn't."

"Never in a million years. But I must be violating some term of my contract. That would be interesting to know. As if I care." She swiveled her hips and looked across the lawn to the Turgersons'. The top of Saul's new tree was just visible, spreading its broad, pale leaves from spindly dark branches. The sight of it brushed Henry, but beside his wife, in the success of the day, he felt the tremor move through him quickly. "And you still don't think," Ilse asked, her heated arm around his waist, "there's a danger?"

"To whom?"

"To him. Or you."

"He was so sick, it wasn't going to hurt him much. And now that it's actually working, I'm going to keep it up no matter what happens."

"You should tell Charlie."

"Charlie doesn't want to know. But he's not going to say anything."

Left unspoken between them was the very real chance now that Henry might be on to something profitable. It was, when he thought about it closely, faintly unsavory. He was not a businessman. He had no head for negotiation. Orphaned, he had sought to prove himself valuable to the world, but he found it awkward when called on to state this value. Like so many basically good men, he mistrusted his own heart and felt that official accountings of himself invariably overstated his worth. But now he felt a surge of power, of possibility. He could *cure* people. He had never felt this way before. He could do anything. Say anything. He felt a businessman's blood rising in him, confident, capable, assured. "So, no," he told his wife, there on the twilit driveway, "I think we're okay."

He was — as long as nobody said anything. In this area he would have to rely finally on the forbearance of those who might talk. Charlie. Gary might eventually catch on. Justine Jones might. Chin or Victoria, just conceivably. And Lisa, who had guessed about Thomas, had already hinted that she thought something was going on. Of these people, Lisa worried Henry the most, especially because she was not one to keep her theories to herself.

But the truth was that everyone in the Health Sciences building had his or her own project, and if they thought of Henry at all, they thought of him as a solid doctor, a little on the fringe of things once in a while but certainly ethical. He had earned this reputation. And Lisa was known as a gossip, which helped; Henry would be able to deflect people — for a while — by saying in a friendly way, "Lisa's got an exaggerated idea of things" and leaving it at that.

But since Lisa had talked to Gary, Gary had probably talked to Gunnar Peterson. This was not a bad thing, necessarily. He could use Gary as a messenger. And it wasn't long before Gary called him back.

"It's not six weeks yet," Henry protested halfheartedly.

"Yeah, I'm calling with a heads-up, Henry. You heard from Peterson? I think somebody gave him the news about your boy."

"Somebody! I wonder who."

"Listen." Gary lowered his voice. "I had to tell him something. I guess he'd heard from somewhere else. I told him the condition's too rare to allow for an asymptomatic positive, which it is — I mean, the odds are astronomical. So I might have bought you a little time before you hear from him. Maybe."

"You told him."

"Shit, Henry, he was going to find out anyway. Please. You know what you've got yet?"

"It's a new helicase. I think it's repairing the Hickman damage, at least. But I have a feeling it does something else too."

Silent, Gary waited.

"You're not repeating this, I hope."

"No," said Gary feebly. "Scout's honor."

"I think we've got some kind of global repair mechanism. Some sort of preservation engine. This kid's cells are brand-new, this asymptomatic positive's. It's like he's got the same cells he was born with. The telomeres are long. His cytochrome oxidase levels are normal, but they don't make any mutagens, or maybe the mutagens are somehow destroyed by this protein. Anyway, we can't find any. We can't even force this kid's cells to make neoplasms. Not from mesenchymal cells, not from epithelial cells. We put his cells under UV and they're damaged, and then two days later they're repaired and we can't find any damage at all. Nothing. Put them through X-rays and we can kill them, but if they're not absolutely dead they regenerate." *Don't mention William,* he had to remind himself. *Do not.*

There was another long moment of silence as Gary took this in. Then he said weakly, "You need some facilities."

"I know. But I don't want to give it up to anybody. It's the most exciting thing I've ever seen in my life."

"Sounds like it."

"You should see this kid."

"Henry, please, make a deal. Everybody wins. Gunnar'll pay. He's got the money. He'd hire you tomorrow if you wanted — he hasn't got half the people he needs, you know that. He's thinking of setting up an office up there anyway. You could run the thing if you wanted. *Do* it, Henry. He'll pay. You doing rodent trials?"

"We've just started. They're not picking it up for some reason, which bugs me. If we're encoding some kind of superpowered helicase, we'd see it there, wouldn't we? But we don't. The mice are still dying. So I don't know what's going on. I'm tempted," he said suddenly, "just to give it to William."

"Oh god, Henry, no. That's a terrible idea."

The urge to confess was enormous. But he couldn't. "I know it is."

"Yeah."

"Remind me why," he said. Playing the part.

"Well, first, you don't know what it does. You could actually hurt him, you realize. It could cause him terrible pain. I mean who knows what it could do? You've got no idea. And second, you'd get in trouble. What would you do if they found out? They'd make you leave!"

"But what if it worked?"

Gary's voice dropped, became measured. "Listen, you understand he's going to die no matter what you do. He's a sweetheart, I know. But they get to that point and their hearts are so weak it's just a matter of time. They're too far gone."

But maybe not. "I've got this thing staring at me, and I've got William staring at me, and I'm sitting here not trying it."

"Yeah. Not trying things is half the job. Don't do it."

"I'm not," Henry answered.

"You should leave it that way," Gary warned.

Strange, how the temptation to confess was almost overpowering. Like the temptation to commit suicide, he thought. *I have something to say.* But if Gary found out, Gary would undoubtedly tell someone, and a week later they would be shutting down the laboratory and sending Gretl packing and upsetting the education of Chin; they would propel gum-chewing Victoria out into the world again; the cartoons on his door and the contents of his file cabinets would be appropriated for investigation and he himself would be the subject of a special bulletin in the *Journal of the American Medical Association*. Even with the secret so closely guarded, it was frightening, terribly frightening, really. The humming laboratory, the delicate clinking of beakers and pipe racks, the swishing of distilled water down the enameled drains — it was the music of his life. He would do it all again. Still, it was terrifying. No wonder he was talking in his sleep.

It was hard not to feel a little guilty when Giles came in with his mother. The boy was unchanged, and at age three he would be stable for a while. But how much better would it be to arrest his decline now — today? Would the helicase act more quickly in a patient with less extensive chromosomal damage? And was William really going to get better, as it appeared he was? How was that possible, if information on the boy's chromosomes had already been miscopied — where was all that lost information stored? Was there some overarching somatic bookkeeper that maintained a master file somewhere? Were corrected copies taken from uncorrupted cells? And how did the mRNA know how to do this?

"He's sleeping okay?" Henry asked Giles's mother.

"Yes, he likes the pills."

"They're not making him sluggish?"

"No, no."

"Feel okay, buddy?"

"Fine," Giles said from the stool. His hooded eyes flicked around the room.

"And Thomas is looking well."

"He's a terrible . . ." Hélène said, and gestured into space. "*Ffff.*" Terrible what? "Yeah, he's seventeen."

"Complains, complains, complains. He wants a job, but no one wants to hire him." She shifted her shoulders. "I was thinking you could possibly pay him. He has to come all this way once a week. You want him to keep coming here? He could use some money. One hundred a week, maybe."

"A week? Come on."

"For all this — ?" She gestured around. "You rely on him, correct?"

"Yeah. But really. It's not like we haven't paid you guys."

"Moving is expensive."

"And it's not like Giles isn't going to get some benefit from it."

"He's very special?"

"Thomas? He is." Should he tell her what the arrangement was, the fifty-fifty split? No; he had talked too much today already, so he held his tongue. "He's very special."

"One hundred dollars isn't so much."

A shakedown. What else would you call it? "Okay," he said.

"Yes. Okay, good." Mrs. Benhamouda nodded briskly. Deal done. "She is a nice girl, I think, but much too nice for him."

"Sandra."

"She is so *big*. Very tall."

"She has her mother's height."

"Your wife is big?" asked Mrs. Benhamouda, gathering up her bag and standing.

Henry, looking up at her with a rush of relief, said, "She's perfect."

18

I N A REST STOP south of Olympia they swapped the driving, and Sandra was allowed to aim the Accord down the middle of the highway with the cruise control pegged at seventy through the long, flat, rural miles. Boring driving. But better than nothing.

"Do they talk about things like Columbine at school?" her mother asked after sitting in silence for a while. "When I was your age we worried about the Russians coming, as they had in Hungary. We were given papers to carry around, to prove we were citizens. But we didn't think they would actually come into the school and shoot us dead. They would come maybe in the middle of the night."

"People sort of joke about it."

"But you don't worry?"

"They've got metal detectors."

"But what if the killers come in a window?"

"I don't know." The car surged; the gas pedal, under its ghostly command, sank to the floor. "We had that assembly."

"You don't worry? Even after Mr. Harstein?"

Sandra said, "I don't see what the two have to do with each other."

"Nothing," her mother admitted. She rearranged her long legs.

"Are there tall boys at this camp?" she asked after a while, looking at her sandals.

"Well, duh, usually."

"Black ones, probably."

Her mother could just say things like this, as if she expected an answer. "Usually," Sandra said.

After a minute her mother asked, "Do you think about Mr. Harstein much?"

"I don't know. Sometimes."

"Does what happened frighten you?"

She was suddenly aware of the feel of the steering wheel in her hands: a knobby rubber bone. "Do we have to talk about this now?"

"No, sweetheart."

They drove on. "What I can't believe is how nobody can figure out why he *did* it," Sandra said, with more feeling than she had intended. "He should have at least left a note or something."

"It's frustrating, isn't it?"

"Maybe it was an accident — he was like cleaning his gun or something in bed, and it just like went off? Or he was pretending and forgot there was a bullet in it. But obviously that's stupid," she said, mostly to herself. Her father's parents had died when he was not much older than she was now, and imagining the world without her parents opened a swinging trap door in her gut: Where would she live? How would she go to college? "We better not get a gun," she said.

"Of course not." Her mother rearranged herself, tugged down her shirt. "We have no need for one."

They didn't, her mother meant, because their neighborhood was a safe one. Did Thomas's parents own a gun? Possibly. He would be the sort to show it off, too.

"Now, the Whites have a gun," her mother was saying, "I happen to know, because they're afraid their Oriental carpets are going to be stolen. Apparently they're worth thousands and thousands of dollars — they actually had to buy some special kind of insurance. Or didn't *have* to, of course, but decided to. And then they got a gun too, as if someone would break in while they were at home and roll up their carpets and put them in the back of a van!"

"It's possible."

"They think it is. It's like people who are afraid they're going to be hit by lightning."

Sandra was still fighting the image of Thomas with a pistol in his hand — fighting the urge to duck as, in her mind's eye, the barrel found her. "Could we maybe like drop this subject?"

"Okay," her mother said, without protest. "Dropped."

She drove all the way to Eugene. It was a wet, changeable day, shot through with long shafts of sunlight that seemed, as they angled out of the clouds, to be fingering their way along the ground, picking out hills and power lines, considering them — illuminating them — and then moving on. Rain showers came and went. Far away across the glowing fields, white houses stood beneath clusters of trees. She loved traveling; in particular she loved traveling through open countryside like this. Her mind could wander, wander, into the imaginary grandeur of her future life. *Woolgathering* was the term for it, and she felt sometimes that she could spend her whole life this way, staring at the yellow line in front of her. The fat letter arrived from Harvard, she was drafted into the WBL, she walked onto the floor of Key Arena with the enormous scoreboard hanging above center court and felt, in her tripping heart, the truth of it, the arrival of the glory that was her due. Her unlived future life was grand and full of wonder. It was traveling that did this, loosed her mind into fantasy, and in such moments she seemed to be invested with so much vision and sentience that she was animated by something beyond herself — some gesture of consciousness that could grasp from the air the best of things and show her what was possible. Or that anything was possible. She was sorry, really, when they had to pull off the freeway in Eugene.

The Sonny McMaster Basketball Camp was held at the University of Oregon. There was a girls' floor in the basketball dormitory, and a boys' floor above it, and the coaches had a floor to themselves on top. "So here you are, sweetheart," her mother said, setting down Sandra's second duffel in the lobby. "Thanks for driving so much. I get so used to the scooter, the car seems so big, like a boat."

Flush with the glory of the drive, Sandra said, "You should stay overnight, Mom. Be fun. We could have dinner and whatever."

"You don't really want me to."

Didn't she? "I do," she insisted. "You have like four hours going back."

"I don't mind," her mother said lightly. "Hug now. You cannot still be growing."

"You're just shrinking."

"The old take up less space — it is one of our virtues," her mother said valiantly. But she did feel fragile in Sandra's arms, she and Sandra's father both. "You must remember, have a good time," she instructed, and she was off down the sidewalk to the illegally parked car. She wore white plastic sandals, and Sandra could see her yellow heels puckering as she walked steadily away. A big woman. The hair on the back of her head was mussed from the Accord's headrest. As though feeling Sandra's gaze, her mother lifted her hand to smooth it, then waved as she got into the car. "Bye," they said together, and she was gone. Sandra was seventeen, but she still felt a thick pulse of sadness in her throat. She had been left alone.

But the feeling passed in moments. She too was getting older.

Sandra's roommate again this year was Kimberly Spires, a white girl from Tacoma. Short and quick — quicker than Sandra would ever be. Kimberly had arrived that morning and taken the bunk by the window. She smoked, and was holding an illicit cigarette out the window. When Sandra entered, she lifted it in salute. "Shit, you again," she said. The plastic mattress was still bare and crinkled under her. "Thought maybe you got fat and stayed home."

"Hi."

"I took the good bunk. I thought you'd want me by the window anyway. I cut down over the winter, but as soon as the season ended, *boosh*." Kimberly exhaled into a fist and smelled her breath. She was pretty, in a hacked-haired, bottle-blond way, and wore a lot of purple eye shadow. Gazing up at Sandra, she had to tip her head back, exposing a throat with a surprising amount of pale fuzz. "So you get that one."

"What if I want the one you've got?"

"Too bad."

"Thanks."

"You *want* this one?"

"No."

"I got here first."

"It's fine," Sandra said. She didn't care, actually. "They'll kick you out for smoking."

Appraisingly, Kimberly looked at her. "You six?"

"I think so." Sandra forced down a smile. She'd been saving the new measurement for today — you got weighed and measured every year, and Sandra's yellow stat card, now eight summers old, came out annually from the camp's filing cabinets. "I don't know yet."

"I saw you got first squad. That's cool."

"It's okay."

"*Okay. Okay.* It's all right to be like excited once in a while. I brought you something." From beneath her bed Kimberly extracted a purple box of condoms. "I thought you might actually want to have some fun this summer."

"Oh my god."

"You on the pill?"

"There's a hundred forty-four condoms in there."

"It's family size! Or anti-family size, whatever."

"Did you bring any for me?"

"Shut up!" Kimberly's voice was raw, and her laugh was gravelly. "Fucking height, if I was as tall as you, I'd be first squad."

"You should stop smoking."

"I did. But it was *hard.*" She exhaled through the window. "It's not worth it. I like my smokes."

"Stunt your growth."

"Fuck, too late." Kimberly shrugged.

Last year, after Todd Grimm dumped her for Lisa Block, Sandra had arrived in Eugene in a shitty mood, feeling fat and titless and ugly. There'd been a guy, Bradley Quinn, who'd been nice to her, whom she'd developed a crush on, and eventually she had made out with him a few times. Bradley was from Astoria, Oregon, and had worn a faded pink tank top saying *Indians — 16,* and on court he'd sort of poured along, as though he were made of some secret military substance that was simultaneously liquid and solid. He was back this year, and approached her in the cafeteria line that night. "Hey," he said, prodding her. "You're tall." His hair was white: dyed.

"Oh my god," she cried, "what happened to your hair?"

"Nothing. What're you talking about?" He looked around, innocent. "Me?"

"You look like an albino!"

"Don't you like it?" Hurt, he put a broad palm to his head. "I'll shave it, then."

"Good idea."

"Seriously?"

"Don't you dare. You'd look like Chris Mullen. Please don't, for your own good." She heard the combative note in her voice. *Thomas,* she thought. She didn't like the way it sounded. "Actually, I like the white," she said.

"I can tell."

"No, I like it. It's cute."

"*Actually.*" He pretended offense, she saw, but like so many boys he was vain and easily complimented. "Really?"

"Yeah. It's nice." That was better, she thought; better to be nice.

The camp took eight- to eighteen-year-olds, two hundred total. Twenty-five staff members, most of whom knew Sandra from her seven previous summers here. This was one of the pleasures of getting older, she was discovering — you stuck around long enough and people just knew you. She'd always had difficulty making friends, no matter where she went, but she liked being known today, at this evening's first shoot-around, after dinner, as she walked across the lawn to the gym and stepped for the first time onto the almost empty first-squad court wearing her cut-off sweat shorts and her Garfield tank top, her hair in a scrunchy, the familiar Oregon Duck looking down from above the scoreboard. Such an embarrassing mascot, god. Who would ever go to Oregon, to be called a Duck? To wear *Ducks* on your chest all season long?

The girls' first squad consisted of the five best girls at the camp, and this year all the others were seniors, having finished high school and come back for one last year. Sandra was the only junior. "Fuckin' A," said Angela Pond, who was six-foot-six and had signed a letter of intent for Oregon State. The Beavers — even worse than the Ducks. But Angela Pond was frightening. In the post she was gigantic, with her big white round shoulders right at the level of your forehead. "You made it," said Angela.

"What'd you expect?"

"You look stronger, Moss."

"Kick *your* ass."

"Yeah. You love me. You want to be me." Angela embraced her. "You've been lifting."

"A little."

"Yeah? You could play the four. *I'm* not playing four." Angela reached out, felt Sandra's bicep. "That's good, girl. Maybe you'll be useful for something finally."

"Shut up." But she fought another smile.

The other first-squad girls arrived: from Portland, from Olympia, from Sacramento, all black — Jacquelynn Gibson, Theresa Williams, Lisa Marks. Sandra knew them all from earlier years, and among them she was happy. As the youngest, she felt conspicuous. They greeted her with surprise, but they knew her. They knew she was good. And together with her teammates she felt herself examined by the ninety-five girls who were not allowed to use the first-squad court — oh, it was wonderful, she thought, to be this big white girl with tiny breasts and big arms who was now easily at work, from the right side, on her baseline turnaround, which tonight was falling, falling, under the eyes of everyone, one shot after another, as though she would never miss again, as though she had always been meant for this one lovely thing and nothing else in the world.

The first night was always in some sense the best. Eugene was warm by now, so everyone could walk around in shorts. After the shoot-around the gym doors were left open to the cool evening, so moths fluttered to the ceiling and were lost to sight against the wire-caged bulbs; and that first night, after all the campers had been seated in their rows, the eight-year-olds, in their identical blue McMaster T-shirts, had to stand up and be sung to by everyone else, deafeningly:

> Welcome to McMaster camp!
> Welcome to McMaster camp!
> Welcome to McMaster camp!

to which the ten babies sang back,

> We're so happy to be campers!

which always made everybody laugh. After the great roar of the group as a whole, their ten little voices — so *cute!* — hung perfectly tiny and shy in the enormous gymnasium.

Then Sonny McMaster stood up on his bony legs, his Afro now mostly gray, and held his enormous hands up for silence, and took a basketball to half court, and turned, and breathed deeply, and with an unfolding heave like a heron taking flight sent the ball arcing to the distant hoop, where, as it did every year, it missed. He had not made one, everyone said, in twenty years — twenty-one, now. And this brave, hopeful shot, made before Sandra's own eyes every second Saturday in July since 1992, made her think of Sonny McMaster with a great wash of affection, because twenty-nine years ago he had missed a free throw in the NBA Finals to lose a crucial fifth game, and he was famous for it, as far as he was remembered by anyone at all. Every year she hoped he would make it, but with everyone else she laughed when he never did. Glorious in his gangly imperfection, he turned to them all, bowed, and shouted, "Welcome to McMaster Camp!" And they all shouted back, two hundred strong, "We're so happy to be campers!"

The next morning when she checked in for measurement, she was six feet, one inch tall in her socks. She wrote it herself on the worn yellow card and signed it with a blue flourish, *Alexandra Entwitten Moss,* and then, as she was allowed to, *first squad.*

Curfews were enforced and lights were out by midnight, though no one was remotely tired. The boys could be heard one story up, hooting out the windows into the darkness, their voices enlarged under the spreading maples of the quad. The nights here seemed vast, as though the sky were higher and could accommodate an enormous quantity of darkness. Crickets sounded in the grass. Rain could come at odd hours before dawn, but by breakfast the sidewalks were dry and a green smell of summer would be rising from the lawns, the most perfect smell in the world.

She loved it all, as she always had. Eugene was a smaller town than Seattle, and the dormitory was smaller still. Everything had about it an extra shine, the shine of temporary possession, and she did not mind that plastic mattress crackled like an enormous diaper when she rolled over, or that the showers were too strong, or that the water stung her skin, or that the white gymnasium towels, too old, smelled punky and sour. She did not mind when at night Kimberly lay in bed, smoking with her arm out the window, the red tip of her cigarette glowing like a brake light in the darkness; she talked, long after midnight, about her boyfriends in Tacoma.

"I was with this one guy," she said, "who got paralyzed in a snowmobile accident like a month later. It was weird. He got paralyzed below the chest, which means you can't ever have sex again. And so I was the last one he ever did it with, ever."

"Bet he was sad about that."

"He came back in a wheelchair." Kimberly exhaled. "He still looked pretty good, but. I mean he'd have to strap something on, I guess."

"Gross!"

"What? That's how lesbians do it."

"Gross! You'd know."

"My dad," Kimberly said, "has these like nasty porno magazines everywhere. For your information."

Kimberly slept noisily, with a smoker's rattle in her throat. From the window every night came the humming of a nearby cooling system and the echoing squeal of tires in the parking garage a block away. Trucks on the freeway growled, downshifting, far away in the enormous night. Footsteps sounded in the halls. Adult laughter came drifting down from the third floor, where the coaches lived — laughter, and the sound of ice falling into tumblers, like little windows breaking. To Sandra, as she lay unsleeping, this was the sound of paradise.

The previous year, when Sandra had been in the throes of her crush on Bradley Quinn, she'd spent a lot of afternoons driving around in his car. They'd drive off to Taco Bell or wherever, and she had spent most of the time wishing Kimberly Spires hadn't been in the back seat with *her* crush, a tall black guy named Arthur Dix, who'd almost never spoken but instead shrugged and *psssh*ed and draped his enormous arms out the car windows. From Oakland, Arthur had always seemed uneasy here in Eugene. "The *country*," he'd insisted on calling it, in his drawling voice. "Trees and shit."

"This isn't the country, you dummy," Kimberly told him.

"It — is — the — country." His wide palm slapped the sheet metal of the door.

"It's not the country!"

"You never seen a city, then," Arthur said.

"I live in *Tacoma,* you dummy."

"That's the country too."

"You've never even heard of Tacoma."

"Some country place."

"It is not!"

Arthur Dix was back this year. He too had made first squad as a junior, and on the adjacent court he could be seen flowing smoothly to the hoop. One, two, three steps from the top of the key to the basket. He was not the tallest guy on his team, but his body seemed to move with the least effort, as though heavily lubricated at all its slender joints. And he'd grown, Sandra saw. "Six seven," he told her at a break, walking over to see her. "You're all big too."

"Six one exactly."

"That's a big girl." He was sweating riotously, though not breathing hard. Above her, his elongated head with its heavily veined scalp suddenly furrowed. "I was about to say, you look different," he said.

"Really?"

"Older or something." Idly, he palmed the basketball he was carrying, waved it around over his head. In his armpit was a tight little tuft of black hair, nearly as sparse as her own. "You got a car?"

"No," she said. "Still."

"I got one this time."

"Really?"

"Yeah, I killed some dude. No, my brother sold it to me." He shifted his shoulders, rearranging his tank top. "Ugly, though."

"You look different too," she ventured.

"Cause I got a car suddenly."

"No."

"I got four more inches." Embarrassed, he looked away. "Taller. I don't want to be nasty with nobody."

"Taller," she agreed.

For the first few days she tried writing letters. But what could she say? *Dear Thomas, I am fine, how are you? Dear Thomas, I'm six-foot-one. Dear Thomas, My roommate has 144 condoms.* After the first line she was always faced with a long empty sheet of paper and nothing to tell him. It began to nag at her, and then she decided to forget about it. Would he actually care? Probably not.

Mail was distributed during the afternoon; on the second day she began to get postcards from her parents, little colorful flags left on her pillow:

Dear Sandra, We miss you very much. We have sold all your clothes, though. We're now all dressing in purple muumuus. Moo! Love, Mama

Dear Sandra, I found some dead squirrels in your dresser, just left them. Thought you were working on something? If not, let me know. Love your father. Love, your father.

Her brother sent one, crammed to the edges:

Hey sista, Things are totally the same here, no surprise. Sorry I didn't write sooner but I wanted to send you a funny picture. Instead here's a Space Needle for your collection. Whoopdy doo. I bet you forgot what it looked like. Well, anyway, this is not the best postcard ever written is it? I'm up to ninety pounds BTW, I am getting ripped! I hope you're having a good time and making all kinds of baskets. I would be there too but I'm too good for those guys, I would SCHOOL them with my Monsta Jamma! Love your brother Quentin Darrentino

She put them on her mirror and wrote back:

Hello, family members, Thank you for the mail. If Dad is wearing muumuus I'm never ever ever coming home. Those squirrels were going to be snacks for the road but I forgot! Oh well. Tell Darren he can have them.

This seemed a little sour somehow. She added *I love you,* but there at the bottom of the card it seemed too earnest, too dorky. Was it? She tore the card up and rewrote:

Hello, lovely family members, thanks for the cards. I knew Dad would eventually start wearing muumuus, but now I don't want to come home! Well, that's not true, I'm homesick as usual. Tell Darren he can have the squirrels. Love, The Queen of McMaster Camp

This was sufficient, she thought happily, and dropped it in the box.

When she returned to her room before dinner the next day, she found a letter from Colleen, whose square printing marched in heavily inked rows across the envelope and across the paper inside:

Hello hello!? So I thought I'd send you a letter, since you probably wonder what's happening back here. Well, nothing!!! Except my parents told me last night I was a perfect dove of heaven, and told me to guard the key to heaven with my love of Christ. Then they looked for my RING which I had stupidly taken off while I was beating my clothes on the rock by the riverside. Or maybe I was washing dishes, I forget. They made me go get it and put it on. I did. Am I a coward or just practical? Maybe both? Anyway, I seriously think this was the talk about SEX. They looked very serious, and as usual they thought I was very serious too because I was trying so hard not to LAUGH. Oh my god, to coin a phrase. This was after dinner and before prayer number 3,495,781 of the day together. I am evil sometimes, thank you very much, so I said I use that electric toothbrush as a vibrator when you guys aren't here. Well, not actually said it but I SAID IT with my EYES. I hope you find tons of guys there and bring one back for me. Would you mind terribly, darling? Just make sure he has 1. tattoos 2. a prison record 3. some kind of disease or 3a. a missing limb 4. a really fast car.

After a week Sandra didn't think of Thomas much at all. When she remembered him, she saw his shirtless form on the carpet in front of her in the broken sunlight and quiet of that dusty basement — the most perfect boy she had ever seen. What did he want with her? It was hard to say. In the mirror she was the same Sandra: tall, titless, big around the hips. No letters arrived from him — not a surprise. She would have winced to read them, she suspected, and was happy not to have to do so.

His gravity, Sandra discovered, was weak. It did not extend with its full force the three hundred miles to Eugene, and besides, he was probably already with some other girl anyway. Who? Simone Whitman, that cow. Probably. Picturing it, she was pierced by a stab of jealousy, sharp and merciless as a nail. But then she thought of Bradley Quinn and Arthur Dix, tall, loose-jointed, funny boys who were close at hand, and put Thomas out of mind.

Dear Colleen, she wrote,

I'd bring you one back, but they all want me. What can I say? Somehow I don't really miss checking out basketballs all day long. STRANGE! I'll pass on the toothbrush thing to my roommate, who's very into sex. Who isn't, I guess?! Tell your parents you're the Hand of Satan and that you're going lesbian and moving to San Francisco. You can blame it on me!

Arthur Dix's car *was* ugly, an old white Cutlass Sierra, and he was a terrible driver: hunched over and much too slow. "Hey, grandma," Sandra said, "watch out for that piece of air right there."

"I'm a black man," he said. "What'm I supposed to do, just drive to the jail every day?"

"I guess your brother's a pimp, with this car."

"No. That's racist, by the way."

"You actually got a license somehow?"

"Yeah I got a license. I got a license, I got insurance, I got this like flare kit my mom made me get." With his sinuous arm he gestured into the back, then grabbed the wheel again. "For highway safety, like I'm not just about to get dragged to death by a bunch of redneck motherfuckers if I get a flat tire. This state makes me nervous."

"You, nervous. Like a — a building gets nervous," she said, feeling stupid. "Like a tree."

"You never been in it except around here. It's just full of motherfuckers waiting for me to break down. Like I got a bunch of people just following this thing around on the freeway, like replacing my spark pulls or whatever they are, spark *plugs*."

"It's the country," she said. Fighting a smile.

"It — is — the — country."

They were alone, driving around the campus, through the generous leafy neighborhoods, on nameless streets. They had two hours free every other afternoon, and Sandra had taken to ditching Kimberly and Bradley — leave them to each other, she decided — and sneaking off with Arthur instead. His head just reached the ceiling of the car, where a coaster-sized bald spot on the red velour had already been created by the brushing of his round skull. He was most nervous, she saw, on these harmless residential avenues where the lawyers and professors and doctors lived, the neighborhood that was most like her own. But he was also nervous in the rundown part of town, where the black people lived, as though he were expecting to be recognized and flagged down. He was least nervous on the anonymous one-way arterials that ran the north-south axis of the city, past the McDonald's and Wendy's. This was where all the police cruised too, but Arthur was most at ease when he could see them. "That way at least I know where they are," he said.

"I'll just say you kidnapped me."

"Right out the house." He nodded. "That's good. Get me shot. They would, too. Look at that dude driving up to look at me."

"Wave."

"Wave, like I'm about to take my hand off the wheel." Steadily he aimed the car at the center of the lane. "Just don't start yelling."

"Help!" she cried under her breath. "I'm being carjacked!"

They had somehow agreed between them — without saying a word — that Kimberly Spires was not to be mentioned. Neither was Bradley Quinn. Last year's news. With Arthur, Sandra felt a companionable jauntiness; even when they were just cruising the strip at three in the afternoon in his Cutlass Sierra with its burned-oil smell filtering through the vents, she was happy. The red cloth seat was fuzzy beneath her thighs and gave off a faint, interesting odor of cigarettes and cologne, and the wide sun-baked arterials of Eugene suggested to her satisfied eye the nameless outskirts of some unknown city, where in her imagination she and Arthur lived, not exactly roommates but unquestionably together — a two-ball team, driving from one asphalt court to another. The ashtrays stank, and when she flipped their flimsy lids she found the sooty remains of a million butts.

With his enormous, agile fingers, Arthur manipulated the radio. "Not even a tape player," he complained mildly. "Ain't no good music around here."

"I think there's some Christian rock."

"Yahh," he cried softly.

He did not seem to be interested in her sexually, but it was hard to tell. For one thing, he never really looked at her, even when they were alone in the car; but she wondered if this inattention — his eyes so courteously misdirected — signified a kind of interest. His dark, involuted ears were snug to his skull in a way that made her want to feel them, and once she did, reaching over and bending down the top of his ear. It was firmer than she had expected, more rigid. "Quit," he said mildly, and ducked his head away.

"You don't like me?"

"I like you," he allowed.

But although they had plenty of time to themselves and hundreds of shady side streets where they might have turned off and parked, if he wanted to kiss her, he never did. It was disappointing. The sun-struck streets wheeled by, one after another, and then they headed back to camp for the afternoon games.

It might have been the fact that she was watched by Arthur and Bradley Quinn, or that she felt obliged to live up to the expectations of the first squad, or that she had finally reached the height she believed she deserved — had at last grown to inhabit the body she had always imagined for herself, and so could use it exactly as she pleased — but she was brilliant this year. Fast off the pivot. On the wing, shot after shot feathered itself through the net. Angela Pond set brick-wall picks and allowed Sandra to scoot free to the hoop or slide to the corner, where she had all day to shoot. The ball arrived in her hands and then it was gone again, not hers to keep. It was beautiful. Every afternoon she came off the court feeling she'd left some bright, complicated presence behind her — some intricate contraption made of light and geometry — and she was afraid, almost, to turn around, to see what was now suspended over the varnished floor. There was nothing, of course, when she turned: nothing. But there *was* something, a bright, beautiful, real object they had built together, now hanging invisibly in the air. It said nothing to her; it asked nothing of her. But it was there. Who could she talk to about this? No one.

> Dear Sandra, This is a real quote from Freda: "You are a hostile man. I can tell by your haircut." Just like your grandmother! We miss you. Love, Dad

Love, love — it was so easy to write. She answered:

> Dear Dad, You're not hostile! Guess who really IS though? Wait'll she sees my new buzzcut! (Just kidding.)

Love, she wrote, and watched her pen hesitate above the card. *Love. Sandra.*

Then, late one night, Sandra was awakened by a knock at the door from the proctor, a smoke-smelling, middle-aged woman. "Somebody for you on the phone," she was told. "He says he's your father."

"On the phone?" She sat up in bed. "What time is it?"

"Two," the proctor told her. "Come on."

"Is something wrong?"

"He didn't say."

Kimberly, a shape beneath the sheets, sighed into her pillow. Standing, Sandra put on her robe, and with a tendril of fear developing in her chest, she followed the proctor through the hallway and down the stairs. Her father? Had her mother died? Had her brother died? Still blurry with sleep, with her heart clutching beneath her ribs, she picked up the black receiver from the desk. The lobby, stark in its middle-of-the-night emptiness, its couches rearranged before the television, the carpet swiped with vacuum marks, seemed a frightful place, where anything might happen, unobserved.

"Dad?"

"Hey," said a voice on the other end.

"Who is this?"

"Nobody."

"Thomas! You asshole!"

"*Sha.* What're you doing?"

"What do you want?"

"What're you doing down there?"

"I'm at camp. How'd you get this number?"

"Guess where I'm working now."

"I don't know. Where."

"I got your job. Norma's a lez, you know."

"Really."

"Sha, she's okay."

The proctor eyed her from across the room, her arms folded.

"Congratulations," Sandra said.

"When're you coming back?"

"A week."

"You know what else?" Conspiratorially, he said, "I still got that other job too."

"Yeah."

"You want to know what it is?"

"Sure."

"Sha, I can't even tell you."

"Oh, darn."

"You all playing basketball all day?"

"Yeah. I'm all playing basketball all day. That's right."

"You got another boyfriend there?"

"None of your business," she said.

"Some tall dude? Some tall black dude?"

"Yeah," she said. "I do. Okay?"

"You do? What's his name?"

"Arthur Dix."

"You do it with him?"

"Every night," she said. "Fifty times."

He took a breath. "Really?"

"Yeah."

"You nasty bitch." His voice tightened. "You serious?"

"Yeah." The thread of fear twisted in her again, but from this distance and at this empty, lightless hour, she was able to taunt him. "Yeah," she whispered. "I'm serious."

"You know what I am? Bitch? You know what I am?"

"What."

"*Everything*," he hissed.

She said nothing. The proctor, suspicious, began to cross the room toward her.

"I'm *everything*," he repeated. "You want to know what you are?"

She hung up before he could say it, but she heard the word anyway, following her up to her room, into the dark, where Kimberly still slept above the whirring of the air conditioner. It followed her into the gymnasium the next day, even as Arthur Dix practiced thirty feet away, his slender body twisting into the air; around the sunny streets it followed her, hovering like a cruiser in the Cutlass's blind spot; and only when Arthur finally pulled over into a wooded dead end at the edge of town and, closing his eyes, nervously began to kiss her, and allowed himself to be groped, and permitted his shorts to be slid down around his knees, did it begin to fade. He had brought condoms, and without saying anything about it they had sex in the back seat, quickly and not totally painlessly, the flare kit pushed aside. Naked, Arthur gave off a healthy, sweaty smell. His penis moved timidly in her, cautious. Surrounded by trees in its hiding place, the car was filled with a deep, rural, sun-green illumination; and as Sandra embraced Arthur Dix with her thighs, the car creaked and moved like an old mattress, just a little, beneath them, rhythmically. In this way the word *nothing* was replaced, in Sandra's mind, with the noise made by the rusty creaking of the seat, which seemed to say instead, *Hell-o, hell-o, hell-o,* in a kindly old voice — the voice of a troll from beneath a bridge, the voice of a toad from the bottom of a well. Arthur had short red strands of something in his hair, she saw. Fabric, she realized, from the ceiling of the car. *Dear Thomas, Guess what?*

19

S HE SAW IT a quarter mile away — a black Labrador trapped on the grassy median. Running back and forth, with its head bobbing up and down, it was looking for a break in the traffic. When it finally ran across the road a hundred yards in front of her, Ilse clutched the wheel. Up ahead a blue pickup hit the brakes, began to swerve, then straightened and hit the dog with a hollow, metallic thump.

The spray of bright blood was immediate. One lane over, the dog was churned beneath the wheels of the truck and emerged as a scruff of bloody fur, dead. She passed it a second later at seventy miles an hour. And Ilse, in that instant, was presented with a kind of vision: the dog's eyes, as in a comic strip, appeared to have been replaced with two Xs. She recoiled at the shock of it. In the rearview mirror the body receded, a black tuft, cars swerving, hitting it, smearing blood on the asphalt.

In that elongated instant Ilse remembered something she had not thought of in twenty years: the night Gregor Hals had come home drunk, carrying a large round package wrapped in butcher paper. It was heavy, solid, as big as a turkey. Silently, with a deadly look in his eye, he'd picked apart the twine and peeled away layers of brown paper as though preparing an artichoke. At the center of the package was a pig's head, dead white and waxy, pink only at its great rubbery snout and two eyelids, where the puckered flesh collapsed into the empty sockets. "So," he announced proudly, when it stood exposed, "this is what you turn me into. A dead pig. So I decided, why not just give you my head to keep around the apartment, since you've taken everything else already?"

"I have?" So young, she would have believed anything! "What do you mean?"

"I mean," Gregor informed her, "that you have no sense of fun." Satisfied, he turned away, picked up his keys, and disappeared for a week.

Good heavens, she thought, driving home from Eugene, had she ever lived like that? Was it possible? But yes, these very hands clutching the Honda's steering wheel had wrapped the head again and carried it four stories down to the incinerator, where she had pushed it whole into the flames. Expecting the smell of bacon, she had been disappointed; the furnace, an enormous iron octopus, had a tight seal and vented — not a surprise, on reflection — through the roof, where no one was allowed to go.

No sense of fun. But it hadn't been true then, and it wasn't now. Driving north alone, she felt a sudden press of happiness against her ribs. How far she had come from that sad basement! And how good things were, really! What on earth was she waiting for? She would quit Kreutznaer, of course. She would make something new of her life with Henry. She would let herself out of her glassy aerie and into the city again. She would rent a little storefront office in the International District and become neighborhood doctor to the poor. Or if not a doctor, at least an adviser of some kind. She could help people do their paperwork, tell old ladies which tests were necessary and which weren't. She could have a little file cabinet, a metal desk, a window, a telephone!

Yes, a filing cabinet, and brand-new folders, and a drawer of pens, and a pencil sharpener! Oh, she could! The bricked-over plaza at Testarossa rose in her mind's eye. As is true of most people, her early days as a free adult held not just a nostalgic but an instructive value; the person who had done what she had done then — moved to a new city, lived alone in a sunlit apartment, tended to the ruined bodies of the old — seemed the truest and best version of herself. It was the self that Henry had fallen in love with, after all, so wasn't it a self that deserved unearthing? Oh, it was. The heated draft of her sudden happiness rushed up the long stovepipe of her body and lifted — lifted! — the roots of her hair. Oh, what sudden and unexpected happiness! Oh, poor dog!

She couldn't quit work immediately, and she didn't want to announce her plans immediately, but she began making secret arrangements. She turned her glass-topped desk so she faced south. The workmen had finished their riveting on the roof of the new baseball stadium, and from the window she could now see tiny players in white and gray, like seagulls, practicing their footing on the new sod. White flecks — early spectators — spotted the green grandstands in the late afternoons.

"This'll be a good place to watch the Kingdome go down when they blow it up," Miriam said, at her side. The plan was to bring it down next March. "We could sell tickets."

"You would think they'd find some use for it, wouldn't you?"

"Oh, I know." Miriam, piously, stepped away from the window. "Half a billion dollars for the new one. Well, you should bring Darren to watch. He's fourteen? He'd love it. With Brian? First it was construction equipment, then it was guns, then it was exploding things, then it was girls. Thank god he got out of the house before we got an Internet connection."

"How is Brian?"

"Wonderful, I guess. Richer than ever." Miriam's son, twenty-five, worked for an on-line drugstore. "Of course it's all on paper. I keep telling him to sell. And he says, Mom, it'd be criminal to sell right now, I'd be a laughingstock. The earnings curve is — you know, he says it grows exponentially. And I tell him, What do I know, but the price-to-earnings ratio is all out of whack, there aren't any earnings. But that's the *point!* he says. Of course, it's his money. He doesn't spend it on anything. He still wears these awful clothes, although he did get a nice tie the other day — he didn't have a tie. I don't know. Maybe he's right."

"How many shares does he have?"

"Twenty-two thousand."

"At how much?"

"The stock's at two eighty-one. So that's . . . five point one million."

"Oh, Miriam."

"I keep telling my husband I'm in the wrong business," Miriam said. "But it can't last."

That figure — it was shocking, though it would have been more shocking two or three years ago. Now everyone — almost everyone Ilse knew — was at most two degrees separated from this kind of money, and not in a speculative, uncertain way as Henry might eventually be, but really, actually. On paper, at least. "It does make you wonder," she said.

"If you had money right now, would you buy stocks?" Miriam's voice lowered. "I'm not sure I would, to be honest."

"I'd buy a little bit of Amazon. Or — no," Ilse said, considering, still alight in her happiness. "I think I'd buy HomeGrocer and Kozmo. People like having things delivered. Especially all the professionals having their babies."

Miriam smiled. "I like Kozmo. We use them for movies. When I talk to Brian I try not to be a mother, but it's very hard. He doesn't believe it can all go bust underneath him, and I can't believe it won't."

"Five million dollars."

"Well, plus," said Miriam.

That's what it was like now. Money was everywhere. Every third person seemed to have retired on his investments. But were people happier for it? Some of them seemed to be. Like the Whites: Kevin no longer worked, and Jackie spent her days supervising the remodeling and maneuvering her new Suburban up and down the narrow street, a black-and-silver hulk, thousands of pounds of metal and rubber that drew Ilse magnetically in the evenings after she returned from running. Like so many evil things, it was very attractive. The bumper was a convenient height to stretch her hamstrings, and the dark metal, glowing under the crepuscular sky, held polished depths that invited her touch. The mechanical stillness of the enormous car was palpable in the diminishing evening. Moving, it was a hippopotamus, but motionless, it had the menacing grace of a panther. Warm from the day, the metal shaped itself to her palm. If the SUV gave Jackie pleasure, was it really a bad thing? Yes.

And they were everywhere, the neighborhood was full of them. One of the many pleasures of running was the long trip away from her house. She was too old to think poverty had any inherent virtue, but the trip down Union and Yesler was a relief. On Jackson the old brick hotels still stood, renting out their rooms by the hour. The indecipherable Asian signs that Jackie White hated so much filled Ilse's heart instead with a pang of longing, because she could not read them. Some version of her — some ideal version — could read Chinese, Vietnamese, Thai. Would she really want to buy dried mandrake root, salted fish heads, tea with tapioca balls bobbing in it? No. But if she set up a little office here, the rent would be minimal — it was far enough from the new green-glass blocks — and she would have any number of old women to look after.

It was possible, wasn't it? She could be a sort of medical social worker, someone with connections to all the hospitals in town who could advise the old ladies about what to eat, which doctors' recommendations to ignore, which ones to follow carefully. She could explain things to them that the doctors themselves did not care to explain. Crossing against the light with their string bags full of mysterious produce, these old Asian women did not look up to see her, a white woman in sneakers standing not quite six feet tall on the curb. They were stooped, all of them. Hunchbacked. The Asian diet did not provide much calcium.

Eighty years ago this had been a tony neighborhood, and the buildings still held remnants of their old style: ribbons of white brick worked into the red masonry crowns, marble floors in what were now insurance offices and travel agencies. Puget Sound was visible, and the salt air was spiced with the smell of frying dumplings. It was very nice. And office space *was* for rent: there were signs here and there.

One night while she was running, a sign caught her eye — a yellow printed cardboard notice in the bottom corner of a vacant storefront:

HARSTEIN PROPERTY GROUP
CONTACT _____

She stopped dead. To see the name here was a jolt. And to see below it the unsettling blank was worse. "Oh," she said aloud.

The storefront was a long dark space with a checkerboard floor, absolutely empty. The ceiling was hung with pipes, which had been wrapped in white paper. Traffic passed, reflected in the window. If Saul had not shot himself, she might have ended up in this very office, but now it was a corridor of her life that would never be opened, a corridor whose size and shape corresponded exactly with this tall, narrow space going back into the unlit depths of the building.

Experimentally, she looked up Harstein Property Group in the white pages and dialed the number. It had been disconnected.

She could still read the file on William Durbin, though there were large patches of opacity where Henry's work was beyond her and his notes were inscrutable. To encounter these blanknesses within herself was not particularly frightening; his work had always been far more involved than hers, and the science had advanced over the years she had been out of medicine. His handwriting was no neater than it had ever been, and paging through his notes, she had the sense of being inside his hands, the blue pen making its looping and untutored way across the page: *oc. fer. .027, mtl 1.22, p-oxide 7.81, calc. clear, ur. .0023! hmstel −3.45. Better.*

Better. It was thrilling to sit and look at the notes with Henry, his stubby finger occasionally landing on a particularly notable number. *"That,"* he said, "right there. That's impossible."

"What about the mice?"

"Still nothing." But this wasn't too unusual, and it did not diminish his excitement. He paged through William's file the way he paged through the album of Sandra's first year, with an expression of happy disbelief and a lingering fondness.

There was no question his work had changed him. He babbled, and he would stand at the window in Sandra's empty room, gazing out benignly at nothing, like a house guest waiting to be called to dinner. His own children were perfectly healthy, but his attachment to William Durbin had worn at him like a wasting illness. Hickman patients often suffered cognitive decline of one kind or another, and to Ilse it seemed that Henry had been affected sympathetically, becoming marginally less rational and more driven by emotion than he had ever been in his work. Why else the secret experimentation, the really quite profound violations of established ethics? *Disinhibiting* was the term. That William's death seemed to have been forestalled was great and beautiful news. But it had come at some cost, and William's death could not be avoided forever. Or could it? Neither of them knew.

But she was terribly proud of her husband and still took pleasure in him, in his body. For all her running, she had lost exactly six pounds, but the muscles in her legs and back now seemed to use their tension to alleviate the pull of the earth on her; her center of gravity had been lifted a few crucial inches and had arrived somewhere in her guts. The Greeks had imagined that thinking occurred in the intestines, that intestinal bubbling and groaning were the products of thought as the body turned food directly into mind. How sensible this was, really — how sensibly material! How unlikely that the inert goop inside the skull was anything more than a sort of oily ambergris thrown off by the eyes and nasal passages, the winding canals of the ears! Had she been a Greek, she would have believed it.

As her runs had lengthened, a stillness had entered her muscles; even sitting behind her desk all day she felt perfectly calm, the excess energy that had once hummed within her having been entirely spent on the Yesler hill. Sex was more fun with this solid, calm body to use, and after she left Henry prone in the attic, the big downstairs bed embraced her. With her nose at the open window, she inhaled the summer smells of earth and air, one fine, harmless breath after another. What was this tonic spreading through her? How far had this air traveled, to be taken into her lungs? *Einschlafen* did not describe it so well as the English did: to fall asleep. It *was* a fall: the consciousness letting go of its high perch in the skull and plunging deep, deep into the body. Into the gut, and out of sight.

Part of this happiness, she knew, came from exercise, and part of it from Henry's successes at work; but part of it also seemed to be coming from Jackie White. They had begun to see much more of each other, and the regular workout of Ilse's muscle of outrage was doing some good; unlike her other muscles, this one seemed to be diminishing with use. Jackie was not quite a friend. But what was she? A therapist, maybe.

The pillaging of Jackie's house was ongoing, and Jackie faced Ilse's continuing rebukes with a complacent wag of the head. "Eighty years ago is a long time, honey. You realize they were still putting horsehair in the plaster?" A shaggy chunk of this had fallen on the porch on its way to the dumpster, and Jackie shook it in disgust, a piece of bone with the hairy scalp still attached. "Horsehair in my walls! Not happening."

"So you're just blithely going around ripping everything down. What if they did that in Europe? Historians are going to be appalled."

"Oh, let them. See how much nicer this is? Very smooth." Inside, the harsh light of bare bulbs illuminated the new sheetrock in the dining room. "You know, eighty years ago people like you were complaining about the poor horses not getting enough exercise now that everyone suddenly had a car."

"That's another thing."

"Don't start talking to me about public transportation. Honestly, don't."

"Well, I think what you've done here is just . . . heartbreaking. Heartbreaking. Look at it! You've completely destroyed your house."

"Not completely. The fireplace gets to stay."

"A house like this is a public trust," Ilse said. Was she really this angry? She had felt guilty for saying these things at first, but it obviously didn't bother Jackie at all, so what was the harm? "Architecture is a public matter, even the architecture of your house."

"But surely not the interior."

"Of course the interior. Everything."

"You're so funny!" Jackie grasped her forearm and leaned toward her, exhaling a great warm breath. "You're *so* funny. And I know you mean it. Actually, you know, your place could probably use a little attention, speaking frankly. How long has it been since you replaced the wiring? We thought we were fine, and we found little charred parts everywhere." Jackie tipped her ringed hand at the walls. "We'd been having little fires all along and never knew it. Thinking about it now gives me the chills, ha ha. All that wood, the wainscoting — half of it was split and ruined anyway, and the rest would have just gone up in flames, *whoosh*. Really, it was no one's loss."

What was it about Jackie that attracted her? *Attracted* was not the word, exactly. Fascinated, maybe. Jackie was, if nothing else, very vivid.

While her husband Kevin was not. Now that he had retired from Microsoft he had the distant and distracted manner of someone who had walked out of a movie theater and been surprised to find himself in the light of day. He was a tall, stooped figure with a grave long face, with deep lines etched on either side of his mouth and eyes that drooped at the corners. His voice was deep and thick, and he migrated from one room to another with a somber nod and an air of recuperative self-regard: it would take at least another year, Jackie said, for him to recover fully from working there. "It gets in your bones," Jackie whispered. "He was in charge of the whole Windows Ibex team, which is why it took him so long to get out of there. They just wanted him to stay and stay and stay, and they kept offering him, you know, more and more money, so it just got harder and harder to go. The thing about money is that it's obviously never enough. I mean, you don't turn it down when it's offered. More is always better, no matter what — it's not like food. It's *money.*"

"I'm not dead, you know," Kevin said from the stairs.

"Not quite, muffin."

"I'm resting," he said. "I think I deserve a few months off."

"Of course you do." She turned her fluffy head to watch him come into the room. "You can take the rest of your life off if you want to."

"At least I didn't put a gun to my head."

"You would never do such a thing." She turned to Ilse. "They didn't get along, Kevin and Saul."

"We got along all right." Kevin drifted toward the doorway. "We weren't friends. He told me once I was a small man in a big man's body."

"As if he would know. I think you fit your bones very well."

"This was ten years ago." Kevin lifted his gaze to the ceiling, counting. "Eleven. I'm shorter now," he added. "I hardly talked to the guy for a decade. You all stayed with him," he said to Ilse, edging toward the doorway.

"Just once. He wasn't there very much. He was very nice to the children. He had a beautiful house."

"Unlike us, she means," said Jackie. "She thinks we're ruining our house as a historical document."

"The wiring was shot," Kevin said.

"I told her."

"We're totally rewired." He twirled his finger in the air. "We're on a T-1 line."

"And now they're both on-line all night long," Jackie confided, her chin down, "and don't ask me what they're doing, because I don't want to know what either of them is looking at."

"Oh, I'm sure it's nothing too dreadful," Ilse said. Was she sure? She seemed to be. Her new benignity apparently extended here too. An unforced concern for the shell-shocked Kevin, the neglected Jonathan, and the heedless Jackie rose in her like a breath. What would become of them? What would they do with the rest of their lives? None of them had the faintest idea, it was obvious, and to Ilse this suddenly seemed very sad.

Yes, Jackie and Kevin struck her as a strange couple, but there were lots of strange couples in the world. Her own parents, to begin with. In Ilse's memory, her parents had spent their entire lives at opposite ends of their apartment and had communicated by leaving notes on a pad by the telephone. Was this right? When she next spoke to her mother, she felt the question rising in her, but it was, as she knew it would be, an impossible question to ask. "Are you healthy?" she asked instead.

"What sort of question is that? It's none of your business. Of course I am."

"Do you need anything? Money?"

Her mother barked with laughter. "Don't worry about me," Freda said.

"I do sometimes."

"Oh, you do not." A ferry's round hoot sounded behind her. "Besides," she said archly, "I can live on next to nothing."

Were you happy, Mama? No, Ilse couldn't ask, and there was only one person left who might know the answer. She telephoned Tannie.

"We are having an interesting summer," Ilse said uncomfortably into the humming ether, and described the suicide and her new Vespa, Sandra's boyfriend Thomas, her mother throwing the dishes. "One after the other," she said and, having exaggerated by accident, felt compelled to soften it: "She didn't mean anything by it."

"She was making a point."

"Of some kind," Ilse agreed.

"Her point is, she can do whatever she wants."

"That's just what I thought!"

"You were right," Tannie told her. "Exactly right."

It seemed a generous thing for her sister to say, and into this opening she asked, "And you, sweetheart? What's been happening there?"

Sweetheart. Her sister turned the word around in her mind — *Liebling* — before saying, "Happening? Well, Jörg Haider is happening. The Freedom Party is happening. Even after Walter Reder everybody loves him."

"How are you feeling?"

"Me? Oh, the same. The grocery boys, they talk about Haider, they call him Jörg, as though he's a friend of theirs who will show up and give them something to do. It feels very familiar. Mama thinks so too — she says it's the same. It's the bravado he has. He has the same secret that everybody knows."

"You've been talking to Mama. Good."

"We talk all the time." Tannie sniffed. "More than you talk to her, she says. I don't know, I have no opinion about you two. She told me all about the man who killed himself. Horrible. Your poor children."

"Your legs are better?"

The satellite sent Tannie's answer back strangely hollowed, as though she were speaking down a long tube. "You're changing the subject."

"I want to know how *you* are."

"Since you ask, I have a spot on my arm that refuses to heal, no matter what I do. My feet hurt. And if Haider wins, I'm leaving. I'll be coming to stay."

"Coming where? Coming here?"

"You do sound excited at the idea. But why not? I can live with Mama. I'll rent out this place until someone else is president. I cannot live in Haider's Austria — it will simply kill me to turn on the television every night and see him acting as though he is not a monster. Waldheim, now Haider? No, no, no. It's too much, I'm too old. I'll get too angry and I'll have a stroke."

"What about Papa's things?"

"Everything can go in a box."

Here was her opening. "Were they happy, Tannie?"

"Happy? Mama and Papa?" Tannie paused. "I don't have the first idea. I don't think they operated on that principle. As you know, she often prefers good function to good form. If things are working, she doesn't much think about them. Papa never objected to anything in his life, so I think she assumed everything was working. What a funny question."

"Is it funny? I was just wondering."

Tannie was sharp. "It's Henry. Something's wrong."

"No! Just the opposite. I was just feeling sort of sorry for her, because I'm so happy with him."

Her sister calculated the truth of this and said, "Sorry for her. Well, if you must. It won't do either of you any good."

"But it's just too sad," Ilse said, feeling foolish, "to think of them living together all that time if they weren't happy!"

"Everyone's happy sometimes," Tannie said offhandedly. "I'll send you something you can use. When she's being proper and terrible, you pull it from your pocket and show her and she'll just pop like a balloon."

"What is it?"

"A weapon," Tannie said.

Two weeks later a stiff, flat envelope arrived, sealed with strapping tape and plastered with airmail stamps. Inside, Ilse found a flat package wrapped in layers of pink tissue. She undid the tissue, layer by layer.

Her sister had sent her a photograph. The photograph was of their mother, naked, reclining on a couch, facing the camera with her chin up. She was not smiling, but a liveliness in her face suggested she had just finished speaking. Her eyes were bright. She was resigned to having a body, her expression said, and having been saddled with such a thing, she might as well resign herself to its pleasures as well. She was propped on an elbow, with her hair in a complicated mid-thirties curl-and-drop. She had not been a large woman. Her breasts were small and dark-nippled, and behind her eyes was the terrible innocence of any historical figure, looking out through long-vanished air. If she was twenty-five, then it was 1934, and the world was already burning.

The photograph had yellowed slightly over sixty-five years and had curled at the edges, and in the open air it smelled richly of their father's library. And oh, how that room rose before Ilse — the window with its view of the tiled rooftops, and the cobwebs in the high corners that shivered when the sash was lifted! She did not recognize the sofa, but the picture had been taken in their apartment, without question: there in the background was one of their radiators. Had they been in love? They must have been, to do such a thing, and to keep such evidence for so long. Her mother. Not a weapon, exactly, but a means of disarming her.

Ilse, feeling tender and fond, had the photograph framed and took it to work, where she hung it above her diplomas. From the wall this girlish Freda gazed out the window at the water, as she did in life ten blocks away. Tannie here too? It wasn't that hard to imagine. Maybe Tannie would take over this job, with the elevator, the view, the light, the water. Why not? The Entwitten women, whatever their faults, were really very adaptable.

20

WITH SANDRA AWAY at camp, his son had unlimited access to her weight bench and had set about improving himself in earnest. Deep-toned clinking and measured, thoughtful grunts could be heard most evenings now after dinner, coming from Sandra's open doorway. Like any other boy, Darren was prone to fads, as though an entire culture were contained within him — as though he were not a person but a society of several million wherein sudden attractions were founded, nourished, and eventually discarded, burned out like a prairie fire that had consumed the available grass. When Darren was nine, Henry remembered, he had shaved his head with Sandra's help, not for any social advancement that Henry could tell but in order to see what it would feel like growing in. *Fuzzy,* he reported. At ten he had begun a coin collection, and Henry, to oblige him, had bought forty dollars' worth of pennies, Darren handing over the curled currency with a tradesman's confidence, knowing he was certainly not losing money and speculating that he could in fact be turning a profit, if he should run across a 1909 S-VDB or a 1955 double-strike or another such marvel. The exercise was repeated three times and turned up a dozen wheat pennies, none of any real value, and the pennies found their way into the bottom of Darren's desk drawer, worthless but unspendable, trinkets from the wreck of time. Henry remembered those sorts of childhood impulses and had fondly watched Darren come into them and leave them behind.

In this way it was especially strange having a teenage son. Henry felt that his old adolescent urges — to know everything, to collect everything, to have sex with everything — were buried in a very shallow grave. Darren was braver, more forward, than he had ever been; Henry had been more isolated, without a sister, thrown more on his own resources. As a result, he hadn't had a girlfriend until his senior year and had instead cherished the worthless odds and ends that made it to his room: a photograph of the Supreme Court, which his father had somehow acquired and passed on to him; a worn leather case for spectacles inscribed with the gold monogram BTR (the glasses themselves were missing but the case smelled richly of leather and another life); a heavy iron stapler that fanged huge stacks of paper with a predatory inevitability. For Henry, childhood had been a time of personal poverty, and like poverty, it had tended to highlight, and impart value to, the material possessions that happened to be at hand.

But Darren was different. He talked to girls late at night on the telephone. He had dates at museums. He lifted weights. He experimented occasionally with good manners. He improved himself. He watched Henry — Henry could see him doing it — when they were out in public together, absorbing the position of his body, the way he shook hands with the plumber, opened the mail, swept the porch. Watched him on the phone with the Durbins — watched the care he took, observed the joy he felt at William's improvement. It was cautious, but it was joy, and it made Henry happy to be able to show his son this, that you could be happy in the world.

Yes — that you could celebrate a little. He himself had never seen his father celebrating anything, and he still found it embarrassing to do. But he did it for Darren. And Darren watched him, watched him, and pretended not to be watching, and Henry went along, pretending with him. Acting natural.

But to see Darren at work on himself like this in the passion of his adolescence struck Henry a continuing blow to the heart. Four more years and his son would be off into the abundant world, taking his oversized jeans and backward caps and goofy music with him, never really to return. Would he even live in Seattle? Maybe, eventually. But Darren often seemed more comfortable in the world than Henry ever was. Older than Henry, in this way. He could live in New York. London. Murmansk.

Imagining this, Henry called the Durbins and got permission to ask Darren to go with them all to the planetarium, on William's first outing since coming home from the hospital. Darren, when Henry mentioned the idea, gave him a pained look, as though wondering what he had done wrong. "You don't have to," Henry offered, backpedaling quickly. "I just thought you might like to come."

His son's glance flicked around the room. "Why're you asking me? I thought he was like really sick."

"He's feeling a little better."

Darren pursed his lips, considered. "Yeah, okay."

"Okay you will?"

"Sure." He sat up from the red vinyl weight bench, his arms hanging. "Can he walk?"

"He'll probably be in his wheelchair."

Darren looked at him blankly. Was this too much, like the blood in the mattress? "I could push him," Darren suggested.

"Sure," Henry said. And his heart clanged in warning. Maybe this wasn't a good idea. If they became friends and William died, Darren would be one more person to miss him. It occurred to Henry, driving across town with Darren, that he was using his son as a good-luck charm. That he was obliging William, by introducing him to Darren, to stay alive — to keep them all happy. "We can turn around if you want," he said.

"Nah," said Darren, scratching his foot, "it's cool." And then, later, "Oh my god, their house is *huge*."

On the porch Darren shifted and pulled at his belt, but when Lillian answered the door he stood perfectly still and extended a hand to shake. His arm, Henry saw suddenly, was banded with muscle and as long as a boom. "Pleased to meet you, Mrs. Durbin," said Darren.

"Well, we're so happy you could come along. William was very excited to hear you were coming."

"Cool," Darren said. "Nice house."

"Thank you very much." She was dressed in a green linen blouse and her wrists were empty of bracelets; she was ready for an outing. "Bernie's bringing him down," she said to Henry, and then behind her came the sound of footsteps and Bernie appeared on the stairs, carrying William in his arms.

"Look who's here," Bernie said, and settled William on his feet in the foyer.

"Hi," said William.

"What's up," said Darren.

"Not a lot," said William.

"Cool," said Darren. The boys stood four feet apart without moving, and Henry resisted the urge to intervene, to explain each to the other, to justify his idea of having them meet. Bernie had vanished into the depths of the house and returned with the low-slung, black-tubed wheelchair.

"Doesn't he look good?" Bernie asked, and Henry had to agree, he did. Was it his imagination, or was there more hair on William's head? He had been standing there upright for almost a minute without showing any distress, and when he lowered himself onto the leather seat of the chair, it was a slow, controlled descent, and to all appearances painless. Thomas's enzyme was swirling in his bloodstream and giving the kid's cells a chronic kind of health, and if it was working this well, there was no reason to think it wouldn't keep working forever. "And Darren looks good too," Bernie said, extending a hand. "Not to be left out."

In the driveway under the clouds — it was a warm gray Saturday morning — William glowed with a brilliant pallor. He had never liked wearing hats, and the great exposed ball of his skull was a perfect vegetal white, like a bulb that had been turned up to the air. Together Henry and Bernie levered him into the van. "I want Darren to sit next to me," William announced when he was settled, and Darren did, folding himself into the seat.

"Have you ever been," Darren asked politely, "to the planetarium?"

"Not for a while. Now you" — William pointed at Henry — "on this side."

Henry put himself next to William opposite Darren and inhaled the scorched chemical scent of him, the fire that still smoldered in his cells. "Just make sure you stay on your side," he said.

"You stay on *your* side."

"Okay, but," Henry said, as grandly as he could, "you're touching me."

"I am not," said William gravely. "You're touching me."

"I am not." Henry grasped William's leg. Hard and frail, the skin a liquid envelope slipping around the bone. "I am *not* touching you."

The boy laughed — a reedy, strangled sound — drawing back his dark lips to reveal his blunt, grayed-out teeth. "Mom, he's touching me!"

Henry extended his arm along the back of the seat and rested it on William's shoulders, feeling with his palm the peculiar broadened shelf of the boy's clavicle. "There," Henry said. A few inches more and he put the hand on Darren's shoulder too, the hard musculature of it. His boys. "Now nobody's touching anybody," he said.

"I don't think so," William said. Rustling, he inched himself closer, then sank comfortably against Henry's chest. When the van began to move they were pressed together, William rolling helplessly against him; for a moment they were closer than they had ever been, William's dry papery scalp shoved beneath Henry's chin. Then William recovered and leaned forward and said to Darren, "To answer your question, it's been a long time."

In the parking lot there was a minute of fuss while the wheelchair was reassembled and Lillian loaded her bag, and then the five of them were rolling up the white wooden ramp and then down, taking two switchbacks into the darkened municipal hush of the Science Center. Red walls rose in the dim lobby. Oceanic music played around them. Henry had not been here in years, but the place was unchanged in its unironical sixties décor — the gold metal balusters and starburst chandeliers, the perforated gold lampshades standing in the corners. Everything became history eventually, if you just left it alone. Glowing signs directed them to PLANETARIUM and SCIENTARIUM and GIFT SHOP.

The group slowed, Bernie gripping the handles of the wheelchair. "Which way first?"

"Planetarium."

"No Scientarium?"

"I don't exactly have enough hair," William explained, "to stand on end with the static ball."

But the planetarium had shows only every half-hour, and for twenty minutes they wandered noncommittally through the Scientarium. The place was filled with children, most of them younger than William, some of whom crept close to peer at him with innocent rudeness until their parents came and sheepishly pulled them away; but the parents gave him a second glance too.

William didn't notice, or didn't appear to. Rapturously he watched his father climb onto a stationary bicycle and generate electricity; Bernie managed to illuminate eighteen of twenty light bulbs while his expression changed from nonchalance to real concentration. "Damn," he said, breathing hard afterward, "I used to be able to hit the top," and William said, "You're *old*, Dad," to which Bernie said, "Look who's talking, pal." Then to the gyroscope, where Lillian stood holding a spinning bicycle wheel on a rotating platform. "Oh, god," she said, getting off, "I forgot how dizzy that makes me." Then to the shadowbox, where Henry leapt into the air in front of a white screen and shut his eyes when the bank of lights flashed. Behind him his figure was preserved on the photosensitive fabric of the wall: a comic, ungraceful silhouette, his jacket flaring and his shadowed fists clutched over his head. "Boy," he said, "is that what I look like?" His son, seeing an opportunity, said, "Usually you actually look a little geekier than that, Dad," and Henry was happy to leave the shadow behind, like the others feeling himself subtly betrayed by these experiments, as though his measurements had been taken and compared to the flat perfectibility of the universe and found wanting.

Only Darren did not subject himself. A dark surge of guilt went through Henry; Darren did not really have a place here, he saw, and asking him along had been — hadn't it? — another sort of cruelty. He had embraced William; he had not embraced his own son, and Darren had watched and noted that too, as he noted everything.

When they were finally let into the planetarium, it was a larger, more public space than Henry remembered, with a high domed ceiling and rows of black seats arranged around the central, spiny projector. William did not want help getting into his chair, and tried to shake his mother's hand away, and scowled angrily when Bernie clattered the wheelchair shut in the aisle. But when the five of them were installed in the seats and Henry pulled the lever that allowed him to recline, he remembered immediately what he had liked so much about the place — the sudden privacy that descended once you were horizontal. You couldn't see anyone else unless you lifted your head, and the great black stretch of the ceiling, which looked much farther away now, an immense screen, curved into a bowl like the sky it mimicked. "Cool," said Darren beside him, and Henry said, "Totally."

When the lights went down, the room was sunk in perfect blackness for half a minute. Next to him William whispered, "Here we go," and slowly the night above them was filled with stars, one by one — a sky of prehistoric clarity. "Four thousand nine hundred stars are visible to the naked eye in the Northern Hemisphere," said the narrator, a woman, in a voice that thrilled Henry to the bone. Where were these women, with these siren voices? "Of these, the closest is Alpha Centauri, about twenty-five trillion miles from Earth." The names of the brightest stars were read — *Sirius, Canopus, Arcturus, Rigel, Procyon, Capella, Betelgeuse, Altair, Deneb, Vega, Hadar, Antares*. William was whispering the list to himself, and when it ended he continued: *Spica, Pollux, Fomalhaut, Mimosa, Acrux, Regulus, Adhara, Gacrux, Shaula, Bellatrix*.

The sky above them swerved, and Alpha Centauri blazed above them, and then they were moving toward it, racing through space. The star grew larger and brighter until it filled a quarter of the sky — such a distance covered at a gallop! They circled it, paused, considered its blazing corona, and passed on. They sailed through wispy nebulae and into the blinding bright heart of galaxies, each anchored at its center by a black hole of titanic size and appetite. They approached a mindless quasar that was beating out its signal a thousand times a second — the thrumming filled the room with a great cosmic roar — and then pushed off for the edge of the universe, where the seam of matter somehow did not edge up against nothingness but was itself the edge of everything. How could that be? How can there be an edge to everything, if there is nothing on the other side?

Halfway through this William reached out and clasped Henry's hand. William's hand was a bony, lumpy thing, with hard patches and roughened imperfections, a lion's well-used paw. Henry, guiltily, clutched it in the dark. His son did not notice, or did not appear to.

After twenty minutes the projectors showed them turning for home. They fell from immense heights to the plane of the Milky Way Galaxy, then swam through the stars to the familiar territory of the solar system, where unbeautiful Pluto tumbled in the blackness. They stopped briefly at backward-rotating Neptune, at Uranus. They swept through the icy rings of Saturn and hovered above the Great Red Spot of Jupiter and looped low along the red dusty deserts of Mars, so like Earth and yet not, a world that seemed fitting and useful but that was, as in a dream, missing something. Nobody home. A dead planet. Then back to Earth. Projected above them, it was a blue brightness darkened by brown continental shadows. Closer, it was seen to be swarming with tiny self-sustaining systems that walked and hunted and ate things, and larger systems that delivered rain to the prairies and snow to the mountains; the planet seemed in this view as magnificent and complex as the rest of the universe put together, and sailing along above its mountains and valleys and waterfalls, sinking into the depths of its populated oceans, Henry felt he was entering a kind of green, many-layered paradise, where you could breathe without trouble and rest your unprotected body on a patch of grass without dying of cold or heat or radiation. The narration had ended. It went without saying: a beautiful world.

Then the show was over and the lights came mercilessly up. Bernie levered William's seat upright again. William, leaning forward, said, "That was so cool," and made no complaint when he was loaded into his chair. He looked exhausted, as though he had really traveled all that way. Back in the car he fell asleep against Henry, his fragile avian chest rising and falling under his shirt. They drove in silence up the hill, under the trees to the Durbins' big house.

Henry watched the city unroll around him. Darren, on his other side, sat without touching anyone, in an inscrutable silence. Had he done this all wrong? William shifted under Henry's arm like a stack of loose papers, and Henry felt a perilous sadness rising in his throat. Oh, he knew he was too close to William. It had affected his judgment, and now it was too late.

But he loved William, and instead of closing, his heart was opening, inflating, swelling, until it seemed to fill his chest. Love and sadness joined in him, and with a painful self-consciousness he clasped the sleeping William closer. The boy weighed nothing. Dry as paper, brittle as ash, he took one shallow breath after another. Beside him, Henry's healthy son stirred. "Is he okay?" Darren whispered, and Henry, whispering back, said, "He's sleeping."

Darren nodded, leaned forward to see him there against William. Then he reached a hand to Henry's knee, once, a gentle touch, and took his hand away again. *All is forgiven,* Henry hoped it meant, not *What about me?*

Summer was ripening, producing a spicy, bitter odor in the side yard. The ash tree was making its little green berries, and nameless brown birds lived in the branches, flitting through the early morning unseen by anyone but Henry, high in his attic perch. From his window he could see down onto Saul's roof and into his yard. The neighbors had decided to mow his lawn, and from time to time a package would arrive and sit for a day on his front steps before Jackie or Kevin picked it up for safekeeping.

"They're not opening them, which, frankly, surprises me," Ilse informed him one night. "I would think they'd be eager to pry. I guess the police can stop the U.S. mail, but UPS isn't an arm of government. Not yet, anyway."

"Who are they from?"

"There're only three so far." Ilse, naked on the futon beside him, propped herself on her elbows and began to count. "There's one from Land's End, one from something called Group Sales Incorporated, and one from Amazon. He must have had things on back order."

"I wonder what."

"I'm dying to know, but it can't be anything that interesting, can it? I don't remember him having very many books. Were there books?"

Henry recalled the bloody stink of the hallway. "I didn't really notice."

"I guess you wouldn't," she said. "Oh, you look funny suddenly. I'm sorry. I didn't mean to bring it up. Do you want some slightly interesting news on a totally different subject? Say yes."

"Okay."

"Okay. I think I found an office to rent."

"Already?"

"It turns out you sort of have to move fast, Henry — it's not like buying a lawnmower. If you want something, you have to just decide. You don't mind?"

"How much is it?"

"Almost nothing. Less than you'd think. Nine hundred dollars a month. I haven't signed anything yet, but I did the math," she said hurriedly, "and there are grants I know I can get that will easily cover the rent and all my salary besides, especially when you count my pension after I quit."

"You're really going to do this?"

"Of course I am, darling."

"What exactly will you be doing?"

"Assisting the old ladies with their needs," she answered. "Whatever those of a medical nature may be."

The guilt he had felt riding home from the planetarium had diffused but had not disappeared. *Why love William when you could love someone who isn't going to die on you?* "Can I see it?" he asked his wife.

"I don't have a key." She checked her watch. It was only eight; the sky was still bright. "But I guess we could drive by and look at the outside."

In the car she steered with unusual care and temperance, as though giving him time to prepare. Her yellow hair was in eruption around her ears, and she swiped slowly at it with alternating hands. "I think the best grants will come from the NIH and the Chinese American Benevolent Society. I'd never heard of them before, but they have so much money, Henry, it's unbelievable. Now, for the first year I think we'd just be getting to know people. We could even do house calls — wouldn't that be fun? Although something I worry about is barging in on everyone and trying to fix everything all at once, so this is all going to have to start slowly." She caught his questioning look. "We'll be helping people understand what their doctors tell them."

"Like social work?"

"Yes, medical social work, and helping them fill out their forms, and giving them rides and things. I guess we're going to need some interpreters."

"I can ask Chin."

"Ask everyone." She steered gently downhill into the International District. "Wait till you see it."

The building was brick, on a corner, five stories high. They parked. Advertising circulars had been dumped in the lobby, and Ilse bent to gather them up; there was no trash can, and she waved them vaguely in either direction before folding them into her back pocket. The lobby was dusty and smelled faintly toxic, as though a beaker of poison had been spilled and not entirely cleaned up. A board with white letters was mounted on the plaster wall.

"We're in 307." Ilse rapped her fingernail on the glass. "We would be. It might just be open — do you want to come upstairs?"

"That sounds like a proposition."

She eyed him levelly. "You can't be horny again."

The stairwell was just as dusty as the lobby, with the same poisonous stink. Insecticide, he decided. Roaches. The poor frogs and their fraying zona pellucida. Grit scratched beneath the soles of his shoes; he would wipe his feet before getting back in the car. His wife climbed the stairs beside him, and alone in the stairwell with her he felt they were mounting an older set of stairs, climbing to her ancient apartment on the rue Georgienne twenty years ago, his nametag still affixed to his shirt and a felt-tipped pen knocking around lost in the lining of his sports coat. What of the world had awaited him then? His children, his wife, his life, had all once awaited him at the top of those stairs. It was a precious memory, and why would he not want to remember such a thing forever and ever? What additional stores of good might be added to the world by thousand-year-old men who remembered such kindnesses as Ilse had showed him since that day?

The third-floor corridor was long and dim, with a creaking fir floor. "Jackie would hate this," she said under her breath. She led him to a frosted door with a delicate gold doorknob. Black letters had been scraped recently from the glass, and the ghostly printing teased the eye but did not quite resolve into legibility. She tried the knob, and it turned under her hand. "Ah!" she cried, pushing the door aside. She threw the light switch. "Ta-da."

Together they stood in the doorway. "Wow," he said, after a minute.

"That's just what *I* said."

"This is how much?"

"Nine hundred."

"It's enormous."

"There's more," she said, giddy, and danced ahead of him into the room. The walls were brick. The ceiling was high. The floor was scuffed and worn, with black nailheads rising here and there from the floorboards like burned matches. The windows were made of dozens of tiny rectangular panes and showed a long slice of dark blue sky. The room was as big as half a tennis court and re-turned their voices with an echo. The floor creaked musically underfoot. "See this door?" Ilse opened it and scooted through, then reappeared. "Another room just like this."

He leaned in. "This is part of the same deal?"

"It's all one place."

"We could move in here."

"Isn't it wonderful?" She danced away into the open room. "Isn't it perfect?"

"What was it before?"

"Who knows? A sweatshop maybe. Yesterday there was a big pile of tennis shoes in that corner, but they were all left shoes. Not just left behind, I mean left *feet*. I thought it was art, but on second thought I guess it was just shoes. Now, through here," she said, leading him across, "there's a little bathroom, so you don't have to pee in the plants, and then down here there's another little back room, which could be an office or storage or something." The hall was narrow and blue and opened onto a small windowless room at the end, where a bare bulb hung on a cord from the ceiling. "This is where the boss sits, I guess, telling them to make more shoes."

"You're sure it's only nine hundred bucks?"

"Look at the neighborhood. No one wants a place without an elevator. There's no parking. It is sort of rustic. There's no air conditioning. It's hard to find unless you already know your way around. It's cheap, so people think there's something wrong with it. The landlord is Chinese, and he's very hard to understand."

"But he said nine hundred."

"The advertisement said nine hundred, I said nine hundred, he said nah hunda. I have to decide by tomorrow, Henry — there's some kind of design company that's second in line after me. So. This first room, you come in, sit down, say hello to your friends, and I'm next door, sitting at my beautiful, beautiful desk." She took three long steps and entered the second room. "And I say, Hello, yes, can I help you? And they say, What does this say? And I look over my shoulder at my friend the translator and say, Can you explain arteriosclerosis, please? I guess eventually I should learn Chinese."

"Where does that go?" A white door stood against the far white wall.

His wife turned. Stopped short. "I don't know. To a closet, I guess."

"You didn't notice it before?"

"It was a quick tour," she said.

Together they walked across the creaking floor. Their shadows crept forward ahead of them. The knob was black porcelain and polished like an eightball, and when his wife reached to turn it, Henry felt his heart rising in his throat. The door was unlocked, and the knob turned easily under her hand. What would they find? An immense, lost room, grand as a lost world?

She pulled the door open.

Behind it another long corridor led away to a pair of distant windows. "Well," she said, and together they stood, looking in. No voices. No noise at all, and a dusty, ancient smell, as though the air within had not stirred in months. "Do you know," Ilse said idly, "ghosts are usually said to live on stairs and in hallways? They are places of transition."

"Like rest stops," he suggested.

"I don't think ghosts drive very much."

They waited again. No sound. "Does this come with the rent too?" he asked.

"I imagine it does," Ilse said, stepping forward.

He followed her into the silent corridor. There were no doors, only the set of windows, which drew them forward. The light was very dim. Orange rectangles stood on the ceiling, cast by the streetlights below. An extra accumulation of grit crackled under his shoes. The windows were old, two square panes fastened with a latch. At the windows the hall took a sharp left turn and ended at a brick wall. A wicker lounge chair stood here by itself, coated in a layer of white fluffy dust. "This," Henry said, "is really where the boss sits." The windows looked down on the street; it seemed a street in a different city, in a neighborhood they had never seen. Their car was nowhere in sight. Was there anything more, another secret passage? No, the walls were solid. Henry swiped his hand at the cottony dust on the chair; under his touch it seemed to be made up of millions of tiny white threads, which fell from the wicker in a weightless clump. "From the shoes," he guessed.

"Possibly. But then why isn't there fluff everywhere?" His wife eyed the long hallway back. "I don't think anyone's been in here in a long time. Look, there's dust on the dust."

"I think," he said, "you should take it."

"Well, I think we'd go absolutely insane remembering it and *not* taking it." She inhaled, a deep, tasting breath, and said, "Will you help me write grants? I forget how. And what about desks and things — will you help me carry things up?"

"Darren and I can do it."

"Don't tell him about this part!" she cried, turning to him. "Is that silly? Don't tell anyone." She leaned against him. "We're so lucky, Henry," she said into his ear. "Isn't it just *awful*? We're so lucky!" She was laughing into his shoulder, big huffing gusts. "What did we do to deserve it?"

She was serious, he knew. "Mum's the word," he promised.

She put two fists on his chest. Her eyes were shining with happiness. "It's going to be *wonderful*."

They turned out all the lights, shut the doors, and on the drive home they took a slow detour into the warehouse district. "This is where I turn around on my runs — right here is exactly four miles from our driveway," Ilse said, and pulled a sudden U-turn in the middle of the empty arterial. "And if we go up this hill a little bit, look! See that? That's where Kozmo lives! That's the headquarters. Look!" She put her palm on the window. A scooter was pulling away from the loading dock. "There goes someone right now with a jar of olives and a movie called *Predator 3!*"

"Godspeed!"

"Godspeed, heroic driver!" Ilse cried, as the scooter roared past them.

William's outing laid him up in bed for a day, Bernie said over the telephone, but now he was walking downstairs in the morning and seating himself at the breakfast table and drinking his protein shake with celebratory gusto. "And you know that stuff tastes like shit. Hey, there's a medical question for you — why does everything that's good for you taste so terrible? Don't tell me: evolution."

"Natural selection," Henry said. "Every question you ask about biology has the same answer."

"Yeah." Bernie sighed. "By the way, the preliminary papers are back. On your patent. Came in this morning."

"Everything okay?"

"Oh, yeah, it's all routine. No worries. They didn't even blink.

They know Justine by now. You should see some of the crazy stuff they patent, Henry, they publish a summary every couple months. You know what they patented this month? Wait, let me get it." He shuffled some papers. "'A Means to Swing from Side to Side.' I shit you not. This is the stuff that makes my day. Actually, the patent office is the best-run government office in the world, in my opinion. It's very pure. Pure invention. Like pure mathematics — nine tenths of the stuff they approve never comes close to seeing the light of day. Pure physics. Of almost zero use to human beings, but you know — possible. It's like law, you know? If you can make a decent argument, you can make it come true."

"He's walking downstairs?"

"Henry, I am not kidding, he is walking downstairs. You should see him, he's got this goofy look" — Bernie's voice thickened — "like he's just the neatest guy in the world, like he invented it. It's like when he was a year old and first learned — he just thought he was a superstar."

"You know Gary Hauptmann?" Henry said. "In Berkeley."

"Sure."

"I'm going to send this kid Thomas down to let Gary look him over."

"Yeah? Okay. We could spring for that."

"No, we can cover it. Gary's going to put him up on the other end. But it's safe to do now, right? I guess is what I'm asking."

"Safe," Bernie said. "You mean proprietarily. Yeah, you're fine. You were fine the second you signed the papers. This kid doesn't know you're dosing Willie, does he?"

"No. Nobody knows."

"Yeah." Bernie sucked air through his teeth. "I'm assuming this is to audition for Gunnar Peterson."

"I think that's pretty likely."

"They don't know about William, correct?"

"No."

"Because if they do, they could sink you, Henry, if they wanted to."

"I know." He struggled to keep the fear from his voice. But what was the point of that? He was scared. He said so. "I'm talking in my sleep, I'm so scared."

"Yeah, but you know what? They don't know. You know why? They don't want to. Because if it comes out that he knows you've been sort of diddling on the side with this stuff and Peterson's shown to have bought it from you anyway? It's going to look bad for him. So he'll do everything he can to avoid learning what he doesn't want to know, as long as it doesn't look like he's been negligent or hasn't done his due diligence. What he'll do is rely on your reputation, which is a reasonable thing to do, and most likely it hasn't even occurred to him you're doing it, right? I mean, it is a strange thing for you to be doing."

"Yeah."

"So I think you're fine."

"Really?"

"Really. Relax. In my experience, these things are never as scary as they could be. If somehow it gets around to those assholes on Review Board, you guys can always come live with us."

"I want that room in the back."

"You, my friend, can have your pick," Bernie told him.

It was all unnerving. His wife left him alone on the futon to talk to whomever he was talking to, and in the summer's heat the attic rafters gave off their resinous smell of timber, and Bryan Suits on the radio put him gently to sleep, and every morning he woke to the sound of the contractors' trucks rolling up to Jackie and Kevin's house. Only once recently had he woken in the middle of the night. A rustling at the garage below had drawn him to the window. Dark, dark, the rhododendrons swayed as something moved among them: an animal, sliding silently along on all fours. Bigger than a big dog. What the hell was it? Deep in shadow, it had a long, narrow head, no tail — a patch of white near its head. A wild pig? A wayward bear? In the darkness, in the shadows of the brush along the driveway, it looked like no animal he had ever seen. *Saul,* he thought with a shiver. Soundlessly the shadow slipped down the driveway, beneath the branches of the shedding ash tree, out onto the road, and vanished from his sight.

21

IT WAS POSSIBLE — if you pushed the clutch at the top of the driveway — to roll the Vespa all the way down the driveway and past Mr. Harstein's house and then down to 29th Street without having to either start the engine or push uphill more than a few feet. After school was out for the summer, Darren stole the scooter almost every night. No one heard him — the wind rushed through the hemlocks, and the jets roared into Sea-Tac, shifting their gears overhead, putting down their flaps — and no one saw him, because he didn't dare take the machine out until the house was entirely silent, his restless father having at last succumbed to sleep. By that hour the summer air had cooled, no one was outside, and the houses of the neighborhood were dark and still.

Like any theft, it was easier to accomplish than seemed decent. Taking the silver keys from the bowl by the door, he would creep out into the back yard in his Tevas and unlock the garage. Hanging on the wall like a toy moon was his mother's helmet, which fit him fine. Its squishy leather padding had been permanently infused with his mother's flat smell of foundation and lipstick, and the fact that it fit him so well seemed, as he lowered it over his head, a kind of permission. *Thank you,* he would think.

Always helmeted, never speeding, always signaling, he was never pulled over. It was in his nature, he thought, to be cautious and stealthy. That parking lot could hold a cop. That narrow rut in the road could spill him. The summer rain left the roads fragrant but slick, and darknesses loomed down all the side streets, threatening to send out a tendril and ensnare him. As a younger boy he had been afraid of the basement and its quiet emptiness; going down to retrieve a roll of paper towels, he had kept the monsters at bay with the power of his rational mind, but once his back was turned to the darkness it swelled and became a palpable thing, with its dancing fingers just behind his neck. He would run upstairs silently, so no one would know he was afraid, and burst into the light of the kitchen with his neck still tingling. In the same way the scooter swept him along, faster than the darkness could find him, but with the sensation that he was seen, groped for, and always on the verge of being taken.

Most of the time he didn't go anywhere in particular. Up the maple-lined street to Union, west on Union in the middle of the night, passing with averted eyes the clusters of thugs who gathered outside the convenience stores. North on 23rd Avenue, past the YMCA and HeadHunters Salon with its tin-foiled windows. Then west on John to 15th, down 15th past the all-night Safeway and the darkened Wine Shop with its grated white door, and into the neighborhood again, past the enormous brick houses along the edge of the park, which stared down at him in magisterial silence. Volunteer Park was full of gay guys who had sex in the bushes all night — supposedly, anyway. *What do you do when you drop your wallet in Volunteer Park?* To give himself a thrill he slowed and peered into the underbrush, but he saw nothing. *Kick it home.*

Then he drove down the hill to the drawbridge, where the narrow tires wormed and wiggled on the steel bridge deck. Then past the stadium, where even late at night the enormous banks of halogen lights were shining. Past his dad's hospital. North into the nameless, orderly neighborhood that lay beyond. East again to Lake Washington, where the water churned gently against the stony banks. He often stopped the Vespa at Matthews Beach, straddled it, pulled off his helmet, and inhaled.

Here at the lakeshore he was always alone. The sky was orange with the city's glow, and far away, around the rim of the lake, houses were glowing with an ever-burning light. The wind that tossed the hemlocks on Hynes Street was here a broader, cooler, more oceanic instrument, finding its way unimpeded over the hill from Elliott Bay, smelling of the sea. What a shuddering, all-encompassing feeling he had, while the scooter ticked between his legs! He would not be found missing at home; he never was. The cold summer lake rolled a dozen feet away, and way out on the water something would be winking: a spy boat come to signal him, a drug deal being enacted. Or nobody, on the way to nowhere, winking his lights for no reason.

The nights he didn't take the scooter out he stayed up reading Philip K. Dick and Kim Stanley Robinson until two or three in the morning, just because he could. His father's oddball, longing looks had not gone away, but ever since the trip to the planetarium his father had been especially peculiar, telling him every night, very seriously, how much he loved him. "I know," Darren would call back into the hallway, waiting for a punch line that never came. What was up? It had something to do with William, Darren guessed, but exactly what was hard to tell. His father wasn't saying. Darren had the urge to arm-wrestle his father, to tackle him from behind, but he never dared. It was a physical longing to be closer to his father, to dispel whatever weirdo thing was going on, but he never acted on it.

Instead his mother picked up on it, and now kissed him whenever she had the chance. He ducked away and squirmed out of her arms as quickly as he could, but secretly he didn't mind. He didn't want to admit it, but in her arms he felt the comforts of the world descend upon him, and he knew that if he let himself, he could stay there forever. In the end it was always he who broke their embrace, and he always felt guilty about it afterward, and regretful. But he knew his mother loved him; what he wanted, more than anything, was his father.

He had given himself the mummy's tattoo — three parallel lines cut into the top of his foot.

As he had seen done in movies, he had taken a heavy darning needle and heated it on the stove, then broken open the barrel of a blue Bic and collected the ink in the bottom of a paper cup. For safety he had swabbed his foot with an Oxy-10 pad, to kill the bacteria. Then, with a slow, rocking motion of the needle, he had gouged fifteen holes in his foot, three lines of five. It did not hurt as much as he had feared, and when he poured the ink over his foot, fifteen little blue dots were stenciled into his flesh. Not identical to the mummy's tattoo, but near enough that Tanya would recognize it. It was sore, and itched for a week, but it didn't get infected, and Darren considered it with the same admiration he now felt for his arms.

He had not seen Tanya since that day at the museum, though, and he was getting worried. They talked once in a while on the phone, and she had even called him twice, once to ask what he thought of the name Michelle for a cat and once for no reason at all. Bored, he imagined. To be sixth out of ten — or possibly higher, if he allowed for some probable demotion of his competition — was not bad, and he imagined that the tattoo, when he displayed it, would move him up at least one notch. But to just tell her about it would drop him a notch. Points off for bragging.

He knew where Tanya lived and rode by her house regularly at night. She lived two miles away, in a small frame duplex near Montlake. Her bedroom, he knew from conversation, was upstairs in back, and by sidling the scooter down the alley, over the heaved asphalt and past the stinking trash cans, he could see her darkened window, the white shade pulled snug to the sill. To rev the engine of the scooter was to risk discovery by the neighbors. The back yard was a tangle of weeds and discarded wood. He wanted to show her his tattooed foot, but when would he see her again?

So instead of sneaking into Tanya's house and facing her weirdo father and his two billion buttons, he decided to finally go visit William Durbin. The house was an immense stone pile at the top of a long stretch of lawn, the biggest house he'd ever seen in person, and it was easy enough, having arranged it over the phone, to park the scooter around the corner at midnight and let himself in a side door that William had left unlocked, then creep upstairs into his bedroom.

After the initial shock of meeting him, Darren was prepared for what he saw: gigantic bald head, tiny jaw with basically no teeth, a frail, paunchy little body that stopped halfway down the bed. And that helium-inhaler's voice. "They're asleep," William said, greeting him. His look was frightened, wondering, happy, as if he weren't sure whether Darren was there to talk to him or to murder him. "Did you really steal it?"

"I borrowed it."

"Where'd you learn how to ride it?"

"My mom showed me."

"She lets you?"

"No, she'd totally kill me if she knew," Darren said, and felt a little *ping* of guilt. Not the thing to say. "It's not that hard."

"You should take me out on it."

"Then *your* mom would kill me."

"So?" William slapped the covers with his gnarled hands. "You deserve it. We could go cruising. We could go to Canada."

"Yeah, right."

"We should."

"That's like a hundred miles. My ass would fall off."

"Let's go to Dick's."

"You want to go to Dick's?"

William nodded. "The one on Broadway's open until two A.M."

"You want to go now?" This was not what he had come for. "Wouldn't that food like . . . kill you?"

"I can eat whatever I want." William closed his eyes and raised his beaky nose into the air. "It's none of your business what I eat."

"You seriously want to go to Dick's? You're not even dressed."

William threw back the covers. Jeans, a sweater, white sneakers. "The one thing I don't have is a helmet."

"You can't be serious."

"Why not?" William widened his crinkled eyes, lifted his trembling arms. "It's like the Make-A-Wish Foundation. My last wish is to go to Dick's."

"I thought you were feeling better."

"It's probably only temporary," William said. "Besides, I want a deluxe."

"A deluxe weighs like ten pounds."

"No it doesn't."

"Yeah it does."

"You're thinking of Kidd Valley, dummy."

Darren knew the difference; he just didn't want to do it. "People are going to think you're like five years old, you realize. We'll probably get pulled over."

"I don't care."

"Yeah, well, if I get arrested, I won't be able to get my license until I'm like seventy-five."

"I don't care about that either," said William.

Darren sat in an armchair and took off his shoe. "I have to

show you something," he said. He had to show someone. So he peeled off his sock and lifted his right foot into William's bony lap. "Check it out."

William eyed his foot. "You can count to fifteen."

"I saw this mummy," he explained, "and it had the same exact tattoo, and I thought, man, that's cool. In a museum. Well, not exactly the same, his was just lines, but I couldn't do the lines, I just did the dots. With a needle."

"You did this yourself?"

"It's easy. You just heat the needle and rub some ink in and it sticks. It's like when you stab yourself with a pencil — you ever do that? And the lead just stays in there and gives you lead poisoning."

"It's not lead, it's graphite."

"Duh, I know."

"You can't get lead poisoning from graphite."

"I was joking," Darren said. William was examining his foot, and ran a hard, callused finger down each short stripe of dots. It almost tickled, but not quite.

In a quieter voice, William asked, "Did it hurt?"

"A little bit."

"What kind of mummy?"

"It didn't say. It was like off in the corner under these stairs, I don't know. It looked like they were trying to get rid of it or something. I don't know. It didn't have a card or anything."

William poked the tattoo. "Does it hurt when I do that?"

"Nah, it was like three weeks ago."

William touched it again. "I wonder if he killed three people."

"Yeah, but then why'd he put it on his feet? He'd like put that on his arms, wouldn't he?" Darren flexed his biceps; he felt them harden. "I bet what he did was he like traveled someplace three times. Walked. Like if he was living by the ocean or something, he probably walked to the mountains three times. That's why it's on his feet."

A pause developed, and the room seemed to enlarge around them in the silence. William's bed was against the window and had a view of the water and the hospital with its blinking red light. It was strange, being here — this new view through the window, this unfamiliar hour of the night. Darren had never done anything like this, not remotely. A little lamp was burning on a bedside table. The floor was carpeted. A huge television sat at the end of the bed. Pretty normal, mostly.

But there were other things too: that acrid, incendiary smell; syringes in a glass beaker on the dresser; a stack of white hand towels next to them, for uses Darren did not care to guess at. And William himself, who did look — it was uncanny, really — exactly like an alien. In his sweater and jeans and white shoes he somehow looked more alien, as a dog in a plaid coat looked more like a dog.

In the silence William turned and put his feet on the floor, leaned forward, pushed off the mattress with two hands, and stood. "Does it vibrate?" he asked. "The scooter."

"A little bit. Yeah, I guess it does."

William tugged up his pants, which hung low around his hips. "You realize I usually wear diapers." A stricken, pleading look was in his eye. "So I think I should get one on."

"A diaper?"

"Because of my thing."

"Yeah."

"So I'm going to go put one on."

Darren couldn't help it — it climbed the column of his chest and burst out: a laugh. "That sucks," he said into his hand. "Oh, my god, that sucks so bad."

"It's either that or I'll pee all over your butt."

"Oh my god."

"Shh, be quiet."

"I'm sorry."

"Especially," William noted, "if it vibrates." He was in and out of the bathroom in two minutes. He wrote a short note and folded it and put it on his pillow, then tottered over to Darren to take his hand. "Stairs are still hard," he told him, "so you need to carry me."

He did? "Okay," he said. So he leaned down and lifted William into his arms, cradling him. William was peculiarly light, as though his big head were actually filled with helium and his bones, fragile already, were hollow. Under Darren's nose the acrid scent of him was unmistakably the smell of something burning, and Darren held his breath.

From his arms William reached down and turned the doorknob

leading into the hall. "They won't wake up," he whispered, and he held on as Darren carried him down ten steps, across the landing, down another ten.

"Which way?" Darren whispered.

"The same way you came in."

They crept through the dark kitchen, and William leaned down to turn the knob again, and they were out into the night air.

The side of the house faced a bank of ivy, and its dark, bitter smell rose from the earth. The moon was up. The neighborhood was silent around them. Darren found himself standing there on the concrete not wanting to put William down, and William made no struggle to be released. Past the gas meter and the basement windows and the garbage cans he carried him, around to the front of the house and along the lengthy front walk, across the broad lawn, down to the sidewalk. William was a rustling, delicate package to carry, and when Darren finally lowered him to the street he put out his legs tentatively and stood holding Darren's elbow. Was this going to kill him? But now that they were out in the street, Darren couldn't ask such a thing, couldn't turn around. "You're going to have to hold on to me the whole way, you realize," he told him, and William said, "No shit."

"You have to wear the helmet."

"I'm not wearing a helmet," William said.

"One of us does, and if people see you they're going to drive off the road. Like in *E.T.*" He settled the helmet on William's head. It fit. "Okay?"

William flipped up the visor. "This is so cool." His voice was muffled by the padding.

"Yeah. This is like by far the dumbest thing I've ever done in my life."

"After we go to Dick's, I want to go to Canada."

"I hope you brought a spare diaper."

"I did" came the muffled answer.

Darren didn't know what to say to this. He grasped William under the arms and hoisted him to the seat, balancing him like a book on edge. "Don't fall," he ordered, and climbed quickly aboard himself and pulled William's arms around his waist. "Okay?"

"Roger," William said, muffled.

"I'm going to roll downhill so we don't wake up your parents."

"I told you, they never wake up."

"Still." Darren pushed off and steered them downhill, past the huge dark houses; coasting, he was able to go three blocks without starting the engine, and when he did it sparked to life easily and the noise was absorbed by the roar of an airplane overhead. William clung to his waist around curves and was an awkward weight on the back of the scooter; Darren drove slowly, and when they climbed a long hill he leaned forward so William could rest his head on his back, which he did, the hard globe of the helmet rolling against Darren's spine.

At this hour cops were everywhere on Broadway, and Darren was sure they would be pulled over, but he found he didn't much care. A strange, hopeful happiness was filling him. What was the worst that could happen? He took the side streets across Capitol Hill, passing the great watery darkness of the reservoir and spending only half a minute on Broadway before pulling into the Dick's parking lot. Pigeons bobbled on the pavement under the fluorescent lights, eating French fries, and the parking lot was barely a quarter full.

"Stay here," he told William, and climbed off. It was one o'clock in the morning, and the crowd at Dick's was thin; only a few drug-addict types were sitting in little clusters against the building. He walked up to the window and ordered two deluxes and two fries.

"That your little brother?" the guy behind the steel counter asked, in a not unfriendly way.

Darren looked over and had to say, "He can't sleep." Perched on the back of the scooter, wearing the huge white helmet, William looked exactly like an alien, an alien in a space helmet. When Darren was handed the warm, grease-spotted bag, he slid his change off the counter and hurried back and said, "I know a place we can go eat."

"It's safe here."

"Not exactly. Hold this," Darren said, and backed the scooter out and started it up again and drove them across Broadway, past the reservoir, and down the side streets to the Miller Field tennis courts, where the tires made a quiet adhesive noise against the composite surface. It was dark, surrounded by trees. "Perfect," Darren said.

Sitting beside him on the damp courtside bench, William unwrapped his hamburger and lifted it to his nose. "This basically just smells like cheese," he said.

"I'll eat it if you don't want it."

"That's okay." He took a bite, chewed, swallowed. "This is much better than a protein shake," he said, "and there's actually protein in it."

"Supposedly."

The scooter ticked as the engine cooled, and they ate in silence. It was a warm, hazy night, with occasional breaks in the cloud cover, through which pinpricks of starlight showed. Beside Darren, William made little huffing noises in his throat and loudly chewed his food. As the silence grew, Darren sensed the unasked questions he had been accumulating. *What does it feel like? Do your bones hurt? What do you think about?* After another minute he asked, to break the silence, "You like my dad?"

William swallowed. "He's only like trying to save my life. So yeah."

"He is?"

"It's a secret," William said. "You can't tell anybody."

"What do you mean?"

"It's this thing, it's like illegal or something? They're experimenting on me, and they're not supposed to be."

"Why not?"

"I'm not really sure," said William. "I never quite understood that part."

"It's illegal?"

"Or not illegal, but he could get fired."

"Fired?"

"That's what my mom said. They're not supposed to experiment on people."

"Is that why you're feeling better?"

William turned to him, shrugged enormously, lifted his hands. "I don't know, man," he said. "Probably."

Suddenly it all clicked for Darren: all that strange behavior suddenly had an explanation. "Hey," he said, "that's why he's so totally freaking out. He's totally like talking in his sleep now."

"He is?"

"Totally — it's hilarious! My mom made him go sleep in the attic finally, but you can still sort of hear him if you stand at the door." This did not feel like a betrayal; in fact, in a flash, Darren felt another surge of violent affection for his father. How many people could say their fathers risked their jobs to cure incurable diseases? Very few. And in the next moment he knew what he would do with his life: he would be a doctor. *Click, click, click* — things in his head were locking together. What else was worth doing? Nothing. He had thought of it before, but suddenly it was obvious. At this, a lightness entered him: his own bones seemed full of air. "Yeah," Darren said, "he just goes *Ba ba ba ba ba ba ba ba.* God, that totally makes sense. Okay, I've got another question."

"Okay."

He felt a thrill of fear, but despite it he said, "Are you afraid?"

William shrugged again in the darkness. "Of what?"

"You know. Being . . ." Darren said. "You know."

William finished his hamburger and put the square of orange foil into his pocket. "I have this theory, actually. Okay, you know how you probably think I look like an alien and I really do look like an alien? My theory is this. I mean, it's not a theory, but it's possible. If I look like an alien, then basically that's saying that aliens look like me. And if aliens look like me, then maybe they actually *are* like me. I mean, maybe they're like me except they've got the fix, the fix your dad is giving me? And so here's my theory. In the future, everybody wants to get the injection. So everybody gets it. But then it makes them look like me, so eventually everyone in the world ends up looking like me. And then the aliens that people are supposedly seeing, if they're real, they're just the people who're coming back from the future to see what people used to look like before they all injected themselves. Like in *The Three Stigmata of Palmer Eldritch*? And maybe also they want to get some other DNA from the past for people to use in the future for something." William picked up the helmet and put it on his lap. "That's why people think they never see time travelers. You know? Like the question always is, if time travel's possible, then where are the time travelers? Why aren't they here? The answer is, they're the aliens. But they're not aliens, they're just people who turned out to look like me."

"Those guys in the book were artificially evolved."

"But so am I. Don't you think that's possible?"

It sounded loony. But what did he know? "Possible, I guess," he said.

"You think it's crazy?"

"I don't know."

"Sometimes I can't tell if what I think is crazy or not."

"No," Darren felt he had to say, "it's possible."

"That's what I think too." William put the helmet aside. "I'm going to take a whiz," he said, and stood up. He turned away, dropped his pants. There was a ripping sound as he undid what had to be the diaper, and then he peed in a rattling arc, through the chain-link fence and into the underbrush. "On to Canada," he said.

"Yeah," Darren said.

It was a short ride home under the shifting trees, and William rested his head on Darren's back again. They traveled unseen down the dark side streets, passing house after house, all of them quiet. *But are you afraid?* The night air enveloped them, brushed Darren's face, tossed his hair, whipped the sleeves of his T-shirt. A doctor: that's what he would be. His father would love him for that, and it all seemed perfectly right to him, right as few things ever had, and now that it was decided he felt he could do anything. The idea would always be there.

He parked, lifted William from the scooter, put William down, lowered the kickstand, picked him up again. Back in his arms, William was quiet, his eyes moving from Darren's face to the sidewalk and the side door and then the stairs as they climbed again to his room. Everything was as they had left it. William removed the folded note from his pillow and tipped it into the trash, then sat down on the bed. He was tired, Darren could see. "You cool?" he asked, and William nodded. It was an obvious effort to move his head, and when he lay back on the pillow, still in his clothes, he shut his eyes and said, "I'll call you, okay?"

"Okay."

"I'm all right," he said. "I'm just tired."

"Okay."

"You should probably go."

"Yeah," Darren said. "That was pretty cool."

"Coolest thing you've ever done," William said, "by far."

Darren knew he shouldn't tell anyone what he'd done, but the settled happiness that had entered him on that bench did not go away. He looked at his father with new eyes. No wonder he was so weird these days! His sister, home from camp, looked him over and said, "What're you smiling at?"

"Myself. I am righteous," he said. "I am a righteous dude."

"You weigh like a hundred and twelve pounds."

"All man!" He showed her his arms. "Man of steel!"

"Oh," Sandra said, rolling her eyes, "my god."

"I can bench ninety pounds!"

"Yeah," she said, and in half a second had him in a headlock. It was impossible to extract himself, and she pulled him halfway across the room by the neck, then thwacked the tip of his chin, very deliberately, with her thumbnail. "All what?" she asked.

"All man!" he cried.

"All what?"

"All man!" He tried to tickle her, but when he did he felt the skin of her back and belly go taut and lose all resemblance to skin. "All man," he said.

"All monkey."

"All man," he insisted. His voice came out gurgling and strained. "I feel sorry for you, this is the best you can do." This tightened the grip around his neck, and he had to laugh: she was so much stronger than he was, it was funny. Why did he have to have the six-foot sister? "All man," he said.

He tried tickling her again. No luck, and her grip tightened again. Her sweatshirt was bunched under his nose, so he smelled laundry detergent. The angle of his head required him to stare at his shoes and the carpet and his sister's bare knees. The longer this went on, the more likely he was to sprout an unintentional boner, and just the act of thinking about it was enough to get it going, and that would be bad. And then it was going. "Half monkey," he said hurriedly.

"All monkey."

"All monkey," he agreed, and she let him go. He shook down his pants and she pulled down her sleeves and Darren had the fleeting impression that she had been thinking the same thing, that she had suddenly noticed him as a physical body under her arm and wanted to be rid of him before something happened. Creepy.

He stayed in his room until he was sure she had gone to bed, then sneaked out to examine himself in the mirror. He looked the same. Future doctor of America. Son of a doctor. A righteous dude.

In this mood he called Tanya, who answered with a hopeful hello but sounded distinctly less interested when he told her who it was. "Oh yeah," she said. "Hey."

"Hey. So," he said, "you busy tonight?"

"Tonight? It's like eleven o'clock."

"I mean later. Like one in the morning."

"Uh, that's actually when I usually like sleep."

"Stay up," he said.

"Why?"

"Because I'll come pick you up."

"On what, a bicycle?"

"No."

"On what?"

"Something."

"You're crazy."

"Stay up," he insisted.

She made a long exhaling sound. "You're not going to TP my house, are you? Because my dad would be so pissed off, he'd think I wanted it to happen. Kenyon keeps saying he's going to TP my whole house and I'm like *don't*."

"Oh yeah, Kenyon. Is that Kenyon Poopinhatz?"

"Kenyon who? No!" She laughed. "Kenyon who goes to Roosevelt."

"I know this other guy named Kenyon Peepeejar, is that him?"

She laughed again. "You're so gross," she said. "I'm serious — don't do anything to my house."

"I won't."

"You better not," she said. "Can I ask you something, by the way?"

"Okay," he said.

"I'm not trying to be rude? But why do you keep calling me?"

"I don't know. You called me twice."

"I did?"

"You know you did." This was not a good sign. "You called once about your cat named Michelle and you called once two weeks ago for some reason, and we talked about Mrs. Melgard. Because I like you," he said. "And I'm not going to do anything to your house. I just want to come and go for a ride."

"On what?"

"I forget," he said. "No, it's a horse."

"It better not be, I'm afraid of horses. I'm always afraid they're going to bite me."

"Do you even remember who I am?"

"I remember who you are."

"You gave me the little horse for my birthday."

A long pause. "Don't do anything to the house," she said finally, "or else I'll get grounded for like the entire summer."

Not a good sign. But if she barely remembered him, it would be hard to make a bad impression. She could be just pretending not to remember him; that was possible. Would that be good or bad? Could be either, he decided.

Tanya's back yard was as overgrown as ever, and an old bathtub had been added to the clutter, sunk up to its curved lip in the weeds. It was exactly one A.M. when he arrived and saw Tanya's shade pulled tight to the sill, just as it always was. He waited a long two minutes, with the scooter shut off, the wind sighing in the trees and dashing the tips of the grass back and forth. The scooter had a horn, and he touched it lightly, briefly, so a little reedy *blip* came out. He winced. If he had to, he could be gone in ten seconds; if any lights went on anywhere, he would go.

Her blind moved. She pulled it aside and looked down at him, a pale pretty face brushed with dark eyebrows. Then she dropped the blind again and disappeared. He waited. Her house, seen from behind, did make an attractive target for vandalism; it seemed half abandoned already, and the magnetic appeal of Tanya made you want to reach out and rip off the doors and windows and take her out and drag her away. Failing that, you could throw toilet paper everywhere.

Was she coming out? She was. She crept out the back door and closed it silently behind her. Black jeans and a black T-shirt. Hair back in a ponytail. But no glasses: she had prepared herself. A good sign. He pulled off his helmet and handed it to her. "Hey," he said.

She looked at him speculatively, as though trying to match the voice to the face. "Is it yours?" she whispered, weighing the helmet in her hands. "Whose is it?"

"My mom's."

"You're insane," she whispered, and slipped the helmet over her head.

He knew the less he said the more she would think of him, so he didn't say much. She sat behind him, her feet on the footrests, as close to him as she could be without taking her clothes off. Her thighs were warm around him and flexed when she leaned with him around the corners. She rested her head against his shoulders. She smelled of a bright, flowery soap, a smell that was now almost literally under his nose and that he inhaled along with the fragrant night air. The moon was out again, hiding periodically behind broken clouds. She was quiet too. Now and then he took a long giddy turn, in the middle of which she would squeak and hold on tighter, or he would steer them with gathering speed down a steep side street that sloped away into the darkness and she would let out a long anticipatory sigh, the trees passing darkly overhead as they bottomed out on another quiet block and passed unnoticed along another stretch of lifeless houses. On these back streets the sensation of being with her was particularly acute, and every shadowed driveway, every half-acre park, invited him to pull over and kiss her. But it was too soon, he thought, and he kept going.

He had no plan at all. Unlike with William, in whose company he had felt a great protectiveness, Tanya's presence made him daring. They drove boldly down brightly lit arterials and roared through the hilly, double-ended parking lot of the Greek Orthodox church with the engine spitting angrily beneath them, his hair buffeted by the breeze. Once in a while a cloud of gnats would hit him like a tiny shower of rain and he would spit, calling back, "Bugs!"

But she didn't want to talk either. She was content to ride with him, leaning against his back with her head on his shoulder, and when he angled his mirror to see her, he found she had closed her eyes behind the visor and her mouth was frozen in a dreamy kind of smile. Now and then her thighs tightened around his for balance. This was the girl he had imagined, this was the sensation of intermixing with the universe that he had felt in bed; it was a sensation he had imagined so often that it now felt like a kind of memory even while it was happening, and instead of being nervous he felt entirely calm and knowledgeable and without worry. He did not fear Tanya's parents, and even to be pulled over would not be a disaster, as it would make him intriguing in Tanya's eyes, and the incident would become a story that could be told about him among her friends, something that would improve his reputation without doing him any actual damage or offending his natural caution too much.

When she finally lifted her visor and called to him, "I want to get off!" they were halfway through the winding, forested reaches of Interlaken Park, where enormous trees met overhead and tiny wooded trails snaked away into the underbrush.

He stopped and turned the scooter off, and a silence descended. When they dismounted, both of them were shaking. There were no houses in sight, no lights except the orange glow of the sky through the branches, and the air smelled winy and rich from years' worth of fallen leaves decaying in the damp. A bitterness drifted from the hundreds of ferns that grew on the steep hillsides. Looking over the edge of the embankment, they could see into a small ravine where a stream trickled; a path led down into the darkness. Tanya pulled off her helmet. "There's probably like a million derelicts down there," she said.

It was a dare, maybe, so he took her hand and led her wordlessly into the trees. The path angled down steeply. Matted leaves made the footing slippery, and he righted himself once against her chest and felt against his shoulder the funny hard-softness that he had first felt months ago, in a similar darkness. Maybe it was that first overstepping that had kept him in the game somehow; but here, to-night, with her, none of that really mattered. Her hand in his was sweaty and hot.

At the bottom of the path the ground leveled in a clearing and the creek rattled invisibly against its rocky bed. They were alone, and looking up, they could see a patch of clouds. Superstitiously, he moved them into the center of the clearing, three or four feet from the water, and when they were positioned correctly they could look up together and see around them a perfect circle of sky. It was a circle that seemed to fall directly into the clearing, as though they were standing at the bottom of a dark silo. Here it was easy to kiss her, and easy for her to kiss him.

They were almost exactly the same height now: he was growing. Her lips were cushiony and worked on him with a slightly worri-some expertise, first inhaling his top lip and biting a neat row along its underside and then taking the bottom in and doing the same, as though finishing an ear of corn. Then she inserted a long pointed tongue into his mouth and ran it along the roof of his mouth and then his gumline. It would not pay to be too cautious here, he told himself, so he felt around for her butt and got it solidly in two hands and pulled her against him. This did not seem to bother her, though they could plainly feel between them his boner like a roll of quarters angled in his front pocket. "This doesn't mean anything," she told him in a distressingly normal tone of voice. In the darkness her face was a white shadow marked with a pair of dark eyebrows: hard to read. "We're just doing this," she said.

It was still obviously better to say nothing. Now and then an airplane went overhead, tearing the night with its whining roar, red lights blinking. His hands drifted to her waist, to her shoulder blades, then slowly migrated forward until she pressed down with her elbows and upper arms and trapped his hands against her sides. Another dare? He didn't know. Better not push it too far, he thought. Against his chest her breasts were perfectly firm and high; they seemed to push against him with a desire of their own. They wanted to be touched, he knew it, but he dropped his hands to her hips again and kept on kissing her. She tasted like toothpaste. The contacts, the flowery soap, the toothpaste: she had planned it all. She was in control of the situation, he suddenly understood, and anything they did together would be done because she wanted it. It was not a bad feeling. In fact, it was a sort of relief.

When she finally broke away and led them back up the path to the bike, he felt he had been given his weekly allotment of her and was not to ask for anything more. He feared that the scooter had been stolen during their half-hour at the bottom of the ravine, but no, it was there, glowing white in the dimness, with the polished toy-moon helmet shining with real moonlight, all of it untouched. They mounted the scooter without a word, and when he dropped her off, she handed him the helmet with a long kiss. "I'm glad you liked the horse," she told him, and went off through her weedy back yard. He watched her slip silently into the house, and when she lifted her blind he waved and rolled away, over the humped asphalt, into the neighborhood. He could taste her, smell her, feel her weight still behind him on the bike, helping him lean into the turns, her head rolling on his shoulder. Oh, it was a great summer.

22

IN THE BASEMENT of his dead parents' house Henry had found
— when he returned from Ann Arbor, full of shock and sadness, to deal with their deaths — his father's pole-climbing
spikes. Their basement had been notably empty of memora-
bilia; his father had not been a sentimental man. But the spikes
were there, alone in a cardboard box on a high shelf, out of harm's
way, and though the box was even then covered with dust, Henry
liked to think of the old man keeping something aside for himself, a
reminder of what he had once been. Henry sold the house, kept the
spikes. He still had them. Now on a similar high shelf in his own
basement, they were hardened and useless — the leather brittle,
the rubber soles split along the arches — but the inch-long metal
cleats were still dangerously sharp, ready for action. Tested against
a finger, they could leave a little puncture.

As the summer went on, Henry found himself thinking more of
his father. Watching his own son entering adolescence, and seeing
William responding to the treatment as he was, and protecting his
secret so successfully for so long — these things made him proud.
He felt he was doing things right, and he was happy, and he wondered whether his father had ever felt this way.

It was hard to tell. His father had been a mild, watchful, unre-
sponsive man — a sinewy, narrow-shouldered, hollow-eyed Celt,
born the year the *Titanic* sank, whose first memory was seeing a

shipload of soldiers off to Fort Casey, where they would train on the cliffs to invade the Kaiser's France. "All kinds of hooting," he had remembered, "and the women were all beside themselves." He had not been capable of much joy, or so it had seemed to Henry. This appeared now to be a terrible handicap. What sort of life must he have had? What sort of pleasures had it given him? In Henry's presence, his father had been quiet to the point of rudeness. His youth spent stringing telephone line was one of the few things he had liked to talk about — stringing line, the problem with Eisenhower (Kennedy, Johnson, the first two years of Nixon), and the mulish stupidity of the bosses at City Light. Though he had been twenty years at a desk, he had always seen himself as a lineman, someone brought indoors for a season, and he tended to dismiss the untested, management-trained men around him. Stringing line had been a good job in the Depression. Hot, lonely, difficult, dangerous, but a good job, and a sort of primitive shame had forever attached, in his mind, to sitting indoors. It was that sort of man who had got the country in trouble in the first place, and only a war had got them out of it. When Henry told his father he was interested in medical school, he had looked at Henry, looked at the sky, looked at the sidewalk they were standing on, and said, narrowing his eyes, "That's a nice long time to spend indoors." In other words, not a real job. It had been maddening, Henry remembered. But now he reflected: his father had been ashamed of his work, of sitting inside all those years, and it was this shame, probably, that had contributed to his joylessness.

He himself was a better father than that, Henry knew. But what sorts of strange things was he inadvertently teaching his own son? It was one more thing he would never know. They lived in a neighborhood of lawyers, computer wizards, doctors, in a city that was flush with money and civic pride, where the public schools taught marine science and constitutional law to tenth-graders if they wanted it, and Darren seemed to accept it all as naturally as Henry had accepted his father's reticence and the empty, listless, hazy days of his own childhood. No one in their neighborhood had what his father would have considered a real job. Not him; not Gerald Turgerson, retired from the city manager's office; not Saul Harstein when he was alive; not Ted Bell, a land-use lawyer; not Kevin White, who though supposedly retired was now consulting for a venture-capital group in Kirkland.

"We could set you up with some HotFoot," Kevin had told him one afternoon in his sepulchral voice, over the laurels. "It's just a five-figure buy-in."

Five figures. "The first four figures would have to be zero," Henry told him.

"It's a hell of an opportunity," said Kevin. "You can't turn up a little play money, maybe?"

"That doesn't sound like play money."

"You'd get it all back," Kevin intoned, "I can just about guarantee."

"I don't think so," said Henry, and turning to go up the sidewalk, he found himself hot with embarrassment. Everyone else had money to burn. Not him. But every father had his own shame, he supposed.

What little extra cash he did have he was giving to Thomas Benhamouda. A hundred dollars a week. More expensive than smoking, not yet a cocaine habit. Thomas now appeared in an array of new clothes: the same baggy jeans and baseball hats that Darren favored, to Henry's mystification. It didn't make him look good, did it? Well, it must, in someone's eyes. Thomas had returned safely from California, carrying an envelope in which Gary Hauptmann had placed copies of his own series of tests. On top of the stack was a big yellow Post-it that said only "!" in heavy black marker. Enough said. "That man's *depressing*," Thomas told him, accepting his cash. Five twenties, with Jackson's big face, off-center, folded into his shirt pocket.

Henry flipped through Gary's photocopies: the same tests, the same sequence, the same glaringly impossible findings. He and Gary had both calculated Thomas's mutation rate as 1 in 10^{22}, which was so far beyond the normal results it was difficult to comprehend. The normal rate was 1 in 10^9 — still a vanishingly small number, but when you added up the number of cells and the amount of mitosis they underwent, it was enough to make you get old and die. If mutation rates were the only variable, Thomas would live an unthinkably long time: millions of years. Whether this was actually possible was another story. And it couldn't be possible. It couldn't be. But why not? Here it was, in Gary's chaotic and wandering hand.

To have his findings confirmed like this was not, Henry found, much of a comfort. In fact it made Thomas seem a little frightening. Terminally ill patients were frightening, and Thomas was terminally healthy, and it amounted almost to the same thing: he inhabited a very different country, with entirely different rules. What would you do first if you knew you would live to be a million years old? What would it matter what you did? What would you care about? Nothing. Yourself.

"Depressing?" Henry asked.

"Yeah, I mean he's got like all these pictures on his wall of all these people who died, all these kids, and he's talking about 'em and whatever, and then he's like 'You're a very lucky shit, Thomas — you should be dead by now.'" His mimicry was perfect, and Henry had to laugh. "Sha, he *is,* man! He's always talking about his wife doesn't love him anymore and his dog's about to bite him and whatever, and when he sticks me with the needle it hurts, man — he's *rough.*" He extended his bare arm, but it was unmarked. "Just *pah-pah-pah-pah,*" he said, jabbing himself. "No touch."

"You like California?"

"They put me up in this hotel. It was all right." *Aaiight.* "They didn't let me go anywhere."

"You like their open MRI?"

"Sha, y'all should get one of them! I was just sitting there like when's it supposed to be happening and they're like, It's over, and I'm like, Say what? And then they unstrap me and I'm like, Man, that was easy."

"So you're healthy," Henry said.

"You say so." Thomas rolled his shoulders, said, "But I was thinking something."

Uh-oh. "What's that?"

"Don't call me stupid, all right? But like what if somebody meant for my parents to have a kid with this, and I didn't get it so it's not me, it's Giles?"

"That's not how it works."

"I'm not talking about how it works, I'm just talking about *fate.* I'm talking about the way things should be. I think, if you ever cure him? Then I think you should give it to me instead. Make me old."

"I don't think we know how to do that."

"You could like" — he wagged his head — "*research* it, man. Because what if I *want* to get old? That dude Gary thinks I'm gonna be like this forever." He gestured dismissively at his slender frame. "Like I'm never gonna grow up, really, I'll always be the same as I am right now. That's why that girl never calls me anymore, 'cause she met some older dude in Oregon. And I want to go to college, and instead I'm just going to be this whatever, look like I'm fourteen and whatever all my life. I can't even get into movies, man, and she's all like talking about how stupid I am."

She met someone? "You can go to college, Thomas, you're not frozen in time."

"Am I ever gonna get bigger than this?"

"We don't know. There's never been anyone like you."

"Can't you like guess or something?"

"We can guess. Physically, you take after your mother in other ways. She's a small woman. You'll probably be a fairly small adult man."

"I try to lift weights and whatever, but nothing happens. I mean, I get toned but I don't get any bigger." He lifted his shirt, flexed his abdomen. "*That's* all right. But I got no arms."

"Some people are just like that. It might not have anything to do with what you've got, it might just be who you are. Who you would have been anyway."

Thomas shook his head. "But what about my brain, man? I try to read shit like what that girl's got, or like I'm listening to the news and whatever, and I just don't understand it. I mean, they're all talking about Russia and . . ." He gestured hopelessly. "I don't know, whatever, like Clinton and this and that, and I just don't understand anything they say."

"Have you ever been tested for a learning disorder?"

"Sha, so I am stupid."

"A lot of people have them."

"Nah, man, I think it's my *brain,*" he insisted. "I don't think it works right. I think maybe I got a tumor or something. Like I used to be able to do all kinds of shit, like in math? In fourth grade? I was like the top whatever, we had these groups? I was in the Hummingbirds. But now up at that school I was in that retard class and I didn't even know what the man was talking about."

"We know you don't have a tumor." But cognitive decline was possible. Behaviorally Thomas had deteriorated too, according to his parents. But still: he had changed schools. The schools in Detroit were probably inferior. There would be peer pressure against success. "We can run some more baseline cognitive tests, which might help. We could see where you are now. Then do the same tests again six months from now, see if you're getting better. You had a little trouble fitting in at Garfield, it sounded like?"

"Man, don't talk to me about that school."

"Did you make any other friends? Besides Sandra?"

"No," Thomas said. "People don't like me up there."

"You think next year'll be easier?"

Thomas waved a tired hand. "I don't even want to talk about it."

Henry changed the subject. "Listen, when you were in California, did you see a guy named Gunnar Peterson?" With a nervous flick, Henry called the Allied Genomics site onto his monitor. "That guy?"

Thomas looked at the screen. "That dude smelled nasty, man. Like not BO, but funky."

"He was there."

"Just sitting there." Thomas shrugged. "Lot of people there, man."

"Well," Henry said, "you might be seeing more of him."

"I got to fly more?"

"Probably."

"Oh, man." Thomas grimaced. "Why I got to do that?"

"They're the other experts in this disease," Henry told him. It was not quite untrue. "They may be taking over your case eventually."

"You all just flying me around the world for no reason, man. I hate being up in that plane."

"It won't be very often."

Now Thomas was getting angry. "Man, you all pretend to help me, but you don't even care about who I am. You don't even know who I am at all. You all think you can find shit out, but I'm just sitting here like, *Whatever,* I'm just like walking around and you all don't know shit about me. You know what that girl did at that camp?"

"What?"

"That girl. That *girl,* you know? You want to know what she was doing at that camp?"

Sandra. The older guy in Oregon. No, he didn't want to know. Not from Thomas. From the laboratory came the whirring of the PCR machine as it gently heated and cooled, heated and cooled its strands of DNA. Glass beakers clinked against the metal racks. A drawer was pushed roughly shut. "Listen," Henry said.

"You want to know what that big old fat bitch was doing?"

"Listen —"

"You want to know, bitch?" *Bee-yatch*. His head was held perfectly still, upright on a slender, flawless neck. "You want to know what that bitch was doing?"

"Stop it."

Thomas's voice was soft with menace. "You want to know, motherfucker? You want to know? You all think you know everything." He stared at Henry.

Henry said nothing. A long silence followed. The PCR machine beeped, announcing the end of its cycle.

"I thought so. All's I'm about to say is there's some shit you don't know," Thomas said finally, extending his perfect arm for the needle. "That's all's I'm about to say — there is some shit you do not know."

So Gunnar Peterson had been there. He had met Thomas. Gary and Peterson and Thomas had been in the same room. Henry could see it in his mind's eye — Peterson's mild pink face, observing from the corner; Gary's manic exclamations as he peered into Thomas's flawless ears. And then what? Peterson and Gary sitting down, looking over the files, deciding what the boy was worth? He struggled to imagine this part of it. Thomas glowering from the corner, hating the world?

After work he drove by the Durbins' house, found Bernie in a green apron, the smell of garlic in the air. "That's good news," Bernie told him reassuringly. "Means the fish is on the line."

"I haven't heard anything."

"You're about to panic, Henry." Bernie put a hand out. "This is very common."

"Now that you mention it, maybe I should."

"Listen to Bernie. There is nothing to worry about. Right now they're down there putting together a proposal. Everybody's going to be very happy. And I have a surprise for you, by the way."

"A good one?"

"A good one." Bernie took his arm and led him into the depths of the house, through the glowing, fragrant kitchen, onto the sun porch in the back, where William sat in a wicker chair reading *Red*

Mars. "Lo and behold," Bernie said, "the boy. Meet William. William, I'd like you to meet an old friend of mine. What was your name again, sir?"

William patiently put down his book and looked up. In the day's gray light he still looked old — unspeakably, unnaturally old — but his color was better. Bright splashes of pink had appeared across his cheeks. "You're such a nerd, Dad," he said.

Bernie nudged Henry. "You hear it?"

"*Yes.* Holy crap." William's voice — Henry could not quite believe his ears — had changed. Deepened. It was still reedy and thin, but deeper. "That's incredible."

"It just started a couple days ago. I thought he had a cold at first."

"Hey, say something." Henry knelt in front of William's chair. "Tell me what time it is."

William cleared his throat. "Luke," he said, "I am your father."

"Does that feel different?"

"No." William shrugged. "I don't know. No." Embarrassed, he looked away. "It just happened."

"It doesn't feel different?"

"No."

Testosterone. He took William's hands in his and examined them: little dark hairs had sprouted here and there on the withered skin. Hard to believe, but there they were. He counted them: six, ten, a dozen, twenty. "Looks like you might be hitting puberty, my friend."

"Oh, great." William rolled his eyes. "That'll be interesting."

"Yes, it will."

"I'm going to get dates with eighty-year-old women."

"Don't knock it till you've tried it," Bernie said.

"Gross, Dad."

"Me? Me, gross?" Bernie turned, his arms out, appealing joyously to the audience beyond the windows, declaiming to the overcast sky. "I ask you, me?"

Henry was still holding William's hands, kneeling before him, and when Henry met William's gaze again he felt a surge of love, a crushing thunder of it. How brave William was! How remarkable a boy!

But William was not looking at him with love. No: there in the wicker chair he wore a look of terrible fear. It was a private expression, a brief one, meant for Henry alone, and when Bernie turned to them again it vanished. But Henry had seen it. It was unmistakable. Fear. *What happens next?* he was asking. And Thomas was right about some things. *I don't know,* Henry had to tell him silently.

Ilse had gone to Goodwill and eyed the furniture and picked out a room's worth of desks, filing cabinets, and old office chairs. "I told her we would return it covered with mud," she said, putting a set of unfamiliar keys on the counter, "as a courtesy."

The Suburban keys. "I don't know if I can drive that thing," he said.

"I can — I think my penis is small enough. All the commercials show them covered with mud, but the Whites don't even let theirs get dusty. All the ads show them out in the desert, even though people only use them to go to the grocery store, which a regular car could do without taking up all the parking spaces! All the way to the line!" Ilse put her palms together. "They're all over the garage now, and you can hardly see between them. So stupid. People are so sheeplike."

Henry had not owned a new car in his adult life, and to climb into the big Suburban and feel it surge forward under Ilse's direction was a novel and not entirely unpleasant experience. Darren went along to help move the heavy things up two flights of stairs, and from the far rear seat he called up, "Turn on the TV!"

"Oh, there can't be." Ilse craned her head. "Oh, no, this is terrible. This is the end of civilization."

"On a long drive," Henry said, "it might be nice."

"Yeah, Mom, it'd be nice."

She threw up one hand. "What about car games? What about, you know, guessing what flower I am or looking for license plates or just sitting there being sort of bored and thinking about things, like a person does?" With an idle flip she ran the window down, ran it back up again. "It's too hard to roll down a window," she observed, "so we make it go *rrrrrr* instead. Very useful."

"Mom, you're such a coelacanth."

"Who said that?" She looked in the rearview mirror. "I can hardly hear you, you're so far away."

"A coelacanth!"

"No," she said, "I guess it's just the wind."

It was ten blocks from Goodwill to the office, but they had to make two trips, depositing in the dusty lobby of the Chin Ha building a collection of tatty chairs and particleboard shelving and one immensely heavy steel desk that seemed to have been welded together from the hull of an old battleship. Upstairs, Darren stalked around the empty rooms with his pants drooping and a wide strip of white underwear showing, ducking his head beneath doorways and disappearing down the hidden corridor for a minute before returning. "This is pretty cool," he said. He went to the windows. "What's Mom doing, exactly?"

"Her favorite thing in the world," Henry said, his voice rebounding off the white walls. "Giving people advice."

"Yeah." Darren smiled, a quick secretive grin, then leaped as high as he could, his hand outstretched. No chance: the ceilings were twelve feet high at least. He landed lightly. "You sure there's no elevator?"

"Yeah."

"That desk is like a car."

"A small, efficient car," Henry said.

"Peeble," Darren cried, jumping again, "are zo sheepliiike!"

The stairs were wide but steep, and as they maneuvered the enormous steel desk from landing to landing, Henry grew sweaty and achy, and when the desk leaned against the banister the wood gave a frightening shriek, as if it were an old floor being pried up. "Shit," his son said, laughing under his breath, and helped him wrench the thing back into balance. Darren was strong, Henry saw — maybe as strong as he was. It was astonishing, really, to watch his son's arms at work, to watch his eyes as he calculated an angle and then glanced back at Henry as they made another tight turn. "The master is at work," Darren said, and when they were finally in the upstairs hallway he counted aloud, for Henry's benefit, the numbers on the office doors. Aside from their creaking footsteps the hall was absolutely silent. Down its length the brass knobs on the doors were all polished, like a row of buttons on a sleeve.

The desk fit through the doorway — barely — and when they took it to the windows and stepped back to appreciate the effect, Henry was struck again by how appealing the rooms were and how at home his wife seemed in them, as if she had in fact found some remnant of her early life, an idea that made him happy. As the three of them filled the rooms with the rest of the furniture — a row of metal chairs, a pair of black filing cabinets, an old yellow rug, a low pine coffee table, a dozen particleboard shelving units, a greasy armchair that smelled of cigars — Henry could not help feel he was doing something good.

His wife was bright with excitement, dusting and cleaning everything, and the rooms came to smell of Windex. She opened a creaking window, which let in the sounds of the street. Their gray shadows moved on the white walls, and now and then the reflected light from a windshield put a shimmering pool on the ceiling, a pool that held little grains of shadow, imperfections on the glass three stories down, and then the pool would slide away across the ceiling and vanish.

Every so often, though, William's look of terror would enter Henry's thoughts, and he would feel his own fear rising in him — fear that Gary was right, that William was going to die anyway, and that all the risks he had taken would be for nothing. Then he would turn and see his wife swabbing out a drawer, his son collapsed on the yellow rug, and he would wonder what the hell he had been thinking: wasn't this enough? Wasn't this loveliness more than enough for any man's happiness? But what man would have done anything else in his position? If he had said no to William, to Bernie, to Lillian, could he have stood here in good conscience and felt he was a decent man? No, he didn't think so.

When he had finished wiping down the chairs, he went over and sprawled on the rug beside Darren. The boy radiated heat and a scent of healthy sweat. After a silence Henry said, "You're getting stronger."

Beside him Darren looked at him from the corners of his eyes. "Just in time," he answered, and reached out to feel Henry's bicep. It felt loose under his pincer grasp; the striated fibers were deteriorating. But Darren's look was shy, full of humor. "Somebody's got to move the heavy stuff," he said, and rolled against Henry and away again, leaving a hot imprint on Henry's shoulder and hip. His son, his boy.

Out of sight behind them, Ilse's rag squeaked across the glass.

It bothered him that he should feel compelled to ask his daughter about what had happened in Eugene, and when he finally managed it the next day, she gave him a look of such intentional blankness that he knew Thomas had been telling at least some version of the truth.

"I know you were seeing Thomas a little bit," Henry ventured, standing at her door. "But not anymore?"

"He's gross, Dad."

Gross. "Yeah. Listen, do you mind me asking, was there somebody you met down there?" He tipped his head southward. "At camp?"

"Not really." She shrugged. "I mean, there's always guys and whatever, but."

That was all he could get from her — an evasion. But really it was all he wanted. And she sensed that, he saw, and was doing him the kindness of lying. The summer mailbox was beginning to clog with college brochures, and he occasionally caught her prone on her stomach, staring at a page for long minutes, visibly trying to imagine herself into the scenes of leafy quads and stone buildings. Sometimes she rolled over and held the brochure overhead, as though searching for the secret writing hidden in the margins.

To Henry's eye the brochures were pure joy, photographs of heaven, where all the students were of different races and looked good in tank tops and laboratory goggles. His wife rolled her eyes. "The entire developed world is moving toward one industry, which is marketing."

"Yeah, but look, this is real. This is a real lab."

"Your lab doesn't look like that."

"It would if we had a photographer coming in," he said. "Everyone cleans up a little when they're getting their picture taken. What's wrong with that?"

"Nothing." She grimaced. "Well, no, everything, since they're trying to get our money."

"She was looking at Pepperdine today. She said it looked comfortable."

"Oh my, our little girl. Well, she's right — she wouldn't have to think a new thought for four years."

They were both fairly sure she had stopped seeing Thomas. But did that mean there had been someone in Eugene? Probably, they agreed.

Her friend Colleen was around a lot more too, which might have indicated something: at least twice a week she would come striding across the porch in her canvas shoes and knock three times, loudly, on the front door. A ghostly, incandescent girl, with brilliantly clear skin and a high Elizabethan forehead, every inch of it on display with her hair hidden beneath the square white cap. Mennonite? No, but something like it. How on earth had her parents produced this daughter, who was plainly of the modern world and addressed him with a forthrightness that felt almost like flirting?

"They say you're trustworthy," Colleen explained with a simmering smile. "So I can come over."

"Good to know I'm trustworthy."

"Yes. Because of course *I'm* very *un*trustworthy."

"Oh," he said.

"Not in the usual ways — not in the boy-slash-sex-slash-drugs-slash-whatever way," Colleen said, her eyes jumping rapidly across his face, "but in the ways that would bother them the most."

"That's not a coincidence, I'm guessing."

She put a slender, cool hand on his forearm. "How right you are!" she exclaimed. "No, they would die if they knew what I really thought." Which was what? Henry wondered. But then she went upstairs, into his daughter's room, where they could be heard talking and laughing: two women, suddenly, their voices muffled, confidential, at work on the usual conspiracies, he imagined — boys, parents, fairness, sex.

"No, they talk about how much they love us, Henry," his wife whispered into his ear on the futon. "About what wonderful love-lies we all are."

And then it was happening. "Dr. Henry Moss," said a mild voice over the phone on the second Friday in August, "it's Gunnar Peterson."

"Gunnar. Okay. Hang on." He jumped up, closed the office door, and sat down again. The receiver sat like a little viper on the desktop. *Pick it up.* A virile, cagey spirit entered him: Saul Harstein's canny soul. "Hi," he said.

"Do I find you at a convenient time?"

"Sure."

"I should congratulate you. You have quite a nice little thing up there."

"I guess I do," Henry agreed, "if I'm hearing from you."

"Oh, Dr. Moss, I've admired your work for a long, long time." Peterson's voice was warm, genial, grandfatherly. "All those children. You've been doing such good, good work, Dr. Moss, for so long. We need more of you, in my opinion."

"Thanks," Henry said.

"Now I understand you're interested in talking about a price?"

"I am?" Didn't he need Bernie, Justine? "I don't know. I've got lawyers and . . . so on."

"Oh, good. Good. How about we just talk, to start with."

"Okay."

"Let me first confirm a few things, if that's agreeable to you, Henry."

"Okay," he managed. But this conversation felt suddenly dangerous. He didn't have to agree to anything, did he? "Go ahead."

"All right." Peterson's voice carried a plain, careful Western accent, the same one Henry's parents' voices had had; those vacant childhood lots of Wedgwood lifted momentarily into Henry's vision, his father wrestling obscurely beneath the forsythia, emerging with his glass of beer at a dangerous angle. "Now." There was a rustling of papers, and Peterson began. "He's seventeen, of Algerian parents, American citizen, carries two copies of the Hickman gene from his parents, forty and forty-one. A younger brother, three, also carries two copies of the Hickman gene, exhibits typical, et cetera, while the older brother appears normal, due it appears to a mutation adjacent to the Hickman gene on the same, et cetera. Speak up when my information fails me."

"Sure," Henry said.

"Please do stop me. Since April your laboratory has worked with this asymptomatic boy in an effort to determine why he is asymptomatic, and to that end you've turned up an anomalous protein produced by his mutation, a protein that you have of course reproduced and that you've called AAC32, right? All of this is correct?" Henry said nothing, and after a few seconds Peterson cleared his throat. "This is of course one of the things we've been interested in lately. Has Dr. Hauptmann been in touch with you? Dr. Hauptmann has just agreed to come work for us — I don't know if he has told you."

"He has? Really?"

There was a careful hesitation. "I guess he was in a mood to make a change. I imagine he wouldn't mind my telling you — he mentioned that you two were fairly close. I'm surprised he hasn't called."

"When was this?"

"Very recently. Anyway, Henry, I'm ready to make you an offer. Depending on what you've got, what you can show us vis-à-vis the rodents, we're thinking somewhere in the neighborhood of eighty-five thousand, depending, for all rights, beginning to end."

"Eighty-five thousand?"

"That's our standard rate."

"Dollars?"

"We would distribute it in three parts, Henry, for tax reasons, so you'd see approximately — what? Twenty-eight thousand a year for three years."

"Yeah."

"And it's not only cash, it actually amounts to quite a bit more in eventual goodwill dollars when you consider the publicity that will accrue to the condition should our research lead to a viable treatment. Money becomes much easier to come by once the end is in sight, as you know. Everyone loves the light at the end of the tunnel. That's why everyone's always going off prematurely about their AIDS vaccines — it's at least as much publicity as it is science. I was a researcher too, Henry. I suppose you know that. I used to fill out grant forms and send them off to the March of Dimes and sit around waiting for my rent check to bounce. Or worse, to have it be cashed." Peterson's voice was measured, quiet, insistent. Around its edges was a whispery rushing sound, as though he had too much wind in his lungs. "Those were the days," he said.

"We've signed a deal." Eighty-five? That couldn't be right. "We've got the kid exclusively."

Peterson became warmer, friendlier. "Of course you have. What else would you do?"

"You want all rights?"

"That's how we do things here. Beginning to end. All products, all patents, all programs. Any copies of the thing we'd ask you to hand over. Just pack it all up in a Cold Crate and we're in business."

A dark shaft of despair went through him. "Don't you usually do royalties?"

"Royalties?" Peterson said, stumped.

"Royalties on future returns?"

"Royalties. I suppose once in a while, if it's something worth bothering over. Frankly, I think eighty-five thousand is a little much for something that addresses the problems of exactly sixty-eight people on the planet. You can't expect us to make much money from it, after all. It's a nice thing to do, that's all — it's a sort of boutique item for us. It's not cancer, Henry. It's Hickman."

"Then why do you want it at all?"

"As I say," Peterson answered, "it's a nice thing to do."

He was bluffing. He had to be. "You're not serious," Henry said.

"No?"

"You know what we've got? Reduction of replication errors by at least ninety-nine percent. No matter what we do to the originals. This isn't just surveillance, it's like Scotchgard. This kid's got the cleanest genome in the world. You want to sequence somebody? Sequence this kid. No junk mutations. Nothing."

"Yes, it does sound like you've got something. He's a remarkable boy, Benhamouda."

"We've been publishing confidentials with the NIGH all along. Dick Ottergard's got a dozen sealed envelopes in his vault, I guess. God knows what he thinks is in them — he's always thought I was a little crazy."

"But does it work on non-progeroids, Henry? The mice?"

"Not yet," Henry admitted. Down the hall, the mice continued to show no effects at all. The progeroid mice were still sliding unaltered toward their early demise, creeping around the edges of their cages, their cells degrading exponentially. The healthy mice were still healthy but showed zero diminishment of their mutation rate. So it didn't work on either healthy mice or progeroid mice, not even after weeks of constant injections. William was getting better — there was no question about it. His rate was down to around 10^8, considerably better than it had ever been. It worked. It undeniably worked, at least on one progeroid patient. But this was information he could never use, never bargain with. "We're still waiting," he said.

"So no, in other words. And that *is* the question, isn't it."

"It's a question."

"Oh," Peterson countered, "I think it's *the* question. If the protein worked as a hypercatalysis in a normal cellular environment, it would be really quite a find. But the value of the thing is minimal otherwise, isn't it? Say about eighty-five thousand dollars? And the notion that it might work outside of the progeroid population seems to me very unlikely, Henry. Otherwise we'd have seen something like this before. One would think. It's just the odds, Henry — they're awfully long. If it doesn't work on normal mice, it won't work on people."

"That's not necessarily true."

Peterson huffed, a little impatient. "I hope you're not really waiting on those results, because I have the feeling you'll be waiting an awfully long time. And then you've possibly delayed the availability of treatment for all sixty-eight children and even possibly lost yourself a nice little paycheck for no reason at all. Let us take the gamble, Henry. We've got the facilities. We could be running enormous studies within the week. That's what corporations are for. And we can write you off if we need to."

"Thanks a lot."

"You want me to appreciate your work," Petersen stated. "I do. You've done a marvelous job — you may have found something that's quite wonderful after all, with some very interesting narrow-targeted applications in the long run. But you've heard my best. This is it. First chance, last chance. You needn't answer now. Or is there someone else? You have another offer? Or you've already done the human studies? The review board upstairs is full of your stockholders and lets you do exactly what you want? That's almost certainly not true. Larry Rich and Stephan Wernerheit are very conservative men. Certainly you can't be already experimenting on humans with any approval from them." Hearing no contradiction, Peterson said, in consolation, "We could name it after you, if you like."

"Name it after William Durbin."

"The Durbin Treatment. Durbin's Treatment. Whatever you like." Peterson's voice grew light and gentle. "You must love him very much. I hear he's very sick now."

Henry let the line hum between them: there was that temptation again, to confess. But also it was the urge to celebrate, to exult in William's improvement. Did Peterson suspect anything? He might. And now Peterson was giving him the opportunity to admit everything, and the lure was powerful. Obscurely, Henry felt he deserved to be reprimanded, humiliated, punished: it was his orphan's due. But he resisted. "He's doing a little better this week" was all he allowed himself.

"Lovely. Lovely," said Peterson. "Shall we meet sometime, all of us together? Your lawyers, my lawyers, et cetera, et cetera, et cetera?"

By the time Henry put the receiver back in its cradle and cleared his desk with shaking hands, it was after five. Victoria had gone home, leaving him the afternoon mail, which he flipped through. There was nothing of interest: equipment catalogs, subscription offers, nothing. Unthinking, he threw it all away on top of the remains of his lunch; taking a patient breath, he retrieved the mail and slid it, instead, into the recycling bin.

Eighty-five thousand. Eighty-five. Minus expenses, divided in two, minus taxes. It was almost nothing. What would he tell his wife? The vision of Saul's body mounded beneath the quilt had risen in his mind's eye. William, carried down the stairs in his father's arms, then standing in the soft green light of the foyer. His own son, rolling against him. His daughter behind her door. Gretl at work at the far bench, her head bowed. Had it been worth it? If he were any sort of decent man, he would take the money. It was what he had waited for, wasn't it? He would pick up the telephone and do the decent thing — call Bernie, call Justine, do the deal, and let some other man take things over. Pack up a Cold Crate. Send Thomas and his venom and his brooding ferocity out of town, out of his life forever.

He would never own the sequence again, a thought that struck a sad final note in him. But he had always felt strange about owning it.

And he had done his work. He could just hand it over now to the people who could reproduce it, who could run the studies faster and on a larger scale than he ever could. Allied Genomic would do good science. And he would be involved in some way or other. He could work for Gary, who would like having him to boss around. It was enough. He had done enough. Eighty-five thousand dollars waiting for him on the other end of the telephone. *Quit,* he thought, *while you're ahead.*

He would. He would, he promised himself. But instead, with a thumping heart, he removed a syringe from a drawer, filled it with Thomas's enzyme, clenched his fist, and sank the silver needle deep into his arm.

FOUR

23

THE NEEDLE was visible as it lay in the blue tunnel of his vein; when he depressed the plunger, the fluid vanished into his blood. *Safe journey.* The angle of injection was awkward, and when he removed the spike the wound began to bleed. He cursed under his breath, held his dripping arm away from his pants, set the needle down on his desk. Quickly he laid a pad of gauze across the little hole, taped it down hard, then lifted his arm over his head and pressed his fingers against the gauze. Okay. Done. A healthy patient? Here he was. Live forever. Never die.

He didn't expect anything to happen immediately, and nothing did. He sat for a minute, waiting, his hands emptying of blood above his head, his shoulders tiring; they still ached from wrestling Ilse's desk up the stairs. Was he taking a risk? Yes, of course he was. If the enzyme did nothing to mice, it would almost certainly do nothing to him — Peterson was right about that. But there was a possibility, very remote, that he would keel over and die in the next few minutes from some unforeseen interaction.

A minute later, when the bleeding had stopped, he rolled down his sleeve and stood up. Gingerly he tucked the empty syringe into the *NEJM* stacks — sharp side in, so no one would stab himself inadvertently — and made his way into the lab. Afternoon traffic, he saw, was clogged on the 520 viaduct. He took one deep breath. Another. Nothing. If anything, he felt a tiny wave of nausea. But he could only be imagining it, so soon after.

Gretl was on her stool in the corner of the laboratory, tending to her computer.

"Listen, that was Peterson on the phone," he said to the back of her head.

"Oh?"

He felt sick, sicker. Swallowed. "So guess what? Gary Hauptmann left Berkeley. He's at AG."

"No." She swiveled around on her stool. "He *isn't*." Her mouth opened in astonishment. "But he loves Berkeley. He loves the idea of it. He loves being Gary at Berkeley. That's what he is. It must be the money."

"That, and Gary's always had that tendency to swoon. So Peterson offered us eighty-five thousand dollars."

Gretl started. "He did?"

"You think it's enough?"

"Enough for what?"

"I don't know." A heat — could it be? — was gathering in his elbow, strangely, as though a hot pad were being held against it. "Where's Chin?"

"Henry, you look peculiar."

"I don't want to end up selling short."

"You think eighty-five thousand dollars is short?"

"I have no idea," Henry said. "He wants all the rights to Thomas."

Gretl's eyes shifted. "The sooner we get him out of here, the better."

"Somebody's been giving Peterson an awful lot of good information — I guess it must be Gary. Or maybe Lisa's been more persistent than I give her credit for."

"Or Chin. Or me." She lifted an eyebrow. "I would have, if I thought we could get rid of Thomas that easily."

"Listen, I just took some of it myself. Just now."

It took her a second. "Oh, no, *Henry!*" she cried. She touched his arm, stood. "How do you feel?"

"Oh, you know, about the same."

"How much?"

"Just one."

"Why? Why would you do something like that?"

"It's worth more," he said, "if it works on me too."

She stared, stunned, and dropped her hand. "That's the most ridiculous thing I've ever heard in my life. You and Gary, both of you absolutely losing your minds." Her wire-rimmed glasses had slipped far down her nose. "We could have gone around collecting aluminum cans if it's that bad."

"I don't think it's going to hurt me."

"Probably not." She was thinking. "I'm going to take some blood," she decided, and quickly put together a syringe. "Make a fist," she said, swabbing his arm. "We want some unaffected samples. How long ago?"

"Two minutes."

She inserted the needle with a technician's clean confidence, and when the vial was full she withdrew it painlessly and handed him a tissue. "I can't believe you did this."

"It won't kill me."

"As far as you know. I'm too old to drag your body down the hall to the incinerator. I'd probably slip a disk. Look out." She inserted the needle again, lower on his forearm this time. "You could have asked me to do it," she said. "I'm light enough so you could just put me in a garbage bag and take me down to the dumpster."

"The mice are okay."

"They're mice, Henry." She fixed him with a glacial stare. "Mice! They're analogs. We haven't even tried it on pigs yet. It's insane."

The adeno-associated virus, carrying its load of precious information, would arrive at its target within minutes, he knew, and begin infecting him, possibly, with health. Was one dose enough to lower his mutation rate? He doubted it. It had not been enough in William, and Thomas had been exposed to the enzyme literally since before he was born. Could it maybe give him a version of Hickman? The thought sent a sudden chill into him. But no, it couldn't happen; the missing nucleotides that resulted in Hickman were present in his cells, and the sequence delivered by the virus produced an exquisitely sensitive repair mechanism, not the disease. No. Still, he shuddered at the thought.

"Salk did it," Henry said.

Gretl grimaced. "Oh, what do you need with more money? I suppose you want to get into the market."

"William Durbin says the market's going to tank."

"William. *That* was a reasonable thing to do. This was not. This was greedy and reckless." She taped two pads of gauze to his arm. "Say aah," she said, and with a hard metal scraper took five samples from his cheeks. She was quick but gentle, tilting her head back to see into his mouth, then daubing each sample into its own petri dish, tapping the scraper on the Plexiglas twice to remove the little clots of cells, pink blobs no bigger than a letter on a page. She would culture them, watch them mutating naturally as they aged, calculate their natural mutation rate, then compare that number with the number she would get from later samples now that he had injected himself. More work for her, he realized. She capped the dishes, labeled them *HM cheek 1* through *HM cheek 5,* and set them on the wire rack in the refrigerator. "You know, it just might really work on you," she said, closing the glass door on its rubber seal. "And then what? Do you really want to live forever?"

"Don't you?"

"Then you'd have to give it to Ilse. And then the kids. But how do you know they want to do it? What if they don't? Then what do you do? And what if they have friends — then what? And what about me?" She adjusted her glasses. "You realize you could never run this place without me."

"He wanted it all. He wanted all our samples, all our work, everything."

"It's called lowballing, Henry."

Of course it was. Of course. How stupid of him. "But it was just *so* low."

"It's an opening offer — it's supposed to be terrible. You're expected to negotiate." She put a hand up to his sore cheek. "Go home. Lie down and drink some water. Bernie will take care of it."

"Sha," Henry said.

"Sha," she answered grimly.

Both his forearms ached now, and gripping the steering wheel he could feel the site of his injection throbbing against his sleeve. Lowballing. Of course. What would Saul have done?

Poor Saul. Poor dead Saul.

He steered toward home, under the trees.

What had William felt? Slow — empty — calm. Was this, Henry wondered, the beginning of it? A pleasant, easeful feeling, as though he'd had a strong martini on an empty stomach. The nausea was gone. He drove, watching the traffic part around him.

He drove. In the afternoon's light the city seemed a pleasant encampment, the city of his youth, where water held the land in place and where the land had been cultivated to grow its orderly crop of houses on its sensible grid. Where the city made a dip into a hollow, the grid of streets dipped and twisted out of true to match the terrain. Mount Rainier was out, visible in brief glimpses as he made his way south, a great white cone against the haze. "It is an alp!" Ilse had cried, getting off the airplane all those years ago. Calm, empty, slow. And a creeping . . . what? Elation? But that could have been the conversation with Peterson, or it could all be psychosomatic. That was the problem, he reflected, with having no control group — you never knew what the hell you were looking at.

It was not until he parked the car at the bottom of the driveway that he began to feel really peculiar. Weirdly perceptive, as though his brain had been washed in a very clear, very cold and turbulent stream, then reinserted into his skull, refurbished, with all the fusible links scoured of their grime. The dashboard of the faithful Accord could be seen to carry on the drops and rises of its textured surface a coating of bright brownish dust, which in turn could be seen to be made of individual particles of various colors, green and red and black and white, tiny pixels that if derandomized could be compacted and rearranged to construct the flags of Liberia and Venezuela. The steering wheel with its knobby protrusions felt interesting under his hands, manmade material bent for an organic use and nearly organic in the shape it created in his mind, soft and rigid in a curiously fleshy way; and his keys were a slick tarnished pile of odd-shaped coins that he could trade for cars and rooms and the contents therein. Not quite like a morphine high, this feeling, but he could see what William meant.

The heat in his arm had spread up his arm, across the yoke of his shoulders, and up the back of his neck. As he stepped from the car he saw the yellow light hanging high in the perilous hemlocks as a kind of paint, a paint that was simultaneously transparent and tinged with the bright new green growth at the tips of the branches that hovered and dodged without hurry in the evening breeze. The car's engine ticked in the driveway. Each inhalation as he stood there seemed to gently excavate a soft double hollow in his chest, a sensation that was enjoyable but slightly frightening too, as though the light in the trees was also filling his lungs, making them visible through his ribcage and the cotton weave of his shirt.

He looked down at his chest: same old Henry. It felt odd, as though he were being microscopically invaded by the world. It was *working*. It had to be. He rolled up his sleeve and peeled back the tape, the gauze. The site of the injection was red and worried-looking, with a tiny flyspeck of a scab, and was faintly sore. He watched it for a long minute, waiting for it to heal. Across the street Saul's house sat empty, shadowed beneath the hemlocks. He turned his mind to it and felt nothing: it was a wall of shingles, a set of gutters, a series of windows now dull with the dust of summer, a roof sprinkled with needles. Looked back at his arm. No change.

He found Sandra in the living room, e-mailing. To the boy in Eugene, whoever he was, Henry intuited, and when she flipped quickly over to a game of solitaire, he knew he was right. The living room was dim and Sandra's hair glowed blue in the light from the monitor. Her hair was wispy and lifted away from her head in staticky agitation, and two or three strands lay horizontally across the air, attracted to the screen. She was a very big woman, he saw, round-shouldered in her T-shirt, thighs taut with muscle beneath the thready cuffs of her cutoffs, ankles strongly articulated and spreading into wide, agile feet that were bare on the carpet, curling with pleasure against the nap of the rug. She did not turn to see him come in, and as he approached he felt he was passing through a series of buffers that she had constructed around herself, buffers he could sense as variations in the pressure of the air; as he got closer the density of the atmosphere seemed to increase until at her shoulder he felt he could hardly lift a hand to touch her.

"What's his name?" he asked.

"Who?" She turned her face up to his.

"Whoever."

"I forget," she said. "Arthur something."

"Arthur."

"Very good, Dad."

"What's he like?"

A quick smile flashed across her face. "He's funny."

"Funny ha-ha, or funny strange?"

"Funny ha-ha," she told him. Her voice was different — some new settled note had entered it, a low tone of earned confidence — and Henry saw in a flash that she had had sex with Arthur. Of course she had. His heart clenched unpleasantly. Seventeen. Too young. But not that young, not these days. Someone she had found it worthwhile to stay in touch with — was that good or bad? She would delete all their e-mails now, he imagined, but wouldn't a sentimental streak command her to print them out, store them on a disk, keep them around in one way or another? Surely. Did he want to find them? No, he didn't think so. Thomas had offered to tell him and he had not wanted to hear it from him either, in whatever scrambled and tainted version he would have had to offer; Henry was a private enough man to appreciate his daughter's desire to keep certain things a secret. And a large part of him just didn't want to know about it at all, he realized — it was too terrible to think of.

He saw all this in a flash, a second in which his heart clenched, hardened, then relaxed again. He left his daughter and searched for his wife, but found her nowhere. As he passed from room to room, the objects of the house seemed extraordinarily distinct and present to his eye, and he saw as though for the first time the drifts of dust along the baseboards, and the tiny pebbles in the old plaster that cast their little shadows, and the wire racks that held their oatmeal boxes, and the plates and coat hooks and photographs on the walls, and the silver garbage can with its black piano pedal — everything seeming to hold within itself its perfect alternate form, a form that kept threatening, as he watched, to make itself known, as though the ideal Platonic toaster would at any moment appear in the room, responding to the wave that Henry's factual, approximated toaster had sent out, as lightning is drawn to heat. He closed his eyes. *This is some shit,* he thought, and for a second he was worried: what if it never stopped?

Upstairs the rooms seemed to be full of a kind of shimmering potential, the same potential he had sensed in the open houses he had visited with Ilse, an erotic infinitude of possibility. Infinitude. Live forever. He had felt all these things before, it seemed to him, but never with this kind of clarity, and never had things seemed to be so sensible to him, or so immediate. The odd bits and treasures in

Darren's room all seemed to be made of a weighty semiprecious alloy, the wills and longings of his adolescent son, and he examined each one with a fearful love. He should check himself in the mirror, he thought, and turned with care to the wall. He saw nothing unusual. Himself. His face intact.

He did not find his wife. "Where is she?" he asked the air as he went gingerly back downstairs, and Sandra called over her shoulder, "Outside." It was not that he could not feel his legs but that he felt them too distinctly, every muscle and tendon, every one of the bones of his feet as they bent, held, flexed, rebounded, bent again. The blood as it coursed through his heart, the wind in his lungs — he was a living wonder. In the ash tree the birds were hopping from branch to branch, arguing, and their song seemed a language he had been born knowing, a language he had forgotten but whose phrasings and melodies exactly fit some ancient structure in his brain, and it seemed if he listened long enough he would remember it all. Boy, he was high as hell, he thought, looking down at his hands. Gray hairs. They had been there before. They had, he assured himself. He was fifty-one.

The pear tree was full of hard little fruit; a few green ovoids had already fallen into the grass to nestle among the weeds, imitating frogs, and suddenly the grass looked very inviting. Henry went down on his knees and felt it with his palms, the wispy living hairiness of it shivering against his skin, the dampness of the earth rising through the knees of his corduroys. He lay down in the grass, on his back. What loveliness this was! What utter loveliness! His wife could be heard clattering around in the garage, but this seemed miles away, around the corner of the rhododendron bush. He would never tell her what he had done, never. It had been an act of rash irresponsibility, and he would hide the fact from her forever. This seemed the kindest course of action, and to have decided such a thing made him happy.

Beneath his head the earth was damp and cool. The sky above was blue but held faint tracings of white cloud, summer clouds visible above the globe of the ash tree and sailing over the soffits of the house, over the telephone wires, the wires turning in the breeze and the black rubber insulation flashing black, white, black, white, in the sun. In an instant Henry saw something else: his parents driving into the hills above Chehalis to find — Henry could see it as though he were there — one of his father's old lines, a nostalgic and sentimental mission for a quiet and unexpressive man. That's what they had been looking for — his father's old lines, strung through the timberland. They would have found them if they had made it to the top of the hill, would have seen them against the sun as he was seeing them now. A rational part of his brain knew this was not exactly knowledge, but it felt like knowledge to Henry, it had the certainty of knowledge. His mother had been in the passenger seat, along for the ride. With this sudden understanding came a flood of happiness: so he had inherited this from his father as well — not just a cautious nature but a sentimental one, and in this sense he was his father's son; if his father had been asked to dose William Durbin, he would have done so too. Henry closed his eyes and saw his father, thin-lipped, stepping out of the car at the top of the hill. If only.

His wife appeared overhead, a shadow. "Henry?" She held a roll of black electrical tape. "Are you awake?"

She was silhouetted against the sun, and in her shadow the day was cool. Her hair stood out around her head like a nimbus. "Sure," he said.

"You've been talking in your sleep out here."

"I was asleep?"

"For a few minutes. Did you know Darren has a tattoo?"

Asleep? He propped himself on his elbows. The back of his shirt was wet, soaking. Time had passed. "He does?"

"He did it himself. It's three little dotted lines on his foot."

"He did it himself?"

"With a needle and a ballpoint pen." She collapsed into the grass beside him. "Now he wants an eyebrow ring." She lay across his stomach, peeled a length of tape from the roll. "And if you say anything except *Oh, no,* I'm going to tape your mouth closed."

"Oh, no," he said.

"I agree with you entirely."

She was a warm shape against him. *It worked,* he thought. At least it had had some effect on him; he could not have imagined such an experience, could he? He could have, but he didn't think he had. What would his cells show in the weeks to come? Had he added another week, another year to his life this afternoon? Could he prove that something had happened to him? Only if his mutation rate had dropped, and only time would tell. There was no control group. He closed his eyes again. The peak of the buzz appeared to have passed with his unnoticed nap, and now he was merely agreeable and profoundly, deliciously relaxed, so much so that when they went inside he made his way through the dim living room to the sofa and fell asleep again in his damp shirt while Sandra continued her *tap-tap-tap* on the keyboard.

There on the sofa he dreamed he was speaking German to his wife. It was a familiar dream, one he seemed to have had on many occasions before; together they were debating, in the kitchen, whether to paint the walls or just wash them again. He wanted to paint, she wanted to wash. How rude it had been of him, his dream self thought, to have gone so long without learning his wife's native language! But now he had done it, and the sensation was surprising on his tongue; he was surprised, as one is in dreams, that he was so good at it, that the words he needed would come so easily to mind and that he was able to make one very convincing point: that in order to paint they would have to wash the walls anyway, so why not go the whole distance? Ilse in his dream considered this and answered, in German, that she was fond of the present color because it reminded her of a cake made of dogs. *A cake made of dogs?* It is an idiom, she told him. It meant vibrant, living, robust. He was still learning.

He woke, still on the sofa. Sandra was gone. Another hour had passed. He felt almost normal again, more like himself. Peeling back his bits of gauze, he discovered that his wounds looked as they should, red, a little bruised. No miraculous healing.

He found his wife upstairs, reading in bed. "Guess what? I know what I've been saying in my sleep," he told her.

She looked at him over her glasses. "Oh?"

"I've been talking to you in German."

She tipped her head. "Henry, how sweet. What do you say?"

"Normal things. Everyday things. Just now we were talking about painting the kitchen."

"*Anstreichen die Küche?*"

"And washing the walls."

"*Waschen die Wände?*"

"Something like that."

"What a nice thing to do. It is looking a little grungy in there."

"You should teach me."

"No," she said, putting her glasses aside. "Then you'd understand all the things my mother's been saying about you all these years, and you'd throw her off the balcony. Did you just realize this?"

"Just now. I must have been having this dream all along."

"And now you remember it." She kissed him. "Very good. Now you can come back to our bed and sleep with me again. Have you been trying to tell me something and haven't had the nerve? Are you joining the Merchant Marine? Are there pumas in our garage? Henry, are you really a woman?"

"I talked to Gunnar Peterson today."

"Oh?" She became still. "And did you die?"

"We should be able to make a few dollars. Not a whole lot, but some."

"Some is still good."

"He offered eighty-five. But I think that was his opening bid."

"That is low. He'll go up," she assured him.

"Whatever it is, then it's minus expenses, minus five percent for Carrier, minus the legal fees, then split the rest in half and give half to the Benhamoudas. Although then there's also a royalty deal for future earnings. Gunnar didn't seem to know what I was talking about, but I think it was just an act."

Ilse had rummaged around in the bedside drawer and come up with a calculator. She began doing the math. "Say two hundred, minus expenses?"

"For fun," he agreed. Two hundred thousand. "Say ten for expenses."

"Minus the legal fees."

"Say thirty."

"One sixty, minus five percent off the top, so one forty, divided in half." She nodded. "Seventy thousand."

"Minus taxes."

"Do you know how much Jackie White paid in taxes this year?" She looked at him sadly. "Three hundred thousand dollars. I keep wondering what they're doing in our neighborhood, but maybe I should start wondering what we're doing in theirs. Seventy thousand. Well, it's still not bad."

An idea appeared in his head from nowhere: the last little flicker. "You know, we could blow it all and buy Saul's house." What was impossible, after all? "You think?"

"What a macabre idea. We could never afford it."

"I don't know. We could maybe swing it. Clean this place up."

"Paint the kitchen."

"Yeah, and sell it and then blow it all and move across the street."

She turned the calculator upside down. "What was it?"

Feeling very sinister and strange, as though conjuring spirits, he leaned over and punched in the numbers with the eraser end of a pencil: 7734. Ilse turned the calculator upside down. Together they looked at the word there for a second in the liquid crystal display before Ilse abruptly pressed Clear. But not fast enough: it felt suddenly as though a word had passed between them, something they regretted saying but could not get back — as though a figure had stood for a moment at the doorway, then vanished.

24

Henry, it's Bernie Durbin. Hope I didn't wake you there. Bernie *Durbin*, Henry."

"Bernie?" Sitting up in the unfamiliar bed, beside his wife, Henry was momentarily disoriented. Whose house was this? Who was this pale woman beside him? But there was his musty robe on its hook, the papers on the nightstand. His forearm was still sore. He had no hangover from last night. "Is everything all right?" he asked. No, it couldn't be, not at this hour. Just past seven in the morning.

"Henry, sorry — sorry, Henry. William died."

Ping. No. Not possible. "When?"

"Yeah, well, last night." Bernie took a deep breath. "This morning, we went in — we, you know, we found him. Elaine doesn't come on the weekends, so we went in, and he was on the floor, ah, by the door to his room, Henry. I think he was trying to, you know, come see us." Bernie began to cry. "He was just this little guy, you know, just lying there on the carpet, and I guess he must have felt something happening at the end, he had his little fridge open, and then he made it part of the way, you know, across the room, and then he just *fell,* I guess, just . . . He just died and we didn't even *hear* anything, and he was just all alone all by himself, he got out of bed trying to come see us one last time, and he just died there all by himself, all by himself there on the floor, trying to come see us, he *died,* you know? He wanted to come *see* us!" Bernie's crying came in great whooping bursts. "So I had to call you, we just found him a couple minutes ago. Should we — what should we do?"

"I'll call the hospital. Oh, Bernie, I'm sorry."

"He was *too old,*" Bernie cried. "My *son* was too *old.* We picked him up and we put him back in the bed and he was like my old man was, he was just bones, he was so *tiny,* he didn't weigh *anything.*"

Ilse, sitting up, looked at him gravely. "William died," he whispered, his hand over the mouthpiece. She made a sad mouth and put a hand on his leg, then rolled out of bed and left the room. He watched her go, pleaded with her silently to come back. It wasn't possible. William had been getting better.

Henry said, "I'll come over, and then we can call an ambulance. I'll be there in twenty minutes."

"Yeah." Bernie was hoarse. "We should do an autopsy, right?"

"You don't have to decide now."

"We should, yeah, we should, but if we decide to do it, that means you can't bring him back, right? There's no way you can bring him back, if you do an autopsy?"

"Back?"

"To life?"

"Bernie, I don't think we can bring him back."

"I shot him full of that stuff, I loaded him all up with it, he had one in his hand so I just used all of it, all there was, I shot it right into him. I thought maybe it'd do some good but nothing happened at all, he just lay there on the floor."

"I'm coming over."

"But what do we do now?"

"Right now?"

"I'm sitting down here in the kitchen. Oh god," he choked, "he's up there right now!"

"You don't have to do anything."

"He was on the floor, does that have anything to do with it?"

"I don't know, Bernie. I'll be there in twenty minutes."

"Oh, god!" Bernie cried, and hung up the phone.

William was in bed, the covers drawn up to his chin. The great ball of his head lay against the pillow; his eyes were shut, his mouth open, his head tipped back just slightly as though to get more air into his lungs. Silent. Motionless. His teeth were little gray nubs, worn, eroded in their sockets. Henry put his hand on William's forehead: cool, waxy. Dead. William dead. "Oh," he said, and withdrew his hand. William was not his to touch.

Bernie was sitting on the bed beside his son, his hand on William's chest. The day was bright, and the morning light was slanting into the room. "Okay," Bernie was saying soothingly, "okay, okay, okay, okay." Lillian was sitting at the foot of the bed and was stroking Bernie's back, up and down. She was wearing a set of white pajamas; her blond hair fell over her shoulders. Around the carpet were scattered empty glass vials, and Henry got up to gather them in his pockets. They clinked softly in his corduroys. Dead. He looked again, from the other side of the room. The same scene. A van rolled by outside, shifting gears as it made its way to the top of the hill.

"We should call Charlie," Lillian said.

"You don't have to do anything right away. There's no rush."

Bernie abruptly stood and went to the window and opened it. A gush of summer morning air came in, smelling of the dewy lawn and the sea. Gorgeous, pregnant, perfect air. "Ah, jeez," Bernie said, and made a wide circle around the room, his hands clasped behind his head. "Sheez," he said, exhaling, and a new cluster of sobs came on. Lillian stood and removed the blanket from the bed, crumpling it into a ball. William was wearing blue pajamas and white socks. His body was an abbreviation, not quite four feet tall. She took the balled-up blanket, went to the closet and tossed it in, then shut the closet door with a soft click.

William's hands were clenched in fists at his sides, and his feet were arched, the toes pointed. He had resisted all the way, from the look of him, and Bernie turned to see and abruptly turned away again, his hand on his scalp. Henry could not help noticing the black hairs on William's hands, even as he began to cry himself. Heart failure, it had to have been; but had Henry caused it? It was too terrible to contemplate. No: William had been getting better, measurably better. "Goddamn it," Henry said. Too late. Gary had been right. Too late.

Lillian returned to stand at the foot of the bed, her hand on the rail. The clipboard hanging there swayed and she stilled it with a touch and looked at William on the sheet, then slowly sank to the carpet, cross-legged. Her feet were a dull white, her toes twisted from years of wearing fashionable shoes, and she clasped the balls of her feet for a second before she leaned back and stretched herself out on the floor. Then she covered her face with her hands and sighed, a great deep exhausted sigh from the bottom of her lungs, a sad enormous final sound. A strip of white belly showed where her pajamas had lifted, and Henry fought the urge to lean down and kiss her, to take her head in his hands.

It fell to Henry eventually, some minutes later, to call for an ambulance. "Use the phone in our bedroom." Bernie pointed. "Two doors down." It was a big, black, old-fashioned machine refitted with new wiring, hefty and substantial in his hand, a suitable instrument, Henry thought, for making such a call. The Durbins' bedroom was small, green, cozy, stuffed with bookshelves in which the books were slanted and upside down and laid on top of one another, law books and novels and medical texts here and there. The sunlight touched photographs of William as a younger boy, with that brave look, the birdlike smile. Henry had to turn away. The void, opening beneath him. He made the call.

The ambulance would take William to whatever morgue they wanted, Henry told the Durbins when he went back to William's room.

"You want to do . . . ?" Bernie, sitting on the floor with Lillian, twirled his fingers. "A . . . ?"

"It's up to you," he told them.

"You want to do one?"

"It's probably a good idea," Henry said.

"Okay. Okay. Okay," said Bernie, and stood up and went over to William and sat down beside him, patting him again. "You did such a good job," Bernie said, addressing himself to William's hair, arranging it behind his ears. "Oh, buddy, you were such a good guy."

Lillian placed herself on the other side of the bed. Henry turned to leave, but Lillian called, "No, you can stay." She ran her hands over William's pajamas, over his stony, sunken face, and cupped his ears. Then her fingers went to work on the buttons of his pajama top. His chest was stark white, bony, fallen. His skin — they could see it as she undid the buttons, one by one — was decorated all over with felt-tipped pen drawings: blue, black, green, red. "Oh my god," Lillian said, her breath catching. She laid the pajama top open, put her hands on them, felt them, traced them with her fingers.

He had drawn himself chest hair, a dense black tuft of it on his sternum and across his upper pectorals. A row of green triangles beneath. Red dashes beneath the triangles, and below these blue glyphs, indecipherable imaginary letters. Instructions, Henry saw at once, to the aliens.

Lillian sat William up and maneuvered the shirt off, his head lolling: his arms were dotted with color, densely crowded points, clusters of green, red, and black, and the blue veins of his forearms were traced in blue ink. Lillian pulled down his pants. His legs too were illustrated: alternating horizontal bands of green, black, red, blue, striping the circumference of each thigh. Kneecaps outlined in red circles. Vertical lines from his knees to his ankles. She tugged off his socks. On the top of each foot stood three dark blue stripes, half an inch wide and three inches long at least, highlighting the tendons. It was a garish, outlandish sight, the work of hours. He had been able to bathe himself lately, Henry knew. Left alone with his own body at last, this was what he had done.

Lillian, holding his socks, gave a little flutter of laughter, then put her hand to her mouth. Bernie stared, his eyes red, his nose swollen. In the bright light of morning they seemed to have discovered an artifact in the bed, a shrunken tribal boy wildly tattooed below the ribs, something from another place and time entirely. And then it was just William again, poor William, stiff and still and gone forever.

He had seen too many bodies in too short a time, Henry thought, and turned away. At the end of the dark corridor a white shape stood against the wall: just a square of sunlight slanting through a doorway, but for a second it had been something else, something glowing in the dimness, and his mind had been ready to see anything at all. A cloud. A ghost. A boy. He went downstairs, a ringing silence in his ears. It was over. His life. William's life. The world. He had a terrible, invaded feeling, as though someone had broken in and stolen everything he owned. Airless, soundless, groundless; nothing was left. He stood at the curb, in the deafening sunshine, and waited for the ambulance.

Ilse had told the children; he returned to a quiet, polite house. His wife made him coffee and toast, and no one spoke to him as he ate and looked out the window at the driveway. The frogs were gathered there. Talk to the birds, talk to the frogs, tell them to stay out of the sun, avoid pavement, avoid civilization entirely. He had been a part of at least twenty Hickman deaths, but they had all happened out of sight, and he had heard of them only two or three days after the event. Autopsy was the normal procedure, and he had been a witness at several of them: gruesome things, surgery without anesthetic performed in a peculiar, clinical silence, without the rushing and beeping of ventilators and pressure monitors and everything else. Organs removed and weighed, the body hollowed like a pumpkin. William, carved. It was a ghastly thought, and he shrank from it viscerally. No. It was not possible. He would ask to be excused from this one. Gary could have this one. Or someone else — it didn't matter, he didn't care.

When he climbed the stairs to put himself into the shower, he encountered Darren sitting on the top step, waiting for something: waiting for him. "Is he dead?" Darren asked.

"Yeah, he died last night."

"What'd he die of?"

"We don't know." Henry stood below him, put a hand on his knee. "I'm sorry. It was probably a heart attack. It was very fast." But that vial in his hand: he must have had some inkling. He'd had the strength to get up and go to the refrigerator, bend down, take one out. Then head toward the door. Then fall. He'd been so light he'd hardly made a sound. Skin and bones. "He probably never knew what was happening."

Darren was holding his own shoulders in his hands, his arms folded over his chest. "Why'd he die?"

"We don't know, sweetheart."

Without another word Darren leaned to one side to allow Henry to pass.

Henry cried in the shower, silently, into his hand, and then shaved himself with particular care. There it was, his old face: pouchy along the jaw, drooping eyes, the forehead deeply seamed, the corners of his lips undergoing a slow erosion, his ears enlarging, wiry black hairs tufting from their secret depths. His body, his own. His mild and homely face, his own. It showed no hint of anything miraculous — no bloom of color in the cheeks, no brightening of the eyes. He was happy about this. It would have been an offense to have been changed somehow: an offense to William, to everyone who had died already. Terrible.

Dressed in a white shirt, with his hair combed, he looked normal, though he was terribly sad and seemed to have a weight suspended in his chest, a swaying mass that threatened constantly to knock a sob out of his lungs. He carried himself downstairs again, where he was embraced by Sandra. She pushed her hair from her eyes with two hands and said, "I'm sorry, Daddy," then stepped away to examine him. How was he? *Holding up* seemed to be her verdict. Saul, now William — the last two times he had hugged her like this. He remembered the sensation of the day before, when rings of pressure had stood around his daughter, but they were gone now, hallucinations.

His wife was tender. "You can stay home today, can't you?" She snaked an arm around his waist. "You don't have to go to work."

But he did: he needed to tell Gretl, tell everybody. So he put himself in the car and drove down the hill and eventually found Gretl in the back of the laboratory, at work on the first of his own cheek-cell cultures, and when he told her she said, "Oh, no!" and set the dish smartly down on the black PermaCote bench and embraced him in a rush, crying into his ear, her chest shaking. She was shorter than he but not by much, and solid. They stood and cried together. His faithful assistant, his conscience. "Oh, no, oh, no, oh, no," she said.

Later that morning he was embraced by Chin, by Victoria and her cinnamon gum, and, still later, as the information began to spread outward, by Lisa Tung, Danny Rosselli, all the others. "I'm so goddamn sorry," Charlie Calens said in Henry's office, his pop eyes glistening. "God, what a nice kid. One of the best ever." On the black stool Charlie turned back and forth, back and forth, like a figure on a clock. "I was just over there. Those poor guys are . . . " He gestured with two hands into the air. "Sometimes I think it's harder when you know it's coming. You confuse the thing you dread with the thing you want. And sometimes you want the end too, which confuses everything." He slapped his two palms together and stopped his chair. "So, friend, where does this leave us?"

"I don't know."

"You don't think you had anything to do with it?"

"No."

"But you don't really know."

Henry didn't have the strength for this; didn't have the will. He said, "He was improving."

"Yeah." Charlie whistled softly through his teeth. "So you say."

Henry took the folder from the tray, handed it over. Calens looked through it, page by page, in the quiet office. "He liked it, Charlie," Henry said after a minute. "He liked the way it made him feel. He couldn't remember my name sometimes at the end. You ever see the look on his face when that sort of thing happened? He was terrified."

"You don't have to remind me."

"We slowed his mutation rate almost to normal. He knew what we were doing."

"I don't know." Charlie closed the folder. "Who knows, maybe I'd have done the same thing."

"I think you would have."

Charlie flashed Henry a quick look of irritation. "Don't push your luck. Officially, I've still never been told. I don't see any need to get wrapped up in anything if this should come to light somehow."

"That's fine."

"I don't imagine you want to be there at the autopsy."

"Not if I don't have to."

"I'll do it." Charlie extended his flat, wide, pediatric palm and swallowed. "He was a cool kid, wasn't he?" His eyes began to glisten again. "I mean, wasn't he a blast, Hen?"

"I know."

"I just loved him so much. We knew it was going to happen, but god, it's — I mean what the hell are you supposed to do now?" He stood. "What do you do, you just walk out the door and go home at the end of the day and there's your wife sitting there and she says, Hey, Charlie, how about a beer? and you say, Sure, baby, and you sit there and you consider the prospect of the view? I mean, what the fuck are you supposed to do? Why the hell are we doing this — you ever wonder that?" He stepped forward and shook Henry's hand again, then leaned down and embraced him awkwardly where he sat. "God, I'm going to miss him so much," Charlie said, his voice breaking. Then he straightened and kissed Henry on the forehead and left in a rush, so quickly that the cartoons taped to Henry's door lifted in the breeze, and for what seemed the hundredth time that day Henry began to cry. He got up and shut his door until it was over. Not until later did he think to mention the pen drawings. "They're all over him," Henry said, into the man's answering machine.

The boy's heart had failed. The arteriosclerosis that every Hickman patient developed, and that William's MRIs had progressively revealed over the years, had reduced his right ventricle to almost nothing. The enzyme had never touched the plaque on his arterial walls, and time and chance had done the rest. Dr. Calens, unknown to Henry until he read the autopsy report two days later, had considered for months *the possibility of coronary artery bypass surgery with percutaneous transluminal angioplasty,* but William's weakness had mitigated against it. Patient had been *in good spirits recently* and had *drawn designs on his chest, arms, thighs, shins, calves, and feet with felt-tipped pens.* A recent upswing in his general health had *offered some hope, but myocardial infarction occurred before sufficient strength had been gained to operate.* So Charlie had still wanted to do that bypass; these procedures were rarely but occasionally done on Hickman kids, though almost always before they were ten years old. Was this why Charlie had been willing to conceal the helicase? Had he been hoping to do some late-stage experimentation on William? Maybe so. He too had been attached to William, he too had been willing to consider an unlikely and desperate measure to prolong his life. There was no mention of Henry anywhere, no mention of experimental treatment. So he was safe on that front.

It was a slender black folder; the photographs were stark, brutally focused, and Henry could hardly look at them. He did, briefly. Made himself. Avoided the photographs of William's lifeless, staring face — covered it with his thumb when he had to. The photographer had taken pains to document the pen drawings; in black and white they looked especially anthropological. Ilse peered at them through her eyeglasses. "You're right," she said. "How strange."

"Those letters."

"You're right, it *is* alien writing!" she cried. "Oh, the poor boy." She turned to Henry in sympathy. "Do you think he really thought he was one?"

"He liked to imagine he was."

"Oh, I can't stand it." She shut the folder and handed it back.

It was a quiet, windless night, and the smell of the garden was rising through the open window into the bedroom. Alyssum, thyme, lavender. A few frogs were singing in the ivy, and every few minutes a jet would thunder dinosaurically overhead and when it had gone the frogs were audible again.

When the lights were turned off the room seemed immense, and Henry clung to his wife in the dark. A flap of abdomen peeled aside. The sternum sliced in two. The brain removed. Dead. He shut his eyes to it. Could not stop seeing it.

"I remember once," Ilse began, speaking into his ear, into the darkness, "when I was married to Gregor, we had a friend who lived in the apartment across the hall from us. An older man, but not old, maybe forty. Once in a while we went over to his place for dinner, and sometimes we had him to our place. His name was . . ." She paused, remembering. "Mathieu Stenner. He was a technical person of some kind who worked for a factory — I don't remember exactly. He had a very nice apartment and he lived all by himself, and he had a collection of very old radios and things like that, old cameras, and they were all neatly dusted on long shelves, and so sometimes he would turn on one of the radios and we would listen to it for a while, you know, just to be polite. And sometimes when he came over to our apartment he would walk around and look at our things, which weren't very much — we just had the usual lamps and chairs and things like that — and sometimes he would say, 'You are very neat people, yes?' and what he meant was that we didn't have any *things* like he did." She moved closer to him, her hand on his hip.

"So one day he brought home a woman, and after that the woman was always there. Her name was Marie, and she was very, very stupid but very beautiful, like a model, tall and thin, but stupid to a degree that was difficult to believe, Henry. For example, one day she told me that trees move! I said, 'Oh, I don't think so.' And she said, 'Yes, there is a tree in my mama's garden that has moved forty feet since I was a girl.' 'You don't say,' I said. 'Oh, yes, it is a documented fact, everyone knows it.' 'How astonishing!' 'Well, if you came from where I come from,' said Marie, 'you would know all about it.'

"Marie and Mathieu were very happy together for a long time, and sometimes you could hear the radios going in their apartment — sometimes they would turn them all to the same station and sometimes to all different stations, sometimes very loud but not very long, so it sounded like a party, Henry, with music and talking and all sorts of noises coming out of the apartment. Well, so. She was not a very demanding woman for being so beautiful, but she wanted one thing, which was a dog, a little dog, you know? A little tiny dog. You weren't supposed to have them, but they got one anyway and no one complained, and eventually it got pregnant somehow, and then there were some puppies."

"Big puppies or little puppies?" asked Henry.

"Little puppies."

"I like the idea of trees moving."

"The way she said it! I'll never forget. You couldn't do anything but agree with her, she was so sure of herself. Well, puppies. She sold some and gave some away and kept two for herself, and then there were three dogs, and people started to complain about the noise, so she had to get rid of them all."

"I hope this has a happy ending."

"She offered them to me and Gregor and to everyone, but of course no one wanted them, so eventually she gave them to her mother, who lived out in the country with the moving trees. But then she was angry at everyone and forced Mathieu to leave the apartment with her, and they packed up and moved away and we never saw them again." Ilse's voice had fallen to a whisper and her hand had climbed to his chest. "I don't know what made me think of them — I haven't thought of them in years and years. It's so long ago! The dog was named Fuffi. When Mathieu walked her, he would call down the hallway, *Fuffi, Fuffi, Fuffi!*" She heaved a great sigh, exhaling past his ear. "*Fuffi, Fuffi, Fuffi, komm hier, Fuffi!*"

"Fuffi!"

"*Du bist ein schön Hund, Fuffi!* Do you want to learn some words?"

"*Ja.*"

"*Hund* is dog. *Die Wohnung* is apartment."

"*Wohnung.*"

"No, no. *Wohnung.*"

"*Wohnung.*"

"*Wohnung.*"

He said it again. "*Wohnung.*"

"That's terrible, Henry. You're not listening at all."

"I'm saying exactly what you say."

"No." She put her hand up to his mouth. "Say it again."

Her hand was warm and smelled of her lotion. *"Wohnung."* Her fingers moved with his lips. *"Wohnung."*

"Wohnung."

"Wohnung."

"Less round, make it flat in the middle. *Wohnung."*

"Wohnung?"

"W-oh-nung."

"That's exactly what I said."

"Flat! Flat, flat, flat in the middle. You say *Wonunk."*

"I want another word."

"No. *Wohnung."*

"Wohnung." He kissed her fingertips.

"That's better," she said. *"Wohnung."*

He said it again, kissed her fingertips again. "Close?"

"Do it again."

"Wohnung."

"Once more."

"W-oh-nung."

"Yes," she said, "about half right, almost," and put a finger into his mouth, and then he rolled over and began kissing her, and she sighed and opened herself to him. It was a long life, she meant to tell him, maybe; long enough for anyone.

But the sadness remained, and as Henry stepped across the Durbins' lawn for the memorial the following Friday, he felt a high hot clotting in his throat, a knot of concentrated tears. Ilse clutched his hand. In her black dress she looked grand and European. He was still not sure how she did it: dressed so well without any obvious effort. He wore his one presentable black suit, the clingy soft fabric good for funerals and fancy dinners. "I look okay?" he asked. "You look fine," she told him. In the tips of his black shoes he saw reflected the brilliant sun of August. Poor William, never to see the sun again. Was it possible? The NASDAQ, as though in mourning, had taken a hard tumble that day. The end was in sight, William would have said.

The house was open to the sunny late afternoon, and it was a big crowd, two hundred or so, mostly gray-haired, trim, sober. No music, just the rumbling of a hundred conversations at once, and everyone trying not to smile too widely or laugh out loud, while Lillian and Bernie lurked here and there, appearing in doorways and promptly being hugged by everyone they spoke to. "We want to see everybody," they'd said over the phone, and how could anyone turn them down? Navigating the big living room full of well-dressed people who leaned against the green walls and propped themselves on the champagne-upholstered sofas, Henry felt terribly raw and vulnerable; the swinging weight had not left his chest, and behind his eyes was a constant pressure of tears. So this was what the world looked like after you were dead: the same, the same, the same. Sadder, but the same. The carpets were just as soft underfoot, and the afternoon light was just as lovely, falling through the mullioned windows onto the furniture, but you were not there to see it.

While not a guest of honor exactly, Henry was well known in this crowd; he was the geneticist, whereas Charlie Calens was only the pediatrician, and everyone had one of those. Henry had met a number of these people over the years, the Durbins' stable of fancy friends: donors to the foundation, some of them, and others he recognized vaguely — from the newspaper, from television? — but did not know by name. Sympathy cards were everywhere, including one from Gary Hauptmann. A tabletop held photographs of William, and Henry lingered there. William had looked entirely normal as an infant, and in those baby pictures was a ghost of the boy he would have become: good-humored, dark, querulous, shy. And then Hickman had begun to take effect, and that boy was edged out of the photos, until at five he was entirely phenotypic. Strange to see it. There were photographs of the older William swimming. William on the lawn. William standing at the edge of a group of Hickman kids, sticking his tongue out.

No, it was too much. He turned away into the crowd. Gretl was there, and he embraced her. "You know," he said, "I keep thinking he's got to be here somewhere. I keep looking to see if he's hiding behind someone's pant leg."

"Me too," she said.

They regarded each other sadly. "I'm going to sell it," he said after a second.

"I know."

"It was a stupid thing to do."

"You're the boss." She took his hand. "We need to draw some of your blood, just to be sure."

"How about now? Is now a good time?"

"Monday will do," she said airily, but she did not drop his hand; she held him with her fond and serious gaze. Like his mother, he could not help thinking. That urge to tell his parents things had not gone away, but there was no one there to tell, just an empty shape in the air.

Ilse had found Lillian Durbin in the sun room, and together the two women made an apt couple, both tall blondes, broadly built — sisters, they could have been, looking up in unison as Henry approached, Lillian's head rising as though on a string, her expression vacant. Valium, Henry suspected, or something stronger. "Your beautiful wife and I have been talking," Lillian told him slowly, "about Vienna."

Ilse said, "Henry, I want to go back. I miss it so much suddenly, you can't imagine. I'm going to take her back with me."

"I've been hearing about that marvelous apartment," Lillian said. "It sounds just like a place we used to stay. I wonder if it isn't even the same building."

"*Wohnung*," he said.

"*Wohnung*, Henry. You and I will go to all my old places, sweetheart — we'll be two good American tourist ladies. We'll walk in the fountains and be flirted with, go to the Musikverein and leave all the men behind, and we won't think of anything except eating cakes and drinking wine."

"It was fast, wasn't it?" Lillian looked at Henry. "He really didn't know?"

He said, "It was fast. His heart stopped."

"Just like that," she said weakly.

"It's very fast at that point. Four or five seconds."

"He didn't want it to be fast." Her eyes were filling. "He told me that, he told me that over and over again." In the bright, spare room she was brilliantly pale, embracing herself with both arms, her eyes red, her expression exhausted. "He wanted to *know*, he wanted to know it was happening! And he was so hopeful. He wasn't ready." She inhaled roughly. "We didn't let him get ready."

"You did everything right."

"But shouldn't we have had somebody there to watch him?

Shouldn't we have had an alarm? Shouldn't we have had him wired up so we could know when something was happening?"

"You let him be a kid," Henry offered. "That was very brave."

"Wasn't it terribly stupid, though?"

"No."

"Are you sure?"

"This wasn't something you could have prevented. We were afraid it would happen, and then it did."

"Is it going to work?" Lillian swallowed. "Is it going to work on other children?"

"I think so."

"Are those other boys all right? The Benhamoudas?"

"They're fine. Giles is still just three."

"So he has time," Lillian said, looking at the carpet, at nothing, her face drawn. "You still have time to help him."

Bernie was leaning against the maple kitchen island, watching the caterers arrange their trays. His face, usually shining under his broad, bald forehead, looked bloated and old. "Doctor Moss," he said, embracing Henry. "Thanks for everything, yeah? Above and beyond. So it's over. I keep thinking." He inhaled sharply. "Over. Is it, really? It was going on so long, it's hard to imagine. I keep — you know, looking around for him."

"Me too."

"Yeah. I can't really bring myself to go in his room. Boy, oh boy, do I miss him. A son! Henry, I had a *son*, goddammit." His eyes filmed. "I had a goddamned son, and he was a good goddamned brave little guy."

"The best there was, Bernie."

"You know. You knew him better than anybody in this house. Hey, it's a madhouse out there, isn't it? See what I mean? About how you can't turn around in this town anymore? Everybody I thought was gone is back suddenly." Bernie sniffed. "And they're all in the living room."

"It's nice."

"I knew I'd just crumple up and blow away if I didn't see people, you know?"

"They loved him too."

"Not like you did." Bernie put down his drink and embraced Henry again, pressing his squat front against Henry's black jacket.

He stank of whiskey, and there was a light sheen of sweat on his scalp. Wordlessly, Henry hugged him back, watching the caterers over his shoulder. Dozens of tiny pastries emerged from the Durbins' enormous stainless steel oven in a production line; for a long minute Henry and Bernie stood there, not moving. "Oh, goddammit, Henry," the man finally whispered. "Just put me out of my fucking misery, would you?"

As they were leaving, hours later, drunk, Henry caught a glimpse of Elaine in a corner on a chair, holding her wineglass at an angle. Where would she go? What would become of her? Her long, athletic legs were sprawled across the carpet and she was looking at the ceiling with a pained and distant expression, as though memorizing the shape of the box beams, the chandelier. And Bernie and Lillian — would he see them again, and when? What would they have to say to one another? He could not quite imagine it.

Outside, it was twilight, and the hospital's blinking bright eye greeted him from across the water. But oh, what did it know? What did it know? William Durbin lay carved and dead in a freezer in the basement, it told him, in the endless language of red, red, red, red.

25

I N THE DAYS AND WEEKS that followed, Henry found it a great comfort to be in bed with his wife, to discover her there when he woke in the middle of the night, her warm bulk beside him. She was a sound sleeper. A happy creature these days, readying her new office, and Henry absorbed some of this satisfaction from her, this calm. As the weeks passed his sadness became less raw, but it did not diminish much in size; a block of ice in straw, it lost its sharpest corners but would take a long time, he knew, to disappear entirely.

Upstairs they moved the futon from its place under the attic window and installed, with Darren's help, an old desk that had been sitting neglected in the garage for years. Ilse had a phone jack installed in the attic wall — Henry watched the U.S. West guy clamber fearlessly up the ladder, his belt laden with tools — and at this desk she worked late into the night, finishing her grant applications, printing them out, sealing them into envelopes; then she came back downstairs and laid herself against him. His wife, his companion, the fellow traveler of his days. *Poor Saul, alone in his bed,* Henry found himself thinking. Alone: how did anyone stand it?

In the heat of late August Ilse left the attic windows open all night long, so in the morning a cool sea-scented draft would come pouring down the attic stairs and into the little second-floor hallway. Morning air. Getting up before the children — they slept late all summer long — he could feel the cool air eddying around his ankles as he went down the hall to the shower.

His own mutation rate had not been altered by his single dose; he had not really expected that it would be. "Nothing," Gretl told him, looking up from the PCR machine. "You're still good old mortal Henry."

"Tell me about it."

"Of course, it was just a single dose." She turned her lower lip inside out, regarded him. "Maybe it has a cumulative effect."

"He stopped mutating, right? He really did — I'm not imagining that."

"No." Her own sadness was visible. "You're not. He did."

"And I had such an intense reaction."

"Sure."

"It felt like something. It felt the way he described it."

"But that makes me more suspicious than if you'd had some other reaction." She pointed her pen at him.

"I know. I've thought of that."

She rotated gently on her stool. "Placebo response."

"I know."

Together they gathered the petris of Henry's cheek cells, the later cultures, the records of the cultures, the files they had kept on him, the blood Gretl had taken, everything. Walked down the hall to the incinerator chute without a word. NO EXPLOSIVE MATERIALS. NO RADIOACTIVE MATERIALS. NO SHARPS. Swung open the heavy steel chute door and dropped it all in. They could hear the plastic and Plexiglas clattering down the long metal channel, tumbling to the basement, two or three seconds of banging and then a sudden silence — like dropping a rock into a bottomless well. "Never again," she warned him, "or you can just go find yourself a new buddy." Never again, he promised.

When he next spoke to Gary, it was to congratulate him on the move.

"Jeez, you should see this," Gary crowed into the phone. "There's a carpet in my office. An actual carpet! You should have seen it when I told Etterbee, Henry, it was priceless. He sort of looked at me for a second, and it was like I was talking Chinese to him — he couldn't fathom it. You could just see the gears going around and around, and you know what he did?"

"Offered you money."

"Which just killed him to do! Oh, I felt sorry for him. Having to deal with me for so long and then having me jump like that. But you know what? I felt guilty for about twenty minutes, and then I thought about all the shit committee work he had me doing and the — god, the politics of that place. Who's going to be the star of the new funding initiative, who's going to get to be featured in the brochure? I mean, we all got used to it, but suddenly I don't have to do it anymore." He laughed. "School's out."

"You like San Antonio?"

"It's awful. Awful. That was the one hangup for me, actually. Talk about coming down in the world. But they're talking about setting up a Livermore operation, so maybe eventually they'll send me back to civilization."

"You know, we're pretty much ready to hand this off to you guys. I talked to Peterson a couple weeks ago."

"Yeah," Gary said. "That's what he told me."

"Did he tell you what he offered me?"

"Whatever it is," Gary suggested, "make him triple it."

"You think?"

"This is my advice to you. You would not, not, not believe the money that changes hands around here."

"So I guess I'll have my people call your people."

"His people," Gary corrected. "I don't have any say in how all that works. How are you doing, by the way?"

He meant *How are you feeling,* Henry knew, but after destroying all that evidence, he heard it differently. "Better. You know, it's slow. I miss him."

"The parents?"

"Slow." He paused. It was a vivid summer day beyond the windows. "So you like it there, though?"

"As long as I don't go outside or try to find a bookstore," Gary said. "God, they've got this wing here, the E wing, and you know what it is? It's all bioreactors. It's like a brewery. There's a zillion different things they're working on here — it's just brilliant. And you know what the big thing is right now? It's a secret, but I'll tell you, okay? Six months ago they found a population of Inuits who've never had a case of leukemia, ever. They just don't get it. I mean, this is a population they've been studying for something like a hundred years, right? But it just now occurs to somebody maybe there's something going on beyond just a diet of whatever they eat, blubber or whatever, so they go up there and take a bunch of samples and they've got a marrow gene, Henry — they've got a mutation. These people don't get leukemia. They can't. It's like the rain forest, you know — the biodiversity out there is just staggering." Gary's voice was warm, hurried, happy. "And everybody comes here because this is where they can study it. It's utopia, you know?"

"As long as you don't go outside."

"God, the heat. I like a little heat, but Jesus. There's a siesta sort of mentality that I can get into, but it always means you're at work until seven-thirty. There's a place here for you, you know, if you want it."

"Kids," Henry said. "Wife."

"Yeah, okay. Well, maybe think about it. Let me figure out what we have to do on this end for this thing, all right?"

"Congratulations."

"Yeah, it's different, you know?" Gary said. "It's not the same."

"You miss Berkeley?"

"Just . . ." He searched. "I guess it's strange to buy everything instead of having it just come to you." There was a drop of regret in his voice. "It's not the same feeling. I mean, there's a lot I'm not going to miss, but I'm going to miss the sense that the institution was doing it out of the goodness of its heart. I mean ha ha, right, but there was some of that. And right now Peterson's buying everything he can, but realistically he can't do that forever. So some of it's going to get lost in the cracks."

"Not this, though."

"No," Gary stated. "That's why I came here, Hen, so we could do this right. That's why I took the job. I promise you, that's why I came, so there'd be someone here to make sure it all happens the way it needs to."

This conversation did not make Henry envious exactly. He had enough, did he not? He did. His wife was happy, his son, his daughter. As his own sadness lingered he felt it becoming a deep, tender part of himself, a bruise to the bone. Was this something like what Saul had felt in those days before he shot himself? Was this what the man had been hiding, even as he thumped around in the back of that truck? Had he been secretly bankrupt, or was he miserable for other reasons, reasons Henry would never know? Henry had thought of calling Steve Sundstrom to ask, but in the end he did not. Saul was dead, and there was nothing he could do about it, no amount of information that would resurrect him. He doubted that anyone would tell him anything anyway. "Thank you," he told Gary.

These days and weeks were also taken up by the creation of a most-likely-market-value report for Justine Jones. It was half invention, half tedious compilation of man-hours, equipment costs, prorated calculations of the lab's subscriptions to *Age* and *American Journal of Human Genetics,* an invented but fairly accurate tally of the "thought hours" Henry had spent thinking about the new sequence while not at work (2.5 hrs/day), a long description of Hickman lifted from the entry he had written for the *Encyclopedia of Human Genetic Disorders,* a calculation of the man-hours lost to society when Hickman patients died, a calculation of the loss of fellowship for parents whose children died, a calculation of the medical expenses Hickman patients accrued over a lifetime — on and on. When it was not painfully reminding him of William, it was pleasantly boring work, not particularly demanding. "Don't worry about being accurate," Justine told him. "Just put something together that's in the ballpark." So he did.

It was this report that he submitted to Justine and Bernie, and the next time he saw Bernie was when Gunnar Peterson's lawyers flew in and put themselves up in the Grand Olympic Hotel downtown. Henry met Bernie and Justine on the front steps. Bernie looked the same: short, solid, well made, well dressed. Sadness moved in his features, and when he saw Henry he embraced him. "Long time no see," the man said.

"How are things?"

"Things are what they are." He shrugged. "We're alive. You know you didn't have to come for this, right?"

"I know. I just wanted to say hi. Cheer on the team."

"You forgot your pompoms," Justine told him, her eyes glinting. This was an exciting day for her, Henry saw, the deal day. "And your skirt."

"I'm assuming you don't want me in the room."

"Oh, Jesus, hell no," Bernie said. "It's like watching surgery. If you don't know what you're looking at, you can't believe the patient's going to live through it. Justine and I have done this a couple times before."

"Bernie likes to be the butcher," said Justine.

"We have a routine. She's the reasonable one, I'm the hothead. Good cop, bad cop. If you were in there with us, you'd be stepping on our lines all day."

They went inside, climbed the wide staircase into the carpeted lobby, a vast space that extended away in all directions. At the far wall was a row of clerks, and overhead multitiered chandeliers were suspended from the ceiling at regular intervals. Bernie pointed at the hotel bar. "You might want to find a comfortable table," he suggested. "This is going to take us a while."

"Good luck," Henry said, shaking Bernie's hand.

"Yeah, something like that," said Bernie, and together he and Justine went off to the bank of elevators.

The bar was almost empty: it was the middle of the morning. Polished wood and brass, windows overlooking the street, a long mirror behind the bartender. Henry stood at the bar and ordered a cup of coffee and took it with him to a corner table. He watched the traffic climbing the hill. Taxis, limousines, tour buses. Men in suits. Below him stood the city of his youth, though it was not, really; the cruel old waterfront city he had grown up in had disappeared almost entirely. No, it was a softer, richer, larger, less backward sort of place now, a place where immense fortunes were being made, titanic deals struck every day, and Henry, as he sat there, felt a kind of happy regret for the state of things. And he was part of it, wasn't he? Right now upstairs they were negotiating to sell something he had discovered, that he had hoped to discover for decades. It was a strange, slightly dirty, uncomfortable feeling, as though he were negotiating to sell a memory, or a limb.

Traffic lightened, increased, slackened again. His parents would hardly recognize anything downtown, he realized. He had been here for the city's latest transformation, and he felt the strangeness of the event deep within himself. From his table he could see, within the anonymous outlines of half a dozen downtown office buildings, the humble stone structures that had been knocked down to build them; within the ugly triangular Sinking Ship parking garage downtown stood, like a shadow, the Seattle Hotel, which had been demolished on that site in 1970 — rambling, ornate, Victorian, doomed. Every city was like that, he imagined, but this one was his. Had been; would be.

He finished his coffee and had a beer and read the newspaper. He ate a sandwich, had a glass of lemonade. Time passed. He was nervous sitting there, he was jumpy; he went out to walk around the block and hurried back to see what had happened. Nothing had. He took a seat, the same one, for good luck. He had to pee half a dozen times, and every time someone entered the bar he looked up into a stranger's face, hoping to see Bernie and Justine and hoping not to. The bar filled for lunch, emptied again; Henry grew more nervous, less nervous, more nervous again.

Finally Bernie and Justine returned, with their poker faces on. Henry's heart leapt, sank, enlarged, contracted. He stood.

"Okay," said Bernie, "we did good."

"We did? We got royalties?"

"We got royalties."

"We got a number?"

"We got a number." Bernie swallowed. "Two twenty-five."

"With royalties?"

"With," Justine said.

"That's good." Not a million dollars, but good.

"Yeah, that's good." Bernie nodded. "And you can work with the enzyme too."

"I can?"

"They were happy to let you."

"Free labor," Justine noted.

"And I can do that?"

"We had to write it all very carefully," Justine said, "but you can."

"The royalties brought the number down, you understand."

But still. Two twenty-five. When they sat down at Henry's table, Bernie took out a two-inch stack of paperwork and said, "Here's your copy. Make sure you read every single page. Ha!"

"It's done?"

"It's done. That right there," Justine said, "is what you call billable hours."

Two twenty-five. And he could work with it. "Was it like sur-gery?"

"Always is," Bernie said levelly. Suddenly he gave a great, explo-sive sigh, and a thousand pounds seemed to fall from him. "Yeah, it's great — it never fails. I mean the funny thing is, everybody basi-cally knows going in what kind of number we're talking about. That's the thing with a kind of built-in monopoly like this — there aren't a lot of surprises. Or bidding wars, unfortunately. So yeah, you sit down and you name a number, and they name one, and basically you both end up where you knew you would, and every-body can say they fought the good fight and argued the other guy down or screwed the other guy for however many hundreds of thousands of dollars, and everybody in the room knows going in about how long and how hard they should fight before getting there." Beer arrived in a tall flutes. "Oh, heavenly father," Bernie said, "hallowed beer thy name. Cheers. To a deal."

It would be a long time before Henry saw any returns on the royalty end, if he ever saw them at all. But Allied Genomics, with Gary running the program, would be able to run huge rodent tests and would immediately begin to try to create progeroid pigs and chimps, and eventually — three or four years from now, if every-thing went well — it would begin human testing. It was fast, in other words. As an entity operating in the United States it was bound by the Helsinki Declaration as well, but because it was an independent corporation with its own funding, its oversight proto-cols were more streamlined than the university's could ever have been. So it was a good thing really, as long as the results continued to be promising, as Henry expected they would. If results began to sour, there was the danger that AG would defund the project, which would leave the sequence patented but unresearched, in limbo. But Gary was there now, and Gary would see to it that this didn't happen, or so Henry believed.

"Yeah, I think we're okay," Bernie told him. "At least they sure seem to know what the hell they're doing. One of the things we asked for was a potential future project assessment — basically asking them what they were going to do with it."

"A PFPA," Justine said.

"Make sure it went to a good home," Henry said.

"That's it. A good home. So you know about Gary — they brought him on, which I think is step one through ten, and then steps eleven through twenty basically deal with how much dough they're going to throw at it."

"How much?" His heart lifted.

"Millions," Bernie said.

"Yeah?"

"Yeah," Bernie repeated. His eyes were wet. "I mean, that's how I could stand to get myself out of bed today to do this, you know? That's why I wanted to be here. To make sure I liked what I heard from them. They're on our side, Henry. Oh, Jesus, have another beer, Bernie. Thank you, I will. Don't mention it."

Justine gathered herself. "I'll let you two celebrate," she said, and stood. Henry stood with her. "Congratulations," she said, and embraced him, her beads clicking against his ear. "You did a very nice job with the MLMVR." Then she was gone again, into the lobby; it felt to Henry like another cleaving.

Together he and Bernie drank. It was a strange, melancholy, happy moment, and Henry decided to relish it. Bernie's eyes watered and dried; he wiped his nose on a napkin, balled it up, fished in his pockets for a handkerchief.

"Well, it's a good thing," Bernie said. "It's a good thing. Hey, here's something. Don't laugh. We found out about this operation that puts your ashes into orbit. You hear about these guys?"

"They just did Gene Roddenberry or somebody like that."

"Yeah, that's the other guys. These guys not only put you into orbit, they'll send you to the moon." Bernie laughed, blew his nose, cleared his throat. "I just think Willie'd get a kick out of it, you know?"

The idea! Henry had to laugh. "They can do that?"

"They can do that."

"I hesitate to ask what it costs."

Bernie put a hand flat on the table. "It is not cheap, my friend."

"You going to do it?"

"I think we are." Another gust of sadness was building in the man; Henry could see it. "Yeah, I think we are. I just think he'd just love to, you know" — Bernie began crying again, his voice high and pinched — "you know, go up, out there. It's all he used to talk about, you know, so yeah, I think we are. You can go down and watch him take off and everything, just go up in his rocket and go to the moon, and I think that'd be the best thing, to go down and wave goodbye to him like that. You know — watch him go off like that?" He laughed. "Biggest waste of money there ever was," he said through his tears, "but what the hell, I don't care. What am I saving it for, anyway?"

Henry couldn't say it: *Nothing*. But they were both thinking it.

Two hundred twenty-five thousand. On the drive home, Henry did the math. Two twenty-five. Minus thirty, Bernie had said, for Justine's billable hours, and for the rest of the work from the firm. That left one ninety-five. Minus eleven for Carrier's AAV. One eighty-four. Minus the fourteen thousand he had claimed in lab expenses, which would go directly into his lab's general fund for the year and be soaked up by new supplies, new equipment. So one seventy. Divided in two with the Benhamoudas. Left him — eighty-five thousand dollars. Before taxes. He laughed aloud in the car. Oh well. But plus the royalties, whatever they came to. Plus the millions of dollars AG was going to throw at Gary, millions Henry could never have got his hands on, never — and some of it would end up filtering down to him, one way or another. So it was a good thing, all of it was. And he was safe.

Ilse was waiting for him on the porch steps, and when he pulled the car into the driveway she stood and walked over to hear the news. "That's a very nice piece of change," she said, patting his lapels. "And maybe more to come?"

"Exactly."

"Well done, darling. How do we celebrate? You smell like a bar."

It was a warm afternoon, and up and down the block Henry could hear the sounds of sprinklers. Above them the enormous hemlocks stood like sentinels against the sky, dark green and ragged. Old trees.

"What should we do with it?"

"Go to Paris," she said. "We have to now. You can break it to the children that they'll have to stay with Freda."

"We can go shopping," he said.

"I think I forget how!" his wife cried, grasping his shoulders. "I'm terribly out of practice!"

"I think you just keep walking until you run out of money."

"That sounds very appealing. We can go to Galeries Lafayette, if it's still there. Oh, it must be," she said dreamily. "Do you want some new clothes, Henry?"

"It is a lot to hope for," he said, "from a tie."

"But two ties," she said.

Ted and Nora Bell, having accepted the offer on their house, were moving that weekend, and Henry and Ilse went down to the corner, past the Turgersons', to say goodbye. The little white house was set on the large corner lot, behind a mossy white picket fence. A nice place, a cottage. The little porch was crowded with boxes, and the interior was open, airy, and empty. Sun entered the windows and fell uninterrupted to the blond floor. Bright squares revealed where the carpets had lain for decades. Henry and Ilse did not know the Bells very well, but it felt good to kiss Nora and shake hands with Ted and accept an offer to visit them in New Mexico. They would never go, Henry knew, but it didn't matter. The new neighbors would be young, computer people of some description, with a two-year-old son. "They bought the place for the yard," Ted told them. "I guess they've got big plans for the lot."

"Oh, don't tell me," Ilse said.

"They can't exceed the current footprint," Ted said. "But they can go up."

"How high?"

"Thirty-five feet."

Ilse gasped. "But that's a tower! That's a" — she groped — "a silo!"

"You won't have to look at it," Ted said, "but Millie's going to send me a poison toad through the mail, I guarantee it."

"Oh, Ted, I love your little house."

"Little," he noted, "is the problem."

But Henry didn't care, and as it turned out, neither did his wife, really; she subsided quickly, and when it was time to go they said their goodbyes gracefully and left the Bells to the last of their packing.

Gerald Turgerson was on the sidewalk, watering the idesia. It had put out a set of shiny black berries. "I like them," Gerald said, nodding up into the broad, pale leaves. "I kept wondering what they tasted like, so I bit one. You know what it tasted like?"

"What?" Henry asked.

"Shit," Gerald said, laughing at himself. He was an old, frail man, his shirt sitting loose around his neck, his pants belled out around his sunken waist. It dawned on Henry suddenly that in a few more years, he himself would be older than his father had ever been. The thought affected him strangely — as though he were being twirled on a tether, about to be let fly. Jettisoned. His father had died at fifty-eight. Not old.

It was a long walk up the Turgersons' front lawn with the hose, Henry saw, so when Gerald was done watering Henry coiled the hose over his own arm and took it up to the house himself. He hung the coiled hose on its stand and turned the water off, wiped his hands on the seat of his pants, and looked across the Turgersons' lawn at his own house. It was the side view from here, the same view he had been given on the night of the neighborhood meeting. There was his bedroom window, high above the lawn. There stood his house beyond the fence: small, shabby, worn, the place of his days. His world, continuing. Oh, eighty-five thousand dollars would go a long way, but how could he bear to spend it on a paint job, a new roof, a new home for wayward frogs? He couldn't. No, they would go to Paris.

As though signaling agreement, a window shade in the attic flew up abruptly on its own, with a sudden bang. *Pow.* He stood there, waiting to see if all the shades would do it — all of them at once. He waited for a moment, expecting it. He could see it happening in his mind's eye, a whole house full of windows signaling to him. But nothing happened. The house was still, silent, dark under the hemlocks. Feeling as though he were being watched, Henry turned and went downhill to his wife on the sidewalk and kissed her.

26

SHE WOULD MISS MIRIAM, Ilse decided.

And what else? Okay, this view. The water, shining on a day like this.

Yes, and the orange cranes. Oh, and the big navy ships — she would miss seeing them camouflaged against the gray water, slipping out of Bremerton like tenants sneaking out of a lease. It had been a long way up to this office, in a sense. One decision made, then another, another, and eventually she had been lifted into this lofty, unhappy place, this big high room with the views of everything.

She herself was not being allowed to sneak out. No; they — oh, they tortured her, really, with a party, the sort of thing she had always tried to discourage. There was a kind of happy malice in this. A case of red wine — everybody was drinking the reds now and nobody drank white ever; it was part of the rustic Italian thing that was happening everywhere — and a cake that said *We'll Miss You Ilse,* which she suspected was not exactly true, though it did have a cute picture of her in icing, in the upper right-hand corner, dressed all in white, with bushy yellow hair standing out around her head. First thirty, then forty, then sixty people standing around drinking wine from plastic cups and admiring her view and shaking her hand and congratulating her on retirement.

But she hadn't done anything, she wanted to say. She hadn't

finished anything, she hadn't accomplished anything. She'd been marking time, or so it felt, year after year after year, to a point that it was frightening to think of. How young she had been when she started here! Newly American, newly married; a fearful stretch of her youth had been swallowed up and consumed by this tall glassy building, these papers, these offices, these people. She shuddered to think of it. Poured herself another glass of wine. As a child, she had imagined becoming a scientist, working on something wonderful, being given a Nobel Prize. Why not? It did not seem too implausible. It happened to people. But not to her, as it turned out: she had spent her years here, counting dollars and telling people not to have parties, instructing new doctors about how to be nice to other people. Well, oh well.

But — maybe it was the wine — as the party grew and a real crowd turned up, she began to feel better. Everyone hugged her. Doctors she had not seen since they were just starting out had returned, older and lined around the eyes, to tease her, and finally she began to feel that maybe she had done some good after all, that she had trained people to be conscientious and decent, as least as far as was possible. The affection did not seem forced, and now and then someone would actually cry in front of her and she would have to say, "Oh, don't be ridiculous, I'm not dying, as far as I know, although some people here wish otherwise," and this would provoke a little laughter.

And it was a lovely view. The newly refurbished train station, and the funny towers with their girders exposed on purpose, and the brick-solid blocks of Belltown converted into lofts and condos — all of this combined, with the wine, to make her feel brilliant and blameless, and happy too that she was leaving, going on to something new. Standing on her chair to make her speech, she said, "You will not miss me all that much, I happen to know. Tomorrow you can have another party. And tomorrow after that, you can have another party. You will have parties for weeks and weeks, because Ilse Moss is not here to tell you to do otherwise."

There was a round of cheering. Below her, she saw a sea of smiling faces. Were they really happy to see her go? She thought yes, partly. But only partly.

"Finally you will all be so hung over you'll want me to come back. But by then I will be . . . gone away, to become the president of the United States."

"You can't," called Miriam from the back. "You weren't born here!"

"People will elect me anyway, because I am the best woman for the job."

"You're the best woman for *any* job!" Miriam shouted.

That brought another round of cheers, which Ilse faced down. She herself did not feel like crying, but there was an upwelling within her that threatened to gush out in one way or another. Why not cry? What was to be lost? And laugh at the same time. So she did. Lifting her glass to the rear of the room, she said, "*You* should have this job, dear Miriam. You deserve it more than anybody."

This was greeted with applause.

Ilse wiped her eyes. "I think you are all crazy to have been in this business with me," she said, "but now I feel I am crazy to be leaving it, because you will not be coming with me." It was a neat little sentence, one she was proud of, and then, after thanking a few people she felt she had to, she stepped down from her chair. And that — after some more hand-shaking and hugging and one last look out the window — was that. One last time she pressed her fingerprints onto the glass desktop. Tomorrow they would be gone for good.

Her new view was, as seemed appropriate, closer to the ground, and contained a number of things she did not quite understand. The travel agency on the corner seemed to double as a grocery store, as women would go in with nothing and come out laden with plastic bags. The lights in two of the apartments across the street were always on, no matter what the hour was, but they were visibly unoccupied. On the wall of one of these apartments an old poster had come loose at a top corner, and though it was poised forever to fall, it never did. Police were always roaming the streets below, and once in a while the abrupt *bloop* of a siren would jolt her upright in her secondhand chair. The desk was pushed up against the window, and as she was not yet officially in business, she spent her days alone, for the most part, finishing another half-dozen lengthy grant applications and arranging for more phone lines to be put in. At lunchtime she called Shanghai Garden and ordered pea vine with black mushrooms or the hand-shaved noodles with chicken, then walked down the block and picked it up, enjoying the bustle and oddity of this new part of the city.

New to her, anyway. On every other corner a concrete pavilion held a thousand pigeons and a clutch of old men sequestered on iron benches, while around her on the sidewalk women toted home huge cartfuls of produce and paper towels and stuffed animals. Nearly everyone she saw was old. Relatively healthy, for the most part: Asians, like Jews, did not drink much, though they smoked a lot. The gutters were filled with butts, and to her window now and then a dry whiff of exhaled tobacco would rise. It was a good smell, one of many here: frying dumplings, diesel, musty old garbage, fish, and above it all the smell of the salty air, a briny smell of creosote and algae: the sea.

The old people still said nothing to her. "Hello," she ventured to an old woman in the lobby one morning. "How are you?"

The woman eyed her, turned away.

"A beautiful day, isn't it?" Ilse called.

The woman looked over her shoulder, examined Ilse quizzically, and turned away again in silence. It was not exactly encouraging. But maybe she was deaf, or had no English. She would know *hello*, though, wouldn't she? "Have a wonderful morning," Ilse cried as the woman exited onto the sidewalk and hurried away.

She hoped this was not a sign of things to come. When this sort of thing happened, a familiar feeling of foolishness would come to her — what if no one wanted to give her grant money? What if no one wanted her services? What if everyone hated her?

Still — even if it took a long time to get everything running — still, how wonderful it was to be out of Kreutznaer! After two days she did not miss it, not at all, and she settled with pleasure into her new routines: riding an extra mile on the scooter, picking up flyers from the floor of the lobby, greeting the acupuncturist who stood at his door gazing down the hall for his first appointment of the day — "Hello," she would say, and be answered with a wordless, infinitesimal bow — then entering her big bright rooms alone and shutting the door softly behind her. Alone. She laid her purse on the desk and opened the big windows and inhaled the beautiful air. Oh, how wonderful it was! She had installed banana trees, spider plants, little jasmines in clay pots, a passionflower that was doing its best to climb the brick wall, a gardenia that sputtered and dropped its yellow leaves but could fill the room with the fragrance of a single blossom, and ficus trees that broke the sunlight on the old floor — and ferns, ferns, aligned in rows on the sills and hanging in the windows, so now and then she would hear a rustling and look up to see the ferns turning gently from side to side, as though examining the view with first one eye, then the other.

She had quite a lot to do before she could open for business, not the least of which was hiring interpreters, so she photocopied request forms and hung them in the Japanese grocery store and put in a call to the Chinese American Benevolent Society. Eventually she would have to hire a secretary, and then she would see what else she needed. *Ein Laufbursche* — what was the word? Errand boy. Spending all day alone, saying almost nothing, she felt her English receding — it slipped away like the tides and revealed a neglected understructure of German, worn and rotted and eroded and altogether gone in parts, so that by the end of the afternoon she could reach for a word and find absolutely nothing there: no English, no German. A perfect blank. Then the word would return. *Appropriate. Degenerative. Destitute. Preventive.* She was getting older, of course, though to judge by her mother, she had a long way to go yet.

Her days here were quiet and unhurried, full of a benevolent optimism, and sometimes she would rise from her steel desk and take a walk around the office, always finding herself drawn to the secret corridor, to the window at its end, where she could stand and look down at the street, her street. Below, her scooter sat bolted to a parking meter. The real work of this second part of her life had not yet begun, she knew, and her days were her own to spend as she pleased. In this there was joy, but a sorrow too, that she had not arrived here sooner. What had she been doing at Kreutznaer all those years? What had she been thinking, when there had been *this*, all along, to do instead?

When she described this feeling to Jackie, the other woman sighed and nodded. "Believe me, I know what you mean. You just feel there's so much more you could have done with your life!"

"Exactly."

"Well, it's true and it's not, I think." Jackie's living room was now a wreck: the walls were down to the studs and the windows had been removed, so the sensation, as they stood looking out at the lake, was of being in a ruin, an old temple on a hill. "I think it's a very common feeling, especially with women who have families.

I don't think any woman I know is ever really satisfied with herself. Happy — some of them are happy. But I don't know about satisfied."

"I keep thinking I should have done it years ago."

"Think of it this way: you wouldn't have been as good at it then." Jackie made a benign gesture with her wineglass. "You didn't spend all those years up there doing nothing, honey. You made contacts. You paid your dues."

"I wasted my time."

"Have it your way. You're wrong, though." She turned and gestured to the hall. "Do you want to see the top floor? It's finally done."

Ilse did not, but out of politeness she followed Jackie across the room and up the staircase to the second floor, then up again to the top of the house. She smelled paint here, new wood. It had been an old attic with a slanted ceiling, unfinished, dingy, and now the ceiling was high, painted white, full of skylights. Closets and bookshelves lined the walls, and a new bathroom was tucked into a dormer, with a view of the street. The new pine floor extended uninterrupted to a bank of high windows, which were open. Beyond them a balcony overlooked the lake, the view, the treetops, the roofs of the neighborhood. The whole third floor would be Jackie and Kevin's bedroom.

"Oh, Jackie," Ilse said, envious, though she didn't want to be. "It's very nice."

"Oh, ha ha."

"No, it really is."

Jackie turned to face her. "You're not serious."

"I really do like it. It's very private."

"Private! I guess it is. Not that it matters anymore." Jackie sighed. "With all Kevin and I do, we could sleep in the front yard and it wouldn't be any more scandalous. Oh well. But I do like being up so high, it's like living in a tree. You really like it?"

"Yes. And now you can spit on anyone you want to."

"Don't think I won't," said Jackie.

"It must have cost you at least fifteen dollars."

"Fifteen and a half. No, I won't tell you what it cost, you'll just get mad." Jackie leaned against the balcony railing and looked down into the cluttered yard below. Drywall and sacks of concrete sat everywhere, and someone had spray-painted a section of the grass orange, where a guest cottage was going to be built. "But oh well. If you've got it . . ."

Ilse could peer around the corner of the house and see the street behind them. There in the rhododendrons, under the hemlocks, sat her own little house, in need of paint, the chimney slanting to the south, the roof awash with tiny brown hemlock needles. She would never have this sort of view, she realized, not unless she went back to her office at Kreutznaer. "I'm sure you're giving at least that much to charity," she said.

"Oh, *fff*, charity." Jackie shrugged, looking serenely at the lake. "Let them eat cake."

Jackie's balcony put Ilse in mind of her mother, and one day shortly thereafter she left her office and rode her scooter along the waterfront to the market, where she bought salami from DeLaurenti's and smoked salmon farther down the arcade. She then rolled the scooter across the street and into her mother's garage.

"What do you want?" her mother asked at the door, and Ilse was able to say, "Mama, be nice," and lean down and kiss her. Her mother went reluctantly to the refrigerator and took out a tall bottle of wine, and they sat together on the balcony in a little breeze. "You might as well stay for a while," she said, opening the wine, and together they ate and drank and looked out over the afternoon water, where the white ferries were cruising in from Bremerton. The cedar smoke from Etta's stained the air in a faint, wavering, fragrant column, and as the ferries arrived and departed, hooting, Ilse and Freda drank the entire bottle of wine and began another one, this one not as cold.

"She keeps threatening to come," Ilse said, exaggerating, her feet on the railing. "But I don't think she will." Tannie, she meant.

Her mother shrugged dismissively, a tiny, familiar gesture that Ilse noticed with pleasure; it was an American gesture, one her mother had never had before. Her mother had also been drinking, was relaxed. "I think it is very unlikely," Freda said. "In the last few years she has become very neurotic. It happens to women when they hit sixty, if they haven't anyone else in their life. They turn inward, as a man would. Like cancer of the ovaries in nuns — they get eaten up."

"I could go over there, but she seems only occasionally interested in me."

"Ha. Tannie was always much more interested in your father than in anyone else." This was unthinkable, Freda's expression said. "She was more interested in that man than I was, often. They had a very, very unhealthy way of relating to each other. That's why she's so sexless. I believe it's why she never married. She already had a husband."

"Mama, really."

"Really! It's entirely true. He encouraged it, of course. Your father and I did not see eye to eye on a good number of things. In fact, did you know this? I left him once."

"No."

"Yes. After you were born, he decided, in his perfectly terrible way, that I had become too much of a mother. He did not approve of the way I had abandoned my profession to raise children. He was very forward-thinking for a man of our generation. He thought he understood exactly what made a person happy. But he did not always understand what made *me* happy."

"She misses you."

"No, Tannie misses no one. Tannie was independent from the beginning. *Independent* is not the word. She was *isolated*. In her classrooms as a tiny girl she expressed no interest in the other girls and boys whatsoever. You, on the other hand" — Freda placed her tough claw around Ilse's forearm and squeezed — "you had no fear of being utterly at the mercy of other people. You would give of yourself so absolutely that it used to frighten me. I was afraid you'd grow up to be either something very, very romantic, like a nurse, or some kind of prostitute."

"That was a long time ago."

"No." She flicked her head sideways once, shut her eyes. Drunk. "You are still very romantic."

"Me?"

"Yes, but for some reason you don't like to admit it. I didn't know what to do with you, after Tannie. You looked to me for everything. You two were so different. And you looked to your father, for all the good it did you. I'm afraid he scarred you by not paying you enough attention." Freda leaned away, regarded Ilse, then straightened again. "You see? Even now you have that terribly sad look in your eyes when I mention him. He never amounted to much, but he had a good life, as he saw it. I know you always felt sorry for him because he had to put up with me, but he did love me, despite everything. Just as you love Henry."

"I don't love him despite anything."

"You see? The romantic. Of course you do. You think he is too involved in his work, that sometimes he cares as much about those sick children as he does about his own."

"Well — sometimes."

"When I left your father," Freda said, "I went to London."

"You did?"

"Yes. For two months. You and I and Tannie all packed up our things, and we moved to London to live."

"I don't remember this at all."

"No, you were very young. Not quite two. Tannie would remember it."

"What did we do?"

"Well, what else? I watched you two children." Her mother's face became strict and plain. "You walked around and burned yourself on the radiators, and Tannie was tutored by an Englishman with an artificial leg. Also, I had an affair."

"You did? No!"

"Yes. With another Viennese. In the long run, I think it did me more good than not."

"Did Tannie know?"

"I think so. You had no idea, of course. He was a poet — can you believe it? That is, he claimed he wrote poems. No one had ever heard of him, including me, and no one has ever mentioned his name again in my hearing, so he must not have been very good, but in those days he looked very much the poet, and that was almost all the battle. He smoked a pipe, like your father, and had a lot of rather elegant hair."

"What was his name?"

"That is for me to know and for you never to know, or to discover accidentally in my papers when I die. I threw out all his letters, but I may have missed one or two. I don't want to leave the impression it was a serious thing." Freda waved her hand loosely. "I was doing it because it was expected of me, and after it was over I was perfectly happy to go home again."

"Did Papa know?"

"Never. Never." Freda looked sadly at the water. "I was saving it for a good moment, when I needed some big ammunition. But I never had the heart to tell him."

"I miss him."

"He missed you too," said Freda neatly. "He never understood why you came here."

"To follow Henry."

"To run away from everyone, especially Gregor," corrected her mother. "You were a lovely girl, Ilse. You had great potential, and you have not made enough of yourself. This new office of yours is a nice idea, but in a way it is too little, too late. But I suspect you know that and don't really mind all that much. Some people are like that."

Stung, Ilse snapped, "I'm very happy."

"Happy. Happiness is not everything. There is duty, and courtesy, and all sorts of good things you can do, none of it having to do with happiness."

"You're drunk, Mama."

"So are you." Freda pursed her lips. "Now that you have a little extra money, you will probably forget all about me. You know I could have given you money, if you wanted some."

"You haven't got any."

"I have," she asserted. The thought of money — or of dying, maybe — drew her upright in the chair. "Would you like to guess how much?"

"Where would you ever have got any money from?"

Freda eyed her craftily. "I will tell you after you guess."

"A million dollars."

"No."

"More or less?"

Freda swallowed. "More."

"Oh, Mama, you're lying. Where on earth would you get a million dollars?"

"Do you know, when you condescend, Ilse, you look just like Gregor."

"Oh! Well, I suppose I learned it from him. Or from you."

"I do not condescend. I educate."

"Two million."

"No."

"More?"

"Yes, more."

[394]

"Three million."

"More."

"Mama! Don't be ridiculous."

"I am not being ridiculous." Placidly she finished her wine. "I am trying to tell you something. I have been thinking of how to tell you this for some time now. Years."

"I think you're trying not to tell me something."

"Yes," Freda said consideringly, "that might be true, now that you mention it."

Ilse poured herself another glass of wine, though in fact she was already very drunk, in a way she had not been in — well, years, she supposed. Her lips were numb, and far back in her throat she felt a kind of chemical insult, as though she had burned herself. She found suddenly that she was nervous. "Does Tannie know?"

"About the money? No, she knows nothing. Why do you think I came all this way? Why do you think I ran away from that place? Because I knew that once your father was dead she would come back home, and in six months she would have strangled me with one of her stockings. She knows nothing about this. I . . . well, wait here."

Freda stood and leaned heavily against the iron railing of the balcony, then turned and disappeared inside the condominium. Ilse could not have followed if she wanted to; she was experiencing one of those drunken stupors that she had forgotten about, the sort that sneaked up on you, caught you sitting down and entered your brain heavily, making you consider, with an unfamiliar steadiness, everything you did. She could put her glass down, there; she could uncross her legs this way, like so; she could watch another ferry approaching the dock and sight on its top deck a crowd of microscopic people waiting to disembark, and she could stare at them, like so.

Soon a heavy shuffling sound came from inside, as though a great pile of papers had slumped onto the floor. "Mama?" she called, not turning around.

"I'm not dead," Freda answered, and a minute later the old woman returned, squinting in the light and carrying a single printed sheet close to her bosom. "Now," she pronounced, "this is the latest figure."

"Let me see!"

"No." Freda leaned away again. "First I must say a few things."

"Mama, you're frightening me."

"I still intend to outlive you!" she cried angrily. "Don't get your hopes up." She consulted her paper. "This is a rough calculation, and it includes the value of the Brucknerstrasse place, of course, which is actually rather high in today's money. Though who would really want to live there, I have no idea."

"The Haider boys."

"You *have* been talking to Tannie! Good for you. No — here is the story." Sedately, Freda licked her lips, decided on another glass of wine. The wine was a strong golden color. "The money comes from a long time ago. When you are old, Ilse, you will discover that having money is usually just a matter of surviving and doing nothing too heedless. So. It happened this way. After the war and before you were born, during the four-power occupation, property was very cheap. No one believed the future would come! They were very, very depressed in Austria. So we bought some, because your father had had the foresight before the war to invest in American bonds through a black market broker he knew. I was furious. I was sure they were forgeries. To my eye, they looked absolutely counterfeit. But they were not, and therefore we were able to take advantage of the situation."

"Mama!" A bubble of disbelieving laughter was rising in her.

"Let me finish. This is only the first part. In the sixties, during that wave of renewal you probably remember, we sold the properties, which were being torn down, and invested in a company I knew nothing about but that your father thought was a good idea — a company called Xerox, which you no doubt have heard of. I thought he was crazy, but he was not. We did very well. After he died, I reevaluated our position. I diversified." Her mother held the paper flat against her chest, unwavering, and swallowed half her wine. Her German had become stately and measured. With deliberation she shut her eyes, then opened them again. Gray, lucid, they fixed on Ilse. "Because I was unfamiliar with the American companies, I remained liquid for some time. Then I bought some shares of Microsoft."

"Mama!"

"A year ago I sold half of them and invested the money in Amazon, which I have just this week sold, because I believe things are going to correct. This boom cannot last forever, because nothing does." She exhaled. "That is the first part. Now, the second part is not so much fun. There are some mechanics to consider. When I die, one of the many things you will have to do, Ilse, is see my lawyer and my accountant. They are both very responsible men. We are setting up things so there will not be much damage from taxes."

Breathless, Ilse asked, "What about Tannie?"

"Tannie — what does she need? She has no children. She has no lovers. She has her money from her work, she has her pension. She has left *me* nothing — perhaps that is how I feel. She never particularly loved me." Freda shrugged. "She can have the apartment."

"Mama, this is a joke. This is a practical joke you're playing on me."

"This is not a joke," said her mother, calmly, and laid the paper down between them.

After all that wine — and after such a shock — she should not have been on her scooter. Her extremities as she descended in the elevator felt extraordinarily far away, as though her body had been spread, through some cosmic mistake, over many millions of miles. Clumsily she fit her white helmet over her head. Its cozy padded interior compressed her face, and the helmet smelled nicely of herself, and of industrial vinyl. She inhaled it. Drunk, she was.

From the dim, diesely lower levels of the concrete parking garage she steered her way up, around, making herself nauseated, and at last she emerged into the light. The outdoors seemed simultaneously overloaded with the details of the afternoon — dust in the gutter, iron grates surrounding the sidewalk's little saplings, cars flashing as they passed in the street — and vacant, quiet, uninhabited, with the lowering sun a noiseless, bright oppression in the empty urban sky, commanding everything to silence. The padding in her helmet must be askew, she reasoned; otherwise she would be hearing things better. Or maybe it was that enormous number that had stunned her into deafness.

She had made it to the top of the hill — to the cramped stretch of Madison near Kreutznaer, where fast-food joints and pharmacies alternated down the block — when a taxi eased out into traffic ahead of her. It was an orange Stita taxi, radio-dispatched, EL3409, a Caprice Classic identical to those unmarked detectives' cars that had parked so heedlessly in front of Saul Harstein's house in June. She was going too fast, and she should have been slowing down, because now the rear of the taxi was approaching quickly, but she had forgotten momentarily where the brakes were, so instead she swerved instinctively and the Vespa bucked. The front wheel swiveled with a terrible quick twist, and with a disdainful flick the machine pitched her forward, into the air and onto the rear window of the taxi.

Instantly she knew she had broken her right arm: she heard a neat snapping sound, louder and hollower than she would have thought. She felt a sharp pain. The taxi stopped hard beneath her and Ilse rolled comically up the rear window, onto the roof of the car, then down the front windshield, scraping herself on the wipers. The poor misunderstanding Vespa tried gallantly to follow her; she could see it climbing up the car behind her, its tiny bald wheels still stupidly spinning and the engine still buzzing. It mounted to the roof, gouged long ugly scrapes into the perfect orange paint of the taxi, and at last fell harmlessly into the road, off the driver's side, where it lay dead.

Somehow she was sitting upright on the Caprice's hood, her scratched legs bleeding all over her white tennis shoes, her arm very broken when she dared to look down at it. The sharp end of the ulna was bulging beneath the skin of her forearm, like a tongue in a cheek. A clean break. There was a clamor of voices from the taxi. Filipino, maybe. With her left hand she pulled off her helmet; then she said, "I'm sorry, please excuse me," leaned over, and vomited fragrant, embarrassing wine onto the black asphalt of the street.

"You couldn't stay away two weeks," said Dr. Edwards gravely, manipulating her arm with his big fingers. "Had to come back and bother us all over again."

"Please don't joke."

"Never thought I'd see the day."

"It's not at all funny. It's mortifying."

"Yeah, well. Of all the people in the world who might have done this, you were the last one I would have picked. Retirement is a little too much fun, I guess."

"It is not retirement." He had begun wrapping her arm gently in cotton gauze; in his big dark hands her arm seemed an especially frail thing, now doubly useless.

The X-rays still pinned in the lightbox showed that the radius and the ulna had both been snapped in two; a tidy blackness separated their two neat halves, the bones displaced half an inch from each other. Dr. Edwards had given her codeine, numbed her arm, set the bones gently with his thumbs. That tattoo — scar — was hidden beneath his blue sleeve. What had it been like to live before X-rays? Before you could see so convincingly the plain, graceful, mortal anatomy of your own body? It had been easier to be religious then, Ilse supposed, to believe it was all blood and soul.

"I was celebrating. Very, very stupid."

"You're lucky they didn't arrest you."

"Yes." The police had recognized her — how strange, but true! — as Henry Moss's wife, and this had been their repayment to him, to ignore the boozy vomit on the street and the apologetic, mortified expression in her eyes; they had taken her stumbling as a sign of injury — and maybe it had been; who was to say? Grandly, with a kind of innocent corruption she had not imagined possible in this city, the two cops had rolled her Vespa to the curb and brought her unquestioningly to this ER, ignoring the outraged taxi driver, a boiled Russian in a floral shirt, asking her nothing except her name, writing her no ticket, silencing her when she began to explain. With brief silent shakes of the head they let her understand that they didn't want to know. *It's all right — we owe you one.* Alone, she had passed unhindered through the waiting room, through the ER, looking for someone she knew.

"The worst thing is, I ruined my scooter," she said now. "Poor thing."

"You can get another one."

"That one liked me." Was she still drunk? She had a headache, and that damaged feeling at the back of her throat was worse now that she had vomited. "We were simpatico."

Dr. Edwards gave her a quick look. "I had a little dirt bike when I was in college. Spilled it coming out of a parking lot. Came this close to getting my head run over by a BMW. Saw a black guy on the road and didn't even slow down."

"Were you wearing a helmet?"

"No," he admitted.

"You were very lucky."

"I've always been lucky," he said. Tenderly he began wrapping her arm in QuickCast. As he wrapped the material, it hardened, giving off a chemical heat. "Bike was ruined, though. That was a good bike."

"You see? I'm not completely crazy."

"Never said you were."

"Just drunk," she said accusingly. "I was. Do you want to know why?"

"You were celebrating your retirement," he parroted.

No one wanted to know anything from her — they wanted her quiet, she felt. She felt coddled, tolerated, ignored. "My mother gave me a shock. A series of shocks," she said. "And I hadn't had anything to drink in a while. Weeks, I mean." This was not exactly true, but it could have been.

The hospital bonged benignly around them, and Dr. Edwards continued his methodical wrapping of her arm. Absorbed in his task, he was briefly lost to her. After five minutes her elbow was immobilized and her hand and wrist were sculpted into the cast. When he was done, she was forced to carry her arm heavily and off to her side, as though she were carrying an overweight suitcase.

"You want some pills?" he asked.

"Of course I do. Don't you think I'll need them? I'm not that tough." She sounded petulant in her own ears, and didn't mean to. "I'll write it up myself," she said.

"You can't write," Dr. Edwards noted. "You got a ride home?"

"I'll take the bus."

"What about your scooter?"

"I don't want to see it," she said bravely. "It's ruined. Someone will steal it for me."

"I doubt it." He wrote clearly on his pad. A doctor trained by her staff: keep the prescriptions legible, she'd insisted. "Now that it's damaged goods. You know where it is?"

"On the sidewalk somewhere," she said. "That was the last place I saw it."

"It's still there, probably."

"Can I borrow a dollar twenty-five?" she asked. "It occurs to me I have no money for the bus."

"I'd feel better if you'd call your husband. You look pretty woozy."

"I'm perfectly fine." Affixing her purse to her left shoulder, awkwardly, she scowled. The pain was returning. "I just need some bus fare."

"You want your helmet?" He handed it to her from the side table. "In case you fall over?"

"You're not funny."

"I'm not trying to be."

She took it from him. It was scratched, she saw, its perfect billiard-ball whiteness grooved with orange. "Thank you."

He upended his pockets and handed her his change, enough to get her home. Warm, the quarters and dimes came heated from his groin.

"Hey," he said as she turned to go, "so what do you think?"

"Not a bad job," she allowed.

"I get the angle right?"

"It's very comfortable."

"It was an honor," he said comically, and in his bow he displayed what she had never seen before: his bald spot, dark in the darkness of his hair, round as a coin and a little shiny; and whatever shame she had felt ballooned abruptly into affection, and as quickly vanished into the white air of the hospital. She tried, girlishly, to blow him a kiss, but it was a strange, elderly movement she had to make with her left arm, untrained as it was in such spontaneous motion, and Dr. Edwards had half turned away from her anyway and did not see it.

Big, incurious Sandra was the nicest to her, bringing her a pitcher of water while she sat downstairs watching television, feeling desperately thirsty and ridiculous. "You did *what?*" Henry asked, and she told him, leaving out the part about the wine — and about the money too. It could wait. Besides, she thought it would make her seem extremely flighty and susceptible if she told the whole truth just now. Greedy. She felt a companionship with Darren, with his beady adolescent eyes: he was jealous of her cast. "Seriously, you totaled it?" he said.

"Seriously," she said.

"What'd it look like?"

Dr. Edwards had been right: the Vespa had still been there; she had called a wrecking company to take it away. The front fork had split, and the metal of the runnerboard was bent sadly out of true. "Completely ruined."

"No way."

"Yes. I flew through the air!"

"Cool," he said. "What'd the taxi driver do?"

"He got out," she said, remembering, "and yelled at me in Russian. Then I threw up on the street."

"Nasty!"

"Yes," Ilse agreed, and guiltlessly took another red pill.

She dozed, but woke after minutes, feeling heavy and peculiar. Upstairs in bed, she found it difficult to position herself comfortably with the cast. "Am I keeping you awake?" she asked Henry at midnight.

"A little."

"You want me to go upstairs?" she asked loyally.

"No."

"Are you ashamed of me, Henry?" The news, which had now expanded to fill her throat, would not come out. "I'm sorry. I could have been killed. It was very stupid of me to do."

Henry said, "We all do stupid things."

"But not me," she asserted. "When have I ever done a stupid thing?"

"Good point."

"Mama told me some news. I don't want to tell you tonight, but I'll tell you soon."

"Is she sick?"

"No! No, she's fine."

"Is it Tannie?"

"Aren't you sweet, Henry. No. It's not bad news."

"Is she remarrying?"

"Mama?" Involuntarily, a barking laugh escaped her. "No. She would sooner throw herself off the balcony." The iron railing had shivered under the old lady's weight, she remembered. "No, it's good news."

"It's a secret?"

"For a little while."

"That's all right," Henry said. "Can I try to guess?"

"You can try."

Silently, Henry lay breathing beside her. "Your mother is moving in with us," he ventured finally.

"That certainly wouldn't be good news."

"I wouldn't mind."

"You would, after a week. You'd find your sweaters organized by weight and color."

"I already do sometimes."

"Only when I'm restless. No, that's not it."

"It has to do with her?"

"In a way."

"Well," Henry said, "let me think about it for a second."

Beyond the window the heavy racemes of the ash tree could be heard brushing back and forth in the wind, and after a minute Henry's breathing began to match them: gently irregular, at peace. "Henry?" she asked, but he was asleep. Deeply, profoundly, peacefully asleep, as he hadn't been in ages. She would tell him soon. But it could wait a few days at least, she thought. Days. Or months, maybe. She would have to think about it.

Happy with her freight of sudden wealth — pregnant with it — she turned awkwardly away from him, a heron with one wing outstretched, into the cottony largeness of the bed. Drugged, hurting, she dreamed of her papa, his brown, tarry, fruit-infused smell, his enormous veined hands, hands that had been, unseen by any of them, manipulating things correctly all along; and though in her dream Ilse knew her papa was waiting for her in his study at the end of the hall — audibly rearranging things on his desk, talking unhurriedly to someone on the telephone — it took a long time to reach him, and when she at last arrived at the study the blackout shade was up and the tall brown room, packed full of books, was bright with sunlight and the high window was open to the day. Beyond the window, outlined in huge, cartoonish footprints, she could see the path her father had taken in his effortless escape across the rooftops, away from her into the maze of the old city — up, and over, and gone.

27

WHEN HE FINALLY got up the nerve to ask what had happened to William's body, his father told him it was going to be shot to the moon. It did not seem funny to Darren, and it was not like his father to joke about such a thing. But his father wasn't joking. "Seriously. In a little canister," he said, holding his hands a foot apart. "They shoot you off from Florida or somewhere and just drop you right down on the moon."

"Seriously?"

"Yeah. It's not cheap, though."

"How much is it?"

"I have no idea. Lots."

"Wouldn't it like totally bounce?"

"I guess it would. I don't know. There's no atmosphere, so you don't burn up."

"So like two hundred years from now, when we've got a colony up there, there'll be all these tennis-ball cans of dead people lying around? That's freaky."

"I think it's pretty neat."

"Yeah. If I die," Darren said, "that's what I want you to do to me."

"I don't think we can afford it. We could drop you off at Safeway, maybe."

"What if I saved up?"

"Then," his father agreed, "we would happily send you to the moon."

It took Darren two minutes to find Lunar Burials online and to discover that he would need $125,000 to get his ashes to the moon. Whoa. Never mind. He read that the canister was a foot long and made of

titanium with a submarine-hatch containment system and coated with a dark gray nonreflective surface to avoid interference with terrestrial measurement devices. Each canister weighs twenty-two pounds and is inscribed with the name of the decedent and both birth and death dates and is guaranteed to survive untarnished and uncorrupted in the lunar environment for ten thousand years. Canisters are dropped in groups but requests for specific placement upon the lunar surface cannot at this time be met due to the unpredictability of launch times and the irregularity of the subsequent orbits. Family and friends are informed of the date of launch at least four months in advance to allow for planning. Local facilities are available for services and gatherings, *click here for more information.* The dispersal of human remains is governed by several national and international regulations and Lunar Burials conforms to all appropriate regulations. Lunar Burials does not violate any existing or proposed treaties for the use or treatment of the moon. Space travel is a risky enterprise. Interested parties are advised that while rare, mishaps during launch, orbit, and dispersal are not impossible. Lunar Burials has never experienced a failure during launch, orbit, or dispersal, but in the unlikely event of such an occurrence, refunds are not available. *Click here for full disclaimer.*

There was a roster of photographs of people who had already been put on the moon. Most of them were old men, a few women. No children, not yet. One hundred twenty-five thousand bucks. Holy shit. You had to be seriously loaded even to think of it. Darren studied the faces; they looked normal. It was a clear night, and the moon was visible through his window. He could not really picture what it would be like to lie there for ten thousand years inside a titanium can, like the donkey who wanted to be a stone, but he could easily imagine walking along the surface and finding one — it would have splashed down in the dust and sent up a big spatter of lunar material, making a new crater with a gray tube buried in the center of it. Or it could have bounced, hit a cliff, and rolled to a stop somewhere, leaving behind it a long flat trail, a track in the dust that ended at something obviously manmade. He would lean down, pick it up in his glove. *Dropped in groups.* Around him would be a hundred of them. He would go from can to can, looking for *William Durbin, 1985–1999.* And someone would, someday. That was the weirdest thing. Someone would actually find the can up there, pick it up, and wonder — car accident? Drowning? And probably by then there'd be no one around who would know. It was a desolating feeling.

Darren missed William, and cried when he thought about him for too long. It was not fair, not at all. How could he be dead? He was *cool.* And Darren was afraid he had contributed to his death by taking him out on the scooter, something he would never tell anyone, never ever ever. A heart attack, okay, but maybe the vibrations had loosened some junk in his heart and he'd died. It was possible, wasn't it? He thought so.

He tried not to think about it. If his parents noticed anything different about him, they didn't say so. But he felt different. Worse. His father seemed to be fine, though, so Darren felt he should be too. He could pretend, anyway, and he did.

He did not at first believe that his mother had totaled the scooter — it was completely unlike her — but it was gone. The space in the garage where it had been parked was empty. Instead she dragged her bicycle up from the basement and oiled the chain and spritzed the seat with Formula 409 to get the dust off.

"You should get another scooter," he suggested. "It was totally cool."

"We have enough internal combustion engines," she told him.

"We've got like exactly one!'

"Exactly," she said. "One."

So his nighttime rides were over. If he couldn't save up enough to be buried on the moon with William, he could at least start to save for a scooter. They were only eight or nine hundred dollars, the used ones, and the gas cost hardly anything. Meanwhile he walked a lot or rode his own bicycle or took the bus, and bummed rides from his dad when he could. Often the car sat maddeningly at the bottom of the driveway — his father took the bus as often as not, and his mother only rarely drove it these days. But to steal the car was beyond him. The keys in the bowl by the door were tempting, but he did not succumb.

At least there was a good story to tell Tanya. "My mom had a wreck," he said. "She totaled it."

"Oh my god, really?"

"Yeah. She broke her arm." They were in GameWorks, a gigantic video arcade downtown, with windows four stories high and ramps leading to the upper floors and a great ringing chaos of noise.

This was the first time he'd seen her since the scooter ride, and it wasn't going well. He had been demoted somehow, for some reason. She hadn't answered his phone calls, had come here only very reluctantly. Now and then, when they were out of sight of anyone, she would let him hold her hand. But the place was full, and so far the hand-holding had amounted to about five minutes total, most of it in the hallway to the bathrooms.

He was careful not to seem desperate, but it was a struggle. She was prettier than ever — her hair was lighter, and she was wearing a shirt that was cut above her navel, and her tanned stomach was flat and tan and he could hardly stand it, watching her walk in front of him, her little butt filling her shorts. He could feel his hands fluttering out to touch her and had to tell himself, *Not here.* But where? He shoved his hands in his pockets. He had brought the Spanish Navy rapper's button, or whatever it was, for luck, but it wasn't working. They passed a bank of car-racing games, and his eye was drawn to the spiraling, onrushing road. God, he missed the scooter, that sense of rolling through the world.

"Hey, did you get that tattoo yet?" he asked.

She grimaced. "My dad totally said no."

"You should do it anyway."

She shook her head. "He would *so* freak out. Show it to me again."

"Right now?"

"I just want to see it."

So there in GameWorks he sat down on the edge of Speed-Star2000 and took off his sneaker and his sock. Clean socks, good thing. Showed her the three dotted lines again. She crouched and touched them gingerly, a pucker of distaste on her lips as she felt the rows of bumps. Her fingertip was cool and tickled him slightly. "That is so nasty," she said.

"It feels good."

She stood, looked at him as though trying to place him, then said, "You know what? I like should probably go home."

"We've only been here twenty minutes."

"Yeah," she said, "I know."

It was trouble, he knew. Well, he would take the bus home with her; it was vaguely in the same direction he was going. Together they found a Number 25 going to Montlake. It was a Wednesday, midafternoon, so the bus was almost empty, and sitting in a rear seat he was able to hold her hand and even place her hand on his thigh, which she allowed with a great show of reluctance. Without the scooter, it occurred to him, he was just another boring guy. But what else did he have to offer? Not much. William? No, never. They watched the windows. Downtown gave way to neighborhoods. The bus stopped, started, lurched along. *That your little brother? Yeah,* he'd said, *he can't sleep.*

"I'll walk you home," he said, getting off the bus with her.

"It's fine if you don't."

"I know."

"Because it's seriously not like anything is going to happen?" She faced him. "We should probably like talk about it, actually."

"Okay," he said. The bus had pulled away; they were alone in the middle of the sidewalk. A pair of identical houses looked down on them from opposite sides of the street.

"Because it's not that I don't like you."

"Yeah," he said. But what about that night in the clearing? What about her helmeted head against his spine, rolling her own permanent tattoo on his back? What about all that kissing? He would feel that sensation forever, and the memory of her long, monkeyish hands against his chest would never vanish. But her expression was serious and final. "Okay." He stifled an urge to run, to cry.

"I'm not your girlfriend, okay?"

"Yeah, I know."

She wouldn't meet his eye. "And you're like not my boyfriend, okay?"

"I know."

"I mean, I like you. I seriously always did — it's not like I didn't and just like decided to try to see and like go out with you a little this summer? But it's not like a *thing*."

"Okay."

"Because don't you really feel like we're not really meant to be together? Don't you think there should be a spark when we're together? And there pretty much isn't, and it's not your fault or anything, it's just the way things are right now. Plus," she added, "the summer's almost over."

"Yeah, okay," he said, as lightly as he could. But his voice was wavering. Fuck. What did he do now? She was so pretty. Against her tan, her dark eyebrows were irresistible. His hand lifted and he touched her hair, and after a second she leaned away. Oh, fuck.

With a hot lump in his throat, he turned. Walked away from her. Walked down the block. The street was quiet. The little brass button was a knot against his skin. He would be a doctor. He would show her. And he would walk all the way home — why the fuck not. His fucking mom, crashing the scooter. He turned and looked behind him. She was going quickly the other way, head high, not looking back. He watched her go. He couldn't help it. She never turned around.

For the last week of summer he mowed lawns and pulled ivy out of gardens and basically took all the shit jobs he could. He hosed off driveways, raked the moss off garage roofs, painted old fences, sprayed Roundup on cracks in the sidewalk, scraped algae off the Nilssons' swimming pool tiles with a scrub brush until his hands turned green and clammy, cut down little trees with an ax, and once he not only knocked down a wasps' nest with a blast from a garden hose but managed, to his happy surprise, to get it to land right where he wanted it, in an empty plastic garbage can, the lid of which he quickly slapped down. The wasps were out for the day, but a dry, hollow buzzing could be heard when he put his ear to the lid — a few laggards had been caught inside. He was sorry for them but could not release them, he feared, without getting stung, so with regret he left the lid in place. Two days later he returned and retrieved the nest as a souvenir. A handful of dead wasps were curled in the bottom of the garbage can; he shook the can to be sure, and the little bodies slid back and forth harmlessly. *Sorry*. The nest was crisp and delicate and for its size unbelievably light — a little paper balloon, mottled gray-brown, like an old newspaper left in the sun. He tossed it into the air and caught it with two cupped hands, and when he hung it from his ceiling with a length of dental floss, it drifted back and forth whenever he opened the door or the window, and sometimes it even moved when he took off his shirt or exhaled too heavily. Weightless, almost. Empty. At night the thing hung there like a gray, eyeless head, a ghostly presence in the room above his desk. It had a dark, almost bitter scent, not very strong.

Six bucks an hour was what he charged, and as the week passed he managed to make a couple hundred dollars, all in cash. Without Tanya to blow his savings on, he had very little to buy, which was good in a way, although only in a way. He thought about her all the time as he worked, at least when he wasn't thinking about William. It was not much of a choice.

It was, he discovered, a pleasant thing to iron his money. Heated, the bills released a rich leathery smell, probably from wallets. Under the iron's steaming press they became crisp and taut again, not like new, exactly, but with new money's firm edges. Stacked in his dresser drawer, they made a neat pile.

His sister thought he was nuts. "You should like name each individual one — you ever think of that? Then you could really enjoy its company."

"Shut up."

"Could you iron my change too?"

"No."

"My keys?"

"I'll iron your head."

"You could have like tea parties where you sit them up around a little table and they can talk to each other."

He feinted at her with the iron and she disappeared. The summer had not been a total loss: he was stronger. His biceps were actually defined now, and his stomach was flat and four knots were visible at the top of his abdomen, not just when he clenched his muscles but all the time. His legs were still skinny, but he was starting to fill out in a way that was not altogether terrible. In the mirror, he didn't look much like Edward Burns anymore. What did he look like? He examined himself: front, back, profile. Nobody he recognized.

*　　*　　*

At night he jacked off to the good parts in *Jaws* by Peter Benchley, whoever that was, also to the good parts in *The Game Players of Titan* and *Ubik* and also *The Gold Coast* by Kim Stanley Robinson, which his parents probably thought was science fiction but wasn't, exactly. And sometimes he would just lie on his bed in the dark, watching the wasps' nest turning back and forth in the breeze and listening to the sounds of the neighborhood, quietly playing the Goo Goo Dolls — *I want to wake up where you are, I won't say anything at all* — and waiting for the phone to ring and for it to be Tanya, regretful and passionate. He would lie with his arms above his head, his stomach clenched tight for her admiration, and wait for her to remember him. He could imagine, couldn't he? He liked lying there thinking about her — he could imagine her arriving at the top of the stairs, seeing the careful way he had arranged the horse, the button, objects that would at a glance regenerate whatever feelings she had begun to have for him, and then she would smile at him on the bed in his marvelous pose and throw herself on top of him. As if. But it was better than thinking about William all night long, which he didn't want to do, not at all.

In this way the last days of summer passed. His parents, as far as he could tell, were back to normal, or as close as they ever got. Sleeping in the same bed, anyway. Alone in the house sometimes he rummaged through their dressers, peered into their bedside stands, but found nothing of interest. Funny ointments, earplugs, an emery board, dental floss, forgotten medical magazines now covered in dust, parking stubs. The useless junk of adults.

He was struck, not for the first time, with the oddity of life in general, and his life in particular: that while his family seemed a solid and permanent thing, it wasn't that at all. His parents had not always been his parents; his mom had been married before; his parents had met very accidentally in a city where neither of them had been born, at a conference where neither of them really needed to be. This meant that his own existence had not been guaranteed from the start of things and that indeed he was a very unlikely being, the product of a particular sperm and egg from two random people who could easily never have met. In this way he could be seen as an exceptionally rare and valuable person, the end product of a long chain of unbelievably unlikely events, not just his parents and grandparents all meeting each other but also the dinosaurs dying out exactly when they did and the Earth forming in the orbit it had — all that. It was chance, he knew it, fantastic, unimaginable chance that had led to his being here, on this bed, at this hour, in this year, on this planet, in this body. But for some reason it didn't *feel* like chance. In fact he felt very much at home in the world, enmeshed with it in that intimate and permanent way, and maybe this was the strangest thing of all, that he knew all the facts about his existence but did not *feel* them.

Had William felt the same way? He would never know. Now that William was dead, Darren found he had strange, sentimental, wussy-boy thoughts about, say, the little bits of granola that spilled to the floor when he was getting his breakfast: a weird sorrow that they had made it this far only to fail at the last step, the trip from the box to the bowl. He regarded them sadly against the bristles of the broom. He brushed rice grains from the counter and returned them to the canister. And he ate the little crumbs and parings of cheese that sat unattended on the counter — not that it was bad luck to waste things, but that anything that existed was too precious to waste. Weeds, wasps, whatever. Well, it was stupid, maybe, but he couldn't help it.

Mrs. White hired him to dig a short trench along the side of her house; it took him two days and earned him eighty dollars. She wrote him a check. "Very nice work, Darren," she said, peering up and down the length of the ditch. "You may have a future in manual labor."

He folded the check into his back pocket. "That's really what I'm hoping for," he said. "I was going to join the army, but they make you like think too hard."

"Funny," she said. She put her fingers on her lips and said, "I've noticed you've been around quite a bit. Did your parents not plan any activities for you this summer?"

"Uh," he said, "not exactly."

"Don't you think that's a little strange?"

"No. I didn't have anything I wanted to do."

"Jonathan is very busy. As you know, he's not as old as you, but he just spent three weeks at Leadership Camp in Idaho."

"Yeah."

"That sort of thing doesn't appeal to you?"

"Leadership Camp? Not really. I went to chess camp last year."

"How wonderful."

"It was all right. They had a good swimming pool."

"You don't want to be a leader?"

Was she joking? It was hard to tell. Behind her, Jonathan wandered into the yard, wearing sandals. He was eleven or so but looked younger, and had the mean, aggressive sneer of a dumb private school kid: *I'm better than you.* "Actually, I usually sort of think of myself as a sullen loner," Darren said, for Jonathan's benefit.

"You do?"

"Sure. Totally."

"I don't think that's very healthy."

"Yeah. You know anything about like semiautomatic weaponry?"

She looked startled. "Of course not."

Jonathan was edging closer. "Or explosives?" Darren asked. "I'm trying to do this research project."

"Researching what?"

"Just like . . . research." He shrugged, and locked eyes with Jonathan. "I've got these couple projects in mind."

She frowned, tapped him lightly on the top of his head. "Well, you're joking, of course. But it's not very funny. Not after that horrible thing in Colorado, it's not very funny at all," she said, and vanished into the house.

Leadership Camp. Would his time have been better spent socializing, meeting girls, doing all that? Sandra had a new boyfriend from basketball camp, and he had been to chess camp twice and tennis camp once and had actually enjoyed himself, sort of. So maybe. But it had been a strange spring, a strange summer, and things had fallen apart a little, not that he would have been desperate to go anyway.

He muscled out a last shovelful of dirt, hoisted himself from the ditch, and said to the lingering Jonathan, "Go have a Popsicle, okay?"

"I can't eat Popsicles," said Jonathan.

"Go have a beer, then."

"Duh, I can't drink beer, I'm too young. I'm allergic to Popsicles."

"No one's allergic to Popsicles, it's like being allergic to water."

"I'm half allergic to water," Jonathan said.

"Which half?"

He hesitated. "Just half," he said.

"Left side or right side?"

"That's not how it works."

"I'm allergic to air," Darren offered. "But only in my right lung."

"Shut up."

"Yesterday I was allergic to sunlight, but only on my hair."

"Shut up. I'm not joking. Besides, you don't really have a gun."

"Maybe not," Darren agreed.

"We got to shoot air rifles."

"Yeah, well, I'm allergic to those," Darren said.

Jonathan's face screwed itself into a furious scowl. "Shut up, you fucking dumb motherfucker," he said, and turned on his sandaled heel.

Darren laughed in surprise, watching the boy take angry little steps into the house. *That your little brother? Yeah,* he thought, and inhaled on a suddenly ragged breath. *No.* His friend was dead. Oh, shit, and now suddenly he was crying again. Again. He stabbed the shovel into the earth and left the yard as fast as he could, wiping his eyes when he was behind the laurel hedge, clearing his throat. He walked all the way to the end of the block before he felt he could turn around and go home and take a shower and try to stop thinking about it. *Allergies,* he could say, blinking.

But in the shower he couldn't stop himself, and he cried as the hot water ran out completely, cried with his hands on the shower wall and his head completely under the stream, and even after he climbed out he let the cold water run to cover the sound of his crying, which seemed as though it would never stop. He would never see William again, never, never, never, never talk to him again. Even his body was going to the moon, and Darren would never get there, never in his life. Those little frail hands on his chest — never, never, never again.

28

UP AT MILLER COMMUNITY CENTER, as the summer came to an end, Sandra saw Thomas one last time. "Hey," he said, surprising her, "you like this?" He turned around, modeling new clothes. Heavy denim that hung in swags. A black hat with heavy gold seams. She stood up to see his shoes: expensive sneakers. Beside him, hidden by the high counter, stood Giles.

"Oh, hey," she said. She felt a swipe of fear that quickly passed. "How's it going?"

"Hello," said Giles, piping.

Thomas's lovely, heartbreaking face lit up. "How you like that?"

She opened her mouth to answer. But what did she have to say? "I don't even know what you're asking me."

"Got my brother out."

"He was in jail?"

"Sha," he said, shrugging. "Just got the boy out on a nice day. I said, Let's go check on that girl, see what's up. So?"

"So?"

"So." He rolled his eyes. "Whassup?"

"Could you like go away?"

He turned, deliberately surveying the lobby: the tiles, the Coke machine, the bulletin board. "Away from *here*? Why would I want to get out of *here,* it's like a beautiful work of *art.* Maybe I'll *work* here."

"What do you want?"

Giles squawked, "I want to go home."

Thomas shrugged exaggeratedly, his heavy clothes lifting and settling. "Just trying to be friendly and all that."

"Friendly — that's a change."

"Sha, I was just mad at you."

"Get out of here, okay?" The beige telephone in front of her was programmed to call police, fire, ambulance. "I still can't believe you did that."

"What?"

"Called me like that."

"I was calling to say I missed you."

"No you weren't, you were totally calling to like check up on me."

"Sha. Take it how you want. You think I'm stupid, that's all."

"Yeah, you're pretty stupid."

"Least I'm not all ugly," he said, angry. "All fat, and no titties."

"Get out of here."

Proud, calm, he asked, "You want to see my car?"

"You don't have a car."

"Sha, I got a car," he said, and displayed the keys. "Don't I?"

"Yeah," said Giles obediently.

"Shouldn't he be in bed?"

"Man, that's my brother," said Thomas. "How come you don't like me anymore?"

"Because you called me a bitch."

"Before that, you like went off to that camp and you didn't even call me."

"I don't know." He had shrunk, she remembered: contracted. "I didn't think you wanted me to."

"You got a new boyfriend?"

"I don't want to talk about this, okay?"

"I'm not gonna get crazy." Still calm, he put his two hands flat on the counter in front of her. "You really think I'm stupid?"

"No," she said. She didn't, exactly. But selfish, and he didn't care to know anything more than he did. "I just met this other guy I like better."

He twisted his mouth: half grimace, half pout. "He black?"

"I don't see how that matters."

"He is." Satisfied, he leaned away. "Once you go with it, you can't quit."

"But you're not black," she said. "Look at you. You're not black. You're Arab or something."

"Same thing."

"It is not!"

"I'm blacker than you are!" he cried. "What, you think I'm white?"

"Well," she said, "you're not black."

She saw it coming before it happened — it was just like him to pretend offense, or maybe really be offended but pretend to pretend. Anyway, he pulled off his enormous baggy shirt and stood before her, barechested. "Didn't you want some of this?" he cried melodramatically. "Didn't you want some of this?"

"Oh my god. Put your clothes on."

"You think I'm gonna die?"

Giles cackled, a strange, dry sound. Norma appeared from the back office. Catching sight of Thomas, and then, an instant later, of Giles, her tolerant face flashed irritation, then competence. "Hello, Thomas," she said levelly. "I wondered where you'd been hiding."

With a gesture of comical disdain he picked up his shirt, gathered the fragile boy in his arms, and turned without saying anything. It was a beautiful back he turned on them: slim, narrow, tucked at the hips. The elastic waistband of his underwear gleamed a pure bleached white against his skin, the heavy, expensive jeans bagged at the ankles, and Giles, watching them over his shoulder, laughed in his elderly way as he was carried off — carried too roughly, Sandra feared, but Giles didn't seem to mind at all, his head bouncing as they disappeared down the hall, out the door, into the sun.

"Nice kid," Norma said. "He still your boyfriend?"

"He's crazy," Sandra said dismissively. But she could see Norma hovering there on the other side of the counter, pinned by her fondness for the heedless, callous boys who were even now continuing to rob her. "We broke up," Sandra explained, looking at a box of stubby, worthless pencils, and as she did, she felt a hot lump of sadness swelling in her throat, surprising her. It was sad, she thought, to leave anything behind, even the things you didn't want anymore.

* * *

But she did not miss him. The viperish hiss of his voice over the telephone had been softened, but not entirely erased, by her time with Arthur, and that sinister whisper would be with her always, one way or another, a wormy, writhing thing that moved within her. Yes, he had left his mark. The Benhamoudas were moving to San Antonio — that was the news her father had passed on — and thinking of this caused a narrow spike of jealousy to run through her. Some other girl would meet Thomas and get to do everything with him. Which wasn't fair. At the same time, she really, really never wanted to see him again. It was all confusing.

"What do they think's going to happen to him?" Colleen asked, visiting her at work one afternoon. "Is he all right?"

"He's the same," Sandra said. They were sitting in the sun, on a low brick wall that overlooked the soccer field. Below them a man in a blue tracksuit was throwing a Frisbee, again and again, for his black dog. The man's throws were imperfect and tended to slope off one way or the other, but the dog liked it, and after a while Sandra supposed the man was meaning to throw it that way, so the dog didn't have as far to run. "He's exactly the same."

"Is Arthur coming to visit?"

"I don't know. Probably not. We haven't really talked about it that seriously. Like where would he stay?"

"He could stay at my house."

"Your mom would go insane."

Colleen's white face was shining under her cap, and on this hot, sunny summer day her white blouse, with its dozens of folds and pleats and carefully starched pockets, seemed a particularly ridiculous costume. The lap of her long gray skirt was collecting crumbs from a bag of Sun Chips they were sharing. Beyond the soccer field the neighborhood reached away.

"So they're going to try to make me go to Shoreline Community College — that's the new idea." Colleen brushed her lap clean. "Very attractive campus, very Christian-friendly, very unthreatening, especially to people of minimal intellect and marginal ambition, and then after two years I can transfer, depending on how well I've handled everything, to UW. Meanwhile of course I'll be living at, oh, you know, *home*, basically sitting in my room while all my actual friends go off to actual colleges."

"You better have fun senior year, then."

"If only I could find a way to have sex with a black guy," Colleen mused. "That would probably just about do it."

"Shut up."

"I can't believe they let you like e-mail him and everything. They must suspect something."

Did they? Her father did seem more — what was the word? — jokey with her lately, more suggestive, as though he were unable to keep from thinking about certain subjects. But he was notoriously distractible and could be put off with a word or two, and now that he had stopped sleeping in the attic he seemed to have recovered some of his old composure.

"Seriously, don't go to Shoreline. That would be so depressing."

"Believe me, they have no idea. The only school I'm applying to in this *time zone* is Stanford. And you know the good thing about having parents who live in the nineteenth century? They don't really travel a whole lot, especially when you have to use certain mechanical conveyances that travel through the air, you know, so it's not like they're going to track me down all the time either. You know what else they don't believe in? Debt. Because debt involves interest, and all interest is usury. Fortunately, I can apply for student loans on my own — they never have to know."

"Sinner."

"Look who's talking."

Sandra's break was over, but they stayed on the wall, in the sun. Sandra's hair had been getting lighter all summer and now it was dark blond, and she took a nice tan too, and in her tank top she didn't look too bad, she thought. Her round shoulders were dark and flecked with freckles, and the hair on her arms was golden. Wispy, fine, nice against her fingers.

"Don't you ever feel like just *telling* them?" she asked.

Colleen shrugged. "I told them everything when I was ten years old. I said, There's no God, you can't make me believe in him until you prove he exists, and I'm never wearing these clothes again. And they said Uh-oh, little Colleen has been spending too much time with the nonbelievers, and then it was like *pop*, so much for fifth grade! I think they just figure I've grown out of all that. It's actually sort of fun if you think about it the right way. It's like I'm an actress and all day long at home I play the part of True Believing Innocent Young Colleen, and they just keep buying it for some reason." She sighed and looked at the mountains. She was slender, her skin perfectly clear, her eyes a deep metallic blue. Pretty. Trapped. "You have to promise me something, okay?"

"Okay."

"Okay, I know this is going to sound stupid, but I have this fear that one day I'm going to like wake up and believe everything they say."

"No you won't."

"I know, but what if I do?" Colleen said. "I mean, they've somehow managed to go through their whole lives believing it. What if suddenly I do too? Then I'm going to be a brainwashed knucklehead just like they are, and you want to know what the scary thing is? Okay, the *really* scary thing is that I can like sense it. It's this thing in the back of my head that's sitting there, this big *shape*, you know, and if I keep thinking about it too long, it just rises up and all of a sudden the things they say actually start to make sense, and I know it's just because I've heard it all fifty million times, but still, and then actually there's some of it that's really appealing, and that if I *could* believe in it my life would be so much nicer, like heaven."

"But you know it's not true."

"I know I *know*." In despair, Colleen took off her cap. With a deft twist of her wrists she unpinned her braid from her head, then shook her hair free in front of her face and began rebraiding it, her fingertips flashing. "But you have to promise me that if I start believing it, you'll remind me what I used to be like."

"But you won't, though."

"I'm too nice," Colleen said from behind the screen of her hair. Long, brown, shining. Pretty hair. "I feel so sorry for my dumb parents — it's like I don't want to hurt their feelings."

"You can still be nice and not believe in it."

Colleen's fingers weaved, tucked, straightened. "They're going to be so sad, though, when they finally find out."

"They'll get over it."

Colleen's voice was tiny now. "No they won't."

"Eventually they will."

There was a long pause. Colleen tugged, finished the braid, restored it to her head, replaced the pins, settled the cap again. Her eyes were full of sorrow, a look Sandra had never seen before, a look of absolute, unscreened sadness. "No they won't," she said, and looked away.

Sandra felt sorry for Colleen and did her best to console her, though Colleen was good at consoling herself. Sandra talked her into shooting baskets despite her being awkward and comically overdressed, and after two or three minutes little beads of sweat appeared on her upper lip. "My mom would *die*," Colleen said, airing her underarms. Sandra retrieved the ball from the corner of the gym, rolled it back across the floor. She showed off a little — shot from the three-point line, dribbled between her legs — while Colleen stood like a matron in the middle of the floor. "That's not fair," Colleen said. "You're not wearing a girdle."

"Yeah I am."

A pinched, pained look crossed Colleen's face. "I don't think so," she said, laughing.

A girdle! They had never seen each other undressed, and it was such an unexpected admission that Sandra had to laugh too. "Oh my god, don't tell me."

Colleen said, "I'm serious. Stop laughing!"

"I can't help it."

"Just because I get strap lines all over my butt. It's not funny!"

"Oh my god, it is *so* funny. Oh my god. You don't seriously."

"I seriously do. I get all these like snap marks on my stomach, I look like I got attacked by a giant squid. It's not funny!"

But Sandra was helpless. "Yes it is," she said faintly, leaning over, weak with laughter.

"Wait, watch, come here. I can make it creak." In the empty gym Colleen strained. "Hear that?"

"No."

"Come here."

Sandra went over and stood beside her.

"Listen." Colleen strained again, with a blank, pious look on her face. After a second she emitted a tiny fart. "Oops," she said.

"Oh my god," Sandra said, and collapsed to the floor. "Oh my god!"

"That wasn't me!" Colleen cried, laughing, going red. "It was the girdle!" Then she farted again.

"Oh my god!"

"Shut up!" Colleen said, helpless herself. She was walking in circles, her hands on her hips, her face as red as a soup label. "You're totally making me fart!"

*   *   *

All in all, as September rolled around, Sandra could not remember ever being happier. Thomas was gone, apparently for good, and Arthur e-mailed her at least three times a week, and the college catalogs that now arrived almost daily each contained a description of a possible life, exact and exotic in a way that thrilled her to the bone. She had never maintained anything like a large group of friends, but she saw herself effortlessly at the center of the photographs in these brochures: that was her sitting on a stone stairway; that was her in the grass reading; those were her plastic safety goggles; that was her in the NCAA tournament, working the wing, her hair in a scrunchy. What could be better than this? And she did not have to decide — she did not even have to write her essays — for months still, and she could take her SATs as late as November 17, and she could spend what remained of the summer studying the catalogs and thinking about them in a dreamy way. That's what they were for, right? She took them to work with her, even the lame ones from Central Washington University and Spokane Valley College, because in truth even these had a wonderful allure: that C painted on the grassy hill above the school — what would it be like to walk there in the morning, before anyone else was up? The University of North Dakota had tunnels between buildings; what would they be like in the middle of the winter — full of bustling students, a little smelly, the ceilings hung with steam pipes?

She would go away to school — that was the only thing she had decided so far, and she had not so much decided it as understood that it would be a good thing for her to do. The farther away she went, the easier it would be to present herself as someone new. She felt this vaguely, and had a still vaguer sense of what this new person would be like. Taller? Friendlier, certainly, more outgoing, less private. If she could drive home every weekend, it would be harder to be new. Eugene was almost far enough away, but not quite. Colleen was right: it was important to get away — to get out of reach.

The strange thing was — she thought about this all the time — that no matter where she went, it would change her life forever. By choosing one place above all the others, she would be choosing against fifty or sixty possible lives whose details she could never know, and how was she supposed to decide which unseen life she wanted to live? By the pictures? By the college's record of tournament appearances? It was impossible. And if she chose the wrong life, how would she ever know? She wouldn't. Which is why it was such a pleasure to sit and look at all the catalogs, every single one, to study the pictures and smell the ink and the glossy paper and to feel the nubby texture of the fancy paper some of the better schools used for their cover letter, and in general to pretend she could go to every one of these places and live all the possible lives they presented, all at the same time, and not be forced to choose just one. It was a kind of heaven, this suspension, when everything was still possible — like the moment before her body moved one way or the other, when she was in perfect balance, or like the moment before Arthur had turned to her, nervous, when nothing had happened yet, nothing, but it was about to, and the size, the mass of the event about to happen had seemed to send little waves back in time, little shimmers that she could sense in the air — and then he did turn to her, and what had been about to happen was suddenly *happening,* it had arrived.

He too was thinking about college, she knew, and this was still another reason to study the catalogs endlessly, looking for people like him. She missed him terribly; they talked at least once a week.

"There you are," she said when she called him one night. "I've been calling for an hour."

"Sorry!" he said. "I was out."

She could pretend to complain, but who knew where he had been? She could not picture his life very clearly, though she knew he worked two jobs and was taking a class at the community college called Stress Therapy for Seniors. As in senior citizens. He had a grandmother. "Were you out running," she asked mockingly, "with your homies?"

"Oh my god." He laughed. "What was *that?*"

She laughed too. "Out getting the bling-bling?"

He laughed again. "Hey, I was thinking — you know what?"

"What?"

"I miss you," he said bluntly.

"You do not."

"Yeah I do."

"Well," she said, startled, happy, "I miss you too."

"Yeah." He made a little grinding noise and said, "I'm trying to be totally honest with people in my life now. I heard this like speech by this guy? About being upfront with people? But it's hard."

"You're pretty honest to start with."

"Yeah, but just being like . . . not just honest, but like not holding your feelings back from people. I don't know. It was this guy at school, he was this guy who got shot a bunch of times and then he was dying and he thought, Man, I need to tell some people some things, I hope I don't die, and . . . Now he goes around and makes these speeches telling people to tell people things."

"We had that guy. We also had the burned guy."

"Yeah! We had him too! Guy looks like a sock puppet, man."

Honest. Teasing, she asked, "Was I your first girlfriend after Kimberly?"

"Oh, all right, it's like that then."

"Was I?"

"You don't have to be that way."

"Was I?"

He sighed. "Either way you're gonna think I'm a chump."

"No I won't," she said, now honestly curious. She hadn't been before, not exactly.

"What do you think?" he asked.

"Probably not."

"What else you need to know?"

"Nothing," she said. "I just thought I'd ask."

"Yeah, well." There was a pause. "You got any brothers and sisters?"

How little they really knew each other! "A brother. He's fourteen."

"He play ball?"

"Tennis sometimes. Mostly he just sort of lies around the house."

He paused. "You didn't ask about me. I got two brothers. Older."

"Cool," she said.

"You don't even want to ask, do you?" His voice had become warm, rounded. "You know what you want to ask. Just ask it."

"What do you mean?"

"Just ask it. It's all right."

"Do they play ball?"

"That's not it. You know what I'm trying to say. 'They in prison?' No, they ain't in prison."

"I wasn't thinking that."

"You were. Why'd you just say *Cool*? That's what you meant."

"I don't know — maybe I did." Had the thought crossed her

mind? Maybe it had. "But that's sort of a natural question, don't you think?"

"Ah, see? That's what I like. Honesty. I got one brother who's in community college, I got another one who's thirty, who works up in Berkeley. Phones and whatever, he works in the fundraising department. I mean it's nothing like — he's not a professor." This was said in a straight-ahead, genial voice. "What do you want to be?"

"I don't know," she said. "I guess I could be a doctor."

"Damn," he said, laughing. "I guess."

"Why not?"

"No reason! No reason." She heard shuffling on his end of the line. "You got a boyfriend up there?"

"Not anymore."

"Nobody? You used to have somebody?"

"I used to, sort of. But he was a jerk."

"I don't have nobody down here either."

"Who'd want you?"

"Ah, that's not necessary at all." He laughed. "You think I'm a nice guy?"

"Definitely."

"Really?"

"That's why I like you," she said. "It's not like you're handsome or anything."

"Yeah, you like that Bradley Quinn."

"That was last year."

"You —" He audibly stopped himself. "He says he's gonna try to go to Stanford."

"No way."

"Like a walk-on."

"He's too small."

"Nah, I don't know, they like that kind of guard. My man Brevin Knight's from there. He's struggling, though. See him out there, he's like a child. Also the man can't shoot straight, which is another problem got nothing to do with his height. Quinn, though," said Arthur dismissively, "he's always wanting to post, and I'm like, You can't play that game up here."

"Angela Pond," she said.

"Now that girl's got some skills."

"She frightens me."

"That's part of her skills."

"Hey," she said, "I miss you too."

He smiled; she could hear it. "You should come down visit me."

"White girl in the hood," she ventured.

"Man, I don't live in the *hood,*" he said, embarrassed for her. "We got a lawn and everything. That's racist, by the way."

Undaunted, she said, "You should come up here. We've got a spare bedroom."

"'We've got a spare bedroom,'" he mimicked. "You don't know how funny that is."

"I'm serious."

"I am not making that drive again," he said. "Maybe if I save up money I can fly."

"They let black people on planes now?"

"Shut up. Listen to you."

She was enjoying this: push, pull, give, take. "*You* should be the one at Stanford."

"Well." He made a considering noise in his throat. "I've seen Montgomery's people out here, but I know I'm not that good. I mean I'm good, but I'm not *that* good. The only way I could go there is on a scholarship, and they're not gonna give me a scholarship. I might go to Cal — they're good. They might, *might,* give me one. My brother says."

"You're better than that!"

"Girl, you need to do some more looking around," he said pleasantly. "Lot of us out here trying to get something. Cal's a good school. A great school."

"I know it is. It's just . . ." She feared she had overstepped. "Never mind."

"My mom wants me to go there."

"That's cool."

"What, you think I'm gonna get drafted or something? Cause I'm telling you that's not about to happen. I mean maybe if I grow another five inches. Taller, I mean. Otherwise, you know. Just another" — he hesitated, editing himself — "black man with a basketball."

"Hey," she said, "guess what."

"What?"

Plunging, she said, "I love you."

He snorted. "Girl," he said with emphasis. "Getting heavy."

"I do."

"I got people here listening."

"Who?"

"Nobody."

"Your other girlfriend."

"No."

"I love you," she said again. Saying it felt — who would have guessed? — marvelous. "In case that wasn't already obvious, with what we did."

"Lot of people separate the two things."

"Like your other girlfriends?"

"You're about to be insulting me with all that," he warned.

"I'm just trying to get you to say something nice back to me."

"Well, I do too."

"Really?"

"Yeah."

"Are there really other people there?"

"I'm in the kitchen."

"Who's there?"

"Nobody! Just . . . everybody."

"Say it."

"Come on."

"Say it! Come on. It won't kill you."

"Say what?"

"You know. It."

She could sense him grimacing. "Some people round here's 'bout to kill me."

"Come on."

"Right now?"

"Why not? I thought you heard a speech or something."

"Right *now*? You know I mean it."

"But you haven't said it."

"Girl," he said again. The line between them hissed.

It was never mentioned that she paid for all the phone calls — or her parents did, anyway, in this way maybe signaling their approval of Arthur, or at least the idea of Arthur. It was always she who called him, at times prearranged over e-mail, and always she who paid. So there were limits to what Sandra could say too. And he would either answer her or he wouldn't. In fact — it now occurred to her — it didn't really matter, because *she'd* said it, and that was enough. There was a kind of safety, she saw, in admitting to such a looming, enveloping thing as love. Love, or whatever it was. A crush. Well, something. Anyway, it was liberating. How strange this was to realize, and how her heart opened at the realization!

The copper line between them — or maybe it was a satellite link, she didn't know — anyway, she imagined it as a bright cord, an electric strand illuminated by the current of their conversation, by Arthur Dix's breathing at the other end of the connection; and just as swiftly Sandra saw this cord as the first in what would be an uncountable number of bright lines, strands that she would extend from herself to the world around her, to Arthur and Colleen and everyone, all the people she loved, and this would be a successful life, a good life, to be absolutely draped with these strands, a benevolent figure, loved because she loved people first. What did anything else matter?

In her darkened bedroom, puddles of light stood in familiar corners of the ceiling, wavering when the trees shifted in the yard. She waited, the line open, her heart rising.

"Girl," he said, and told her.

2000

OVER THE WINTER, the building was gutted.
Metal bleachers, hot dog stands, Astroturf, lighting, scoreboards — everything not made of concrete was taken out and sold, or auctioned off, or destroyed. Giant scrubbers scoured away the Super Foam coating that had sealed the roof against the rain, and 44,000 troublesome ceiling tiles, prone to falling anyway, were scraped from the interior like the scales from an enormous fish. When, in February, the building was reduced to an empty shell, demolition crews spent long weeks drilling holes into the vast concrete ribs of the roof and the elephantine vertical supports until it was possible to imagine the structure as a huge upside-down sieve. Into these drill holes were inserted thousands of sticks of dynamite, tiny chemical plugs blocking the building's new pores.

It had never been a handsome thing, everyone agreed. Squat, gray, a monument to a municipal moment that had come and gone swiftly in Henry's city, to those few years when the town — stretching beyond Boeing and Weyerhaeuser, and with the chintzy World's Fair fifteen years gone and Microsoft still an unimaginable decade away — had decided on sports as its next area of expansion and voted to erect a taxpayer-funded stadium. Modest, functional, decidedly unbeautiful. The nostalgic photographs in the papers showed the designers, the builders, the councilmen, everyone with wide lapels and extravagant sideburns, clunky black eyeglasses under hardhats, men standing before a pit of rebar or mounting the skeletal beginnings of the concrete roof that had been an architectural breakthrough. All these men now looked small, and admirably industrious and goodhearted, and all made decent in their vanishing: innocent of the future, and so, Henry saw, innocent of everything.

Now — weathered, exposed, a twenty-four-year-old ruin — the Kingdome looked as though it had been standing for centuries. Overrun by Goths, looted for its metal, for its ribbons and pennants. It had stood through the riots of November, when tear gas had floated through the streets downtown and helicopters had chopped the milky air; it had stood undamaged through Y2K, when the silent city feared a bomb; and now, at eight-thirty A.M. on the fourth Sunday in March, it was set to be demolished with the push of a button.

In Ilse's old office, high up on the hill, the Mosses gathered. The children, Miriam thought, looked older than they had last summer: Sandra more poised, having taken early acceptance to Berkeley; Darren suddenly taller, with a surprising length to his jaw that would make him, possibly, handsome. Ilse was slim and happy, in white, and Henry less vague, his sandy, slack face not quite submitting to its age and his eyes for once not darting nervously around the room.

Helicopters hovered today too, and on every downtown balcony, on the bridges and overpasses, on boats in the sound, people had gathered to watch. In the Kingdome's place would rise another glass-and-brick palace, a football stadium that would be half transparent, designed to last, built by a billionaire and designed to impress, to make money. On the next hilltop south, the chosen at Amazon had stepped onto their high orange terrace; the Smith Tower held on its square observation deck a raft of multicolored observers, clutching the iron railings.

At the appointed hour the radio counted down from thirty. Ilse stirred at the window, straightening the darts in her shirt. At zero, quick electric pulses of light snaked down the ribs of the roof, down the massive support structures, and into the ground, as though the living spirits of the building had been abruptly let go, suddenly released to their old homes within the stony earth; then a series of answering flashes, like flashbulbs going off, ran up and down the ramps and hollows of the place; then began a great harrumphing settling of the roof, and then a massive buckling, and the rest of the fall was swallowed up in dust, a beautiful, titanic, downward slipping, a shuddering surrender to gravity as the building swayed and came undone with a clumsy, weighty grace, a behemoth falling to its knees. The fall was almost soundless from so far away; then, belatedly, came a muffled, rumbling thunder, distant, restrained. *Ka-boom.*

"Oh my heavens," said Ilse.

"Excellent," said Darren.

The cloud of dust rose, unhurried, obscuring everything. Minutes passed; the cloud drifted toward them over the city, driving the spectators on the Smith Tower balcony indoors. Arriving at the nineteenth floor of Kreutznaer, the cloud could be seen to be a swarmy, finely powdered dust, the Kingdome's mortal ashes. On this warm, still morning the ashes settled on the narrow metal windowsills of the nineteenth floor, and in the ventilation grilles of the exterior, and the buildings downtown became covered with a gray film on their southern sides, and even blocks and blocks to the north windshields ended up with a coat of dust, as though they'd been driven for miles through the desert. From their high perch the Mosses watched the cloud rise, approach, and pass them.

When the air cleared, the Kingdome was a tumbled pile of rubble, surprisingly small — as though an egg had been crushed — and, most surprising, they could see the sound through the new gap in the skyline: the blue dark water, the hundreds of white boats bobbing offshore. A new space, as though a new part of the air had been discovered.

In the weeks afterward Henry and Ilse met for lunch downtown a few times, and on some of those afternoons they walked a few blocks west and watched the new stadium rising. When it was possible to do so, they bought — at ten dollars apiece — four hunks of rough-edged rubble to put in the garden, under the ash tree, markers to remember their old city by. Together in their tight ring these four stones outlined a rough circle. Water collected here after a rain, and Ilse threatened to knock the stones apart, not wanting to attract mosquitoes. But Henry liked them as they were, and they stayed.

When the King County treasurer finally auctioned off Saul Harstein's house — to a twenty-nine-year-old woman and her husband, both Amazon employees, who bought it for more than two million dollars — these new neighbors liked the stones, liked the idea of them anyway, when Henry pointed them out, and they jokingly asked to have one. But no, Henry liked the look of them from the kitchen window, and liked the birds that came to drink at the mossy pond — little chickadees and watchful crows, and grackles and robins — and the frogs gathered there too; and soon the stones looked as though they had always been there. Eventually Henry stopped noticing them so much, and after another year in the rain they became entirely covered with lichen and moss, and their edges grew round under the tree, and finally he stopped noticing them entirely.

From his own window Darren could look down on them in the back yard, and it was he who finally moved them apart, releasing a gush of water into the bushes; with some effort, he rolled them away in separate directions under the rhododendrons. It was funny to admit, but the stones had unnerved him — at some point during the hours of gazing down on them from his window, it occurred to him that they looked like four little graves, and having a cemetery in the back yard seemed like very bad luck. But no matter how he moved them apart from one another in the garden, he couldn't stop thinking of them as headstones, and after a while it seemed bad luck to have separated them, so he rolled them back together in a rough circle out of sight behind the ash tree. This was better. But he knew they were there, and from then on the idea of them always troubled him a little.

But there were other things on his mind, too. He too was getting ready for college, and now he felt more acutely than ever that the world was full of a sort of marvelous, overwhelming, distracting possibility; so sometimes he found himself coming into a room with a purpose, only to forget what it was, and as he stood there, suddenly adrift in the middle of a familiar room, each object around him, though mute and motionless, seemed to hold a kind of coded message for him, a vibrating potential that remained unrealized — Was *this* what he had wanted? Was *this*? — and only by retracing his steps, squinting deeply into his own mind, and then coming into the room again would he at last remember what it was he had been looking for.